# The Dragon Moonstone

VJ Garske

ISBN: 9798862988642 (Paperback)
Imprint: Independently published

Cover Design by: Markee Books
Printed in the United States of America

For Owen

# CONTENTS

# CHAPTER 1

## *AND SO IT BEGAN*

I used to think being a wizard would be cool, but I changed my mind as I stared at the handcuffs encircling my wrists.

I rattled the silver bracelets, hoping to catch the guy's attention. "Hey, do you really need to chain me up like this?"

The guy ignored me, absorbed in his phone.

"Are you a cop? Show me some identification."

He didn't look my way, thumbs flitting across his smartphone. I sank into the couch, struggling to wrap my head around how I'd ended up handcuffed in my own home.

My day started like any other, until a stranger in a long, white leather coat barged in. Before I could react, he used slick moves to twist me into a pretzel and clamp cold metal around my wrists. Despite being taller and heavier, I was no match for him. He had the build of a jockey and the hand speed of a boxer. So there I sat, frustrated and confused, holding my head in my hands, baffled by the guy's preoccupation with his phone.

*What's he doing on his phone? Why is he here?*

A few months ago, I accidentally discovered that I had wizard blood running through my veins. An ancient relative was a mage, and I ended up inheriting his mystical gifts. The thing is, I've been stumbling through this magical mess without a map. My Aunt Shirley said that I had raw talent but lacked discipline. Worst of all, my unchecked emotions affected my magic—badly. At the moment, I was more nervous about losing control of my anger than the intruder and his phone.

I concentrated on the cuffs, whispering, "Open says me."

The bracelets prickled and ratcheted tighter, pinching my skin.

*Ouch! Definitely not what I intended.*

I shifted on the couch. "Hey, can you at least tell me what you want?"

The guy fixed me with an intense glare. An old scar traced from his temple to his mouth, leaving a permanent sneer. His high-collared coat added to his already creepy vibe. He reminded me of an angry dachshund, one of those mean little badger-dogs.

I shivered and raised my cuffed wrists. "These really hurt."

He growled, turned his back, and leaned over his phone. My anger smoldered and my frustrated thoughts swirled.

*Maybe he's texting his friends to come party. No, on second thought, he looks like a loner to me. But why is he in my house? He hasn't gone through anything.*

I didn't want him touching my parents' stuff. Everything was how they had left it, since the day they never returned. I pushed away the haunting memory by placing my hands against my chest, comforted by my mother's pendant underneath my T-shirt.

*Stay positive. At least the cuffs aren't behind my back. If Mom were here, she'd probably offer the man coffee and strike up a friendly chat.*

I jiggled the bracelets. "My wallet's on the counter. Take it."

He mumbled, and the handcuffs tightened with a *click*.

*Who's he texting? I can't let him take over my house. Think of something!*

I focused on breaking the links, straining my muscles. The cuffs grew warm before they sparked.

*Zap*!

The metal dug into my skin.

"You're only making it worse," the guy said without looking up.

"They're cutting off my circulation." I hated the whine in my voice.

A car door slammed, and Ranger charged inside as if he owned the place, which was weird because he'd never been to my house as far as I knew.

Ranger Rodrigues was the local forest ranger, known as Ranger by everyone. He always wore reflective aviation sunglasses, and for some reason, it made me nervous when I couldn't see his eyes.

Ranger crossed the room, lips curling to reveal an extra-long canine tooth. "Why'd you cuff him?" Ranger asked, annoyed. "This is my district. What are you doing here?"

The man pocketed his phone. "Your job, apparently."

"What's that supposed to mean?" Ranger folded his arms. He was a gym rat and had the biceps to prove it.

"I'm following protocol. The un-sub has been executing unauthorized magic." The guy scowled at me as if I were a piece of dirt.

"Un-sub—as in unknown suspect? He's Noah Farmer, and you know exactly who he is."

The guy's eye twitched. "This place reeks of magical misconduct." He glared at me as if I creeped him out. "I'm placing this joker under arrest."

"Un-cuff him. He's not going anywhere," Ranger said, his voice rumbling in a low, menacing tone.

"He's my collar," the guy said. "I texted you as a professional courtesy."

Ranger's voice held an air of superiority. "Collar? You've been watching too many cop shows. And for your information, Noah's under twenty-one and a minor in the eyes of the Council." Ranger's unwavering gaze locked onto the guy's. "This is my turf. I won't ask again. Remove the cuffs."

"I'm following procedure." The guy's defensiveness was as glaring as a neon sign.

Ranger's muscles tensed, and a low, guttural growl rumbled from his chest.

As the power struggle continued, I found myself on the sidelines, caught in the crossfire. The room crackled with an intimidating tension. As the standoff peaked, Ranger radiated an intensity I hadn't seen before, like he became a whole new person.

"Okay, okay." The guy lifted his hands in surrender, and the cuffs vanished.

I rubbed the angry welts on my wrists.

"Are you alright?" Ranger's concern shone through his tough exterior.

"Yeah, but—"

Ranger raised a hand, cutting off my words, before dialing a number on his phone. "He's in trouble. Yes, ma'am—I'll wait."

I stood and pointed an accusing finger. "This guy broke into —"

"Sit," Ranger barked.

My eyes shot daggers at the guy in white as I dropped onto the couch with a huff, frustrated and angry. And like a big dog guarding his territory, Ranger positioned himself across the room, his attention fixed on the guy.

My brows creased into a sulk while my mind spun like a dryer, tumbling questions. One of Mom's sayings echoed in my mind—she had a stock phrase for every situation.

*Only fools rush in. Listen and learn, then decide.*

My hands trembled at the possibility of losing control. So, following Mom's advice, summoning every ounce of self-control, I exhaled and inhaled. With each deliberate breath, I repeated the mantra. *I can't control the circumstances, but I can control my reactions.*

Once I could speak without shaking, I headed into the kitchen. "I brewed a pot of coffee earlier. Who wants a cup?" I asked, faking a casual attitude.

Ranger's body language relaxed when I set the coffeepot down. I skipped the cream and sugar—my hospitality had limits. I eased into a dining room chair and breathed in the calming aroma of dark roast. Adopting a nonchalant demeanor, I glanced at Ranger over the rim of my mug. "So, who's this guy?"

"Guy?" Ranger pointed at the man in white, his grin wide

enough that light reflected off his extra-long incisor.

"Yeah, the guy who broke in."

"Guy," Ranger said, sliding into a chair.

I tried not to let Ranger's lack of information irritate me. Still, he tested my patience, and I think he was enjoying himself.

"Who's this guy, and what does he want with me?"

The guy stood rigidly by the back door. "Don't play dumb. You've been practicing magic without a license." His words spat with censure as he wiped the spittle from his mouth.

I flinched at the hostility, my bravado fading. "Ranger, answer my question."

"His nickname is Guy." Ranger sipped his coffee and hid his grin.

"No, it's not. My name is Erik Guyguyum. Erik with a K. I'm a magic enforcer." Erik, *the enforcer*, pointed a long finger at me. "You're under arrest for unsanctioned magic."

"What's that?" My eyes widened with apprehension. My heart raced as I realized Erik wasn't here only to make accusations. He intended to wield his authority. I swallowed hard.

"Ignorance of the law is no excuse." Erik Guyguyum gave me the stink eye. He had not joined us at the table, opting to loom by the door. His long coat billowed around him like smoke.

Ranger cut me off. "Don't say another word until you have proper representation."

Tires pounding gravel interrupted the conversation. I smiled as a vintage black Chevy ground to a stop outside the window.

My great-aunt Shirley swept in, and Ranger and I rose to our feet. She was in her eighties, but you wouldn't know it. Aunt Shirley didn't suffer fools and valued social etiquette, such as when men stood when a lady entered the room. And family was everything—no one messed with her family.

"I demand to know what's going on!" Aunt Shirley's blue eyes went flat, hard. "What do you want with my nephew?" Aunt Shirley may be tiny, but when she's mad—she's scary.

"Miss Shirley, calm down." Erik waved his arms in a placating fashion.

Aunt Shirley's cheeks turned a shade redder, and her nostrils flared. "Don't tell me to calm down. Erik, what are you doing here?"

Ranger offered Aunt Shirley a chair, and before she could acknowledge his polite gesture, I pointed at Erik. "Aunt Shirley, this guy broke in and handcuffed me." I didn't keep the whine out of my voice when I made my accusation.

She sat in the chair with the grace of a queen. "Is that so?" Her voice held a sharp edge.

The air was tense, an emotional volcano ready to erupt. Erik extended his palms in a gesture of peace. "Miss Shirley, I didn't know he was your kin. But we can't let this go unaddressed." He made a sweeping motion. "Ectoplasmic residue is spreading across the walls. The place is dripping with magical waste." He jerked his hand away when it brushed against the wall. His face flashed with disgust, as if my house had cooties.

Aunt Shirley's lips pursed in surprise as her gaze scanned the ceiling. Perplexed, I followed her line of sight, but my efforts revealed nothing unusual.

With a heavy sigh, she whispered, "Oh, dear."

"What?" I asked, my eyebrows popping and my head swiveling.

"It's getting worse by the minute," Erik said with disdain. "Can't you smell the ammonia? It's burning my nose and throat." He wiped his mouth with the back of his hand.

"Erik, please take a seat," Aunt Shirley said, gesturing to an empty chair.

"With all due respect, I'd prefer to keep my distance," Erik said, his voice tinged with revulsion. And as if he couldn't stand the thought of touching anything, he stuffed his hands in his pockets.

"Suit yourself," Aunt Shirley said.

"Aunt Shirley—"

She wasn't listening.

"Where's his sponsor?" Erik asked.

"Ranger has been keeping an eye on him," Aunt Shirley said.

I raised both brows at the revelation.

"No sponsor, that's quite irregular," Erik said.

"He only began manifesting magic a few weeks ago," Ranger said.

"How is that possible?" Erik pointed at the ceiling. "There's several years' worth of accumulated residue." He scrunched his face. "Stalactites of ectoplasmic poison are dangling from the ceiling." Erik shuddered. "One could fall at any moment."

"His parents raised him as a mundane," Aunt Shirley said, as if that explained everything.

"What's a mundane?" I asked.

"Non-magical people," Ranger answered in a rapid whisper, motioning to be quiet.

Erik looked dumbfounded.

"They thought it best to wait until he showed a particular interest or tendency," Aunt Shirley said.

I rapped on the table. "Hello, I'm sitting right here. Would you mind not talking like I'm not in the room?"

"But that's unheard of." Erik tilted his chin. "He's what—sixteen?"

"I'm nineteen, in case anyone wants to ask me."

"He should have chosen a specialty years ago," Erik said.

"He's had no training," Aunt Shirley said, biting her bottom lip.

"No training?" Erik repeated, scrunching his brow.

Aunt Shirley responded with a slight shake of her head.

Ranger shrugged. "When I first met him, I sensed a mere tickle of energy. Now, he's broadcasting magical power like a main event on ESPN."

Erik blinked twice as if processing the information. "So, who's his mentor?"

"No mentor," Aunt Shirley said. "His parents planned to homeschool him."

"I need to speak to them right away," Erik said. "They're negligent and should face charges."

My chair scraped against the wood floor when I jumped to my

feet. My fists clenched as I shouted, "Get out of my house!"

Erik shot me a disdainful look. "Control your pup, Miss Shirley."

"Sit, Noah," Aunt Shirley's eyes had lost their fiery edge.

I snorted and turned my chair around, simply to be annoying. But I knew the situation was grim when Aunt Shirley didn't react.

"Noah's parents, Emma and Eli, passed away a few years ago. After the tragedy, the family decided to delay introducing magic until Noah worked through his grief."

A strained pause fell. "Surely, you're well aware of the danger an undisciplined young wizard poses to himself and others."

"Yes, I know. And don't call me Shirley."

I muffled a laugh, grateful for my aunt's effort to put me at ease with our inside joke.

Erik stiffened. "He's a vulnerable target and could end up like Duncan."

Aunt Shirley's sagged, weariness etched on her face.

"Who's Duncan?" I asked, but no one answered.

"He needs training," Ranger said.

"I'll do it," Aunt Shirley said.

"You're too close. Noah must learn the proper accords of magic until a path chooses him," Ranger said. "Are you willing to let him fail? To let him suffer the consequences of his mistakes?"

Aunt Shirley's eyes watered as she processed Ranger's words. Then she set her jaw, her eyes glinting with determination. "He must go to Dragon."

Ranger leaned in, his expression filled with concern.

Aunt Shirley nodded with conviction. "Dragon is our best option—eccentric, yes, but brilliant."

"But what about learning independently, like I've been?"

Erik sputtered.

"You're transmitting beacons of energy, inviting practitioners of the dark forces to steal your powers, or worse," Aunt Shirley said. "Consider how easily Erik found you and disabled you. If he had a mind to, you'd be dead."

"We can't protect you," Ranger said. "Your magical powers are acting erratic."

I studied Ranger, wondering what part he played in this mystery dinner theater.

"You're ill, and Dragon is your best chance," Aunt Shirley said.

"I'm fine—"

But before I could argue further, Jesse exploded into the room. The screen door slammed. Ranger jumped out of his chair, alert and ready.

"Noah, come quick. Something's wrong with Bandit." Jesse held a cage with a raging raccoon inside—hissing and snarling. I stood to check on Bandit, but Erik blocked my path.

"It's worse than I imagined," Erik said, stepping away until his back touched the wall, and then he jumped as if burned and thrust his palms forward. "Don't come any closer with that—that creature."

Erik took a breath, his expression resolute, as if he had decided. "Okay, I'll do it—I'll take him to Dragon." He sidestepped Jesse. "Ranger, are we good?"

Ranger nodded, and the men shook hands.

Aunt Shirley sighed. "I hoped we'd have more time to ease him into this."

Ranger frowned. "Miss Shirley, Noah's in grave danger."

A wave of emotions crossed my great aunt's face before settling on determination. "Yes, he'll leave today." Aunt Shirley, the powerhouse, had returned. "I'll send word ahead to smooth things over." She paced, making plans. "Ranger, will you assist with the decontamination?"

"Wait a minute, don't I get a say in this?"

They responded in unison, "No!"

"Jesse and the raccoon also need cleansing, so take them with you," Ranger said. He motioned to Jesse. "Pack a bag, and plan to be gone for a while."

"Okay," Jesse said, running down the hall to the guest room. He had been staying with me after learning his stepmom was an evil witch. It was just like Jesse, not to question, but to jump in with both feet.

"Get your things." Aunt Shirley gave me a slight push, moving me forward.

I looked around my room, stuffing items in my backpack. When I spotted my grandfather's-grandfather Ezra's journal, I wrapped it in a soft cloth before placing it in my bag. I named the book *Mischief* because of the trouble it had caused. Besides, *The Book of Potions and Mischief for Beginners* was too long a title.

Five minutes later, shouldering my pack, I shuffled into the dining room, relieved that Bandit's rabid snarls had ceased. Nestled in a ball, the raccoon lay fast asleep, emitting gentle snores from within his cage. Jesse sat on the kitchen counter, tapping his foot. With his fiery red hair slicked down and an adventurous gleam in his eyes, he bubbled with excitement.

Meanwhile, Aunt Shirley banged around in the kitchen. A whirlwind of activity, orchestrating a symphony of clattering pots and pans, and then, with a satisfied smile, she emerged. "Food for the road trip," she announced, handing the bag to Jesse.

"What's going on?" I asked.

Aunt Shirley looked at me as if I was the dullest knife in the drawer. "We're sending you to Castle Dragon. I'm calling in a favor. Still, it's a long shot if Dragon will help you. Dragon hasn't taken a student in many years."

"Not since Duncan," Erik said, interrupting.

Aunt Shirley sent Erik a scathing glance. Confident that Erik received the message, she continued. "As I was saying, if Dragon decides you're worthy, I expect you to be humble, grateful, and to do your best."

"So I'm off to see the wizard," I said, putting on the charm.

"Noah, this isn't a joke," Aunt Shirley said.

"Why can't I stay here?" My stomach flipped at the thought of being sent away from the last of my family.

"I'm sorry to rush you, but you need urgent medical-magical attention." Then, with pensive eyes, she said, "Things may seem dark, but after you hit rock bottom—the only way is up."

I gulped. "I don't understand."

"Of course not, dear. I wish I could do more to prepare you." Aunt Shirley tilted her head as if she had an idea. "Do you have your mother's amulet?"

I patted my chest and felt its warmth.

Aunt Shirley rose on her tiptoes, pulling me closer so only I could hear. "Always keep it close. It will be your guiding light. Where's the Raven Moonstone?"

"It's in my pocket." When I handed her the brooch, it emitted a subtle hum.

Aunt Shirley grabbed the wizard staff leaning against the wall and expertly affixed the Raven Moonstone to its hilt. Both arcane artifacts had originally belonged to the wizard Ezra, my great-great-great-something-grandfather, our family's patriarch. But I had no idea what it was capable of. I stood thunderstruck, my mouth hanging open, as Aunt Shirley twisted the hilt of the staff. The etchings glowed as the wood transformed into a gleaming blade. With swashbuckling flair, she sliced the air.

Grinning, I rocked back on my heels. My amusement turned into a snort of surprise as she shrunk the staff to the size of a flashlight. Aunt Shirley handed me the telescoping wizard's staff. Upon examination, I discovered an array of configurations akin to a Swiss Army knife for wizards.

"This is a family heirloom. Honor the Raven Moonstone's power," Aunt Shirley said.

Erik's eyelid twitched. "Is that what I think it is? Stars have mercy. What's wrong with you people, entrusting arcane power to an ignorant mundane?"

"Mind your words, Erik Guyguyum."

Erik blinked, stepping away from my aunt.

Ranger stepped forward. "It's time to go," he said.

Conflicted, I gave Aunt Shirley a bear hug, and a lump formed in my throat. "I have a cross-country bike race next week. Can't I go after the race?" I said, trying one last time to change her mind.

Aunt Shirley's eyes softened. "This is best. Study hard, learn the ways, and choose wisely."

"What about my goat business? The Airstream—"

"I'll bring the goats to George, and the Airstream camper can stay at the campground," Ranger said.

My mind swam. "It's too sudden. Everything is moving too fast. I can't think."

"Let me make this perfectly clear—you and your friend must leave. You're a danger to yourself and anyone near you," Erik said. "We need to get your abilities under control or neutralized."

*Did he say neutralized?* Something like panic twisted my stomach.

"Think of it as an adventure," Jesse said, picking up Bandit's cage and following Erik outside.

"Safe travels. Come back to us as one of the good guys." Ranger grinned, handing me his card. "Call me if you get into trouble."

"Wizards and Werewolves Anonymous, Chief Security Officer —Ranger Rodrigues," I read aloud and flipped it over. "There's no number, so how do I contact you?"

"Kid, you're so green—it's hard to believe you're not a vegetable. If you put your thumb on the postage stamp barcode, it'll summon me." Ranger tilted his aviators. "But no crying wolf."

Aunt Shirley released a half-hearted chuckle. "You mustn't keep Erik waiting. He has a short fuse." She hugged me again. "This is for the best, but be careful who you trust." She shoved me out the door.

# CHAPTER 2

## *ON THE ROAD TO CASTLE DRAGON*

My roots ran deep in Sweetwater, stretching back for generations. My house sat on an acre of the original homestead. Uncle George continued to farm, as evidenced by the round bales dotting his south field. Aunt Shirley and Ranger stepped onto the porch while I kept Erik waiting in his white Jeep with oversized tires.

Not exactly eager to leave, I lingered beside Felix, Aunt Shirley's 1959 Chevy Bel Air Impala Sport Coup, admiring the fine lines and craftsmanship. Childhood memories of Felix, the monster car, reframed the Chevy's taillights and pipes to appear like predatory eyes and fangs. I blinked away my childish musings.

Aunt Shirley shuffled across the lawn and flashed her signature grandmotherly smile, reassuring me as always. Shielding her eyes from the morning sun, she gazed over the hayfield. A dark mass distorted the horizon. At first, I mistook it for a flock of barn swallows engaged in a ballet, but then I sensed brooding magic. I squinted to get a better look.

"It's begun," Ranger said, hurrying toward me—his expression grim.

I tilted my head, puzzled yet drawn to the swirling blackness.

Aunt Shirley thrust out her hands, shooting a blinding light. Thunder rumbled. The air charged with electricity, and my arm hairs quivered. She chanted ancient words, harnessing nature's forces, and sent a whirlwind of fog to repel the black mass.

Dazed, I felt the darkness beckoning me closer while Aunt Shirley's lightening-infused fog pushed against it. I rubbed my face. Never had I suspected my aunt possessed such tremendous power.

"I saved you the shotgun seat." Jesse stuck his smiling face out the side window.

Taken aback by Jesse's obliviousness, I slowed my steps, hesitating. *Was I the only one who felt the pull of the dark summons?*

Ranger grabbed me by the arm, dragged me across the yard, and shoved me into the front passenger seat. Slamming the door, he pounded on the roof. "Drive!"

Tires spun, and gravel sprayed as Erik's Jeep rocketed out of the driveway. My heart raced as lightning exploded. The engine roared, drowning out the thunder. A dense fog swallowed the car, but Erik didn't reduce his speed. He drove as if staying on the road was an afterthought.

My head bounced against the window when Erik hit a pothole. "Do you have to go so fast?" I didn't expect an answer.

Jesse leaned forward between the seats, his hot breath on my neck.

I elbowed him away. "Sit back and fasten your seat belt. The last thing we need is for Erik to slam on the brakes, sending you flying out the windshield."

"Ah, you're such a nag," Jesse complained, then pressed his face against his window. "This is crazy. I can't see beyond ten feet."

"Miss Shirley summoned fog to ward off the phantasmal invasion," Erik said, his voice clipped.

"The fantastical what?" Jesse asked from the back seat.

While Jesse peppered him with questions, Erik careened down the road like a madman and casually provided answers.

It didn't surprise me Erik responded positively to Jesse. Jesse had a knack for turning any situation into an adventure, and people gravitated to his carefree nature. Jesse reminded me of a red golden retriever—loyal, intelligent, with boundless energy and an eagerness to please. I envied his easygoing ways. While I struggled to make friends, it came naturally to Jesse.

Erik seemed fine with the backseat banter, even if I wished for a more focused driver who kept both hands on the wheel.

"You talk like a professor," Jesse said.

"When I'm not chasing rule-breakers—" Erik scratched his chin. "I teach a class in Parapsychology." He continued before Jesse could ask. "The course explores the psychology of magic, the conceptual and historical concepts of paranormal sciences." Erik met Jesse's eyes in the rearview. "I also conduct magical self-defense classes."

"That's cool," Jesse said with genuine enthusiasm. "And I suppose Noah's the so-called *rule breaker*?" Jesse snorted, shaking my seat.

"Cut it out." I knocked his hand away. "How was I supposed to know?" I muttered.

"The ectoplasmic crystals coating your house and yard should've been a clue," Erik said in the angry voice he reserved for me. "Wizardry leaves a residue, but professional practitioners leave no trace."

"Like green or environmentally friendly magic," Jesse said.

I rolled my eyes at Jesse, the teacher's pet.

"Sure, you could call it that." Erik nodded approvingly before his face took on a stern, commanding expression. "Your friend lacks discipline. His powers are progressing at an unsteady rate. He's been practicing magic without a clue, polluting the sector and attracting supernatural pests. The bottom line is that the kid's magic is unstable, and therefore, he's a menace." Erik's lips pressed tight, and he glanced at me with contempt.

I scowled, sulking under his criticism. *It wasn't as if I wanted to cause magical disturbances or attract pests, but it was more complicated than Erik 'the enforcer' made it sound.*

Erik growled. "I ought to haul you to jail, not some exclusive school for pampered wannabes. Kids like you using connections to shirk responsibility and dodge consequences—it's sickening."

"Hey, don't sugarcoat it. Why don't you tell us what you really think?" I clenched my jaw, twisted in my seat, and glared out the window.

Jesse, always the peacekeeper, leaned forward, his seat belt long forgotten. "Since we're in this car for a while, we should get along."

"Good try, Red." Erik glanced at Jesse through the rearview mirror. "But I don't plan to stick around. I'm splitting as soon as I dump you and your delinquent friend off at Castle Dragon."

As we barreled toward Dead Dragon Divide, a seven-hundred-foot canyon, the road deteriorated into rutted tracks. Recognition dawned—we were heading straight for the gorge.

Fear ran up my spine, my eyes as big as saucers. "Slow down!" I yelled, stomping my foot as if slamming on the brakes.

Erik hit the gas, letting loose a maniacal laugh.

Jesse shrieked as we plunged over the cliff.

We nosedived, and the canyon floor rose to meet us. The Jeep tumbled through an arctic vortex, and a biting cold filled the cabin. My stomach flipped, bile bubbled up. But to my astonishment, we landed with a mere thump, like hitting a speed bump.

This defied physics, considering the gorge was at least five miles wide. Since the daredevil Evel Knievel couldn't make a quarter-mile jump over Snake River Canyon, we shouldn't have been able to jump Dead Dragon Divide. But we did.

"Dude, how insane was that?"

"What just happened?" I said, running a hand through my hair and wincing at the headache stabbing my temple.

"We crossed over," Erik said. Erik, with a K (*maybe K stood for Knievel)*, eased off the accelerator, but not much. We continued at a reckless speed, driving through a narrow ravine where the scenery blurred in the side windows.

"Are we dead?" Jesse asked incredulously, voicing my thoughts exactly.

"No, we traversed the veil. Dead Dragon Divide is a portal to the Otherlands."

"You could've warned us," I said.

"Where's the fun in that?" Erik flashed a self-satisfied smirk.

Jesse burst into laughter while I folded my arms in annoyance.

We drove out of the canyon and zoomed along a mountain pass through forests unfamiliar yet eerily similar to home.

"Are we there yet?" Jesse asked.

"See that faraway mountain—we're headed to the top."

"I thought we were headed to this dragon guy—No one mentioned crossing into some other realm," I said.

"You never asked," Erik said, letting loose a rusty laugh. I wasn't sure what he found so funny. But then he got all condescending again.

"Castle Dragon is in the Otherlands." Erik shot me a sidelong glance. "Seems you don't quite grasp the situation, kid. You're spewing thaumaturgic ectoplasm. Your magic is on overload, and if I don't get you to Dragon, you'll burst."

"As in explode?" Jesse asked in astonishment.

"Yes, precisely. Your friend is manifesting poisonous magical waste. He's also broadcasting electro-magical signals to ectoplasm-eating bugs across the spirit world."

I wondered about the black mist over the hayfield, but I didn't ask because my stomach lurched into my throat when Erik stomped the gas. The dirt road narrowed to the width of the Jeep, and I hoped we wouldn't meet a vehicle coming in the opposite direction. There were no guardrails in the Otherlands. Jesse fell silent, allowing Erik to concentrate as he navigated the hairpin turns. Eventually, the road straightened, and we climbed above the clouds shrouding the valley below.

Jesse broke the silence with more nervous chatter. "Are these supernatural bugs you mentioned, like mosquitos and cockroaches?"

Erik went into professor mode. "It starts with micro bugs searching biodegradable organic ectoplasm. They're too small to see until they swarm."

"Like gnats?" I asked, hoping to join in the casual banter, but then a swarm of purple *no-see-ums* splattered the glass. The wipers swished back and forth, sliming the windshield with tiny bug guts.

"I just washed my car," Erik grumbled.

"I've never seen so many glowing gnats," Jesse said.

"The insects are not of your world. If given a chance, this variety will eat flesh."

"Can they get into the Jeep?" Jesse asked.

"Keep the windows closed. I'll try to outrun them."

After a while, Jesse poked his head through the front seats. "Is Noah still oozing ectoplasmic residue?"

Erik affirmed with a nod before yanking the wheel at a tight turn. "And you too, Red."

"Me?" Jesse squeaked.

The rearview reflected Erik's pale eyes and grim expression. "You, my red-headed passenger, are emitting ectoplasm." He motioned with his thumb. "And so is your caged raccoon in the back." Erik pointed at me. "The kid infected you both with the virus."

"Virus?" I said, my voice rising in alarm.

"Well, that's the best word I can figure for it," Erik said, looking at me. "Such a contagion is unprecedented."

Erik took a hairpin curve, pitching us to one side while half the vehicle swung over the ledge. I white-knuckled the grab handle while Erik managed to keep the car on the road—two of the wheels, anyway. The Jeep raced up the mountain, and the relentless swarm of purple bugs stayed with us, splattering the glass. The windshield wash sprayed, and the wipers squeaked while clearing a swath. Nevertheless, visibility remained sketchy.

"We need frogs to eat the gnats," I said. It wasn't the time to joke, but I was nervous.

Jesse chuckled. "Yeah, frogs love bugs."

Erik swerved from one side of the road to the other, dodging what?—I had no idea.

*Thump-thump!*

A bright green frog leaped onto the hood, and then more and more. A hailstorm of multicolored amphibians battered the Jeep.

One landed on the windshield, and its webfeet scrambled to grab hold before the wipers flung it off. The deluge intensified as larger frogs fell from the sky, turning the road into a slippery, slimy mess.

I had read about the meteorological phenomenon called frog rain. Frogs get sucked into the clouds during a tornado, dropping them miles away when it rains. But it wasn't that, because there wasn't any rain, only frogs.

"Dude, are you causing this weirdness?"

"No," I said, biting my lip to avoid voicing my doubts.

"But dude, you mentioned gnats, and millions of them appear. And now it's raining frogs after you talked about frogs eating gnats," Jesse said. "If it looks like a duck..."

I covered my ears. "La-la-la, I can't hear you, la-la-la." I know it was a childish response, but I was afraid of what would happen if I thought about ducks.

"Zip it! Not another word," Erik said, shooting me a look that sent a chill down my spine.

"It wasn't me," I said.

"I'm warning you, keep your mouth shut unless you want me to close it for you," Erik snarled.

"I liked to see you try," I muttered.

"Silence is golden," Erik said, flicking his right hand.

"Hm—mmm." My mouth wouldn't open, even when I pulled on my lips. My chest heaved, my body rocked back and forth, a rising panic taking hold. With deep, intentional breaths, I forced myself to breathe through my nose, trying not to hyperventilate.

"Hey, something's up with Noah."

"I glued his lips shut because his words were manifesting deeds." Erik gave me a sideways glance. "Calm down. You're fine."

"So Noah summoned the frogs and bugs—Cool."

*Crack!*

A split ran across the windshield, and more frogs pelted the glass.

Erik slammed the steering wheel. "Everyone shut up. I need to concentrate."

Thirty seconds later. "Ravens eat frogs," Jesse said. "Dude, summon ravens."

Erik sped through the downpour of amphibians. Frogs thudded against the Jeep, hopping off and into the roadside ditch. They nimbly avoided the oversized tires like a demented arcade game.

"Better yet, use your mental abilities and think them away," Jesse said.

With my lips stubbornly sealed, I tried to *un-frog* the rain. But I couldn't *un-think* a thought. Finally, I gave up and tried Jesse's idea to summon the ravens. I pictured a raven with iridescent hues shimmering in its oily black feathers. I imagined gliding on the currents, flying over the land with air rising beneath my wings. A peaceful solitude swept me away as I mentally escaped into my musings. My mother's amulet hanging around my neck vibrated as I envisioned flying with the ravens.

"You did it," Jesse said, thumping the back of my seat and jarring me from my daydream.

The ravens had arrived. And in a ravenous frenzy, they feasted upon the frogs. Erik never let up on the gas, even when an immense raven, its wingspan extending beyond the hood, swooped down and plucked a colossal orange frog off the hood. With the last hapless frog devoured, the ravens took to the trees. One raven remained, flying ahead as if to guide.

Despite summoning ravens to eat the frogs that had eaten the gnats, my lips stayed magically glued. With a groan, I fumed as I tried to make sense of my bizarre day.

*And how come I've never heard of Wizard Dragon? This has to be a dream. No, not a dream—a freaking nightmare!*

Our raven guide landed, and Erik slammed on the brakes as the Jeep skidded to a sudden stop. With an echoing *caw-caw*, the raven beat its wings and vanished into the forest.

The road abruptly ended at a sea of sunflowers, which surrounded the old bones of a castle. The once majestic fortress now stood as a hollowed shell of gray stone.

"We're here," Erik said. "Finally." He slumped in the driver's seat and let out a long breath.

"But there's nothing here," I said as my lips came unstuck.

"And again, you'd be wrong," Erik said.

ΔΔΔ

Wedged within the field of sunflowers stood a stone archway. Although resembling a Roman Triumphal Arch, it didn't convey a welcoming transformation from the old to the new. Instead, this gateway exuded a foreboding presence, with an orb blocking the entrance. Inside the sphere, flashes of lightning discouraged any trespassing.

Meanwhile, Erik preened in the rearview, smoothing his straw-like ponytail, adjusting his collar, and picking at his teeth before exhaling deeply. I winced at his bad case of halitosis.

"Stay in the car. I'll handle this." He swung his short legs out of the oversized Jeep and, without looking back, swaggered toward the mysterious light.

I couldn't resist the surge of defiance. *Erik's not my boss.* I opened the door. Jesse followed and rushed to the tailgate to check on Bandit.

Erik gestured for us to wait before turning to face the oscillating orb. "Greetings, Castle Dragon," he spoke as if he were a knight of the realm. "I seek an audience with the esteemed Dragon, for I bear a message of utmost importance."

"Halt! You're not welcome here," the orb responded. It had a reverberating metallic quality to its voice while it flashed at each word.

Erik motioned with flat palms. "We come in peace. I have an urgent message for the master of the castle."

"I demand you turn back." The light throbbed like a beating heart, each pulse accompanied by a word.

"We are weary travelers seeking asylum," Erik said. "I bring a dire missive."

"Go away!" The intensity of the vibration increased.

Erik continued his argument with the disco ball.

Jesse stood behind the Jeep, wide-eyed with excitement. "Bandit's sleeping," Jesse said before I could ask.

Intrigued by the unfolding events, curiosity propelled me forward for a closer look. The orb only pulsed when it spoke, and the rest of the time, it emitted various intensities of light.

Erik persisted, "With all due respect, we have traveled far and in great haste, seeking shelter and replenishment." Erik's voice resonated with self-righteousness. "It's imperative I speak with the master. Grant me an audience that I may fulfill my obligation."

"No one's home." The orb spun, emitting a high-pitched sound.

I scoffed at the waste of time. *We drove a long way for nothing.*

Frustrated with the lack of progress, I took matters into my own hands. "Excuse me," I said, interrupting the exchange despite Erik's dirty look. But then I hesitated, astonished by the icy blast stinging my face.

"Um—I was under the impression we were expected."

The orb buzzed in a screeching, frenetic gyroscope of light, warning me not to provoke it.

I ran my hand through my hair. "Fine, if we're not welcome—never mind. I didn't want to come in the first place." I motioned to Erik. "Forget it. Let's go."

# CHAPTER 3

## *PAYING THE TOLL*

A door with a luminescent threshold materialized, backlighting an outline of a person. I raised an eyebrow when my best friend stumbled through, wearing a hefty backpack and carrying a package. She lurched as if pushed, but stayed upright in her Doc Martens.

"What are you doing here? Better yet, how did you get here?" I asked, bewildered, but pleased to see a friendly face.

"I'll tell you later—"

"Hello, I'm Erik Guyguyum," he said with a smarmy leer.

"Nice to meet you—I'm Sara Goodness from Sweetwater." Her mouth curved into a soft and easy-going smile. Sara's eyes sparkled with warmth and natural grace, causing Erik to react with an audible intake of breath. This didn't surprise me—Sara had that effect on people. Still, I couldn't help but feel annoyed by Erik's interruption.

The orb, posturing with blinding strobes, broke up the reunion. "You're trespassing. Leave at once!" My skin crawled when the sphere screeched like fingernails on a chalkboard.

But Sara didn't seem surprised by a talking light bulb. "I have a private message from Sweetwater for Dragon," she announced assertively.

"No one here by that name," the orb said.

Undeterred, Sara revealed her trump card. "I brought cookies." Her voice chimed with musical laughter. "Shirley said you had a fondness for my Grandma Mercy's cookies."

The orb calmed, as if tempted by Sara's words. "Shirley and Mercy from Sweetwater? Did you say cookies?" The orb dimmed, and its voice softened to mere wind chimes on a summer day.

"I'm to pay the toll," Sara said, winking at me.

When Sara isn't living on campus, she stays with her grandmother, Mercy, my Aunt Shirley's closest friend. My mouth watered at the thought of Sara's grandmother's Toll House cookies. I hoped she brought enough to share.

"Please come in—Shea will assist you." The light softened into a pleasant glow as the orb withdrew, allowing us entry into the mystical realm. My skin tingled, and my ears popped as we crossed the threshold.

A woman in a purple robe awaited us, exuding an aura of authority. Her robe swirled, even though there wasn't a breeze. Her tight gray curls framed a round face that drew attention to her piercing violet eyes. Pearl earrings adorned her grandmotherly ears, adding a touch of elegance to her enigmatic appearance. A slight smile graced her lips.

Beside her, two magnificent Fell Ponies grazed on the lush lawn. These were no ordinary steeds but majestic beasts that embodied strength, beauty, and magic. With stout, powerful legs, feathering hair covering their hooves, and wild manes cascading beyond their eyes, they stood deceptively relaxed. Their ears perked at the slightest movement while their unmarred white coats shimmered.

The older woman stepped forward. "Welcome to Castle Dragon. I'm Mrs. Shea." She swept her arm in a dramatic gesture, and a medieval fortress materialized.

I gasped when the granite blocks of the derelict ruins rose like a phoenix assembling into an imposing fortress. Before us stood a castle with turrets, buttresses, and intricate carvings depicting ancient symbols and magical creatures. Towers with gleaming copper conical roofs reached toward the sky. I marveled at the stained glass windows, illustrating scenes of legendary battles, wizards, and fantastical beasts. I imagined the towers housing the wizard's library and perhaps Rapunzel herself.

My imagination ran wild, fueled by the countless hours spent reading fairy tales. Not the ones diluted for theme park amusement, but the original Brothers Grimm. I remembered my dad handing me a crate of old books—one of his garage sale finds. Both Dad and Mom loved old-world stories. As I let my mind wander, the grand castle radiated a soft, ethereal glow.

But it was the horses that stole Sara's heart. She handed me the care package and stepped closer. The ponies blew and sniffed her outstretched hand. "Oh, you're both so beautiful—yes, you are," Sara cooed in baby talk while the ponies nickered and nuzzled her shoulder.

After a bit, Sara turned to the elderly woman with a warm smile. "Your Fell Ponies are absolutely magnificent. I just had to say hello to these sweeties. But where are my manners? I'm Sara, and Shirley asked me to pass along a message. Thank you for allowing me a moment with these gentle creatures before we talk."

This pleased Mrs. Shea. "Orion and Altair approve." The woman stroked the horse's neck. "Animals can sense a pure soul."

Erik stepped forward, clearing his throat. "I must speak to Wizard Dragon."

Mrs. Shea dismissed Erik with a wave of her hand. "All in good time. Collect your things and wait here."

She snatched the plate of cookies from my grasp and turned to Sara, smiling warmly. "Come along, dear. So how is Mercy these days?" she asked.

Sara sent me a knowing glance before hurrying to match the older woman's stride. The horses whinnied and plodded behind. Again, I couldn't help but notice the subtle glimmer of magic as the ponies' hooves skimmed across the grass, leaving faint, sparkling hoof prints. When they disappeared behind a hedge, I took it as a cue and went to collect my things.

Erik had also returned to the Jeep. He looked around before speaking in a voice only Jesse and I could hear. "What did you not understand about staying put?"

"Hey, you weren't getting anywhere with that orb thingy, were you?" I said.

Erik's eye twitched. "You need to learn to take orders."

Taking advantage of my height, I leaned in. "I don't need or want a babysitter," I said, forgetting Erik had overpowered me in my house only that morning.

"Look, kid, I'm not the enemy. Once I present you to the wizard, I'm out of here. It's time you grow up and learn to control your powers, or we'll have a disaster of Brobdingnagian proportions."

"Brob-ding-a-what? Who talks like that?" I put my hands on my hips. "My name is Noah, so don't call me kid."

"Then stop acting like a spoiled brat." Erik walked back and forth, fuming.

My anger bubbled with childish insults that I didn't say. *What's with all the white? He needs a splash of color.*

Then, in perfect synchronization, a flock of pigeons unleashed an aerial assault on Erik, showering him with droppings. I leaped aside, narrowly escaping the bombardment while struggling to contain my laughter. Erik yelped and ran for the Jeep, grabbing a napkin and wiping off his sleeve. When he realized he was making it worse, he growled and took off his coat, revealing a white silk shirt.

Jesse's hysterical laughter echoed through the air. Tears streamed down his face as he pointed at Erik and snorted.

Erik retaliated with a flick of his wrist, and suddenly Jesse was hanging upside down from a tree. A web of vines draped from a gnarled oak had wrapped around Jesse's ankle. I flinched at Erik's startling demonstration of wizardry. Erik's gaze swung from Jesse and locked onto mine with an intensity that made me take an involuntary step back.

"Watch your temper." Erik laced each word with simmering anger. "And never disrespect the wardrobe."

I swallowed a laugh when he mentioned his fashion choices. "Hey, don't blame me." I raised my hands in surrender.

Erik's eyes narrowed. His mouth moved as if to speak, but he clamped it shut at Jesse's cry for help.

"Get me down. This isn't funny." Jesse squirmed, twisted, and bucked, but the vines were unyielding.

The man's stern expression showed no signs of softening. "Not until you show some respect."

"Hey, I was an innocent bystander." After flailing a moment longer, Jesse conceded. "Okay, respect, respect. I promise."

A thick vine dropped, offering a lifeline. Jesse swung his body, gaining momentum to grab hold. The struggle continued, but he didn't quit. Finally, Jesse pulled himself up, straddling a branch. He untangled his feet and used the rope to slide to solid ground. Without hesitation, Jesse made a mad dash for Erik. It was subtle, but Erik's body tensed.

Jesse skidded to a stop. "That was amazing," he said, grinning from ear to ear. "I wish I could do that!"

The stern lines of Erik's face relaxed, and his mouth tilted into a thoughtful half-smile. "You're okay, Red."

While Jesse beamed at Erik's approval, Erik turned his stern gaze on me.

"What?" I tossed my hands up in frustration. "It wasn't me."

"You conjured the pigeons."

"No way." I scrunched my brow. "Really?"

"My point exactly—you have no idea. Control your emotions, and definitely don't think, say, or do anything to act upon them," Erik said. "We need to get you into treatment."

"Okay, whatever." I leaned against the Jeep, considering Erik's words. *Was I creating havoc?*

A few pink clouds drifted overhead, and a solitary raven flew across the sky while Erik paced in brutal silence. After a while, Mrs. Shea appeared around a hedge, moving along the grass as if she floated.

Jesse scanned the lawn. "Where's Sara?"

*Good question.* I quirked my brow in response.

Erik leaped to attention and directed his conversation to Mrs. Shea. "I have urgent business with Wizard Dragon."

"Yes, I know—asylum, was it?"

"I'm a magic enforcer, a commander of the guard, and these are my charges. I have explicit orders to escort this young man and his companions to Castle Dragon. The wizard must decide the consequences of this hooligan's blatant disregard for the sacred rules of magic. I insist upon a meeting at once."

Mrs. Shea's eyes flashed. "Don't presume, Commander."

Erik stammered, humbling himself with a bow.

Mrs. Shea put on a neutral face. "Okay, then, let's see to your comfort."

"Are you accepting receipt of my charges?" Erik asked in a subdued, respectful tone.

"Of course." Mrs. Shea moved toward the castle.

"It's getting late, so I'll be on my way." Erik turned toward his Jeep.

Mrs. Shea spun on her heels. "Absolutely not!" Her face grew serious. "You require decontamination and quarantine along with the others."

"Oh, no," Erik said, shaking his head. "I'm not staying. I have pressing responsibilities."

"Not anymore. You've been in contact with toxic magic."

"I'll be fine," Erik said. "Besides, you can't keep me against my will."

Mrs. Shea's eyes darkened, and the air crackled with a clap of distant thunder. "Don't believe that for a minute. You're a guest here, whether you like it or not. Do I make myself clear?"

Erik paused for half a beat. "My apologies to you and your household." He bowed his head deferentially.

Satisfied that she had made her point, Mrs. Shea resumed her swift pace. Erik hurried to catch up with her.

As they walked, Erik recounted the day's events to Mrs. Shea, slinging accusatory words like *reckless*, *irresponsible*, and *ignorant* as he described my actions. In his version, Erik had heroically driven me, the *delinquent wizard*, and my *misguided friend* Jesse to seek medical help. He portrayed himself as boldly piloting his cherished Jeep through a torrent of frogs and other mishaps as a favor for my Aunt Shirley. He spoke as though his noble act was one step shy of global salvation.

I clenched my jaw as Erik continued his verbal attacks, but held my tongue. *There's no point in defending myself. He'd only twist my words to his advantage.* I kept such thoughts to myself and slowed, gaining distance from Erik's annoying voice and slanderous comments.

Soon, I engaged Jesse in lively banter about the much-anticipated opportunity to explore a sorcerer's keep. "At least we'll visit a proper castle."

Jesse bounced on his feet. "Do you think we'll see an actual suit of armor?" He seemed to forget he held an animal carrier with a sleeping raccoon. The cage swung as we walked.

I gave Jesse a playful shove. "Not one that would fit you. The average height of a knight of the realm was five and a half feet. But I know an egotistical magic enforcer who could fit into one." I motioned toward Erik, strolling along the path, his words spilling forth at twice the speed.

"I doubt Erik would wear it," Jesse said. "He's too serious to have any fun."

"Right, and besides, he's more of a tinman without a heart than a chivalrous knight," I said, sharing a laugh.

Jesse's excitement boosted my spirits. We were both looking forward to exploring the castle, imagining the wizard holding counsel with his loyal vassals and the intrigue within the ancient walls. The trail wound us through a courtyard and toward the woods. Our enthusiasm deflated with each step that led us away.

We approached a wooded glen and stopped before a quaint cottage with a thatched roof and a stone chimney. The damp earth mingled with the pine trees, creating a woodsy scent. A vigorous vine with glossy leaves and vibrant blooms clung to the porch, adding to the ambiance of an enchanted forest.

*This cottage nestled in the woods is a scene straight out of 'Hansel and Gretel.'*

I shivered—recalling the rest of the story featured a cannibalistic witch and her oven.

Mrs. Shea clasped her hands and nodded toward the lodgings. "The stonecutter's cottage will serve as the guest house during your stay at Castle Dragon. Make yourselves comfortable and meet me in the solarium in an hour." She turned to leave, but stopped. "Oh, and bring Bandit, your raccoon friend."

Erik carried a duffel bag in one hand and reached for Mrs. Shea with the other. "One moment."

Mrs. Shea pinched her lips, eyeing Erik's hand on her sleeve.

He withdrew his hand as if burned. "Ma'am, where are my quarters?"

"Hm—did you not hear me say you are welcome to stay at the stonecutter's cottage?"

"With them?" Erik stood dumbfounded. "No, this won't do." He shook his head vigorously. "I require separate accommodations."

Mrs. Shea's expression grew strained as her eyes darkened. "You each have your own room and will share the living room, the kitchen, and, of course, meals."

"But—" Erik sputtered, "I need my privacy."

"This is the best I can do on short notice," Mrs. Shea said, her voice rising. "What do you expect when you turn up uninvited?"

"But what about the castle? Surely, a private space is available for a warden of good standing." Erik gestured, asserting his self-importance.

Mrs. Shea's brows lifted, and her purple eyes flashed. "You're fortunate the cottage is available." Her tone grew menacing. "There's always the dungeon."

Her gaze shifted toward the winding trail. "Is there anything else?"

"No, ma'am," Erik's voice went flat. "I appreciate the hospitality."

Mrs. Shea gave a quick nod and continued down the path. I smirked at Erik's awkward moment, wishing I could've heard what Mrs. Shea muttered, but clearly, Mrs. Shea didn't suffer fools.

Erik adjusted his duffle bag. "Well, this is unexpected." Then, straightening his posture, he marched into the cottage.

Jesse placed a hand on my shoulder. "This place reminds me of the fairy tale about the girl in a red cape."

"Little Red Riding Hood."

"Nah, the other one."

Jesse waved off the thought and bounded up the steps.

ΔΔΔ

Sara greeted us with a relaxed smile when we entered the cottage. "There are three rooms downstairs and a loft upstairs." She pointed out the finer details of the guesthouse while playing the part of a tour guide. Sara described our lodgings as cozy, with a beamed ceiling and a massive fireplace.

But I would've preferred a medieval castle with grand halls, enchanted towers, and hidden stairways.

"Dibs on the loft," Jesse said. He placed Bandit's carrier beside the kitchen table and climbed the primitive ladder. "Hey, there's even a TV," came Jesse's voice from above.

"This place is amazing," Sara said, watching me with amusement as my eyes wandered to the bookshelves. We were both bookworms. Truth be told, I had more books than friends.

"We have time to settle in before meeting Mrs. Shea." Sara gave me a friendly shove toward the library.

I ran a hand along the bindings, comforted by their scent and feel. I chuckled when I noticed someone had organized the books not by author or category, but by color. It seemed impractical, yet charming. I plucked an old edition of Grimm's Fairy Tales from the shelf and traced my finger across the embossed cover. A chair beckoned, and I settled into the soft leather, resting my feet on the ottoman.

As I cracked open the book, Erik snatched it from my hand. "Give me that. The last thing you should do is feed your imagination." His expression twisted with annoyance.

I swallowed my retort and heeded my mom's advice about

responding to anger with kindness. “I suppose you're right.” Managing a friendly tone, I added, “Sorry about the pigeons. It was an accident.”

I paused, waiting for Erik to reciprocate and apologize for gluing my lips shut. Instead, he grunted in response and stormed outside.

With a frustrated huff, I went to find my room. It was the only one left since everyone else had already chosen theirs. The ceiling angled to the sides, like an attic room, even though it was on the first floor. In the corner, a simple wood desk with a pitted surface from years of use held a gleaming polish. Across the room, an old wardrobe stood sturdy and tall. Its weathered exterior reminded me of a children's story, where a hidden world awaited discovery. I chuckled at my whimsical notions and surrendered to the appeal of the feather bed tucked within the slope of the ceiling.

As I closed my eyes, the surrealism washed over me. And once again, I assured myself, this was all a warped fairytale dream—None of this was real.

*Okay, I'll run down this dream and go wherever it leads, and when I wake up, everything will be right again.*

It sounded good, but I had my doubts.

ΔΔΔ

I opened my eyes when I heard Jesse's excited voice. Curious, I headed off to investigate. Jesse stood in the kitchen, his gaze fixed on the overflowing pantry.

“Wow, that's weird.” Jesse rummaged through the stock of supplies.

My brow furrowed in confusion.

“These are all my favorite snacks,” Jesse said, his expression a mixture of surprise and joy as he grabbed a box of cheese crackers.

I shrugged, not grasping the significance.

"The pantry was empty a moment ago, and I didn't see anyone come in."

Meanwhile, Sara baby-talked to the raccoon cradled in her arms. Jesse and Sara had been caring for the critter since his injury. To my surprise, someone had dressed him in a little kid's outfit.

"Why is he wearing clothes?" I asked.

Sara's eyes sparkled. "Bandit likes it." Her voice carried a hint of laughter.

"It's undignified," I said, scratching behind Bandit's ears.

Bandit had classic markings with black around his eyes and a bushy ringtail. Faint static rippled his salt and pepper fur as I petted and cooed over the raccoon dressed like a cuddle toy. Bandit chattered at the attention. After a while, he became restless, so Sara set him on the wood floor.

Bandit coughed, a distressing, gurgling rattle, and I thought he was choking. But that's not what happened. Jesse's shocked face said it all.

Bandit rose onto his hind legs, his body elongating as he stood upright. His arms straightened, and his paws spread into fingers as he took on a humanoid shape. In the midst of this metamorphosis, a man emerged, six feet tall with a cropped haircut and a dark beard. He stood barefoot, clad in shorts and a T-shirt. Dark circles around his black eyes gave the impression that he hadn't slept. But it was the thick hair covering his limbs that caught my attention.

Unsteadily, the human-raccoon placed his hand on the table and offered a weary smile.

Sara laughed nervously before addressing the man standing before us. "Bandit, are you okay?"

He blinked, opened his mouth, and shut it again.

Uncharacteristically silent, Jesse rubbed his head, causing his shock of red hair to stick out in all directions. "Dude, you're a dude. I mean, you're human!"

Bandit examined his hands as if seeing them for the first time. "Yeah, I guess I am," he said in a gravelly voice before sinking into a nearby chair.

"And you can talk." Jesse scrubbed his eyes in disbelief.

Erik stormed into the room, causing the door to slam shut. He glanced at Bandit and then, with a searing glare, cast all blame in my direction.

"I wasn't me!"

"That's what you always say," Erik said, his tone filled with accusation. "You never take responsibility."

Jesse stepped between us, flashing a toothy grin, and introduced Erik to Bandit, describing Erik as the magic police. Despite his recent transformation, Bandit stood and extended his hand in a friendly greeting.

Erik's eye twitched, ignoring Bandit's offer to shake hands. "This isn't good. Oh no. Not good at all," Erik said, gesturing as he paced.

Bandit padded into the kitchen. His human form adapted, walking on two legs as if it were second nature. Bandit pulled himself onto the counter, hanging his feet off the side. Then, gnawed open a box of crackers and crammed the cheesy snacks into his mouth.

"Too dry," Bandit said, spewing crumbs.

When Sara handed the raccoon-man a glass of water, he sniffed the glass, assessing its contents before taking a gulp and dribbling some down his chin. Bandit wiped his face with his arm. Then, with a newfound solution, he dunked each cracker into the glass before popping it into his mouth. We watched in silent amusement as Bandit indulged in his innate routine of washing his food.

I gave Sara a cheeky wink and said, "Old raccoon habits die hard."

Then Erik rudely reminded us we had a meeting. "Enough nonsense. Mrs. Shea is waiting, and it's time she begins magical decontamination before Noah causes more trouble."

Bandit slid off the counter and brushed the crumbs off his chest. We followed Sara out the door while Erik muttered to himself, questioning what he did to deserve this.

# CHAPTER 4

## *PEARLS OF WISDOM*

Mrs. Shea stood amidst the blooming hedges, her long handle clippers poised in her hands. The sweet scent of flowers mingled with the earthy aroma of wood chips. Her lavender eyes twinkled when they landed on Bandit. "More shenanigans, I see."

"It wasn't me," I mumbled, scuffing the toe of my boot idly against the ground. "Weird stuff keeps happening around me." A lingering pang of guilt knotted my stomach.

Erik stepped forward, brandishing an accusatory finger. "It wouldn't if you learned to keep your mouth shut and your thoughts positive." The vein in his temple throbbed, and his left eye twitched.

I shot Erik a defiant look, refusing to be bullied. "Maybe you're the—hmm." I couldn't believe it. He did it again. My face flushed with humiliation. Anger surged through me. I glared at Erik with daggers while trying to open my mouth.

Mrs. Shea shook her head in disapproval. "Erik, that was rude." She sounded like my second-grade teacher when she made a *tsk-tsk* noise with her tongue.

"Perhaps, but effective. Besides, the kid's a menace," Erik said as if that explained everything.

I snarled, clenched, and unclenched my fists while spiteful comebacks bounced in my head.

*Erik looks like my neighbor's dachshund with short legs, a long nose, and a permanent sneer. And that dog was mean, too, just like Erik. If I could speak, I'd give him a piece of my mind.*

A blast of energy erupted from my fingertips, and a gust of wind rustled the leaves, spinning the pile of clippings into a dust devil. The dervish engulfed Erik, showering him with sticks and stones. I balled my fists in alarm, stuffing them into my pockets, and the whirlwind disappeared.

Erik's face twisted as if he were about to sneeze. Twigs and leaves clung to his hair, and dirt coated his once pristine white shirt.

"*Woof-woof,*" Erik barked canine complaints.

Jesse's jaw dropped, and Sara gave me an accusing stare.

Even with my lips sealed, I couldn't stop the self-satisfied smirk stretching across my face. *It was only barking, after all. Lucky for Erik, I didn't turn him into a mongrel dog—not that I knew how.*

Erik let out a pitiful howl, the kind a coyote makes in the dead of night. I wish I could say I was sorry, but I wasn't.

Mrs. Shea fought to keep a smile from her lips, but amusement glimmered in her eyes. "You two had better play nice. Otherwise, it will be a difficult quarantine." She pulled a slender rod from an inside pocket. With a flick of her wrist, she tapped Erik's shoulder and then mine.

A tingle spread along my neck, reached my chin, and pinched my lip like a pair of pliers. With an invisible yank, my mouth popped open, making a lip-smacking sound.

Meanwhile, dirt rolled off Erik, leaving his shirt clean and fresh. Sidestepping the pile of twigs, he moved closer, his eyes devoid of humor. "Never do that again," he said, his words cutting like a knife.

I forced an innocent smile.

But Erik wasn't one to forgive, nor did he believe me. He puffed his chest and flared his nostrils. And if looks could kill, well, I would be long gone.

Mrs. Shea intervened, patting Erik on the arm. "Easy now. You know he's unwell and cannot control what's happening. As a professional, experienced practitioner, you need to exercise patience. Encourage, don't discourage."

Erik blinked at the scolding. His expression ran the gamut—surprise, denial, humility—and settled on neutral.

Without further delay, Mrs. Shea glided toward the conservatory. Erik pushed forward, opening the door into a blast of hot, moist air. He graciously held it open while Mrs. Shea and Sara entered, quickly stepping in behind Bandit and Jesse.

With a smirk, he let the door slam in my face.

ΔΔΔ

Glass walls enclosed an ideal habitat for exotic flora, their vibrant colors contrasting against a swirling mist, which bore the earthy scent of a rainforest. But there was something about that place that set me on edge. My imagination conjured lurking predators, ready to pounce, sending an uneasy shiver down my arms. I fought to suppress my anxiety, fearing it might accidentally summon a real monster.

Mrs. Shea led us to a corner patio and served tea. Jesse gagged on the bitter brew. But Mrs. Shea insisted we drink it, claiming her medicinal tea would cleanse us. I pinched my nose and gulped the foul concoction, suppressing my revulsion through sheer willpower. Bandit dunked a sugar cookie, crammed it in his mouth, and washed it down with his tea. He made no reaction to the taste and grabbed another cookie.

Sara wiped her mouth. "That wasn't so bad." But her watery eyes gave her away. She cleared her throat. "When does it take effect?"

"Immediately," Mrs. Shea said. "Use your third eye to see the ectoplasm dissolving into ash."

Sara's face went blank, eyes glazing as she described our auras. I stared, stunned she could use her third eye. *Why had she never told me?*

Jesse crossed his eyes and rolled them around, asking if he had a third eye.

"Everyone does, but it takes practice. You all have various

magical gifts—with training, you can learn to see with your third eye and more."

"Will you show me how to use my other eye?" Jesse asked with his easy-going enthusiasm.

Mrs. Shea nodded. "Close your eyes and calm your mind."

Jesse pinched his eyes tight, unable to sit still in anticipation.

"Relax," Mrs. Shea guided in a soothing voice. "Focus on the middle of your forehead where your third eye resides. Open your mind to the mystical."

I took a deep breath and closed my eyes, but doubts nagged me. *What if I couldn't control what I saw*? I steadied my breathing, pushing aside my hesitation. The flowery scents in the greenhouse faded, replaced by a smoldering fire smell. A feather-light tickle brushed the hairs on my arms.

Before I could stop myself, I peeked—expecting to catch Jesse playing a trick. Instead, I found myself staring into the golden eyes of a dragon, its green scales glinting in the dim light. Ancient intelligence radiated from the beast as it attempted to probe my mind. Pain lanced my forehead when I recoiled from the creature's psychic touch. I yelped in shock, my chair screeching back, breaking the connection.

Around me, the greenhouse swam back into focus.

"Did you see a spider?" Jesse teased, knowing how much I *hated* spiders.

I pressed a hand to my temple, steadying my breathing, unable to explain.

Mrs. Shea continued, as if nothing had happened. "Very well, that's enough for one day." She refilled our cups. "Everyone, finish your tea."

Jesse groaned, pinched his nose, and guzzled. As he set down the empty cup, his face erupted in surprise.

Mrs. Shea smiled. "Only the first cup is bitter. After that, it tastes like lemonade. The tea will boost your immunity and help shed the parasitic magic from your system." Mrs. Shea sipped her tea. "A week of quarantine, and I'll reevaluate."

"Are you drinking it too?" Jesse asked.

"Yes, Noah is highly contagious," Mrs. Shea said. "Not to worry, it's merely a precaution."

I couldn't pinpoint why, but Mrs. Shea's confirmation made my illness feel real. Despite feeling fine, I couldn't ignore it anymore. The sooner I accepted this truth, the sooner I could turn the problem into a challenge—one that I could solve.

*One thing for sure—I would do what it took to learn to control my magic. I refused to be a victim of circumstance.*

While I gave myself this massive pep talk, Sara asked about Bandit. "Does Bandit have the virus, too?"

Mrs. Shea tilted her head and studied Bandit in human form. After a long pause, she said. "We'll have to let the idiomorphic process run its course—wait and see. But, in the meantime, everyone drinks the tea. That includes you, Bandit.

"Yes, ma'am," Bandit said. "It's delicious."

Mrs. Shea smiled, crinkling the corners of her eyes. "As guests of Castle Dragon, you're welcome to explore the grounds, but don't venture beyond the wall or into the fortress itself."

Erik leaned forward earnestly, having run out of patience. "With all due respect, I must speak to Wizard Dragon."

Mrs. Shea set down her teacup with an audible clink, her expression hardening, as she responded, "He's away on business, so anything you need to say to Wizard Dragon, say to me."

"It's my duty to ensure my charges receive proper medical care," Erik said.

"Yes, of course." She waved a dismissive hand. "I have the herbal supplements required to manage Noah's emerging magic, and we've already discussed the remedy for the virus." She rose from her chair. "Go along now. I'm a busy woman. I can't spend all day chatting." If anything, Mrs. Shea was direct. Some might find it abrupt, but I appreciated she didn't mince words. As we prepared to leave the greenhouse, Mrs. Shea touched my arm. "I'd like a private word."

I suddenly felt like I was being kept after school, having failed to impress.

Sara, Jesse, and Bandit rushed outside, eager to explore. Mrs.

Shea locked eyes on Erik, clasped her hands under her chin, and waited for him to get the message. Erik cleared his throat and turned to leave. When he pulled open the screen door, it gave out a mousy squeak, slamming behind him with a loud bang.

ΔΔΔ

Alone with Mrs. Shea, my gaze swept over the menagerie of plants. Despite the stillness, leaves rustled, and vines quivered. Mrs. Shea remained composed, as if expecting me to speak. Since she was the one who requested the private meeting, I waited. Besides, I didn't know what to say and wasn't ready to discuss what I had experienced with my third eye.

I couldn't shake the image of the dragon, its shimmering scales and intelligent eyes etched into my memory like a permanent marker. Questions and concerns flooded my mind, their weight pressing down on me.

*Was the dragon a messenger or perhaps a warning? If so, what message did it carry? Maybe I shouldn't have been so quick to resist when it tried to create a psychic connection.*

Uncertain of Mrs. Shea's true identity and intentions, I guarded my thoughts. My fingers sought comfort in the smoothness of the pendant hanging around my neck. A mix of proverbs came to mind, and I considered their wisdom.

*A wise man holds his tongue. Knowledge speaks, but wisdom listens.*

My family often quoted old proverbs to provide insight into a problem. And now it seemed I had inherited the quirk. But it felt like sage advice, so I buried my questions and put on an easy-going face.

Mrs. Shea stared at me with an unreadable expression while her dark purple robe billowed on its own accord. "Walk with me," she said.

Mrs. Shea glided through the rows of exotic plants, greeting each one carefully, tending to any brown spot or imperfection.

As we ventured deeper into the greenhouse, the plants seemed to come alive, their lush greenery rippling in response. They danced in a chorus line of adoration, their flowers opening as if vying for her attention. As an experienced herbalist, she pointed out specific plants and described their valuable properties.

My irrational fear vanished while touring her magical and welcoming garden. I couldn't help but wonder why my initial impression had been tinged with a sense of foreboding.

We wandered the labyrinth of raised beds and planters. Soon, we stopped next to a massive creeping vine weaving through a trellis. The climber had purple leaves and delicate bell-shaped flowers. With a gentle touch, Mrs. Shea palmed a bell petal, coaxing a glimmering pearl to slip from the flower.

"Hello, my sweet Bella. This young man is Noah, and he requires your pearls of wisdom."

She guided my hand below a bloom. "Now you try. Caress the bell and tip the cone so the bead will release." Mrs. Shea smiled. "It takes a light touch." A warm pearl rolled into my hand. "Thank you, my beauty," Mrs. Shea said like a doting parent.

A sneeze escaped when the heady scent of lavender triggered my allergies. "That would be Bella. She has a scent for every mood," Mrs. Shea said, smiling at my reaction. She reached into her pocket and handed me a glass container. "I want you to harvest the pearls until the bottle is full, and be sure to thank Bella for her generosity." Without a backward glance, Mrs. Shea strolled on, attending to her nursery.

I bit my lip. Aunt Shirley and Mercy often chatted with their plants. Still, I felt silly because it wasn't something I'd ever done.

"Uh, hello, big vine plant thing." I slid my hand under a bloom. "I hope you don't mind if I help myself to your pearls."

Although I followed Mrs. Shea's instructions, Bella didn't cooperate. After a few attempts, I grew impatient and thought I'd give her a nudge. As if shooting marbles, I flicked the flower with my thumb and finger.

*Whoosh!*

A vine caught my feet, snaked around my legs, and lifted

me off the ground. Upside down, I struggled to break free. Bella's runners wrapped around my chest while others bound my hands. I squirmed and kicked, sending a trellis crashing to the floor. The scent of Bella oozed, a hot spice stinging my skin. My eyes blurred with tears as if I'd been pepper-sprayed. Panic surged, and I screamed.

"Bella! Release him at once," came Mrs. Shea's voice.

The vines stopped crawling, and the pressure against me eased. Bella uncoiled with a yank, spinning me like a top before dropping me on the floor. I scrambled, backing away from *Evil* Bella, shaking and gasping for breath.

"What was that?" I stammered, wiping my face with my shirt.

"Not to worry, dear. Bella threw a tantrum. She's okay now," Mrs. Shea said as she adjusted a vine.

"That—that plant creature tried to kill me!"

"Not at all. If Bella wanted you dead, she'd have been much more creative."

"Oh, that's reassuring."

"Bella, that's not how we treat guests," Mrs. Shea said as she re-threaded the vines.

*Unbelievable! The plant monster tries to kill me, and she talks to it like a spoiled brat. If it were up to me, I'd get the hedge clippers!*

"Noah, try again, but this time without patronizing."

"But that vine's a monster," I said, rubbing my neck.

"Bella's pearls are key to managing your magic. It would be best if you'd established a positive connection." Mrs. Shea gave me a stern look. "You're the human, so it's up to you to create a relationship based on respect and trust."

It took a few minutes for me to collect my courage. Despite my lingering doubts, I took a breath and squared my shoulders. No way would I let a freaky flora get the best of me.

I put on a cheesy smile. "Your flowers are beautiful, Miss Bella. The most glorious in the land. May I please have a pearl?" I asked, sliding my shaky palm under a blossom. A soft tinkling bell sounded when a glistening bead spilled into my hand. The scent of cinnamon spice tickled my nose, and I took it as a positive sign that Bella's mood had improved. I dumped the pearl into the glass container.

"Remember your manners, Noah," Mrs. Shea said expectantly.

*What about Bella's manners?* "Uh, thank you, magnificent jewel." I didn't sound convincing.

Mrs. Shea cupped her hand over her mouth and whispered to Bella. Its vines rustled in response.

"Carry on," Mrs. Shea said, gliding toward a potted flower at the end of the row.

A solitary yellow stem, as thick as a number two pencil, held a dangling purple orchid and quivered in anticipation. As Mrs. Shea approached, a second orchid unfurled, and her delightful laughter floated to my ears.

When I returned my attention to Bella, I stood on the balls of my feet, prepared to run at the slightest sign of aggression. All the while, the tendrils of the temperamental creeper danced as if taunting me. Nonetheless, I put on the charm, and Bella cooperated. She rewarded me with a pearl of varying sizes with each word of praise. The delicate beads glimmered, their iridescent hues reflecting the depth of my compliments. The more outrageous the flattery, the quicker Bella delivered. Soon, I had the glass container filled with Bella's precious offerings and went in search of Mrs. Shea.

Mrs. Shea sat on a stool, engrossed in her work. A workbench adorned with jars and canisters of various shapes and colors lined the shelf behind her, creating a mosaic of glassware. Though tidy in the immediate vicinity, the table bore evidence of Mrs. Shea's work, with scattered remnants of dirt, twigs, and powder.

Mrs. Shea glanced up, her eyes meeting mine. "Finished so soon?"

I offered a satisfied smile and placed the container filled with Bella's pearls on the table.

"Are you ready to make your first potion?" She gestured for me to take a seat. "These are for you. The bowl is called a mortar, and the pestle is used to grind."

My face flashed surprise at the unexpected gift, but it soon furrowed in concentration as Mrs. Shea introduced me to the art of potion making. I followed her lead, mimicking her actions, and soon found the knack of keeping Bella's pearl from rolling out from under the pestle. After crushing the bead into a fine powder, we added lavender, mint, and a pinch of saffron. The fragrant scents wafted above our cramped workspace as we worked in companionable silence, our grinding and mixing interrupted only by a whistling teapot.

Mrs. Shea grabbed cups from the shelf, inspecting them with a practiced eye. "The cups were clean when I put them away, but we don't want any spiders in our tea, do we?"

Although she was joking, I shook my head in firm refusal. I suffered from arachnophobia and didn't want to think about those creepy eight-legged creatures. There was no telling what nightmares my mind might conjure. I wondered if my accidental magic was like the frequency illusion—when you first notice something and then suddenly see it everywhere, as if your brain becomes hyper-aware. *Was my magic hypersensitive?*

I thought to ask Mrs. Shea about this theory, but before I could, she handed me a steaming cup of tea, insisting I would also need to drink *Pearls of Wisdom* daily to stabilize my spiritual core. She told me my therapy would include a healthy diet, meditation, and physical training.

I couldn't help but roll my eyes at the all-too-familiar advice. "Yeah, yeah, I know—diet and exercise, the magical cure-all. Your body is a temple, *blah, blah, blah,*" I snarked, adding a smile, so she knew I was teasing.

"Don't be impertinent," Mrs. Shea scolded, though her displeasure didn't reach her eyes. "We are what we eat, and magic manifests according to our attitude. Positive emotions yield positive magic, while negativity attracts the darker elements."

I waved a hand dismissively and smiled. "Alright, alright, no need for the lecture—I'll be a good wizard and eat my veggies." I wiggled my eyebrows and made her laugh.

Nevertheless, Mrs. Shea continued her lecture. Her eyes were bright with excitement as she motioned with her hands. "Physical exercise clears the mind, strengthens the body, and burns magical waste. Such discipline builds character. Healthy habits cultivate positive thinking, which is crucial for developing proper wizardry."

"More platitudes and theory when all I want is to learn how to *do* magic?" I sighed.

Mrs. Shea's expression softened, understanding my eagerness. "The first step is purifying your spirit and opening yourself to instruction. Meditation clears the mind of sludge, allowing for introspection and self-auditing of thoughts. Cull the negative thinking, like a gardener pulling weeds." She tapped her cup against mine in a toast. "Patience."

I drank my tea and pondered Mrs. Shea's words while a sense of peace spread through me. After a while, she told me Bella bloomed only one month a year, and that it was fortunate I arrived in time to help with the harvest.

"We should have enough pearls for both of us."

Confusion flickered across my face. "Both?"

"Yes, I need Bella's medicinal pearls as well."

I gave her a questioning look, and when she didn't share, I asked if there were any side effects to *Pearls of Wisdom* tea. Mrs. Shea said I could expect an increase in appetite and fatigue, meaning I might need to sleep more often. She also warned that, as a novice wizard, executing magic could bring on sudden fatigue. Hence, the reason for meditation and the therapy we had discussed. Since I was always hungry and didn't mind a nap now and then, it seemed worth the risk.

After a while, Mrs. Shea led me to a garden patio with a courtyard view. The eye-catching brickwork complemented the lush green lawn. Broad leaves of a shade tree cast dancing shadows along the stones, and a hummingbird swooped in, pilfering the nectar of a flowering hedge. Mrs. Shea unrolled a yoga mat, motioned to a second mat that hadn't been there a moment ago, and asked if I was familiar with meditation.

I nodded, recalling Aunt Shirley had often talked about its benefits. Mrs. Shea inhaled and slowly exhaled. Following her lead, I closed my eyes and relaxed my shoulders, immersing myself in a state of repose.

"Out with the bad, in with the good," Mrs. Shea said.

My eyes sprung open. "That's what Mom said whenever I was upset or sick."

Mrs. Shea's eyes warmed. "So the young wizard *did* receive training—you recognized *The Raven's Mantra*. It cleanses the spirit of negativity." She stretched her arms above her head before slowly settling them on her lap. "Shall we continue?"

I nodded, dropping my eyelids into a soft gaze. Mrs. Shea's calm voice repeated the familiar mantra, guiding me through the meditation and encouraging me to slow my breathing and clear my mind. I experienced a gradual rebalancing of my body and mind. My muscles relaxed, and my breaths deepened, bringing a sense of calm relaxation.

A warm breeze stirred, and I found myself in a different place. I sat atop a tree with a gnarly trunk, its branches adorned with purple leaves. The landscape stretched before me, with shimmering sand meeting towering cliffs. A dragon with an impressive wingspan took flight. It cast a long shadow as it glided, landing before a cave. When I moved my legs, I slipped, and the disorienting sensation of falling jolted my eyes open to find Mrs. Shea's penetrating gaze set upon me.

She leaned forward, her eyes searching. I blinked in confusion, and as my dream retreated, my awareness of my surroundings returned. We sat on our mats. The shadows hadn't moved as though no time had passed.

"What did you see?" she asked.

"What's going on?" I answered her question with a question. Besides, Mrs. Shea's unwavering gaze was creeping me out.

"You had a vision." Her eyes widened the way people do when encouraging someone to share. "Tell me everything."

As Mrs. Shea locked her eyes on me, I became increasingly guarded. I wanted to keep my vision private until I grasped its significance. And I didn't want to give up the information, not understanding the power it might yield. So I balked. "I don't remember." I pushed the hair from my eyes. "When I try to remember, the dream slips out of reach."

Mrs. Shea regarded me, sensing my resistance. "I'll work on a dream-catching potion to help you remember," she said, her stare unwavering.

"Why remember my dreams and visions?" I asked, genuinely curious.

"Clarity—dreams are a wizard's instrument."

*Why does she keep staring at me?*

Although the outside temperature was cooler than the greenhouse, beads of sweat formed at my temples. I avoided her eyes but felt a tug, as if she was trying to read my mind. Instinctively, I blanked my thoughts, staring off into the distant trees. I refused to budge. Setting my resolve, I stood tall against a stubborn shield of silence.

Mrs. Shea let out a breath. "Impressive—Alright, I'll accept you as a student."

It was as if I had passed a test I didn't know I was taking.

"You must meditate and drink the tea daily," she said. "Record your dreams in a journal. The path of magic intertwines with your spirit. Explore it with an open mind, and you'll discover wonders beyond your imagination." A smile pulled at the corner of her mouth. "I'll teach you and your friends the principles of elemental magic. Your days here at Castle Dragon will be full."

I grinned as the realization of her words penetrated my thick skull. "Thank you! I know I have a lot to learn, but I'll try my hardest."

Then, as an afterthought, she added. "And Erik will provide personal defense training."

"Erik—why him?"

"Why indeed?" Mrs. Shea smiled. "But let's keep that between us until I can speak to him directly." She waved her arm in a dismissive gesture. "Run along and tell your friends. I believe they're in the woods. In time, we'll decide on your quest."

"Quest?"

"No more questions," Mrs. Shea said. "I have work to do. I don't want to be disturbed anymore today."

"Sure thing, Mrs. S!" I turned on my best smile.

"Mrs. S—" She pursed her lips as if trying the moniker on for size. "I like it—it has a nice ring."

With an excited fist pump, I kicked my feet, jumped over the hedge, and ran toward the woods. "I'm going to learn magic!"

# CHAPTER 5

## *SETTLING IN*

The setting sun painted the forest in soft emerald hues. Leaves crunched under my feet as I approached, my friends standing before a sprawling oak with a majestic crown commanding the sky. Amusement swept across their faces as Bandit climbed the tangled branches. He leaped from one limb to another without hesitation. Birds tweeted their approval as Bandit, in human form, traversed the tree with the agility of a raccoon and the style of an acrobat. Upon discovering a cluster of acorns, he eagerly filled his pockets.

When Bandit noticed my arrival, he waved a jaunty hello. Then, he executed a flawless backflip with a ten-point landing. Jesse cheered while Bandit juggled acorns with an infectious grin. He tossed one high and attempted to catch it with his mouth, but I intervened.

"Hold on." I snatched the acorn from the air. "Human teeth aren't strong like raccoon teeth. They're not made for cracking nuts."

Bandit's jovial expression slipped into a frown, and his stomach released a soft rumble. I recognized the *hangry* look and pulled an energy bar from my pack.

"Here, eat this instead." While Bandit munched on his snack, I turned to Jesse and Sara. "You need to watch him. He doesn't know the first thing about being human." I sounded like my father and groaned at the thought.

Bandit waved his hand, dismissing my concern for his safety.

"Only a bit of fun," he said, with his mouth full.

Jesse tossed his hands in the air. "We didn't tell him to climb the tree."

"It's not about that," my words came out stiffly, my concern obvious. "Raw acorns could be poisonous to humans."

Sara furrowed her forehead, pondering Bandit's transformation. "Is Bandit human now?"

"We should ask Mrs. Shea," Jesse said, then took off toward the greenhouse. Looking over his shoulder, he yelled, "Race ya!"

Bandit bolted. Sara laughed and sprinted after them, and determined not to be last, I pushed hard to catch up.

We found Mrs. S mixing mulch. Jesse bounded forward, jumping in front of the elderly alchemist. "We have a question," Jesse said, bouncing on his toes.

I gnawed on my lip, remembering Mrs. S had asked not to be disturbed.

She held a trowel and wiped her brow with her wrist, leaving a smudge of dirt across her forehead. With a sigh, she tossed the garden tool on the workbench and turned her undivided attention to Jesse.

Jesse didn't contain his curiosity, bombarding Mrs. S with rapid-fire questions. "Is Bandit a human or a raccoon? Can he eat acorns? He looks like a regular guy, but Bandit climbs like a raccoon and washes his food like one." Jesse mimicked a raccoon's washing motion with his hands. "Oh, and Bandit likes to inspect shiny things."

Warm, grandmotherly patience settled across her face. "One question at a time," she said, lifting her hand to stop the barrage of words spilling from Jesse's lips. "But you're right. I neglected to give Bandit a proper magical checkup."

Mrs. S cautiously approached, extending her hand, smiling as Bandit sniffed her fingers. She rose on her tiptoes, gently touching his bearded face. It seemed like an unspoken connection passed between them as she patted his arms and chest.

"You look like a police officer patting down a suspect." I held back a snort when Jesse spoke my thoughts.

"Shush, I need to concentrate." Mrs. S paced. "Curious, very curious indeed." She rubbed her chin as she muttered. "A peculiar anamorphism with infused magic throughout his core, which has been progressing for some time."

"Is that because Noah saved Bandit?" Jesse asked.

Mrs. Shea quirked a brow. "Saved him—from what?"

With his usual enthusiasm, Jesse explained how I used magic to heal Bandit's broken leg and emphasized my use of the 'out with the bad, in with the good' mantra. Jesse updated Mrs. S, telling her he and Sara had been taking care of Bandit since then. Today, when I petted Bandit, static crackled with each stroke, and shortly afterward, he transformed into a raccoon-man.

Mrs. S regarded me with a perplexing stare before offering an explanation. She surmised Bandit had been slowly changing, and my leaching magic unwittingly moved it along.

"Is that why Bandit the raccoon has been acting all scared and snarly?" Jesse asked.

Mrs. S nodded her head. "Yes, the initial anamorphic transformation can cause discomfort and confusion."

Bandit leaned against the table, folding his arms and crossing his ankles. His voice carried a hint of curiosity when he asked, "What's the bottom line, doc?"

Mrs. S turned to Bandit. "If my assessment is correct, you have the best of both worlds. The agility and digestive system of a raccoon and the intelligence and appearance of a person. So, eat all the acorns you want." Her expressive eyes grew serious. "Your hybrid nature has both pros and cons. You have a raccoon's temperament—curious, adaptive, and mischievous. But raccoons are also notorious for having a short temper, so no biting."

"If I can't bite, how will I eat?" Bandit deadpanned.

Jesse chuckled. "She means biting people. Humans don't bite each other. It's okay to bite food."

"Got ya," Bandit snickered, splashing a goofy grin.

Mrs. S shook her finger. "This is not a joke. Bandit, you will need to learn to navigate both worlds."

"So, can you fix him?" I asked.

"Bandit's not broken," Mrs. S said, her eyes glistening with compassion. "Either Bandit will revert to a permanent form or transform at will. Only time will tell."

Bandit nodded, his expression unchanging. He received the diagnosis unfazed, displaying his uncanny ability to adapt. But his casual attitude contradicted the gravity of the situation, and I wondered if Bandit truly comprehended how I changed him. I certainly didn't understand the full consequences of my magical mistakes.

Guilt gnawed at my stomach, and I cast my gaze downward. "Sorry, Bandit. I didn't mean to turn you into a transformer."

"I'm fine." Bandit swung his arm around my shoulder in response.

We stood there arm in arm, smiling as Mrs. S continued. "The proper term is therianthrope, meaning Bandit can shift between animal and human form. Whereas transformer is a passive component that transfers electricity," Mrs. S said, embracing her new role as our teacher.

The complex terminology left me bewildered. I had much to learn about this new world.

"We'll review this in our coursework." Mrs. S smiled, deepening the wrinkles at the corner of her eyes. "Bandit, I expect you to take part in our lessons, and I'll help you adapt and explore your anamorphic abilities."

"What lessons?" Sara asked.

"Hmm, Noah has been remiss in communicating our next steps," Mrs. Shea said with a twinkle in her eye.

"I really haven't had a chance—I've been busy making sure Bandit didn't get food poisoning or break a tooth," I said with a smile.

Mrs. S chuckled. "Bandit can take care of himself, so don't worry about him. He's the least of your problems." She rested her hand on her waist. "I've decided to teach an impromptu wizardry boot camp. There's an agenda and curriculum posted in the cottage. I'll cover basic magic and evaluate your skills. We'll have group labs and individual projects. It'll be fun. I haven't taught a class in a while." Mrs. S glanced at her potted plants as if they were beckoning for her attention. Our conversation ended abruptly when Mrs. S picked up the garden trowel and returned to her project.

As we filed out the door, Sara paused and looked over her shoulder. "May we visit the ponies?"

"Yes, of course, dear. Orion and Altair would welcome the company." Mrs. S waved us away. "Go—leave me be."

ΔΔΔ

Time flew by as we settled into the woodcutter's cottage. Each day, songbirds would rouse me from my slumber. I drank my herbal remedies, meditated, and experienced no magical mishaps. Our rigorous schedule had Mrs. S teaching magic in the mornings and Erik conducting combat-sport classes in the afternoons.

Our classes were challenging. Mrs. S introduced us to the concept of the Essence of Things (EOT). The foundational energy for all magic. She described elemental manipulation, herbal alchemy, and the art of mental projection. She taught us how to weave spells and concoct potions. Mrs. S claimed magic was two parts discipline and one part art.

Mrs. S fostered a special bond as she worked one-on-one with us. We adored Mrs. S for her wit and counsel. She helped Sara expand her paranormal gifts, Jesse to harness his control over fire and light, and Bandit to adapt to his shapeshifting abilities. Mrs. S urged me to tap into my latent wizardry buried deep within my core.

I excelled in the theoretical principles of magic, but floundered with the application. Every time we had a lab exercise, I faltered, mediocre at best, unable to produce the desired results. I always choked, and I felt like an epic failure.

Mrs. S, relentless in her pursuit of perfection, was particularly tough on me. I never caught a break. She showered Jesse with praise for a mere spark and beamed at Sara's progress with herbal remedies and her powers of perception. And, of course, Bandit, our ever-faithful therianthrope, could do no wrong.

Despite failing labs, I took detailed notes and could recite the technical aspects verbatim. Unimpressed, Mrs. S criticized my overly academic approach, saying it lacked *finesse*. She even labeled me *magically constipated*, urging me to relax and let the magic flow.

During our free time, Sara honed her martial arts skills with Erik and assisted Mrs. S in the greenhouse. Jesse burned his extra energy by going for long runs, and as for Bandit, he napped.

Meanwhile, I spent independent study buried in magical theory, memorizing formulas and incantations. Yet, no matter how hard I worked, my assignments ended in disappointment.

In one session, Mrs. S challenged me to stir sand with magic, but standing at the counter with a half-filled bucket before me, I couldn't lift a single grain. Mrs. S, her patience waning, scolded, "Why do you resist?" Before I could explain, she raised her palm, silencing me. "No excuses. I want results. Engage with the essence."

Scrunching my brows, I focused my thoughts, exerting mental pressure. The strain built, my temple pounded, and the tension in my neck intensified. I was sure my head would explode, but I couldn't move the sand. Frustrated, my confidence as a wizard slipped through my fingers like the sand that I couldn't shift.

"Observe," Mrs. S said, grinding her jaw. With a series of hand gestures in a rhythm only she could hear, the sand lifted, twirled, and formed a delicate castle.

She shook the box, causing the sand castle to collapse. "Okay, your turn."

"I'll try," I said, uncertainty tainting my voice.

"Don't try. Do!"

My chin quivered as doubt crept in. "What if I lose control?

What if my magic gets out of hand?"

Mrs. S creased her brow, her gaze heavy upon me. "You mustn't let fear be the reason you fail."

I nodded as if in agreement, yet remained unconvinced.

"Doubt will kill your dreams faster than any failure ever can. Believe in yourself. Remember, doubt is the true enemy."

I summoned my will, tapped the essence, and mentally commanded the sand to move. I focused, pushing with my mind until my head throbbed, and I couldn't hold my breath any longer. The sand shifted, but I wasn't sure if it was by magic or from my defeated gasp for breath.

"Don't forget to breathe," Mrs. S said. "That's enough for today —It's time for lunch."

ΔΔΔ

My stomach complained, reminding me of its emptiness. We ate our meals together, all except Mrs. S and Erik. When Erik wasn't teaching, he avoided us.

Back at the cottage, a variety of sandwiches, fruit, and snacks sat on the counter, prepared in our absence by a mystery chef. Bandit eyed an open box of crackers and poured them into his mouth. "Crikey, these are bonza."

I smirked, sharing a sideways glance with Sara as she rolled her eyes at Bandit's sudden Aussie accent. I didn't have the heart to tell Bandit that raccoons weren't native to Australia.

Jesse chuckled at our reaction, filling us in on their late-night movie marathon. Sharing that, he and Bandit had been binge-watching those old Crocodile Dundee films, and now Bandit's convinced he's the next Mick Dundee. "It's actually pretty hilarious," Jesse added, tossing a grape into the air and deftly catching it in his mouth.

ΔΔΔ

Combat-sport training awaited us after lunch. Erik agreed to train us only as a favor for Dragon, emphasizing that he wouldn't typically waste his time on beginners. Erik had zero tolerance for slackers and showed no mercy. He melded various forms of martial arts into his unique style. He emphasized self-defense and using force only as a last resort. We spent hours mastering protective shields and wards. Erik boasted his blend of techniques and principles was better suited for the Otherlands. Nevertheless, Erik was a skilled practitioner, and with the speed and precision of a black belt master, he taught us basic fighting maneuvers.

Erik's compact frame wasn't a factor when he faced off against me. Even though I was a foot taller and carried more weight, Erik had quick moves, understood leverage, and never missed an opportunity to toss me on my butt.

Jesse was fast and had a natural talent for martial arts. Jesse also enjoyed being dramatic, and any chance he got, he'd throw in a backflip or tumble just for fun. His speed gave him an advantage, but when Jesse knocked me down, I didn't mind because Jesse always grinned and offered me his hand.

One afternoon, Erik introduced us to fencing. He handed each of us a thin stick, instructing us to treat it like a sword. We learned how to hold it and the basics of movement. Erik urged us to connect with our sabers, and when I held the birch branch, I felt its essence naturally. The makeshift sword became an extension of my arm—I had found my rhythm. I matched Erik stroke for stroke, our sticks clacking in a flurry of sound. Then, feigning a move, I lunged for a direct hit, but Erik countered by sweeping out my leg. I fell on my back, his mock sword pointed at my chest.

"Hey, that's cheating," I protested, shuffling back on my elbows.

"Gentlemen's rules don't apply in battle. Expect no mercy from your opponent," he said.

*Battle? What battle?*

Before I could voice my confusion, Jesse charged ahead. "Dude, that was epic. Where'd you learn to fence like that?"

"Dunno, maybe I have a long-lost pirate ancestor I don't know about." Brushing myself off, I added, "Who's hungry? I'm starving."

ΔΔΔ

Back at the cottage, the aroma of freshly baked blueberry muffins drew me to the sideboard. I nearly knocked over the stack when I grabbed for the biggest while playfully elbowing Bandit out of the way. I wasted no time devouring the warm muffin. "Delicious," I said with my mouth full.

Bandit grabbed three, juggling them with ease.

"Leave some for me," Jesse said, pushing his way to the table.

"You guys eat like animals," Sara said, then, glancing at Bandit, she added, "No offense."

"None taken, Sheila," Bandit said, dunking his muffin in ranch dressing.

# CHAPTER 6

## *A COSTLY MISTAKE*

The weeks rolled on, one after another, blending into a seamless flow of time. Despite the challenging work, I was learning and having fun with my friends. They were some of the best days of my life, but I should have known it wouldn't last.

It began like any other typical morning, with the sun rising and the world waking up to a new day of possibilities. We sat at our designated workspaces while Mrs. S lectured and paced, her purplish robe sweeping the floor with each step.

"The universe's building blocks are earth, wind, fire, and water." Mrs. S paused and looked up as if surprised we were listening. She was an engaging teacher, and we hung on every word.

"What are some manifestations of water?"

"We drink water," Bandit said in a thick Aussie accent.

A smile graced Mrs. Shea's lips as she turned to Sara. "One manifestation of water is steam," Sara said with enthusiasm.

"Water extinguishes fire," Jesse said, grinning widely.

For my turn, I blurted, "Ice."

"All excellent answers." Mrs. S clapped her hands.

"Whoa!" Jesse started at the sudden appearance of four bowls containing clear water.

Mrs. S cleared her throat. "Sara, your assignment is to change water into steam," she said, "and Jesse, I challenge you to create a fire that water cannot extinguish."

Jesse scrunched his face in concentration and nearly jerked

out of his chair when an idea struck him. "Like Greek fire, invented by the Roman Empire."

Mrs. S nodded in agreement. "Absolutely, but the Romans didn't invent it. A mercenary wizard created the secret incendiary and sold it to the Byzantine Empire, an eastern part of the Roman Empire at the time. But I digress. Where was I?"

We waited while she collected her thoughts. "Ah, yes—Bandit." She beamed at the raccoon man. "Enjoy a refreshing drink of water, and then you're excused."

"Hey, how come Bandit gets off so easily?" Jesse complained.

"Lucky for us, he didn't say bathe," Sara said with a giggle.

"I guess we know who the teacher's pet is," Jesse said, folding his arms, pretending annoyance.

We all laughed when Bandit faked a growl.

"Attention, please," Mrs. S tapped her wand on the desk. "Noah, your lab assignment is to conjure ice. Mind you, I want to see your artistic side, not a block of ice." She spread her hands wide. "Okay, class, you have until noon. And go!"

As the class got to work, Bandit brought the bowl to his lips and slurped. Mrs. S chuckled. "There are still a few acorns left, so run along and enjoy the forest."

"G'day, mates." Bandit saluted the group and headed for the door.

I stared at my ceramic bowl, pondering how to transform the water into ice, but my mind blanked.

*Snip-snip.*

The sound of pruning shears broke my concentration. I chuckled to myself. *I hope Evil Bella gets cut down to size.*

Sara called for Mrs. S as a curl of mist danced across the table, and when it tickled my nose, I fanned the fog away. Sara's eyes lit up as she smiled at her swirling masterpiece.

"Well done, Sara," Mrs. S said. "Orion awaits his ride." Delighted, Sara hugged Mrs. S before hurrying off.

Meanwhile, a fiery sphere burned on top of the water. "Bravo, Jesse, now go find something constructive to do."

"You got this," Jesse said, giving me an encouraging punch in the arm before dashing away.

I sat gawking at the bowl of water.

*Why did I choose ice? Everyone else can do the simplest assignments. What's wrong with me?*

After a while, Erik barged in, his long coat billowing behind him. He took a moment for his eyes to adjust from the bright sunshine to the shadows of the greenhouse before winding his way through the garden maze. He spoke in a low voice. Although the words didn't reach my ears, Erik's body language and Mrs. S's stiff posture told me something unusual was happening. Erik shook his head and pointed toward me.

And that's when Mrs. S noticed my eavesdropping. She put her arm on her hip. "Get back to work. You'll stay here until you complete your assignment. Even if that means missing lunch." Satisfied she had made her point, she turned her back to me and engaged Erik in a heated discussion.

I stared at the bowl until my eyes burned.

Erik plunked down a glass bowl. "Like this—Watch and learn." He drew in the air with his index finger. Fine droplets of water rose from the bowl, spinning into the shape of a spider with eight legs and menacing eyes.

I shuddered but quickly steadied myself, not wanting Erik to know about my fear of spiders. "Wow, that's fantastic. How'd you do that?" I almost sounded like I meant it.

"Clear your mind of all doubt. Your lack of confidence is a weakness holding you back." His mouth moved up a tick as if it might've been attempting a rare smile. "Now, you try—You can do it."

*Maybe Erik isn't such a jerk.* But then I pushed my luck as I surveyed the room and asked, "Where's Mrs. S?"

"Not your concern. Mrs. Shea had to step out and left me to babysit," Erik said sharply.

I bristled at the remark.

Erik headed for the door. "I'll be outside in the shade. Let me know when you finish and be quick about it. I don't have all day." The screen door screeched when he flung it open.

Alone at the table, I searched my memory for a solution, but none came. The sticky greenhouse air suffocated me, and the view through the glass distracted me. The deep blue sky and trees swaying in the cool breeze taunted me while the hard chair gnawed my spine. Stretching to ease the kink, I spied the magic tome, *Mischief*, poking through a side pocket of my pack.

I had discovered *Mischief* was more forthcoming—whether because of the Otherlands or my skills were improving, I didn't know. But when I asked about my studies, pages would flip, and the information would appear. *Mischief* could give me the answer. He could tell me the secret of crafting an ice sculpture masterpiece worthy of my wizard ancestry. I gnawed on my lip at the temptation.

"G'day, mate." My friends had joined Erik on the patio.

*Moo-haw*! Erik's laugh honked like a goose with a cold.

Jesse and Sara erupted in a chorus of laughter. My friends' cheerful chatter ignited my resentment.

*It's not fair—My assignment is ten times harder.*

My eyes darted to *Mischief.* Creative problem-solving possibilities ran through my mind.

*Is this an open-book test? Well, Mrs. S never said it wasn't. Besides, isn't that a skill, researching the information?*

My back cracked as I stretched from side to side. I snatched up *Mischief* and my lab and moved to the floor. Thinking I could meditate and clear my mind, I sat cross-legged and closed my eyes. After a moment, one popped open and spied *Mischief.*

*Maybe, just a hint in the right direction.*

When I whispered to *Mischief* for an ice castle spell, his pages fluttered and opened to a page with three words.

I let out a long breath—my palms sweating as I averted my eyes from the ancient text. Jesse's laughter reached my ears, and I turned away from the window and stared into the water glistening in the bowl. I gnawed my lip, tempted yet torn, my gaze drawn back to the simple phrase.

*Could it be that easy?*

With a furtive glance at the door, I made my decision—*I had to try it.*

So, with a grandiose flourish, I uttered the incantation, "Pruina calor receptum."

In a flash, unbridled cold lashed out from my fingertips. The temperature plummeted, and frost formed on the ceramic bowl. The water rose into delicate ice spindles, and the icy bones of a miniature castle took shape with turrets, towers, and a drawbridge. I was both exhilarated by the enchanting magic and mesmerized by the breathtaking beauty of delicate ice crystals sparkling like diamonds. The frost spread across the greenery, transforming it into an instant winter wonderland where ice fairies would play.

I gaped when such a fairy appeared, offering me the slightest of nods. The tiny sprite fluttered about the ice castle, her wings glistening with frost. When the screen door squealed, she darted into my shirt pocket.

Erik marched over, fury twisting his face. "By Merlin's beard, what sorcery is this—"

The frost swallowed him whole.

I jumped to my feet, blinking and rubbing my eyes at the scene that had unfolded. Ice crystals coated every nook and cranny of the greenhouse. I shuddered, but not from the cold. I trembled from fear and the harsh realization of what I had done.

Sara and Jesse ambled in with curious expressions. Sara's eyes widened at the sight of Erik. She grabbed Jesse, yanking him outside, the door slamming in her wake.

Mrs. S burst in. "My plants, my darlings—ruined!" She stumbled but caught herself. The frost vanished with a wave of her hand, but the damage was complete. Erik stood frozen in mid-step. The garden had withered and turned brown.

Sara cracked open the door, venturing a step forward. Jesse, looking over her shoulder, gave a low whistle. Sara shot me a murderous glance.

My stomach lurched as I began to grasp the full extent of my accidental magic. With a trembling voice, I said, "I'm so terribly sorry, I um—"

Mrs. S raised a hand. "Not now."

She made a clucking sound as she inspected Erik, who teetered mid-step, frozen solid, with an expression of twisted, horrified anger.

"Will he be alright?" Sara asked.

"Too soon to say," Mrs. S responded.

Sara took charge and cleared a spot for Erik on a nearby bench. I looped my hands around Erik's chest, and Jesse grabbed his boots. I grunted. Erik was heavy, like lifting a cement statue or a solid block of ice. "Erik—I don't know if you can hear me, but I'm sorry," I whispered. "I'll make it right, I promise."

Sara bunched a lab coat into a pillow and slid it under his head. Next, she found a blanket and tucked him in. Like a mother hen, Sara nestled Erik on the bench, making him as comfortable as possible, considering the situation.

My brow furrowed at Erik's ashen skin and blue lips. I touched his icy neck but couldn't feel a pulse. "Is he dead?" I asked, swallowing hard.

"No, but he's cryo-magically frozen, and the plants I need to defrost him are—" Mrs. Shea stifled a sob, pressing her fist to her lips. She leaned against a table, wilting like her enchanted garden.

My shoulders slumped. "Tell me what I can do to set things right."

Mrs. S shook her head in hopeless despair.

"What about dragonroot?" Sara asked, raising her eyes in question. Sara had taken an interest in herbal magic and spent her free time studying with Mrs. S.

"Impossible." Mrs. S wrung her hands. "Well—perhaps."

A ribbon of hope flickered between us. "Tell me where, and I'll get it."

"It's much too dangerous," Mrs. S said. "There's no way you're ready."

"I'll do whatever it takes. Let me fix this. I need to fix this." In a pleading voice, I added, "I'm so sorry."

"Enough! Wizards don't whine!" Mrs. S snapped, her voice

cutting through the air like a blade. She pivoted sharply and strode among the rows of shriveled plants.

A profound sense of helplessness gripped me as I trailed behind, the pang of regret sinking its teeth into my chest. I buried my fretting hands in my pockets.

Soft, mournful sounds escaped her lips as she tenderly examined her withered garden. Each sorrowful utterance struck my gut like a physical blow, the crushing weight of my actions pressing heavily on my heart.

After a while, Mrs. S fixed her eyes on me. “Can you tell me why were you on the floor and not at the worktable?”

My pulse quickened when I tried to explain. “My back hurt, and I thought to meditate and use my renewed spirit to remove the heat and form ice.” I didn’t lie, but I didn’t tell the whole truth.

“But you left the table and the protection of the containment ward.” Mrs. S struggled to keep her tone neutral.

“I forgot,” I said, rubbing my neck.

Mrs. S sighed. “We learn more from failure than success.” She squeezed my shoulder, her expression filled with patient kindness. It was more than I deserved.

“With dragonroot, I can reverse the spell and prevent lasting damage.” Mrs. S pulled her spine straight. “Okay then—” she let out a breath, “it’s settled.” Her wrinkles deepened like rows in a field. “Fate has decided your quest, albeit a treacherous one. If you bring me dragonroot before the summer solstice, I can save Erik and restore my garden.”

That’s when the fairy revealed herself and peered over the edge of my pocket. “Well, now, who do we have here?” Mrs. S leaned forward. “Eireann, what have you gotten yourself into?”

The fairy’s voice rang clear and crisp. “I wanted to see the ice castle.”

Mrs. Shea raised an eyebrow. Eireann sunk lower into my pocket as if the cotton of the T-shirt would save her from Mrs. S’s penetrating glare. I braced for a reprimand that never came.

“Eireann, check in with your father. I’m sure he’ll want to

know what you've been up to."

Without a word, the fairy zipped from my pocket and disappeared into a beam of sunlight filtering through the window.

*Crash*!

A trellis toppled as a creeping vine crumpled to the floor. Bella's flowers had wilted, and her once-purple leaves turned black. The air surrounding Mrs. S's precious Bella reeked of decay. Mrs. S fought a scowl, masking her emotions, but tension gripped her eyes, and her face drained of color. "Be ready to leave at dawn."

Outside, Jesse and Sara loitered, waiting. I wished they hadn't. My head hurt, my heart stung with shame, and embarrassment burned my cheeks. When Jesse saw my pained face, he opened the door so I could step through and rushed off to find Bandit.

Sara wasted no time in confronting me. "Were you dropped on your head?"

"Hey, I didn't mean to," I said, motioning with my hands.

"You destroyed Mrs. Shea's life's work. And Erik's a popsicle!"

"I know—I'll get the dragon fruit."

"It's dragonroot," Sara said, her eyes spitting fire. "Mrs. Shea depends on her garden for her medicine."

*Why was Sara berating me? I already felt awful.*

"She can buy some more," I said defensively.

"No, she can't."

"Don't be such a drama queen. It's a bunch of plants." I rubbed my face, exasperated and ashamed. "We'll go on the quest thingy, get the dragonroot, and return to help replant the garden."

"If Mrs. S gets sick, who's gonna help Erik?" Sara said, her hands on her hips.

"Oh, so that's what it is? You have a *thing* for Erik?"

"What? No!" Sara paused two beats, her shock mixed with anger. "I can't believe you said that." Sara threw her hands up in frustration and stormed away.

*Why did I make matters worse by picking a fight with Sara?* I dropped my head in my hands. *Stupid, stupid, stupid.*

When I realized I'd forgotten my pack, I let out a deep sigh and slumped back into the greenhouse. The last thing I wanted to do was face Mrs. S again.

Mrs. Shea grasped *Mischief* tightly, her furrowed brow forming a deep V. "You cheated."

I shook my head in denial. "You didn't say no books. I used my resources."

"Cutting corners is reckless."

I couldn't meet her eyes, knowing she was right. I had acted rashly, and now Erik and her plants suffered the consequences.

"The assignment was too hard. I couldn't get it to work," I mumbled, shuffling my feet. "And then Erik came over, and it took him two seconds to create an ice spider. He made it look easy, and I felt dumb sitting there while he laughed with *my* friends. Then I thought of *Mischief*." I chewed on the inside of my cheek.

"And how has that worked for you in the past?"

"Yeah, I know, but I thought it'd be different this time." I lifted my eyes to meet her weary expression. "I connected with the essence, and it was—beautiful."

Mrs. S pursed her lips.

"It's not that I'm not remorseful—I am. But for a fleeting moment, I had wielded magic, and it felt amazing, exhilarating."

"Perhaps, but that's beside the point. If you can't control the results, you pose a danger to yourself and others," Mrs. S said. "Stop entertaining negative thoughts. Take authority over your emotions," she added firmly.

"I didn't do it on purpose." I tightened my brow, and my voice rang with annoyance.

Mrs. S gave me a frustrated look. "Did you have warm, fuzzy thoughts when Erik walked through the door?"

"Well, no, but—"

"My point exactly." Mrs. S coughed and swayed on her feet. I reached out as if to steady her.

"I'll be fine." She waved me off, her hands trembling when

she passed *Mischief* into mine. "Go, leave me be. I have to make arrangements. Be ready to travel at first light."

ΔΔΔ

I wandered the castle grounds until dark, nausea churning my insides, too ashamed to face my friends. Wrecking the garden had been a terrible mistake, but the thought of Erik and Mrs. S being hurt because of me weighed heavily on my mind—I couldn't bear a death on my conscience.

*Well, I wouldn't let that happen. I'd make this right, no matter what it took.* Those were my last thoughts as I crept into the sleepy cottage and headed to bed.

# CHAPTER 7

## *FELL PONIES AND GRIMM GOATS*

A blaring horn rudely ripped me from slumber, and I cursed the low ceiling as I banged my head. Pain throbbed at my temple, and I flopped back onto the comfy mattress, yanking the covers over my ears in a futile attempt to drown out the noise.

"We leave in thirty minutes," Jesse called from the hallway.

Wiping sleep from my eyes, I stumbled into the dining room and snatched the kazoo from his lips. "What's wrong with you?"

Jesse passed me a steaming cup of coffee. Appearing pleased with his wake-up antics, he said, "Everyone's waiting outside."

ΔΔΔ

The Fell Ponies, resembling miniature Clydesdales, stood ready for the journey as Mrs. Shea handed their leads to Sara and Jesse. Jesse's eyes ballooned. "I thought we'd take the Jeep."

Mrs. Shea chuckled. "It wouldn't be wise without Erik's permission. He's rather fond of that gas-guzzler. Besides, the animals are better suited for where you're going."

Jesse scrutinized the fourteen-hand pony with a worried expression. "I'm too big to ride a pony."

"Not at all. Altair is robust and eager for adventure." She gently brushed the bangs from his eyes. "Aren't you, sweetheart?"

Altair's haunches rippled when Jesse grabbed the saddle horn.

"Mount from the left," I said.

Uncertainty clouded Jesse's face. "Right."

"No, left." I held back a retort, realizing he didn't know how to ride. After a quick lesson on the basics, Jesse mounted, sporting a triumphant grin.

Suddenly, a wooden cart and two massive goats appeared. "Lester and Nester have agreed to pull the wagon," Mrs. S said.

With muscles rippling across their 300-pound frames and long corkscrew horns twisting out of their skulls, they left a formidable impression.

"Are they friendly?" I asked.

"Of course, well, unless they don't like you. But I expect you'll get along fine," Mrs. Shea said, motioning to the goats and back to me. "Lester and Nester Grimm, of the Billy Goat Gruff clan, this is Noah Farmer from Sweetwater and, more recently, Castle Dragon."

"Like the kid's story, *The Three Billy Goats Gruff?*" I asked.

Mrs. Shea's eyes grew cautious. "I wouldn't call it a children's story. Although diluted for the mundane, the tale is mostly true. The Gruffs are a feuding family, so it's best not to get on their bad side. The Grimm Goats are resilient and will take you as far as you need. You'll be in good hands with this handsome duo."

The goats gave me a friendly nudge. I chuckled, scratching their backs while their stubby tails spun happily.

"What an awesome pair of animals," I said, preparing to climb aboard the wagon.

"First, an announcement." Mrs. Shea summoned a small platform in a sparkle of light. As Mrs. S stepped up and leaned on the podium, we formed a half-circle. Her ashen skin and once intense violet eyes had dulled to a pale lavender shade, telling of her weakened state.

"Please raise your right hand." Curious, we all did as requested.

"Do you pledge to respect the accords and uphold the traditions and ideals of magic? Will you promise to abstain from all intentional wrong-doing and do no harm to all creatures, great and small?"

We readily agreed.

Then she called us one by one to step forward. Mrs. S tapped me with her wand. "By the power vested in me, I hereby declare you Apprentice Wizard of Castle Dragon."

I whispered so only she could hear, "I didn't think I'd graduate."

"Technically, you're on probation." With a chuckle, she whacked me on the head with her wand. "So don't mess up."

Mrs. S asked me to extend my arm. She slipped a bracelet on my wrist. The moment the thin band of gold touched my skin, it seemed to come alive. It pooled and spread like ink until it formed a bird-like design. I sensed a sentient magical energy ripple deep within my bones. Before I could question, Mrs. S conjured a stack of packages.

Sara squealed with delight as we rushed to the table like Christmas morning, searching for our names scrawled on the tag. I tore the paper off to discover a gray leather duster. We each received a different color. Green for Sara, blue for Jesse, and Bandit's a muted copper. When I put it on, it magically adjusted to a perfect fit. Stuffed in a side pocket, my hand retrieved a pamphlet. *999 Magical Standards of Compliance.* With a grimace, I quickly tucked the brochure back where I had found it.

Mrs. S rubbed her eyes. "It took all night, but I empowered your bracelets and dusters with protective wards. They'll provide limited shielding from rocks, spears, and bullets. I wish I could do more, but—"

"Bullets?" I interrupted.

"Let me be clear. When you leave the castle grounds, you won't be among friends. And if you find dragonroot, and I mean *if*, you'll have fortune hunters on your trail. Apprentices, yes, but you're inexperienced, so don't fool yourself into thinking you're invincible. You'll be tested beyond your limits. If I had any other choice, I wouldn't send apprentices to do a wizard's job." Mrs. S blinked, appearing distracted, turning her head and looking into the distance.

"You haven't told us where to find dragonroot," I said.

"Travel to the Tree of Apotheosis. Rumor has it that's where you'll find dragonroot. Noah, you'll have to dig deep." She shook her head sadly. "As much as it pains me to admit, I haven't the stamina for such a journey," Mrs. S said, her voice filled with vulnerability. "A more motley crew I never did see." A tentative smile appeared, deepening the lines on her face. But then she straightened with a curious expression, and just as we wondered about her change in demeanor, a radiant, dazzling orb materialized.

"A message from the High Council," rang the orb in a pulsating, reverberating voice. "The Dragon Moonstone is missing." It paused for effect. "Behold, young wizard, Fate has decided your quest. Find the Dragon Moonstone and restore the balance. Beware, your destiny is uncertain, filled with betrayal and treachery." The orb began to fade, and as if an afterthought added, "Not everything you seek shall you find, as knowledge is a slippery slope—Each answer will lead to more questions."

When the orb disappeared, I continued to stare at where it had been, dazed and confused.

Mrs. S broke the stunned silence, sighing in resignation. "Plans of mice and men..."

"But what about the dragonroot?" Sara asked, her face etched with concern.

"Sometimes, we need to do what's best for the greater good at the cost of the individual," Mrs. S said. "Find the peddler. If anyone knows what you seek, the peddler does. Keep your eyes open and ask your questions carefully. The Fae are notorious for hidden bargains." Her gaze swept from me to Sara and lingered on Jesse's bright face. "Guard the true nature of your quest."

Mrs. S's gaze shifted to the horizon. "It'll be sunrise soon. It's time to go."

She sighed. "And don't travel at night if you can avoid it. There's so much to tell you and not enough time." She waved us on.

Bandit stood by the wagon. "Think I'll take a snooze." He yawned before morphing into a raccoon. As his duster shrunk to size, he leaped into the back with the supplies and spun into a circle twice before plopping his chin on his paws. Bandit could choose his form, but only during the magic hour when the sun hovered on the horizon. Once decided, he was unchangeable until the next sunset or sunrise.

I grabbed a handful of treats from a sack and offered the goats a quick snack. I knew the best way to their heart was through their stomachs. "Ready for an adventure, Nester and Lester?" I asked as they greedily scooped up the morsels I offered in friendship.

"It's the other way around," Sara said. "Lester has one brown eye and one green eye."

I patted the goats. "My apologies, guys. I won't mix you up again." I tossed my backpack onto the floorboard and winked at Sara.

"Wait!" came a squeaky voice. The tiny fairy Eireann appeared, wearing a red vest and a floppy hat repurposed from a striped tube sock. "I'm to be the guide."

Mrs. S stepped forward, shaking her head disapprovingly. "This isn't a game."

"But Noah saved my life, and now I'm under his protection until I can return the favor," Eireann said.

"Explain to me how Noah saved your life?" Mrs. S said.

"Well, I might've exaggerated when I told Father about the ice castle and how Noah's pocket provided protection," Eireann said. "Please, don't tell Father."

Mrs. Shea tipped her chin knowingly.

Eireann squeaked.

Behind us, a frollick of fairies danced. Hundreds of winged fairies had gathered. A portly fairy broke formation, landing on the podium. He had long white hair and a matching beard and wore a jeweled crown. The king acknowledged Mrs. S with a smile before addressing me.

"Young wizard," he said in a froggy voice, "the Fairies of Castle Dragon express their gratitude with this humble gift."

A small pouch jingled, appearing on the buckboard's seat.

*Gratitude?* I kept my thoughts to myself so as not to interrupt.

"Eireann was amiss in leading you astray with—" he croaked "—the ice castle incident."

"Sir? But that was on me," I interrupted.

The king shook his head and glared at Eireann, who seemed obsessed with an imaginary piece of fairy dust on her sleeve.

"My daughter should've alerted Mrs. Shea before things—" he looked up as if searching for the proper phrase, "got out of hand. So, to make amends, Eireann will guide you on the first leg of your journey."

King Oberon motioned, and a glass globe materialized in my hands. Caught off guard, I fumbled, and the glass slipped through my fingers like a wet bar of soap. Luckily, I recovered. Sheepishly, I wondered why he'd given me a snow globe souvenir of Castle Dragon. As I waited for the amused smile to fade from King Oberon's face, my brow tilted in confusion.

"Of course, most humans think snow globes are simply tourist trinkets, but they actually are glimpses into the Otherlands." His eyes twinkled. "Give it a little shake."

As the globe's fairy dust settled, a scene unfolded. It revealed Sara and Jesse sitting on Fell Ponies and a buckboard hitched to a pair of Grimm Goats. The depiction included specific details, including the supplies piled high on the wagon and Bandit curled in a ball.

"That's incredible," I said, amazement showing on my face.

The king smiled, pleased with my reaction. "Respect magic, and magic will respect you." And then, in a severe tone, he asked. "Do you accept responsibility for Eireann?"

Mrs. S cupped her hand and whispered in my ear, "Don't offend the Fae. Now, more than ever, you need their help."

I quickly adopted a mature face. "It would be an honor if Eireann joined our crew and quest," I said in a formal tone before offering a respectful bow. I'd never spoken to a king, so I attempted to sound dignified. But when I turned to Eireann, I couldn't help but return to my usual self. "Welcome to the team, Scout."

Eireann clapped her hands. "Scout, I love it. I'm honored to receive my new name."

"Good, it's settled," Mrs. S said. "Hmm?" She leaned forward to hear the king's words, but they only sounded like a croaking frog to me. "Yes, I warned them," she replied, her lips forming a thin line.

ΔΔΔ

The sky tinged a rosy hue as Mrs. S concluded the impromptu ceremony. With a sweeping gesture, she raised her hand and declared, "Godspeed!" Her voice filled with bittersweet encouragement.

I gave a flick to the leather reins, and the buckboard emitted a muted creak as its spoked wheels began to turn. The ponies tossed their heads and high-stepped, prancing alongside the wagon. The frollick of fairies fell in line behind us, playing a jubilant marching tune with blaring trumpets, trilling flutes, and assorted noisemakers, creating a whimsical symphony that filled my heart with determination. Our parade led us through the castle grounds, ultimately halting before a luminescent arch.

Scout fluttered like a butterfly, her wings creating a delicate hum before perching on the buckboard's railing. I gestured questioningly toward the shimmering light obscuring the threshold.

"That's the gateway to the Otherlands," Scout said. "Once we pass through the stone arch, we will be beyond Castle Dragon's protection."

When I opened my mind to the orb blocking the gateway, the air crackled with magic. "Have you ever been beyond the gate?" I asked our fairy guide.

"Oh, sure, lots of times." Scout fidgeted, avoiding my gaze.

"How many times, exactly?" I asked, attempting to replicate Mrs. Shea's intimidating stare.

"Forty-six, forty-eight times," the diminutive fairy said.

"Scout, if we're going to work together, I need to trust you. Besides—you're a terrible liar."

Scout threw her arms up in exasperation. "I know—it's something I'm working on."

*Fibbing or telling the truth?* The snarky comment came to mind, but I swallowed it when King Oberon materialized beside his daughter.

"The animals will lead you through the gateway and into the Otherlands. If all goes as planned, you should reach The Tower of Song by nightfall. Once you arrive, seek an experienced guide to take you the rest of the way." The king smiled at his daughter, his eyes shining with pride. "Represent us well and stay out of trouble. You may accompany the young wizard to the fort, but no farther."

"But Papa—"

"No farther!"

"Yes, Papa."

The king returned his attention to me. "Goblin Valley is a treacherous, unforgiving land, so tread carefully. Don't mistake kindness with weakness. Should a conflict arise, resolve it swiftly."

I bobbed my head up and down, eager to be on our way.

"And don't pick up hitchhikers!"

I arched an eyebrow at the unexpected advice.

The King of Fairies extended his arm toward the gleaming arch. "King's Peace!"

The frollick of fairies erupted in cheers and whistles. Scout kissed her father's cheek before buzzing in circles and diving into my shirt pocket.

My friends sat tall in their saddles, Jesse brimming with excitement while Sara's serene presence bolstered my resolve. She offered me a confident, reassuring smile.

I counted to three to settle my nerves. "This mission isn't going to complete itself," I said, trying to sound bold and leader-like, even though I felt like a pretender.

The Grimm Goats bleated their response and stepped into

the dancing light within the arch. As we passed through the portal, I held my breath and squeezed my eyes tight. It was the longest fifteen seconds of my life. My skin burned as the wind pushed against me, making it feel like my face would peel off. The goats steadily pulled the wagon through the expanse, and the sensation stopped. As I tried to catch my breath, I wiped my watery eyes, blinking rapidly to clear my vision. The ringing in my ears drowned out the thumping in my chest.

Then, discovering Bandit had slept through the pulse-pounding experience, I laughed in surprise. The ponies emerged from the gateway, Altair's spirited neigh announcing them. Jesse grinned like a Cheshire cat while Sara stayed composed in the saddle, absentmindedly tucking a few loose strands of hair behind her ear.

Scout zipped about. "The Tower of Song is a full day's ride. Come on, we must keep moving." I smiled at our fairy guide's enthusiasm and tapped the reins. The goats heeded the command and moved us forward along the road paved with cobbles.

# CHAPTER 8

## *THE MYSTERIOUS OBELISK*

We braved the scorching sun, traveling among the upthrusts of rock and thorny plants. The cobblestone road cut through the brush and followed the river's course. Cacti grew in grotesque shapes, many with razor-sharp fishhook thorns. We kept to the middle of the lane, avoiding the prickly shrubs crowding the edges. The wheels kicked up a cloud of dust, coating us with a layer of dirt.

Scout flew ahead, eager to explore, while the goats plodded along at a pace too relaxed for her liking. She had an appetite for adventure and wanted to see everything in a blink. On the other hand, Bandit was a sleepy companion who preferred to nap. Not that I minded. It allowed me to reflect on my mistakes.

I had to admit that this wasn't a weird dream and that my world had turned upside down. So far, my experience in the Otherlands pushed me beyond my comfort zone and onto the bleeding edge of my panic zone.

I was out of my depth, but determined to figure it out. My mind puzzled over my quest, trying to make sense of the unfolding mystical realm. Thinking about my disastrous lab assignment swamped me with guilt. While I accepted the consequences of my actions, I still believed I could find a way to repair the damages. I chewed my lip, berating myself for my shameful cheating. I shouldn't have sought help from *Mischief*, and I had cut corners to impress my friends, envying their success. But what made things worse was my carelessness had hurt others. My recklessness had frozen Erik and had ruined the greenhouse. Mrs. S was in dire trouble, and I was to blame.

After a while, I reframed my problems into a motivating challenge. If I had to scour every nook and cranny of Goblin Valley to find the elusive dragonroot, then that's what I'd do. No matter what, I'd restore Mrs. Shea's shattered faith in me. Nothing would stop me from fulfilling my promise. I was resolved to focus on the moment and not lose track of the end goal.

"From now on, I'm going to be a help to others and not be a hindrance. I spend too much time in my head and don't consider anyone else's needs," I said to myself. "Everything doesn't have to be about me. I need to step up." After my private pep talk, I felt optimistic, pulling back my shoulders and adopting a posture of purpose.

We halted our caravan near a shady boulder field at noon. Water pooled in a deep crevice, and the animals drank their fill. The nearby river dwindled to a shallow ribbon, nothing more than a babbling creek. Still, the stains on the steep banks told a different story of a once mighty flow.

Parched, my throat stung like I had swallowed a bucket of sand. Yet, I smiled when I climbed out of the wagon, eager to stretch my legs and explore the scattering of boulders. The rocks were a deep shade of red, like pickled beets, and I found their shapes fascinating. One particular stone reminded me of a dinosaur head, with its jaw open as if to roar.

Lost in my imagination, I paused at the sound of the wind's miserable wail. When I heard the wretched groan for the second time, I searched for the source. Around the next set of rocks, my eyes widened as I stumbled upon a hooded figure slumped against a weathered boulder. He let forth a haunted sob, and I felt a flood of compassion as he sat folded over, weeping. A pungent odor filled my nostrils. The scent of creosote mixed with the aura of otherworldliness clung to the figure.

"Hello, do you need help?" I asked.

Scout squeaked and buzzed me like an agitated hornet. I

motioned her away, keeping my attention on the hooded person. He shifted, stretching his arms like he had woken from a nap. "I accept your generous offer," came a hollow voice resonating with an eerie emptiness.

The figure lifted his head, and my heart skipped a beat. Filling the darkness within the robe's pointing hood sat a pair of blood-red Xs. My body tensed, struggling with my flight response as I scuttled back.

Still, empathy urged me to continue. Besides, it was too late —I was already committed. I told myself to stay calm and not let the headless creature see my fear. Summoning my courage, I mustered the strength to speak, masking the tremor in my voice. "Um, what can I do for you?"

Scout gasped, honked like a goose, and tugged vehemently at my sleeve, her eyes bulging with panic, urging me to step back.

"Excuse me." I allowed Scout to pull me out of earshot. "What's the problem?" I asked, letting my annoyance show.

Concern marred her fairy face. "You're bargaining with a being of the Otherlands."

My expression scrunched into confusion. "What are you talking about? I'm trying to help someone in need." *This was my chance to follow through with my new resolution to help others.* But I didn't say that last part.

She scoffed. "I don't know what you tried to do, but you offered not one but two open-ended favors and, worse yet, without a fair exchange." Scout's tiny body trembled as her wings hovered. "You need to fix this." With a quick glance at the hooded figure, she added. "Did you forget Mrs. Shea's warning about hidden bargains?"

The atmosphere grew increasingly unsettling as the power of Scout's words drained my confidence. I had a sudden change of heart about putting others first. My eyes darted to the headless guy and back at Scout. "No worries. It's a simple misunderstanding. I'll use diplomacy," I said, masking my anxiety behind a weak smile.

The little fairy responded with a cynical eye roll.

I returned to the hooded being, clasping my hands to hide their shake. My tongue felt rough as sandpaper. Even though his glowing Xs for eyes unnerved me, I attempted an air of confidence.

"I'm Noah, and we're headed—"

*Don't say head!*

"Um, we're traveling to The Tower of Song. It's up ahead—uh, down the road—We're going that way." I gestured randomly with my hand.

"Pleased to make your acquaintance. They call me Headless Howard," he said, giving a sharp bow.

His plain brown robe draped his compact frame, cinched in the middle with a simple rope. When he stood straight, the tip of his hood came to my elbow while his sleeves fell beyond his hands. I pondered the empty void supporting the intense Xs and fought the urge to stare by pretending not to notice. Still, I couldn't stop thinking about his missing head.

My uneasiness hung heavy until I blurted. "Do you need a ride?" I bit my lip, realizing my mistake.

Howard held his arms behind his back, mimicking my stance. "I'm grateful to share your conveyance," his voice echoed as if it came from deep within a tunnel. "I accept your gracious offer to help," he gurgled, but it might have been a laugh. "You're fortunate I won't take advantage of your youth. You aren't from around here. I wouldn't want it said that Headless Howard doesn't pay it forward, and therefore, I'll grant you one courtesy," he sounded as if he was doing *me the favor*.

"Okay, I guess," I said, scratching my chin as I tried to make sense of his cryptic words.

Scout squeaked in distress and disappeared, but quickly returned with the others. At the sight of the hooded figure, Bandit snarled, his hackles raised, and he took an aggressive stance.

"Easy." I grabbed Bandit by the scruff. "This is Headless Howard, and he's coming with us."

"Greetings, my fellow travelers. I appreciate the lift."

Jesse stepped forward, offering a friendly welcome. He introduced our group and didn't seem fazed by our headless passenger. The addition of Headless Howard to our group was met with a mixed reaction. Jesse marched ahead, delighted by the expanded group and oblivious to the tension. Scout shot me a sour look, making her disapproval abundantly clear. Sara's brows drew together in a questioning expression as she slowed her pace. I dropped back to match her steps, sensing her wariness.

Sara elbowed me hard, speaking through gritted teeth. "What didn't you understand about not picking up hitchhikers?"

I scowled, rubbing my smarting arm. "The guy doesn't have a head. What was I supposed to do, abandon Howie in the desert?"

Sara stared at me, incredulous.

"Don't worry. Everything will be fine," I said, giving her a reassuring smile. "We'll drop Howie off at the next town and never see him again."

ΔΔΔ

As we continued our journey, Lester and Nester maintained a steady pace. Headless Howard joined me on the bench seat while Bandit napped. For a guy without a head, Howie was a chatterbox. He droned on about how Goblin Valley depended on the river for their water and that it mysteriously disappeared a few weeks ago. But I wasn't paying much attention. I nodded as if listening while I took in the unfolding landscape and noodled my own problems. That was until he started talking about how he lost his head in a card game, and suddenly, I was all ears.

Howard claimed the other guy cheated, and Headless was determined to get it back. "I'll show you around town and point out the double-dealer, and then you can figure out how to retrieve my head."

"Say what?" My breath caught.

"You offered to help, did you not? And I want my head back."

His words were emphatic, as if to leave no room for argument.

But before I could argue, Scout returned and made a beeline for my left shoulder, giving our guest a wide berth. Neither one had acknowledged the other. I didn't know what that meant in fairy protocol, but I wouldn't interfere and make matters worse.

"How much further?" I asked, grateful for the change of subject.

"Not long." Scout had lost her enthusiasm, and I had to believe it was because of our passenger. "We're ahead of schedule," she said.

I winced, giving Headless a sidelong glance, but he didn't respond to the turn of the phrase.

As we rounded a bend, the land fell away, treating us to an extraordinary view of the valley. A turquoise river snaked through the canyon, a ghost of what it had once been. Much of the riverbed lay exposed, while the towering cliffs were layers of red, yellow, and white. I stopped to give the goats a break but also to take in the rugged landscape.

"What's that?" I pointed at a shiny black pillar rising above the dry riverbed.

"Interesting," Howard said as he hopped out of the wagon. "Shall we investigate?"

Bandit sat up and yawned as the horses trotted over. Scout left my shoulder and landed on Orion's head. The pony didn't seem to mind.

"Why are we stopping?" Sara asked, climbing out of the saddle.

I wiped the sweat from my brow. "There's something strange about that tall black stone."

"It looks like an obelisk," Jesse said. "Cool! Let's go check it out."

"We should stay on schedule and continue to The Tower of Song," Sara said.

Jesse's eyes brightened. "It could be a clue to the—" Sara pinched Jesse. "Ouch," Jesse whined, rubbing his arm.

Howard ignored the banter and hurried along the incline toward the water.

"Sara and I'll go." When I was certain Headless couldn't hear, I cautioned Jesse. "Keep your mouth shut. The mission is a need to know."

"Oh right, N2K—need to know," Jesse said, scratching his head as a thought struck him. "But isn't Howard a friend?"

"You think everyone is a friend."

"And that's why I have a lot of friends," Jesse said. "What's wrong with that?"

"Nothing, but you can't trust everyone you meet—so keep a lid on it."

"If you say so," Jesse said, but his face showed he clearly disagreed.

"We'll be right back—Stay with the animals. Come on, Sara, let's check this out," I said.

The sun reflected off the river rocks, and I dripped with sweat by the time we caught up to Headless Howard. When we approached the obelisk, rising out of the river bottom, the air vibrated with unsettling magic. Oddly, up close, the air was icy and fogged my breath. Carved into the marble was a foreign script and an imprint of a hand.

"What do you sense?" I asked, hoping Sara's paranormal abilities would shed some insight.

She paused, and her gaze softened. "It's a warning, with a sense of urgency, but no immediate danger."

More curious than scared, I opened my mind to the essence of the obelisk. When I held my palm just over the handprint, my wristband tingled.

Sara leaned in, comparing my hand against the print. "A perfect match."

As soon as I touched the surface, an icy wave of magic drew my hand deep into the stone as if pushing into clay. At first, I struggled, but then I felt a comforting presence and understood I had nothing to fear, so I relaxed. The words tumbled from my mouth.

Next you see me, you will weep,

With cries of thirst, and of grief.

Until the dragon returns, to sleep,

Hunger gnaws, with no relief.

After the obelisk had spoken through me, it pushed my hand away. My fingers tingled as if my hand had fallen asleep.

Sara traced the writing with her finger as if contemplating the poem's message. She put her hand on the smooth stone. "The vibe is gone. I don't sense a presence."

Shoving my hands in my pockets, I leaned closer to the obelisk, but I couldn't feel any magic, and the air had warmed.

Preoccupied, pacing and mumbling, Howard paid us no mind. Finally, after a few minutes, he said, "This is a hunger stone, written in a dead language." Howard's Xs tracked me like lasers. "You have arcane knowingness and a special relationship with the author. When you touched the obelisk, you activated the connection."

I shrugged ignorance. But, I wondered if Ezra, my great-great-great-something-grandfather, was *the connection*.

Before Headless Howard could continue, Jesse came bounding toward us. He skidded to a stop, filling the space between Sara and Howard.

I tossed my hands in frustration. "Why aren't you with the animals?"

"They're fine. I left them with Bandit and Scout." Jesse jumped across the stones and soon scrambled behind a boulder the size of a car. "Hey, there's something over here."

We dashed toward Jesse's voice, scrambling over rocks to a marble cistern nestled into the riverbed. The white stone basin sat level with the sandy bottom. A calm pool of water captured inside it mirrored the blue sky above. As I leaned over the cistern's edge, beads of perspiration dripped from my brow, creating ever-expanding ripples across the glassy surface.

The ripples slowly settled, and a strange vision took shape, as if we were gazing through a window to another place entirely. An elegant study emerged, with a mahogany desk and a high-backed chair situated before shelves of leather-bound books. We found ourselves peering into this room as the last ripples smoothed to glass.

"Is that someone's office?" Sara asked.

"Yeah, but whose?" Jesse asked, crouching to observe the scene unfolding before us.

A woman in a red dress entered, her high heels clicking as she glided across the room and busied herself at her desk.

Jesse waved his arms as if to test if she'd notice. It didn't appear she could see Jesse's frantic motions, but I grabbed his arm and glared at him, silently urging him to stop.

There was a knock at the door. "Come in," the woman said in a silky voice. She turned her head as a man entered the room.

"Carla!" Jesse's eyes were as big as tennis balls.

But it wasn't Carla, although she bore a striking resemblance to Jesse's witch of a stepmother.

"Hush," I whispered. "They might hear us."

"Don't just stand there. Tell me everything."

"There's not much to report," a male voice said. "I searched the backwater town, but there was no sign of the young wizard or his friends."

"What about the aunt?"

"A silly old biddy with a yard cluttered with wind chimes. I asked her about the kid, and she didn't know up from down." The man, tall and sturdy, eased himself into a chair. "Senile, if you ask me."

"Unacceptable! Our sister is missing, and no one knows anything. That Goodall character said the newbie wizard killed her." She slammed her fist. "You must find him."

The man showed no reaction to the dramatic outburst. "Agnes, we'll keep looking. I posted a reward, so something will turn up."

Agnes tilted her head, sniffing. "Do you smell that?"

The man stuck his nose in his armpit and shrugged.

In slow motion, Agnes glided into the center of the room. "I sense sorcery—young wizard blood."

She extended her arms and slowly turned around and around, mumbling under her breath. When she stopped, her eyes narrowed, and her finger pointed straight at us. "You! How dare you spy on me!" she spat the words.

Startled, I yelped and stumbled, falling on my backside. Scrambling, a spray of pebbles disturbed the calm water and dissolved the vision.

Jesse's face was ashen, and he looked like he might be sick.

Sara's eyes brimmed. "We must return to Sweetwater. Grandma and Shirley—"

I placed my hands on Sara's shoulders and met her eyes. "We can't go back—Not until we finish what we started. Besides, it'll be worse if we don't find dragonroot."

Sara gave a single nod and, in a quiet voice, added, "And the Dragon Moonstone."

We looked at each other for a couple of beats, and while I sensed her resolve, I hoped she could feel mine.

Scout buzzed overhead. "Come quick, Bandit's in trouble."

Jesse bolted, and Sara and I raced after him. When we made it up the ravine, the goats and horses were nowhere to be seen.

Beside our buckboard sat a tattered, covered wagon that resembled an old West Conestoga. But mules didn't pull it. Instead, a scrawny bull moose with ribs pushing through his hide stood wearily harnessed to the wagon. The pitiful beast was over eight feet, with paddle-shaped antlers spreading the width of the road.

Two men in denim jackets, with their hands raised in submission, were backing away from a snarling raccoon. My amulet warmed as I marched forward, and a saying came to mind, reminding me to stay calm.

*A short temper will make a fool out of you soon enough.*

A figure emerged from the shadows of the wagon with the grace of a predator. Grizzled with watchful eyes, he removed a chicken bone that hung between his lips. "Hello, friend," he said in a relaxed southern drawl.

I knew in a flash that the man was dangerous.

"Hey, that's our wagon," Jesse said in a flustered voice.

"Strange place to leave a buckboard—looks abandoned."

"You'd be mistaken, sir." I extended my hand. "My name's Noah, and you are?"

"Parker, Zeb Parker." He had a grip like a steel trap. "Them there are my brothers, Max and Leo."

I nodded, keeping my eyes fixed on Zeb Parker. I didn't make any further introductions as Sara moved to stand next to Bandit while Jesse stayed beside me.

"Get on over here, boys. No cause to be rude," Zeb said.

"Howdy." Leo smiled, showing a set of small, sharp teeth.

Max touched the brim of his hat. His unblinking black eyes darted from side to side, taking it all in.

The Parker brothers were stick-thin, with leathery faces. Each stood a tad taller than the other. Zeb looked the oldest but was the shortest, standing six feet tall. Max was in the middle, and Leo looked the youngest. I rarely met anyone my size, so I recognized Leo's height. He stood six-six with a bony build, and where my shoulders were broad, Leo's were narrow.

Bandit quit snarling when Sara petted his fur, but he remained focused on the Parkers.

"That's some guard animal," Zeb said, pointing with the chicken bone.

I let the silence hang between us.

"Well, friend, we stopped to water and rest a bit." Zeb laughed, but it wasn't friendly.

I took a step toward our wagon. "We'll be moving on, but in the meantime, I'd appreciate it if you'd keep your distance." I nodded toward Bandit. "He's temperamental."

Zeb rolled the bone with his lips. "No harm. Found an abandoned wagon and intended to see the property returned to its lawful owner."

Leo scratched his shaggy beard. "I couldn't find your team. What are you pullin' that wagon with?" Zeb shot Leo a scathing look. Leo clamped his mouth shut and busied himself with unharnessing the moose.

Zeb gestured with his chicken bone. "The river's mighty low for this time of year."

The air was thick with unspoken words until Jesse couldn't stand it. "We found a hunger stone."

It was my turn to shoot the dirty looks, but as usual—Jesse was oblivious.

"Is that so?" Zeb's yellow eyes widened, revealing diamond-shaped pupils.

"Yeah, over there." Jesse pointed, immune to my *shut-your-mouth* glare.

Zeb moved toward the river, walking like a much younger man. Leo followed with a lead rope attached to the moose's halter. The middle brother, Max, stayed behind. He slid to the ground, leaning against their wagon wheel. He pulled his hat low as his tongue darted out, licking a fly from his lip.

I turned away to cover my grimace and motioned to Jesse. Keeping our distance from the Parkers, we walked toward Sara and Bandit.

"Where are the animals?" I asked, speaking softly out the side of my mouth.

Jesse moved his hand.

"Don't point—show me."

Sara sat down next to the raccoon. "I'll stay with Bandit. But hurry."

I nodded to Sara and followed Jesse through a scattering of boulders, stopping at a clearing.

"Where are they?" I asked, hoping the animals hadn't wandered off.

"Use your peripheral vision," Jesse said.

"You veiled them!" I couldn't keep the surprise from my face. Mrs. S had taught us people see what they expect to see, and it's at the edges where magic is visible. If we noticed something from the corner of our eye and nothing was there when we looked straight on, then it was likely magic.

Jesse grinned, flicked his hand, and the animals appeared from behind an invisible magic curtain. The goats bleated hello while Altair and Orion chewed bits of grass.

My stomach twisted, and my jaw clenched, remembering yet another assignment I hadn't been able to perform as well as my friends. The task was to hide an object behind a veil. I could cloak my coffee cup for five seconds, but nothing as complicated as what Jesse had accomplished.

*I'm the one with the wizard blood—Why can't I do that?*

Jesse was eager for praise, waiting for me to say something.

*It's not Jesse's fault you're a lousy wizard. Don't let your negativity show—it might crush his spirit.*

I reset my attitude with a calming breath. "Jesse, that's awesome. You sure mastered the cloaking spell."

"I've been practicing in my free time while you've had your nose in a book, but the power booster bracelet helps expand my abilities. Maybe tenfold," he said.

Curious, I asked to see his bracelet. Jesse raised his arm, revealing a plain band on his wrist. I rolled back my sleeve, showing him mine. "It started like yours but transformed into this wrist guard with this wicked raven design."

Grabbing my arm, he took a closer look. "Dude, that's not a raven. See the tail. It's a dragon." Jesse dropped my arm. "Mrs. Shea always liked you best," he said, grinning. "Mine is awesome, too, especially since it makes magic easier."

Jesse pinched his eyes shut. His face turned red while a wavy light descended, and the animals disappeared. Jesse struggled to catch his breath. "It still takes a lot of energy, but it's way easier with the booster."

I gave the space a sideways glance and noticed the shimmering light. There was a slight resistance when I stepped through the veil.

"Feels like a wind tunnel," Jesse said. "But not as harsh as when we passed through the Castle Dragon gateway to the Otherlands."

"You got that right," I said. "I almost threw up."

Jesse laughed. "Me too."

I put my hand on Jesse's shoulder. "This is an impressive display of magic. We didn't disturb the invisibility cloak when we walked through, so if anyone comes along, they won't see us."

Jesse beamed at my honest compliment.

The alcove wasn't more than a jumble of boulders. But it served as a perfect makeshift corral, with shade, grass, and water pooled in a basin. The animals were safer here than where I had left them. Petting Orion, I told Jesse as much. "It was a great idea to settle the animals here, especially with the Parkers creeping about. And the veil was a nice touch. I don't think I could've done as well."

"Oh, sure you can, but it's like something's got you blocked." Jesse quirked a grin.

Holding my jealousy in check, I bristled at the backward compliment. I had to give Jesse credit for working on the challenges and believing he could master them. I grabbed the goat's rope. "Let's get back. I don't like leaving Sara and Bandit alone with the Parkers."

Jesse led Orion and Altair while I coaxed the goats forward. The animals were cooperative and eager to get moving. However, the horses reared when they noticed Max leaning against his covered wagon. Jesse struggled to calm them. Lester and Nester snorted, pawing the ground and posturing with corkscrew horns. I used a soothing voice and kept a tight hold of the rope to calm the Grimm Goats.

Max recoiled at the commotion. "Control your beasties," he said, never taking his eyes off the goats as he slipped into his covered wagon. Once Max was out of sight, the animals relaxed.

I hurried to harness the goats. And when I finished, Sara and Jesse were already in their saddles. Bandit sat on the bench, watching the Brothers' wagon.

"What about Scout?" Jesse asked.

"She probably went ahead, but she'll catch up," Sara said, looking around. "Where's your hitchhiker?"

"Don't know, don't care—Let's get out of here." I shook off the uneasy feeling. “The Parker Brothers give me the creeps.”

“Reptilian,” Sara said, and then giggled nervously.

“Exactly.” I flicked the reins, and we were on the move again.

# CHAPTER 9

## *THE TOWER OF SONG*

Lester and Nester quickened their pace as if they understood my desire to create distance from the Parker Brothers. I didn't relish the idea of Zeb and his crew creeping up on us. As we journeyed along, the vast wilderness unfolded. An array of painted cliffs lined the horizon, where tumbled rocks had slid away to reveal a rainbow of layered soil. A cool breeze made the heat bearable while the sun-baked grasslands swayed to the whims of the wind. I relaxed, enjoying the view, lulled by the rhythmic sounds of hooves and the creaking wagon. Far away against the cloudless sky, a jet-black raven glided on the air currents—or at least that's what I thought it was at the time.

A bee buzzed my ear, and at the last second, I resisted the urge to swat. "Scout," I said, rubbing my neck. "I wish you'd stop sneaking up on me."

The pixie fairy winked, displaying an unapologetic grin.

"How much farther?" I asked, rolling the kinks out of my shoulders.

Scout hovered, her wings a blur, casting a superior glance at Nester and Lester Grimm. "At goat speed, it'll take hours. How can you stand to move so *slooooow*?" She stirred her wings in a sluggish motion, mocking the goat's plodding pace. "Later, alligator." And before I could reply, *after a while crocodile,* she zipped away, leaving me with a smile playing across my face.

The wagon creaked along the cobblestones, and before long, I spotted Headless Howard dozing against a boulder. I had a fleeting thought that we could sneak past and leave him behind. But without a word, Headless nimbly leaped onto the bench, squeezing in beside Bandit.

The sleepy raccoon grumbled at being jostled and retreated to the back of the wagon, curling into a ball to resume his nap. I stole a glance at Howard, impressed by his agility, despite the flowing robe concealing his hands and feet. An icky feeling crept over me as I wondered about his shapeless cloak. *Ugh! Don't even think about what's under that robe.* With a sudden shudder, I snapped the reins. The goats jerked, and I winced at my unnecessary roughness.

The ponies moved alongside, and Sara's expression said everything there was to say about my peculiar passenger. When I retorted with a funny face, she chuckled.

Jesse sat confidently in the saddle, having quickly mastered horseback riding. "Hey Howie, long time no see." Then, with a gleam in his eye, he yelled, "Race ya!" Altair surged forward with a burst of speed, kicking up a cloud of dust.

I slumped in my seat, watching Jesse and Altair disappear around a bend. *How did I get stuck with weird Headless Howard?*

Sara answered my unspoken question with a smirk that seemed to say, *That's what you get for picking up hitchhikers.*

A moment later, Orion, accepting Jesse's challenge, whinnied. Sara's musical laughter tickled my ears and stirred my envy as the spirited horse raced away.

Meanwhile, the Grimm Goats plodded along, displaying no interest in joining the race. And even though I hadn't asked, Headless Howard took it upon himself to explain his sudden disappearance. He had a history with the Parkers and thought he'd lose more than his head if he ran into them in the wilds. "They're a bunch of snakes in the grass." Howard's monotone voice reverberated as if it rose from a void. "I'd suggest you tread carefully around that clan. Stick with me, Greenhorn, and I'll show you the ropes."

I cast a glance at my passenger. "It's as if we're stepping back in time—with Conestoga wagons and buckboards. Why aren't there trains, planes, or automobiles?"

"We have locomotives." Howie flapped his droopy sleeves. "Besides, magic and technology don't always mesh."

Something caught my attention and drew my gaze toward the hillside dotted with bushes. The shape and spacing of the bushes resembled a grazing herd of buffalo.

When I mentioned this to Howard, he emitted a robotic laugh. "Those are buffalo scrub. They roam the prairie, and if you watch them from the corner of your eye, you'll see them move."

Intrigued, I asked, "Are they animal or vegetable?"

"Neither and both," he replied.

As we rolled along, I couldn't resist trying to catch a glimpse of a buffalo bush in motion. It was like the kid's game, *Red Light, Green Light*, where the players freeze when the stoplight is watching. I persisted, and when I finally spotted a buffalo scrub move, I fist-pumped my victory.

The further we journeyed from Castle Dragon, the more I noticed the scenic shift. It felt like being immersed in an altered digital photograph with an added filter to make the scene slightly off-kilter. The colors of the plants, rocks, and things intensified, as if this strange realm of the Otherlands had cranked up the saturation dial. Not only that, the landscape changed dramatically without much notice. One moment, it'd be lush trees and rolling hillsides, and the next, a barren desert giving way to a craggy mountain range. It was an unfamiliar experience, and uneasiness stirred. I didn't understand much about this place. So I asked Headless what we should expect when we arrived at The Tower of Song.

"It's about time for the festival. The outpost gets wild at night." Howard slumped over, and I thought that would be all he'd say. But then, as if someone flipped a switch, Headless straightened and launched into a detailed monolog with renewed vigor. "As you visit the Otherlands, you'll notice the towns have cultural themes you might recognize. They vary from place to place, and the motifs can be anything from Gothic to Renaissance to Post-Modern lifestyles." He grew animated.

"The Tower of Song serves as an embassy for the Otherlands as well as a trading post with an eclectic mix of Arthurian, Maritime, and the Old West, where the various arcane beings get along—for the most part, anyway."

"So it's like my hometown of Sweetwater, where magic and non-magic live in peace."

Howard shook his head. "No, not at all. In your world, my kind is misunderstood and feared." His tone turned anxious, as if confiding a secret. "People fear what they don't understand, which leads to hatred. So they demonize and label us monsters. And since nobody likes to be afraid, they send for monster hunters."

I furrowed my forehead. "But there's a ton of magic in Sweetwater, and I never noticed."

"People see what they expect to see, and children accept until they're taught otherwise. Some magical beings can successfully navigate both realms. But it depends. In the mundane world, physical appearance matters. Take me, for example. My temporary state of headlessness would create quite a stir. It would be like Frankenstein's monster all over again."

"Oh, that's a kid's story." I waved off his comment with a scoff.

"Don't believe that for a moment." Howard squirmed in his seat. "History is filled with tales of monster hunters. Need I mention the witch trials?" He dropped his arms to his lap. "Anyway, magical beings coexist as long as we adhere to certain courtesies. Even so, don't romanticize it. There are real monsters lurking in The Tower of Song, dangerous predators. So be careful whom you trust. It's best to conduct your business and leave town as soon as possible." Howard locked his laser-like gaze on me. "But not before you retrieve my head," he said in a tone devoid of humor.

I gulped and looked away.

We continued our journey in silence while I unraveled my tangled thoughts. I didn't know what to expect, and that made me nervous. The unknown loomed. It wasn't exactly fear, but I couldn't shake the uneasy feeling of being out of my depth.

My amulet hummed as if reminding me to focus on what mattered most. Completing my quest was my top priority. I needed help navigating this strange place, so I had no choice but to trust Headless. Still, something about him felt off, and it wasn't just his head.

After a while, Scout appeared, interrupting my mental gymnastics. She kept her distance from Howie, her wings glistening in the sunlight as she announced we'd almost arrived.

As our buckboard slowly descended the hill, a golden meadow opened before us. I spotted Sara and Jesse resting the horses under a giant tree. Its lush green canopy spread across the road, offering shade from the afternoon sun.

A sense of relief washed over me, and I was glad to be back with my friends. "Who won?" I asked, motioning toward the white ponies, munching grass.

Sara patted her loyal steed. "Orion, of course."

The horse blew, his eyes shiny with a hint of pride.

"It must be the rider." My heart somersaulted when Sara flashed me a radiant smile, and I quickly looked away, hoping she didn't notice my flushed face.

As my embarrassment threatened to linger, Scout broke the tension when she mischievously skipped across Altair's nose. The pony sneezed and flicked his head, sending the tiny pixie catapulting into the air. We laughed and waited for our giggling Scout to regain her composure.

The last mile led us to an impressive stone archway, where two sentries stood watch. The guards were a boxy pair with muscular arms and short peg legs. Their multi-colored uniforms boasted balloon sleeves, tight pants, and pointy boots that curled at the tips. Each guard carried a striped flag on a long pole. They lowered their flags with synchronized precision, creating an impromptu gate that crackled with magic.

"Halt! State your purpose," the sentry on the left demanded. He had a sharp nose and a thick, saggy pelican neck.

"We're here on private business for Castle Dragon," Scout said formally.

"So word has reached Dragon," the other guard said, relaxing his stance. Although smaller than his partner, they had similar large, round, dark eyes.

"Absolutely. I'm pleased to present distinguished members of Castle Dragon." The tiny fairy inflated with each embellishment. "The young wizard is a close and personal friend of Dragon."

I groaned, resting my chin on my hand.

The guards raised their flags. "Welcome to The Tower of Song. The provost will be eager to speak with you. Please stop at the registrar's office," the first guard said, motioning us forward.

"Thank you. We won't need much, a place for our animals and a pillow for our heads," I said.

And then, with a grimace, I remembered Howard's missing noggin. *One more thing to worry about. How am I going to retrieve his brainbox?*

But I didn't have time to dwell on my problems because the guards gestured with their flags and hurried us through the archway.

The registrar's office wasn't far, but the cobblestones took an indirect path. We spiraled through roundabouts that led our caravan through town. By the time we arrived, we had established a following of curious townspeople marching behind us.

The townsfolk, in old-fashioned clothes, wore bonnets and hats that shaded their faces. They gathered, whispering in awe, marveling at the majestic Fell Ponies. Orion and Altair stood proud, their long white tails and flowing manes adding to their regal presence. Lester and Nester stomped their hooves and shook their heads, warning the more adventurous townies to keep their distance.

Scout dove into my shirt pocket when I climbed down from the buckboard, leaving Bandit sound asleep beneath a cozy blanket.

"Make way, make way. What's the commotion?" yelled a round man with a handlebar mustache hanging below a bulbous nose. He waddled through the sea of people, parting the crowd, wearing a tight blue sailor's jacket with a double row of straining buttons.

"Good day, sir, I'm—"

"I know, I know—Emissaries of Castle Dragon." The man's voice thundered over the din of the crowd. "I'm Provost Algernon Flowers." His breath burst in spurts, and a line of sweat trickled down his temple as if the exertion was too much. He extended a sweaty hand.

After a firm handshake, I discreetly wiped my palm against my pants. "We're simple travelers here to trade."

"Why yes, my suit is well made." He smiled and adjusted his collar. "I assume you're prepared to investigate the caper."

I wrinkled my brow, puzzled.

The provost motioned to a giant old-growth tree in the center of town. "The harp is missing, and the music has stopped. We can't be The Tower of Song—without music."

The spectators had doubled, pushing in closer to hear a word or two of gossip.

I scratched my head. "There must be some kind of mistake."

"Of course, the thief has escaped," he said matter-of-factly.

I raised my voice in frustration. "You misunderstand. We're here to pick up supplies and to hire a guide through Goblin Valley."

At the mention of Goblin Valley, the onlookers gasped and took a collective step back.

The provost smiled at the gaggle of townfolk and swept his hand in a grandiose gesture. "Indeed, no one goes to Goblin Valley without an experienced guide if they want to return in one piece." He rubbed his chin. "So you think the criminal is from Goblin Valley? Hmm, makes sense." Provost Flowers gave me a judgmental look. "You should've sent word, and we could've seen to a discreet meeting. Now everyone knows you're in hot pursuit of the thief," he said in his booming voice.

I exchanged a bewildered look with Jesse when he nudged my arm. "My Uncle Garrett was hard of hearing. Let me give it a shot." Jesse cupped his hands to his mouth and yelled. "Sir, we have no authority here."

I rolled my eyes.

"Oh, don't worry, I can deputize." The provost retrieved an iridescent ball from his pocket and tossed it to me.

It was reflex that I caught it, and when I opened my hand, I held a shining star with *Marshal* printed on it. "But, I don't—"

Jesse pulled my sleeve, and I tugged free, scowling.

"This is perfect. We can go undercover and search for the 'you know what' while we investigate the missing harp."

I stared at the provost while I ran Jesse's suggestion through my mind. It was a bad idea for many reasons, but I nodded in agreement.

Provost Flowers smiled, showing a gap between his teeth. He flicked a chubby finger, and the star split into three, then one stuck to my duster like a patch, and the others landed on Sara and Jesse's sleeves.

Jesse craned his neck, twisting to check out his star. "I'm a deputy—Sweet!"

Sara touched my arm and lifted her chin toward the ponies.

"We'll need to stable the animals," I said.

"True, it could be cannibals." Provost Flowers tightened the curl of his mustache. "But first, you'll need to stable your animals, and then we can discuss your theories."

My brows creased, and Jesse barked out a laugh.

"We'd be delighted," Sara said, offering the provost her sweetest smile.

Provost Flowers clapped me on the back. "I have high hopes for you, young wizard. We'll talk more later." The provost snapped his fingers and waved. A man standing two feet tall with an overbite, wearing a nautical suit, scampered down the registry steps. "Salty, assist our guests and see to their accommodations," the provost said in a commanding tone.

"Aye-aye, sir." The miniature sailor kept his salute while the provost pivoted on his heels and marched up the steps.

Suddenly, a shadowy figure shifted at the edge of my vision, and the hair on my neck tingled, but nothing was there when I turned.

"This way, please." The top of Salty's sailor's cap didn't reach my waist.

I bent my knees to meet his eyes. He had a round face, a flat nose, and three straight whiskers sticking out from each side of his upper lip.

"Would you like to ride in the buckboard?"

"Yes, sir, thank you." Salty smiled, displaying two chiclet teeth. He scurried aboard the wagon, and that's when I discovered Headless Howard was nowhere to be seen. I scanned the crowd, looking for any sign of my traveling companion, but once again, he had vanished.

Salty directed us to the rear of the building, where we entered a well-maintained barn.

"These are the stables and barracks. Your property will be safe here." He hopped out of the wagon. "We also have private quarters for our visiting dignitaries. It will be my privilege to assist you during your stay."

Bandit, the raccoon, tossed aside his blanket and eyed Salty hungrily.

Salty squeaked, sucking air through his teeth. Then, as if trying to recover his dignity, he stood straight as a board, his eyes fixed on Bandit, the raccoon.

Bandit lifted a paw. "No worries, mate," he said in a thick Aussie accent. "Crikey, it's chockers in here." He jumped from the wagon onto a bale of hay.

Scout flew out of my pocket, and full of commotion, she buzzed about the stable.

"Wow, a real Castle Dragon fairy." Salty caught himself and put on a dignified air. "It's an honor to be of service to such an esteemed group." He bowed and tipped his hat, revealing a tuff of fur and pointy pink ears.

It was the golden hour before sunset. Sunlight filtered through the gaps in the barn as Bandit strolled out of a stall. Salty didn't mention the transformation, although his whiskers twitched at the sight of Bandit in human form.

Salty held the door open. "If you kindly come this way, our guest barracks are down the hall."

"I'm starving," Jesse said, grinning and rubbing his stomach.

"Yes, of course. I've scheduled dinner with Provost Flowers after your meeting," Salty said. "But in the meantime, I'll send over a light snack."

"A sanger would be ripper," Bandit said and followed after Salty.

# CHAPTER 10

## *MISCHIEF AND MORE MISCHIEF*

Salty led us down a never-ending corridor with portraits of past provosts lining the wall. Each figure wore a gold-braided uniform, a stern expression, and a Napoleon pose. When I caught sight of the ridiculous names engraved on polished brass plates—*Dusty Rhodes, Chester Drorz, Cryme A. River*, and *Seymour Butts*—I wanted to linger in the portrait gallery hall. But our escort maintained a brisk pace, his footfalls echoing against the stone floor. I hurried to catch up with the group.

Salty stopped at a set of double doors, revealing our guest quarters. "We've recently remodeled, so you should be comfortable here."

We found ourselves in a spacious suite adorned with plush furnishings and opulent decorations. The marble floors glistened, and crystal chandeliers sparkled. The apartment was so posh it rivaled a five-star hotel. Salty escorted us to our individual rooms, one more extravagant than the other. When he left me at mine, the master's quarters, I didn't stop to explore the luxurious details, content to surrender to exhaustion. I dropped my gear and launched onto the inviting bed, sinking into a cushion of feathers. Sleep claimed me.

A headless horseman haunted my dreams. He thundered through the moonlit woods on a blue stallion with red eyes, chasing Frankenstein's monster. Not the movie version, but a monstrous green monkey with stitched scars marring its face while clutching a doll by the top of its head. They crashed through the dense forest, snapping branches and cutting a path to my campsite. The monster, still gripping the doll, skidded to a stop. The mighty stallion reared up on its hind legs, its muscles rippling.

As I stood in the doorway, the sky, aglow with northern lights, reflected off the polished aluminum sides of my Airstream camper. The sight of the monsters failed to send creepy shivers, but the porcelain doll with painted hair did. The doll's eyelids rolled back to reveal milky eyes. My knees wobbled, and I grabbed the railing to steady myself.

"Can I use the bathroom?" the dolly asked in an Arnold Schwarzenegger voice.

Before I could respond, the green monster barged past me into the vintage camper, leaving the odor of liverwurst and onions in his wake.

*Thump, thump!*

With a jolt, I sat up, blinking until the bizarre dream faded. Sara stood in the doorway. She had changed out of her dusty clothes. Her long brown hair looked damp, and her face scrubbed pink. A fresh, lemony scent erased the lingering odor of onions. I dragged a hand through my sweaty hair, moving it out of my eyes.

"What napping again?" Her smile sparkled in her eyes. "Salty's here to escort us to the provost's office, so get ready to go."

I smiled at her natural beauty and the graceful way she moved when she turned away.

ΔΔΔ

Salty led us to a dimly lit lobby with drab walls and a foot traffic groove down the center of the plank floor. Cobwebs and grime covered the windows. Wooden benches ran the length, with varnish worn off from years of use. The contrast between this lackluster space and our lavish accommodations left me bewildered. What the public saw was a far cry from the extravagant embassy apartment.

Salty banged on a wooden door with a frosted window and faded lettering, marking it as the Office of the Provost.

"Enter," came the provost's thunderous voice.

Provost Flowers sat behind a weathered desk, scratching out a note before folding and hastily sealing it in an envelope. He struggled out of his chair and shuffled to join us at the conference table. The provost skipped the usual small talk and got straight to the point.

"We have much to discuss. And I'm sure you're tired from your travels."

He shot a quick glance at Bandit, who, in his human form, stood captivated by the oil paintings lining the walls and showed no interest in joining us. The provost cleared his throat, twisting his mustache, irritation flashing across his round face. After a beat, his shrewd gray eyes landed on me.

"You'll want to complete your investigation before the village fills with tourists." He tapped his forehead with his pudgy hand. "But you know this."

I shook my head no. "We're new in town."

"Ruin the town—Yes, indeed." He rubbed the back of his neck, explaining the population would swell with visitors for the upcoming music festival. Once a year, vendors and customers travel from all corners of the Otherlands to trade, buy goods, and attend the festivities.

"This is a catastrophe," Provost Flowers continued, his tone laden with defeat. "Without the harp, the music dies, and the tree won't bloom." He covered his face with his hands, muffling his loud voice. "It's a chain reaction—no blooms, no fruit, and come winter, we starve."

Jesse didn't hide his disbelief when asked, "Aren't there other instruments? What's so special about an old harp?"

Salty's anxious eyes traveled to his boss but then visibly relaxed, realizing the provost hadn't heard Jesse's blunt question.

Salty explained, "The harp holds our legacy—our history, traditions, and heritage. But more than that, the harp is the wellspring of our magic. If you'll allow me, I'll provide some background."

Salty's storytelling skills took hold, enthralling us with his passionate narrative. "Once upon a time, a young man from the misty mountains fell head over heels for a fair maiden. He longed to make her his wife, but her father, driven by ambitions for wealth and status, had a different plan. The handsome lad asked for her hand, and the father refused, intending to marry her off to a wealthy baron's son. Heartbroken yet determined, the lad climbed a tree in the town's square, vowing to stay there until he won his true love. Perched upon a high branch, he plucked the strings of his harp, pouring his heart into each melody. Day and night, song after song, his enchanting music lured countless pairs of winged lovebirds, drawn to join his serenade. Eventually, the father's heart melted. Touched by the lad's devotion, he consented to the union. But fate can be cruel —and in the moment of his greatest joy, the young fellow lost his grip and plunged to his death. Devastated by her true love's broken form, the fair maiden's fragile heart shattered. She perished from grief, collapsing beside her young man. Yet, their love story didn't end there. The harp, an instrument of magic, merged with the maiden's spirit, becoming a vessel for her endless love. Since that sorrowful day, flocks of lovebirds faithfully return. Each evening, as darkness falls, the magical harp strums a bittersweet tune, accompanied by a chorus of lovebirds."

Salty sipped some water. "Enriched with the harp's magic, we believe the spirits of the young lovers dance among the branches, and their love enchants the flowering fruit. As a token of respect, our town assumed the tree's name. The revered tree, known as the Tower of Song, provides the extraordinary magical fruit we rely on for food, clothes, and healing."

The provost abruptly cut in, slamming his fist on the table. "You have until the end of the week. That's when we gather for the festival to honor the harp."

I leaned back at the gruff interruption. "You must have an idea of where to look. It'd help if you'd share your theories."

"Of course, make inquiries." Provost Flowers twisted his mustache. "But I have a theory—it could be a collector."

"Could you tell us why a collector?" Sara asked.

Salty perked at the relevant question. "Our harp is an arcane ruin. Opportunistic treasure hunters and unethical antiquities dealers offer high prices for enchanted artifacts." Salty released a squeaky sigh. "Unfortunately, we were naïve and didn't believe someone would be so ruthless to steal the town's life source."

A headache threatened, hovering along the edges of my brain. *How did I get involved in this?*

I rubbed my aching neck. "We have pressing business elsewhere in Goblin Valley, but we'll keep our eyes open. We plan to visit the market tomorrow, so we'll look around, but no promises—"

Provost Flowers leaned back, smiling. "I'm impressed by your optimism, promising to solve it by tomorrow. That's wonderful news. I'm confident you'll retrieve our beloved harp. It's true what they say about you."

Confusion clouded my expression. *We're not detectives. Who does he think we are?*

"Your reputation proceeds you, young wizard of Castle Dragon. Return our harp, and the village will be in your debt." Provost Flowers rose with a grunt, pushing against the table to lift his considerable bulk. "In the meantime, we have prepared a buffet in your honor."

Jesse shot out of his chair, grinning. "Great, I'm starved."

My stomach chose that moment to rumble in agreement.

ΔΔΔ

The bustling dining hall gave off a cafeteria vibe with clattering pans and a buzz of conversation. The dinner hour was in full swing as we grabbed our plates and shuffled down the rows. My eyes widened at the delicious spread. The choices were plentiful, with hearty stews, pasta, and a savory selection of meats, fish, and vegetables. Bandit reached for the green beans, but Sara smacked his hand away, pointing to the serving spoon.

Her hushed voice held a note of motherly admonishment. "We don't grab with our hands. We use the utensils." She smiled. "It's okay, just follow my lead."

With my plate piled high, I scanned the dining hall and spotted my friends behind a red roped-off area labeled VIP. A dining table draped in a linen tablecloth sat on a raised platform. Maroon velvet cushions adorned the high-back chairs. Provost Flowers lounged at the head of the table, gnawing on a turkey leg. Bits of meat clung to his mustache. He greeted me with a nod.

Bandit had secured a chair with his back to the wall. Jesse sat beside him, and Sara found a seat next to Salty, who stood when I arrived, motioning me to take the seat of honor at the other end of the table.

Famished, I dug into my meal, paying little attention to the idle conversation. I devoured the food like a ravenous wildfire. When I treated my sweet tooth to a slab of chocolate cake, everyone else was still working on their first course.

Bandit savored his meal with moans of delight. He grabbed a bun and made a sandwich with spaghetti, sardines, and pickles. I watched the messy spectacle with amusement until Bandit guzzled a bottle of ranch dressing like a can of soda. My stomach churned and I nearly gagged. I tossed my napkin, excusing myself, claiming I needed fresh air.

ΔΔΔ

Back in my suite, a cool breeze ruffled the curtains while a waxing crescent moon provided a soft light. The midnight sky, tinged with purple and awash with stars, looked like a surreal painting. I smiled when I spotted the Big Dipper. Dad had taught me to identify at least a dozen constellations and stargazing made me feel closer to him. I missed my parents deeply, haunted by memories of lost opportunities to be a better son. Their tragic death robbed my family of more than words could express. I shook off the melancholy and scanned the night tapestry. Polaris, also known as the North Star, perched on the tail of the Little Dipper. Pinpointing Polaris took a while until I realized the stars were shifting. Whenever I looked away, the North Star would jump to another corner of the sky.

When the game lost appeal, I sat cross-legged on my bed and dumped my pack's contents before me. The routine of unpacking and repacking my gear comforted me. I set aside *Mischief* and held the globe the king of fairies had gifted me. When I shook it, flakes swirled like glitter, clouding the glass. After a moment, a miniature three-dimensional map of the village emerged. All roads led to a massive tree in the center of town. On the outskirts stood rows of tents.

When I discovered the glass worked like a touch screen, I used my thumb and forefinger to zoom in and read the signs above the various offerings. Flower stands, bookshops, clothing, rugs, and an apothecary stand filled the marketplace. Some tents were elaborate with flags and banners, while others were nothing more than a few tarps strung together. Once I had mentally mapped The Tower of Song's layout, my apprehension about what lay ahead in the bustling marketplace eased.

I turned to my evening routine of reading *Mischief*. The book was a collection of Ezra's notes, drawings, and potions. *Mischief* was unpredictable. I couldn't count on him to display the same information more than once. So, I'd been transcribing tidbits into my own journal. The practice of rewriting what I had read cemented the details into my brain. I learned this technique in school, which helped me to study for tests. That's when I recalled Mrs. S's cryptic warning—*Don't expect there to be a test, although you will be tested.*

Doubts crept into my mind, crowding my thoughts. "What if I'm crazy, and all of this is a psychotic episode?" I muttered. "No, it's real. I can feel it deep in my gut."

"Perhaps it is flatulence," came an unfamiliar voice.

No one was there when I looked around. *Perfect, now I'm hearing voices.* I pushed my hair from my eyes and sighed.

With *Mischief* on my lap, I settled into my bed. My mind jumped like a hyperactive kid on a trampoline while I bellyached, voicing self-doubt. "I'm not making progress—All I've done is add more work to my already impossible quest," I grumbled.

To help me organize my thoughts, I began making a mental list. "And what about Agnes, the witch in red? She's related to Carla—now, that's a problem." I bit my lip, deep in thought about the witch's involvement.

"Something tells me I should return to Sweetwater and check on Aunt Shirley. I didn't like the idea that the witch sent someone to speak to her. But not until I find the Dragon Moonstone. And no way am I going to skip harvesting dragonroot—That's a matter of life and death. Then there's Howard's missing head, and the provost wants me to recover the harp. Oh, and the hunger stone—Why didn't I think to ask Provost Flowers about the low water levels?" I stretched my arms and yawned.

"When will I learn to say no? How did I get myself into this?"

"One question at a time, lad," a rich Scottish brogue said.

I jerked back, hugging my knees, bouncing *Mischief* to the floor.

"Take it easy. I'm not as young as I used to be," the voice said in a Scottish brogue.

My jaw dropped when I leaned over, staring at a face on the cover of Ezra's leather-bound journal. It sported a prominent nose and a goofy grin. My mind bent, struggling to accept the impossibility of a talking book—I couldn't believe what I was seeing.

"You can talk?" I whispered in awe.

"What, you never heard of an audiobook?" The old book brayed laughter.

My eyes narrowed. Perhaps I'd find humor in it later, but I wasn't laughing then. "After all this time, you can talk?" I snapped, glaring at the book.

"Careful, lad, show respect to your elders," *Mischief* said, matching my tone beat for beat.

I gulped as palpable tension thickened the air. "Sorry, *Mischief*, but it's been a long day." I carefully lifted Ezra's journal, setting it before me. "Is it okay if I call you *Mischief*?"

The book fluttered its pages. "I've been called worse," *Mischief* said cheerfully.

I rubbed my face. "No disrespect, but why can you speak now and not before?"

"I've always been able to talk—It's you—who has learned to listen. But enchantments are easier in the Otherlands because magic is accepted as normal. In the mundane world, people don't believe in magic. Thus, it requires more effort. Mundanes often rationalize magic as a coincidence or dismiss it as serendipity or just plain craziness."

"Ugh, magic's a pain no matter which realm and I'm awful at it—Sara and Jesse are miles ahead of me." I threw my hands up in irritation. "Even after I put in the time, I can't get my spells right. I feel like a total failure at this magic stuff, and I'll never be any good."

"You've set limits on your potential when, in truth, it's limitless. Let go of your preconceived notions of what you can and can't do. Your friends have embraced the idea they have powers and have adapted. Your magic runs deep, but you can't force it any more than you can pull water with your feet. Learn to be one with your magic and tune in to your abilities. You must choose to believe in yourself. If you start off thinking you'll fail, then you already did."

"I'll work on a magical attitude adjustment as soon as I get a chance," I scoffed. "I'll do it on the way to Goblin Valley right after I solve the mystery of the missing harp. No worries." My neck and shoulders tensed as I stared out the window. I heaved a sigh, frustration creeping into my voice. "If I only knew where to start."

"Keep it simple and follow the money," *Mischief* said.

I locked eyes with *Mischief*. "You'll help me?" I asked with a glimmer of hope.

"As much as I can, I'm bound to protocol and what's within my bindings," *Mischief* wiggled his bushy eyebrows, his pages fluttering as if he were chuckling. "But you have to do something for me in exchange."

"Of course I do." My shoulders slumped. "Tell me what it is, and I'll add it to my list."

# CHAPTER 11

## *THE MARKETPLACE*

The blaring PA system announcing the last call for breakfast shattered my restless sleep. Worry and guilt over freezing Erik and destroying Mrs. S's garden kept me tossing and turning all night. With a groan, I peeled myself out of bed, yearning for a few more hours of shut-eye. We had a long day ahead, so I forced my legs to get moving. After devouring excessive amounts of food at dinner, one would think I wouldn't want to eat for a week, but they'd be mistaken. I woke up starving, expecting a feast comparable to our previous night's fantastic dinner. Still drowsy, I hurried to the dining hall.

The mess hall was seconds away from closing when I managed to persuade a reluctant kitchen worker to take pity on me. She generously offered to put something together for such an esteemed visitor. I didn't contradict her when she elevated my status. With a dry smile, she handed me a plate piled high and directed me toward the VIP section, where my friends were seated. I quickly joined them—sliding into a chair, offering Sara a half-hearted smile, and giving Jesse a too-early-for-talking nod.

One condition of Jesse staying with me was that he understood I wasn't a morning person and needed to ease into my day with coffee and quiet time. Cradling a warm cup of coffee, my gaze swept the room. The troops finishing breakfast gave off an intense vibe, something that had escaped my notice the night before. With Salty and the provost absent, no one met my eyes. But that was okay with me. Mornings weren't my thing —I preferred companionable silence until noon.

I breathed in the steam from my coffee and mustered patience to listen to Jesse recount what they had learned after dinner. Apparently, The Tower of Song served as an embassy for the territory, acting as the last outpost at the edge of the wilderness. Algernon Flowers played the dual roles of provost and ambassador. Beyond the fort, the harsh wild land was home to notorious outlaws and uncivilized creatures—the provost's words, not theirs. Consequently, navigating the desolate badlands of Goblin Valley would require an experienced guide.

While Jesse's mouth kept running, my strip of bacon crumbled in my hand, charred to a crisp, in an inedible blackened state. The eggs were ice cold, and a fragment of eggshell stuck to my tongue. I choked it down with bitter coffee, ignoring the grounds sticking to my teeth.

Jesse's incessant chatter grated on my already frayed nerves. When he inquired about Howie's whereabouts, I groaned. No one had seen Howard since our arrival, but I knew he would make an appearance. Headless would never let me out of my accidental bargain. He wanted his head back, and I guess I couldn't blame him for that.

Stress pinched my neck, elevated by my additional responsibilities to recover a missing head and a harp, when all I wanted to do was find a peddler and hire a guide.

I bit into soggy toast while rolling the tension from my shoulders. After wiping away a lipstick stain decorating the rim of my glass, I guzzled my water. Upon discovering a fingernail buried in my banana nut muffin, I dropped my napkin in disgust.

In his human form, Bandit sat across from me. Engrossed in his dry cereal, he dunked each piece into a glass of milk before eating them one at a time.

My teeth clenched, but the words escaped my lips, "What on earth are you doing?"

Bandit looked at me as if a village was missing an idiot. "I'm having my brekkie, same as you."

He tossed a dripping square and caught it with his mouth. Bandit continued his ritual of dipping square after square and dribbling milk onto the linen tablecloth.

When I couldn't take it any longer, I grabbed his glass of milk and emptied it over his cereal. "Use a spoon," I said unintentionally loud.

Sara huffed, glaring at me. A heavy silence fell over the hall. Everyone paused, turning toward the commotion.

"Crikey, you drowned them."

Bandit's sad eyes melted my ire, and I swallowed my embarrassment.

"Does that make you a cereal killer?"

There was a long pause while my mind struggled to catch up.

"Serial killer—You nailed it, dude." Jesse high-fived Bandit. "We've been working on Bandit's sense of humor."

Bandit grinned a sloppy raccoon grin, the way only a man with an Aussie accent, who morphs into a nocturnal omnivore, could. Sara's laughter swept away the last remnants of my crabby mood.

Bandit raised his coffee mug as if in a toast. "Lighten up, and don't worry, I've got your back."

A grin cracked my face, drawing strength from Bandit's confidence. As soon as the breakfast crowd realized there wouldn't be any more outbursts, they lost interest and returned to their meals.

Sara wiped her mouth with a napkin. "So, what's the game plan?"

"After breakfast, or brekkie, as Bandit would say, we should check out the market and ask around," I said, dowsing my blueberry pancakes with syrup.

I flinched when Scout materialized on my shoulder. "Stop sneaking up on me."

"I wasn't sneaking. I've been here the entire time."

"You're eavesdropping, and that's not polite."

Scout landed in the middle of the table with hands planted

on her hips. "I'm polite—besides, it's what fairies do." Her wings pulsated a deep red as she glared at me, challenging me to disagree.

I felt the sudden warmth of my amulet around my neck and ground my teeth while reminding myself not to harbor ill will. *Don't borrow trouble. Scout is what she is—no sense in holding it against her.*

I shrugged and took another sip of coffee, refusing to let my lousy mood return.

"Seems to me Scout has a superpower that could come in handy," Sara said, smiling warmly at the fairy. "She could gather intel and help us compile a list of likely suspects."

Scout sprang into action. She flittered about, weaving a pattern between us, boasting of her fairy connections. Scout fibbed so convincingly that I almost believed her.

"We should split up and see what we can find out about the harp," Jesse said.

"And also, any news on the—" Sara air quoted, "—you know what."

Jesse tilted his head in confusion.

"The object we're looking for, the one we don't talk about," I said, waiting until the answer caught up with Jesse's brain.

Jesse smacked his forehead, chuckling at his momentary memory lapse.

Sara sipped her coffee. "Two arcane ruins are missing—the harp and '*the you know what.*' I can't help but think they're connected."

"Follow the money," I said, repeating *Mischief's* advice.

The group gawked as if it was the first time I had uttered something profound. I smiled smugly and used my toast to sop up the runny egg yolk, choking down my last bite.

"Finish up. We have a long day ahead," Sara said.

"Right-o, sister," Bandit said before grabbing the syrup bottle and squirting a glob into his mouth.

ΔΔΔ

When we arrived at the open-air market, the bazaar's earthy spices and exotic fragrances mingled with our buzz of excitement and eagerness to explore. Shopkeepers welcomed us, and zealous hawkers shouted their guaranteed bargains. A particular vendor caught Jesse's attention, and he and Bandit dashed off to investigate.

Sara and I strolled through the rows of tents. We stopped at a shop called *The Mad Hattery*. Sara browsed the aisles, her eyes lighting up as she perused the diverse selection of enchanted headwear. She drifted from rack to rack, letting her fingers trail over the silky ribbons and feathers. With curiosity and delight, she would pick up a hat, assess it, and move on as if seeking the perfect accessory.

Lost in the fun and good humor, I had almost forgotten about the harp. I reveled in the brief respite. But word of our *so-called* investigation of the missing harp had traveled through the grapevine and caught up with us. The gossip mill churned, and from that moment on, speculation and suspicion followed us wherever we went.

Eventually, we stumbled upon an apothecary shop crafted from a converted freight wagon and canvas tarps. Stacked benches served as makeshift shelves, creating a haphazard feel. As I was about to duck inside, I caught a fleeting shadow from the outskirts of my vision, and a shiver crept along my back. My eyes darted in all directions, but I spied nothing more unusual in the already weird world. Ignoring the uncanny sensation, I trailed after Sara.

Potent magic assaulted my senses as I stepped over the threshold of the eclectic shop of herbs and remedies. A wave of dizziness hit me. I hesitated before steeling myself to move deeper into the tent and keep up with Sara. Behind the precarious racks, a woman in a white lab coat was busy measuring and mixing, paying us no mind. The scene brought memories of Mrs. S's laboratory, where controlled chaos hid an underlying order. Although it seemed chaotic to an outsider, there was a method to the madness.

I wondered if the shopkeeper stocked *Pearls of Wisdom* because I secretly left Mrs. S half of my supply of the medicinal tea. In her weakened state, she needed them more than me. Besides, I felt fine and could ration what I kept. With narrow rows and rickety shelves, I stuffed my hands in my pockets and tucked in my elbows, doing my best to avoid brushing against a display and causing a collapse—it wouldn't take much for the shelving to tumble like a stack of dominos.

The prickle of magic followed me as I browsed the mishmash of glass jars and canisters.

"Are you seeing what I'm seeing?" I asked Sara with a touch of awe in my voice.

Sara responded with a questioning smirk.

"It's strange. Whenever I look at a product, after a few seconds, a thought bubble appears with the name and details, like a personal hologram. It's freaky but also cool."

Sara chuckled, shaking her head no.

"You really don't see the bubbles?"

"It's the tinctures," came a raspy voice belonging to the woman pharmacist. "They're hypersensitive to the wizard's blood."

"Who said I was a wizard? I'm an ordinary shopper."

The pharmacist, with the face of a dried apple, scoffed, drawing closer. "You're anything but ordinary. In the Otherlands, you are what you are. You can't hide from yourself. No matter where you go, there you are."

I stared at her blankly, pondering her words and their cryptic nature. And then, shaking off the momentary awkward confusion, I redirected the conversation. "Do you have any *Pearls of Wisdom*?"

"I just gave you some." She smiled so broadly that I feared her face would split in half.

I gazed at her with a bored expression, not wanting to encourage more lame jokes.

"Oh, such a pity when a youngster has no humor." She cleared her throat. "*Pearls of Wisdom*, you say. The plant that produces such pearls is rare indeed." She eyed me with interest. "If you have any clippings, I'll pay handsomely."

I scraped the toe of my boot on the sawdust floor, pushing the image of Mrs. S's wilted Bella out of my mind.

Sara, quick to come to my rescue, sensing my remorseful guilt, spoke up. "Do you have dragonroot?"

"Dragonroot? I haven't had it for many years," the pharmacist said, her intense gaze shifting to Sara. "You ask interesting questions—ah—you're from Castle Dragon. I expected someone older." She rubbed her bony hands as her eyes sparkled. "How is Mrs. Shea?"

"You know Mrs. Shea?" Sara asked.

"Mrs. Shea was my teacher when I was a young girl."

I wondered about the passage of time as I considered the intricate web of wrinkles sprawled across the woman's face. She appeared twice the age of Mrs. Shea.

The pharmacist's eyes glowed silver. "They call me Peddler."

"Mrs. Shea told us to seek a peddler for guidance. Are you the one she was referring to?" Sara asked.

"There are many peddlers, but yes, I believe I'm the one she meant," the old pharmacist said, leaning in with a knowing expression. "What can I help you with?"

"We need to know where to find dragonroot," I said, my voice brimming with determination.

Peddler's eyes widened, cautioning us against the dangers. "If you find it, beware. Harvesting is not for the faint of heart." The lines on her forehead deepened. "I'd advise against it—much too dangerous." She gestured toward an assortment of tinctures. "Browse and see what you can find here." Peddler turned, appearing as though she wanted to end the conversation.

I wasn't about to let her dismiss us. "It's a matter of life and death. Mrs. Shea sent us for dragonroot."

"Did she now?" Her last syllable ended on a higher note. Peddler swung her head from side to side before cupping her hand to shield her mouth. "There's only one place—Dragon Tooth Cave, deep within Goblin Valley. It's a harrowing journey. I'm surprised Mrs. Shea would send someone so—inexperienced." She hesitated and gave us the once-over. "You must be smarter than you look," Peddler hee-hawed at the joke while displaying a toothless grin.

I smiled to let her know I didn't take offense.

Sara inquired about provisions we might need, and Peddler pointed a knobby finger toward a nearby shelf.

"Tooth powder?"

The old pharmacist cackled at my mistake, gesturing me to the next row.

"Truth powder, interesting," I said, grabbing a package.

Soon, Peddler's persuasive skills came to the forefront as she sold us a litany of items she deemed essential for our journey. The pouch of coins jingled as I paid our bill, and I silently thanked the king of fairies for his generous gift.

ΔΔΔ

Following Peddler's advice, we visited the shops specializing in antiques, inquiring about the missing harp. Peddler warned us that the vendors were a tight-lipped group, but we might persuade them with the right incentive. She had also hinted at the existence of unsavory collectors, though she wouldn't name names. Despite our best efforts, that avenue of investigation proved unfruitful. After visiting dozens of antique and collectible shops, I was ready to call it a day, even though I suspected Sara could've shopped for several more hours.

We turned a corner, and there they were—the Parker Brothers. Their tent displayed colorful board games, woven baskets that reminded me of snake charmers, and a few dozen handcrafted rugs.

"We meet again. You two been shopping?" Zeb asked, chewing on what I hoped was a toothpick, not a small-animal bone.

*Why do people always state the obvious as a question? It drives me crazy.*

Zeb slipped his hands through his suspenders and bragged about his rugs. "Flying carpets—the finest in the region." His face twisted into a wicked sneer. "Come with me, girlie. I'll take you on a magic carpet ride." He motioned with his toothpick. "You can come too, young wizard."

Rolls of carpet stood on end, and Zeb grabbed the nearest one and shook it flat. The carpet floated a few inches off the ground, defying gravity. Sara and I exchanged glances. Although we'd love to ride on a carpet, we didn't like the smirk on Zeb's leathery face.

I ran my hand along the rolls of carpets. Static crackled and sparked as I touched the silk threads of the finely woven rugs.

"Don't touch the merchandise!" But Zeb's shout came too late.

Lightning flashed from my fingertips, and the rolled rugs wobbled, wiggled, and then twisted free from the bungee that held them in place. Rugs zigged and zagged, flying low toward the open fairgrounds.

Zeb reacted swiftly. He spat out the toothpick and grabbed a rope. Then he spun it overhead like a lariat and, as if a cowboy, he lassoed the farthest rug. It resisted, tugging against the noose, fighting for all it was worth, but soon Zeb had the defiant carpet hog-tied like a steer in a rodeo.

Concern written all over her face, Sara moved closer to help.

"Stay out of the way," Zeb yelled.

He whistled sharply, and the rugs froze in place, responding to their master's command. "All right, settle down, back to your stations."

With their leader captured, the other carpets lost their enthusiasm. They returned at a sullen pace, like naughty children being sent to their room.

Zeb pointed his bony finger in my direction. "Starz and nebulas. You could've caused a stampede. Have you no sense to leave the enchanted goods be?"

"I didn't mean to. It was an accident."

Zeb threw up his hands and glared at me.

I put my hands on my hips. "We stopped by to ask about the harp," I said in an authoritative voice.

"What about it?" Zeb's eyes narrowed, his hands flexing at his sides.

"Do you know who took it?"

"How should I know?" His eyes glowed cold as a snake. "Who said we had anything to do with it?"

"No one. The provost asked us to investigate." I gestured to my badge on my sleeve.

"Well, do your investigation somewhere else." Zeb turned his back and stormed into his tent.

We stood outside his store for a moment, letting the dust settle. When I was sure Zeb Parker was out of earshot, I asked Sara, "What do you make of Zeb's outburst?"

"I think there's something snaky about the guy." Sara looped her arm through mine and guided me toward the main exit.

# CHAPTER 12

## *DOUBLE OR NOTHING*

Packages in hand, we set off for our embassy suite. The moment we stepped into the bustling street, a rush of machinery whizzed by. I jumped onto the boardwalk, pulling Sara with me.

"Lighten up. You're too tense," Sara said, brushing off the fact that I'd just saved her life.

"This place *is* intense," I said. "Besides, you have no situational awareness. You could've been run over by whatever that contraption was."

She laughed off my concern, nodding toward Jesse.

"Hey, wait for me." Jesse skidded to a stop, his chest heaving, gasping for breath.

Amid the commotion, Bandit sat on a peculiar unicycle. Not a typical unicycle—this machine defied convention. A motorized wheel spun an outer rubber tire without moving the interior, where with one foot planted on the ground, Bandit reclined in the saddle. In human form, he had changed his clothes and rocked a serious biker vibe.

I kneeled down to admire the fantastical mechanical mastery. "My dad would love this—but what is it?"

"A mono-wheel." Bandit held a cocky grin as he adjusted his helmet.

Sara tucked a loose strand of hair behind her ear and crouched beside me, admiring the motorized unicycle. Bandit offered Sara a helmet, and she raised an eyebrow at the single-seat machine.

Bandit pulled a lever, and with a hydraulic hum, a sidecar unfolded.

"Dude, I've been running alongside you for over an hour, and there was a passenger seat," Jesse said, his face flushing red, almost as red as his hair.

Bandit winked at Sara before responding to Jesse's question. "But I figured you were keen on goin' for a trot, eh?"

I burst into laughter.

Jesse watched them drive off with his hands on his hips. I took a seat on a nearby bench and leaned back against the backrest, closing my eyes to take a nap. After a while, they returned. Sara smiled, and a second later, so did I. We each had a go at driving and riding in the sidecar. Bandit was an excellent driver—Jesse, not so much.

ΔΔΔ

Hunger pangs drove us to the embassy's dining hall, where we discovered the kitchen had closed. Scout picked that moment to return. Disappointed, we trudged to our suite's common room, delighted to learn Salty had stocked the fridge with box lunches. We dug into our lunch, exchanging the little information we had gleaned.

Despite a lack of concrete evidence, the Parkers were prime suspects. Scout, with her fairy connection, unearthed rumors about the gang. Although they had never been caught, the Parker clan was believed to be fortune hunters involved in trafficking arcane artifacts. According to her sources, the brothers operated an exclusive backroom dealership offering private showings of their *art gallery*. She also discovered that the Parkers had several associates willing to pay top dollar for rare magical relics.

"It's the Parker brothers—it has to be. Let's arrest them!" Jesse scooted his chair back as if he meant right now.

"Hold on," I said, motioning for him to sit down. "We can't accuse anyone of stealing based on rumors and a gut feeling. We need solid proof."

Jesse folded his arms in a pout, his box lunch spread out before him.

After a moment, Sara crumpled the wrapping of her sandwich and asked if Scout's fairy contacts managed to peek inside the Parker's tents.

"No, they're sealed tighter than a bag of chips," Scout replied.

I couldn't help but joke, reaching for a packet of salt and vinegar potato chips. "Not so hard, see." With a quick tug, the package ripped in half, sending the contents flying across the table.

Sara shook with laughter, and Jesse nearly fell out of his chair.

"Next time, use your teeth, mate." Bandit grabbed a wayward chip and dunked it into Jesse's applesauce.

Scout wasted no time buzzing around like a dust buster, gobbling up the spilled chips. She finished in a dervish and then flopped on the table. The tiny fairy moaned, rubbed her belly, and let out a squeaky burp.

Bandit slurped packets of mustard and stopped mid-stream when the door flung open. A miserable Headless Howard shuffled in, his hood drooping, having lost its starch.

"You look like you had a rough day," Sara said, motioning toward the box lunches, offering to share with Howard.

This could be interesting. *How does Howie eat without a head?*

Howard waved off the offer and flopped into a chair. His shoulders slumped as if all his dirty deeds had caught up with him.

"What's the matter?" Jesse wanted to know.

Howard kept his head down, his shoulders trembling. "I have a problem."

Jesse gave Headless a long, thoughtful look. "What could be worse than losing your head?" he asked, voicing my thoughts exactly.

There was a drawn-out moment as if to choose his words. "It was a monster hand. I couldn't lose. But he raised, and I didn't have credit to cover it." Howie's voice quivered. "That's when I bolstered my bet with Noah's token."

I jerked to attention. "My what?"

"Your token promise to do me a favor," Headless said with his gaze fixed on his lap.

My mind spun in confusion, struggling to grasp the situation.

Howard started talking fast. "I gambled away your pledge, and now you are beholden to them."

"Who?" I scrunched my forehead.

"The Parkers, of course."

"I'm not following," I said, but I was afraid I was.

Howard made a noise that sounded like grinding gears on a stick shift, but I think he cleared his throat. "The cards had been in my favor, and I sort of owed the brothers' money. They saw me with my winnings piling up and pushed their way in."

"Why'd you let them play?" Jesse asked, questioning with open palms.

Headless gestured with his sleeves. "The Parkers own the joint. Besides, I was on an unbelievable winning streak, and Zeb went all in, trying to buy the hand. I knew I had him beat, so I sweetened the pot with Noah's commitment to do a favor." Howard coughed and mumbled into his sleeve. "And now, Noah owes them."

"I don't owe the Parkers anything," I said as heat crept up my neck.

"Yes, you do," Howard said. "When you offered me help, you never said it wasn't a non-transferable contract. Luck was on my side—I had no choice."

I couldn't believe my ears. "You could've folded—You always have a choice." My voice rose in anger.

"It was a winning hand," Harold yelled, and his red Xs looked like they could shoot fire.

"Obviously, it wasn't," I said, clenching my teeth and not backing down. "It doesn't matter. I won't do it."

Howard's voice grew softer. "The brothers expected you to refuse, so they made me bind my bet to the wall."

The sandwich in my stomach turned into a ball of grease.

"What exactly does that mean—bound to the wall?"

Howard's shoulders slumped further. "You're indentured, magically entangled, and can't go beyond the walls of the outpost until you satisfy your obligation."

"And what obligation would that be?"

"That, I'm afraid, is open for interpretation."

Scout squeaked, her eyes filled with panic. "This is so wrong —I told you so—I knew he was trouble," she said before disappearing in a flash of light.

Frustration surged through my veins as I processed the mess Howard put me in. "Well, you had better un-entangle me and be quick about it." My anger simmered.

"I can't. There's no way," Harold said, deflating into his chair.

The room fell silent as we grappled with the weight of the situation. It wasn't long before Howard stood up to pace, his robe dragging along the floor as he moved.

"Unless—well, it might work," Headless mumbled under his breath.

After a couple of beats, Jesse took the bait. "Tell us."

"We ask for a rematch, and the winner takes all." Howard's hoodie had lost some of its slump.

"Isn't that what started the trouble?" I scoffed, folding my arms.

"Yeah, I know, but it was a fantastic hand." Howard waved his sleeve.

"Don't you know you can't beat the house?" I said, shaking my head. "The house always wins."

Sara's eyes sparked with an idea. "What if it's our house and our game?"

"Howard, what do you even have to gamble with?" I asked.

"Well, nothing, but if I were to hazard a guess, you have valuable trinkets in your wagon." Howard waved his sleeves with a sheepish shrug. "Plus, that pack of yours—ripples with magic."

"You told us they cheated. How do we get around that?" I rubbed away the headache forming at my temple.

"Then we'll be better cheats," Sara said smugly.

"Noah, you're a champion Texas hold 'em card player," Jesse said. The table wobbled as he bounced his leg in excitement. "You won a tournament last summer and learned to spot cheats and card tricks from your uncle, right? You can beat them. Besides, what's the worst that could happen? You're already beholden to them?"

I dropped my head in my hands and groaned.

"Let me make it up to you," Howard said.

"And how will you do that?" My jaw clenched as I struggled to keep myself in check, wondering if this was one of the tests Mrs. S had warned about.

"I've traveled deep into Goblin Valley. I'll be your guide."

"Not good enough." I blew off the suggestion. "You got me into this. Now, get me out."

Howard leaned forward. "I'll pledge my fealty until you complete your quest and return to Sweetwater," he said, sounding as if that was something I'd want.

I shook my head a definite no.

"You misunderstand, wizard—fealty is allegiance. I have resources—I have contacts." His tone softened as he tried to persuade me. "And I can help you deal with Agnes, the witch." Howard slipped into a chair.

Now, it was my turn to pace. At the mention of the witch, my resolve weakened. Again, I knew I shouldn't trust Howard, but he had backed me into a corner. Then again, Uncle George had taught me to play a mean game of cards. Still, I had my doubts. With nervous energy, I cleaned up our lunch mess while I mulled over the proposition. I couldn't stay in The Tower of Song forever—I had promises to keep and quests to complete. Besides, I refused to be obligated to the Parkers. There had to be another way.

"Seems crazy to think we can beat them at their own game—We'll need an edge," I said as I reclaimed my seat at the table.

Sara furrowed her brow, thinking. We remained lost in our thoughts until Jesse enthusiastically shared his idea. With a plan in place, I stepped outside for some air.

ΔΔΔ

As I entered the livery stable, my tension peeled away, finding comfort in the clean barn and the familiar scent of fresh hay. Lester and Nester scrambled to their feet, bleating in annoyance at being awakened from their nap. But they settled down when I fed them bits of dried apple. Next, I grabbed a currycomb and brushed the white ponies until their coats glistened. I had finished washing my hands when I heard footfalls behind me.

"Hey, I thought I'd find you hiding here," Sara said, her voice tinged with worry and her eyes filled with concern as she flipped her hair back.

I could tell she wanted to talk. I blew out a breath. "Yeah, animals calm my nerves—always have."

"What's on your mind?" Sara asked.

"What besides the obvious?" I ran a hand through my hair. "Everything. We're no closer to finding the Dragon Moonstone. Time is running out for Mrs. Shea. We also haven't had a chance to discuss the hunger stone."

"All that, huh?" Sara smiled gently. My heart hitched, and I forgot to breathe.

But then I remembered Agnes, the red witch, and straightened out my spine. "Something's wrong in Sweetwater—I can feel it. And Howard's entanglement only makes things worse."

Sara's lips formed a slight frown, but her gaze remained unwavering.

"Together, we'll figure it out," Sara said, while hesitation knotted her voice. "If only I could be of more help. My persuasive abilities work better with the mundane. I'm not as confident with my new magic here in the Otherlands." She wrung her hands.

I stepped closer. "Sara, you're terrific under pressure, and I'm glad you're here." I motioned toward our supply wagon and looked her straight in the eye. "If things go bad, we make a run for it."

"What about the wall?" Sara's eyes flickered with distress. "You can't leave."

I placed my hands on her shoulders, drowning in her big brown eyes. "If something happens to me, promise you'll take Jesse and Bandit and head for Castle Dragon." A few loose strands of hair fell onto her face, and without thinking, I tucked them behind her ear and felt a curl of warmth around my heart. In that sudden moment, I yearned to express the feelings that had been welling up inside me for so long. "Sara," I began, my voice softening to a whisper, "there's something I've been wanting to —"

"Showtime!" Jesse yelled, bursting into the barn. He stopped short when he saw us standing close. "Am I interrupting something?" he asked, clearly amused.

I stepped back, rassling Jesse in a headlock while rubbing my knuckles against his skull.

He laughed, squirming until I released him.

"Nope, not at all," I lied, offering a reassuring smile. "Let's do this!"

ΔΔΔ

The Tower of Song bustled with a Mardi Gras appeal as visitors packed the boardwalks. Women wore long dresses with hoop skirts, and men donned old-century waistcoats. The styles ranged from the rugged Old West to the charming Victorian age. The scene was straight out of a back lot movie studio with a surreal cinematic feel. Partygoers spilled out of carriages drawn by exotic animals. The scent of adventure hung thick in the air. But I couldn't shake the nagging sense that predators lurked in the shadows.

The sky was a swirl of deep blues with bright, shining stars and a radiant crescent moon reminiscent of Vincent van Gogh's painting *Starry Night*. I scanned the midnight sky for a sign, a clue, anything to show that we were on the right track.

Howard kept going, swept up in a sea of people entering a tented establishment. I didn't want to lose sight of him, so I squared my shoulders, nodded to Sara and Jesse, and we followed. A tinny piano filled the air with Coldplay's tune, *Viva La Vida*, as we swam through the crowd to catch Howard, who had already landed a table.

Over the din, Jesse yelled, "There." He was less than discreet, pointing out the Parker brothers.

The rowdy patrons made it impossible to hear. Even so, I read Leo's lips, "Castle Dragon."

A sense of foreboding crept over me as Zeb turned and tracked me with his reptilian eyes.

Leo hastened to our table. "Zeb's waiting."

I glanced at where our food had been set down. "We already ordered appetizers."

Leo cocked a brow but didn't respond. He simply nodded and returned to his brother, assuming we'd follow.

My instincts screamed, *lousy idea, walk away.* But that's not what I did.

Zeb Parker lounged in a VIP section near the stage where several circus acts performed. Acrobats swung on a trapeze while stilt walkers and juggling clowns entertained. An animal trainer kept a pack of yapping poodles dancing and jumping through hoops.

Once I had my bearings, we abandoned our table and navigated the crush of people with purposeful strides.

"I must admit, I thought I'd have to go fetch you," Zeb said.

"Not sure what you mean," I said as I slid into a chair.

"Sure you do," Zeb said, sucking on a bone. "Saw you saunter in with Headless—shame about his head." A stack of eaten chicken wings spilled over the plate.

"Yeah, hee-hee, tragedy," Leo said.

Zeb swatted Leo on the back of his cap. "Keep a lid on it."

Leo rubbed the spot where Zeb had clobbered him and pushed

out his lower lip.

"So, what brings you to my establishment?" Zeb asked in his country drawl.

"Checking out the nightlife," I said, gesturing to the entertainers.

A cool breeze stirred the stale air within the circus tent. Sturdy straps held the door of the massive tent open. Near the side entrance sat a stack of crates, and on the top was a raccoon, scratching and gnawing on the lid.

"Headless Howard told you of his debt payment plan, I assume."

"He mentioned something." I pulled out a deck of cards and began shuffling. When I glanced at the crates by the door, Bandit was gone. Then I looked around, and so was Howie.

"I thought we could renegotiate," I said, purposely fumbling with the shuffle.

"What do you have in mind?"

"A rematch. Double or nothing."

"Interesting," Zeb drawled as he chewed on a bone, his eyes glinting with greed.

"But with my cards and table stakes," I said.

"Sure, if I choose."

I nodded.

"Heads up," Zeb said without missing a beat.

*Oops, I didn't see that coming.*

Zeb systematically evened the odds. We had planned a friendly game of collusion, where Headless, Sara, and Jesse would stack the chips in my favor. But heads-up was a two-player game. I couldn't back down because I was the one who had suggested the rematch. Zeb waved the waitress over to clear the table. A pit boss who looked more like a pit bull brought us a set of poker chips. And before I knew it, the game had begun.

Zeb dealt first. The circus continued, and soon, the crowd lost interest in our game. We played for a couple of hours—my chip stack increased, decreased, and evened out. We were in for a long night.

While the performances kept Sara enthralled, Jesse fidgeted, bouncing his leg anxiously, shaking the floor beneath my feet. I ignored his twitch and mentally ran the numbers. After all, poker boiled down to math in the end.

Jesse pulled out a metal prong, and it hummed when he drummed it on the table. He fiddled with the tuning fork, tapping out distinct tones. The vibrations set my teeth on edge. Each tap rattled a faint echo from somewhere beyond the tent walls. I tilted my head, straining to trace the odd echo.

*Had Sara noticed—sensed any unusual magic?*

Lost in the mesmerizing circus acts, Sara seemed oblivious to our game and Jesse's restlessness. The weird echo and Jesse's fidgeting threw me. I had forgotten my cards and tipped them up to sneak a peek before bluffing. Zeb called and won a hefty pot.

"Amateur bluff," Zeb scoffed, clacking chips as he stacked his growing fortune.

*How did he know I was bluffing?*

"Only a matter of time, and the game is mine."

"I've still got a chip and a chair. I'm not beat yet," I said, leaning back arrogantly.

But my stack was dwindling. The stakes were high—I couldn't afford to lose. Our wagon, my token, and Howard's head all rode on this game. My amulet hummed, and Uncle George's advice came to mind. *Play the player, not the cards. Everyone has a poker tell. Find it.*

Zeb had to be cheating, but I couldn't figure out how. I didn't sense magic—it had to be something else.

Zeb hissed, an impatient reminder that it was my turn to bet. His unblinking eyes bore into me like a coiled viper ready to strike. I stared at the turn card and realized I'd blanked on my hole cards again.

*What were they? Clubs? Spades? Focus, Noah!*

Jesse tapped the blasted tuning fork for—the fifth time? Fiftieth? I'd lost count. "Knock it off," I snatched the blasted noisemaker from Jesse. The second I grabbed the prongs, a piercing cry knifed through the air.

Pandemonium. The trapeze artist shrieked, missed her jump, and tumbled into the net. Then, the clown on stilts tripped over the crazed poodles. A sudden wind whipped the tent walls as a new high-pitched sound rose above the din. Shockwaves of pain stabbed the airwaves. Zeb covered his ears, collapsing with a groan.

My fingers fused to the screaming, quivering prongs and locked in a death grip. I tried hurling it away, but it remained stuck. Desperate to be free of the bewitched tuning fork, I shook my arm and upended the table, scattering cards and chips across Zeb, who remained sprawled on the floor.

The crates by the entrance exploded, sending splinters flying. With the speed of a falcon, a golden harp with satin wings and sharp talons rose from the ruined container. The harp strummed shrill, otherworldly tones as it flew toward me, yanking the fork out of my hand. As the tuning fork stilled, the distressed harp quieted until, for a blissful moment, silence reigned. At the appearance of the harp, the people in the audience erupted in cheers. The harp glided over the crowd, plucking a joyful melody.

Zeb floundered, trying to stand, and I extended a hand to help. My eyebrows shot up with surprise as I discovered the card table's underside hid a two-way mirror. With positioned prisms, if a player tilted their cards at a certain angle, Zeb could see them.

*That's how he cheats—not with magic, but mirrors.* I released my grip, and Zeb toppled backward onto his butt.

"Make way!" Provost Flowers stepped forward while his crew of guardsmen moved the onlookers back.

"The harp has returned," a customer said.

"It's a miracle," a voice yelled from the crowd. "The young wizard summoned the harp."

"Yes indeed," the provost said, smiling at the harp perched on the acrobat's swing. The provost turned toward me. "Well done returning the harp." He squinted at the scattered poker chips. "What's going on here?"

Jesse plucked the queen of spades from the floor and presented it with a dramatic flair.

"Seize them!" The provost bellowed, jabbing his finger toward us.

Two men dressed in multicolored pantaloons caught hold of Jesse and Zeb.

My wristband *zapped* a guard when he reached for me. The jolt sent a tingling sting up my arm, and I backed away, thrusting my palms forward to warn the persistent officer.

"I won't stand for insolence," the provost thundered, veins bulging. "How dare you resist arrest!"

"Arrest? Why am I under arrest?" I yelled.

"Gambling is prohibited within the city limits." The provost huffed out his round chest. "Come along, wizard. Let's not make this worse than it is."

"But you deputized us—We're working for you."

"And now—I hereby un-deputize you."

At the sound of tearing threads, I checked my sleeve to see if my duster had torn. Luckily, my duster remained unmarred when Provost Flowers revoked my authority. Hot blood flooded my face as he stuffed our glinting badges into his breast pocket.

But Sara caught my eye. She pierced me with a sharp look, palm raised—A silent warning to think before acting. With one last reassuring glance, she slipped out with Bandit on her heels.

"Come along," the provost urged. "We'll sort out this misunderstanding."

# CHAPTER 13

## *JAILBIRDS*

I banged my head, crossing the threshold of the old jail. Stars exploded across my vision, and pain radiated from the lump swelling on my skull. The heavy door slammed shut.

"Get some sleep, boys." The jailer's keys jingled as he shuffled away. A chair scraped against the cold floor, followed by a grunt.

Jesse flopped onto the canvas cot, his arms behind his head. Iron bars split the space into two cramped cells. Zeb Parker occupied the other one, sitting sideways on his bunk and chewing on a piece of straw.

"Hey, jailor!" I shook the bars, and grit drifted down. "I want to speak to the provost."

"He's busy, be quiet," came a sleepy response.

"I want a lawyer."

Zeb let out an amused snort.

"Chill, dude," Jesse said. "Sara will straighten everything out in the morning."

Slivers of moonlight penetrated the gloom through a small window. I peered between the bars and glimpsed a moonlit alley. Beyond it, a thin row of trees bordered the outer wall. I leaned my elbow on the window ledge, and my scowl deepened when I felt Zeb watching me.

"I saw the mirrors. You cheated."

Zeb gave a casual shrug. "Cheaters gonna cheat."

"And you stole the harp."

"You ain't got no proof." Zeb rolled the straw with his lip.

"That tuning fork trick was clever, wizard boy. Impressive how you summoned the harp."

"Why steal the harp, anyway?"

"It's an ancient artifact," Zeb said. "Nothing personal, strictly business. Besides, no harm done."

"Are you serious? The town relies on the tree's enchantment. Without the harp, the tree won't bear fruit."

"I didn't know that." Zeb had the gall to sound sorry.

I prodded for more information. "And what about the low water levels?"

Zeb waved it off. "That wasn't me. Even I'm not that daft. The entire valley depends on the river. It's probably a draught, but if someone diverted the water on purpose, then they're dirty, rotten scoundrels."

Jesse dragged himself upright using the bars. "I suppose you didn't steal the Dragon Moonstone, either."

"The Dragon Moonstone—so that's what you're about. It's a myth—no such thing. Waste of time," Zeb said, sticking the straw between his lips. "Moonstone—interesting."

I shot Jesse an irritated look. *He's such a blabbermouth—So much for extracting intel, and now Zeb knows our business.*

At the sound of shuffling feet, I moved to the door. A stooped jailer with thick glasses distorting his eyes trailed Provost Flowers down the hall. The portly provost stopped abruptly and seemed oblivious when the guard rebounded off his substantial backside.

Provost Flowers had changed into a white three-piece suit with yellow buttons.

"Why am I here?"

"Cashmere?" The provost brushed lint from his jacket. "No, it's linen. I'm glad you like it." His mouth curved into a self-satisfied smile.

I rolled my eyes.

The provost wagged his finger. "Don't change the subject. I'm not here to discuss fashion." Provost Flower's eyes tightened. "You're under arrest for gambling. That's a serious offense, young wizard."

"You asked me to find the harp. And I did," I said, speaking up for his hard-of-hearing ears.

"The harp's return is a blessing indeed," the provost said, lifting his gaze heavenward.

"And didn't you say the village would be grateful?" I shouted.

The provost rolled a finger in his ear and pulled out a sizeable wad of wax. "You don't need to yell."

I let out a breath to reset my patience. "Why are we in jail?"

The provost clasped his hands behind his back, face pinching into a frown. "Gambling is illegal. The means don't justify the end."

"Uh, isn't that the end doesn't justify the means?" Jesse got off his bunk. "Besides, I wasn't the one gambling," he complained.

I glared at Jesse and mouthed, "Stop talking."

Jesse shrugged and busied himself by flipping over the mattress, resulting in a cloud of dust.

My eyes watered, and I held back a sneeze. "How long will we be stuck here?"

"Until the magistrate arrives."

"When will that be?"

Provost Flowers raised his shoulders in a shrug. "Who knows? I haven't seen one in a year."

The guard guffawed, unlocking Zeb's cell.

"Free to go," the provost said. "Max paid your bail."

Zeb hissed out a sigh as he slid his long telephone pole frame to his feet.

"What about us?" My voice cracked.

"Sorry," the provost paused, as if grasping for the phrase. "You're a flight risk."

"How am I a risk when I'm magically bound to the wall—Right, Zeb?"

Zeb snorted, raising his hands in denial.

The provost roared with laughter, and the loose skin on his neck waved like a flag. The jailer snickered, hooking the jumble of keys to his belt.

I grabbed the bars while a sinking feeling wobbled my legs.

"Zeb, you crack me up." The provost hooted, slapping his thighs. "Magically bound—I can't believe you got away with that old joke."

"Are you saying it's a lie?" My knuckles turned white as I tightened my grip.

The provost wiped away the tears of laughter. "Of course, it's a lie. Our wall won't accept third-party bindings. And if it could, an agreement can't be bound based on an illegal deed." The provost put his arm around Zeb. "You're one of a kind, you old gecko." He gave Zeb a friendly push. "Go on now and stay out of trouble."

Zeb's eyes glowed as he tipped his hat. "See ya later, boys."

Provost Algernon shook his stubby finger and turned to leave. "Behave, and I'll put in a good word."

Suddenly, as if enchanted, a folded paper wormed out of the provost's pocket and drifted to the floor. The provost shuffled forward, with the paper sticking to the bottom of his shoe. After a couple of steps, it pulled free, sailing across the floor and sliding into my cell as if it had a mind of its own. A shimmer of light danced at the edge of my vision. My eyes locked on Sara. She put a finger to her lips in the universal signal of shush. Then, with a flicker—poof—she disappeared.

I waited until the provost left before grabbing the fallen note. Jesse tried to see, and I stepped back so he wasn't breathing on my neck. "It's a bounty notice—wanted for questioning—twenty thousand silvers."

"Wow, dude, that's a lot. Who are they looking for?"

"Us," I said, handing the sheet to Jesse while the gravity of the situation sank in.

Front and center was a photograph of Jesse and me taken during a Sweetwater town meeting. Jesse pushed out a breath. "Well, at least it doesn't say dead or alive." A worried smile tugged at his lips.

I rubbed my chin. "This explains why the provost won't let us make bail. He plans to collect on the ransom."

"Ransom?" Jesse studied the sheet. "Who said anything about ransom?"

"Reward, ransom, whatever—we're wanted, men. This can't be good."

"I wonder who put up the money," Jesse said, his brow furrowed.

*Psst*!

Jesse's face lit up when he spotted Scout hovering beyond the window. "You can fit through the bars," Jesse said. "Come in."

Scout shook her head. "No can do. Jails have security wards. Fae can enter, but we can never leave." She flitted about. "Sara says be ready at daybreak."

"Ready for what?" I asked.

Scout's voice rang with urgency. "Someone's coming. Gotta go. Get some rest." The little fairy flickered like a firefly and disappeared.

ΔΔΔ

I lay on the lumpy cot, hands behind my head, staring at the cracked ceiling. A feeble hallway bulb sputtered, casting quivering shadows that danced across the cell walls. Shafts of moonlight seeped in through the narrow window, adding to the ghostly atmosphere. The town had quieted, with only the occasional snore and fart of the sleeping guard to break the silence. Sleep evaded me, but exhaustion must have eventually won out.

I woke with a start. "It's time to go," came the tiny fairy's urgent voice.

Jesse vaulted, ready for whatever awaited us. His mop of red hair stuck out at odd angles. As I rolled out of bed, I couldn't help but marvel at his boundless enthusiasm. How anyone could have so much energy in the morning was beyond me.

Jesse remained on high alert, his ears tuned for any changes in the steady snores of our jailer. Outside, the goats stood ready. Scout extended a rope, which I tied to the bars, before giving a thumbs-up. She nodded and zipped over to Lester and Nester. The goats strained, and the buckboard creaked under the pressure. The goats tugged, and a crack zigzagged along the wall, but the bars remained stubbornly in place.

"Give it another yank. Put some goat muscle into it," Scout demanded.

Lester and Nester gave it a final heave, and a series of cracks spider-webbed the walls. Dust and chunks of brick fell from the ceiling.

My amulet thrummed. With a flash of prescience, I watched the future unfold—we had knocked out a support wall, and the entire jail was on the brink of collapse. "*Congelo!*" I shouted.

Time froze, or rather, it crawled. The crumbling wall and falling bricks were suspended in mid-air. Dirt and sand barely moved.

"Hurry," I said, grabbing Jesse and vaulting through the opening in the wall, and then, in ultra-slow motion, the jail folded onto itself. Mesmerized by the scene, we gawked until a stark realization hit. *The sleeping jailer wouldn't survive the catastrophic collapse*. A spike of fear shot through me. *I had to fix this.*

My mother's amulet stung my skin as my inner wizard asserted control and flooded my senses. I closed my eyes and connected with the essence of the toppled bricks. In my mind's eye, I rebuilt the jail, restoring it to its original state. Then, with a breath from deep in my core, I swept my hands overhead. "*Olegnoc*!"

The destruction reversed like a movie reel played backward. Crackling energy surrounded me as bricks floated into place and mortar fused. But at an agonizing cost. Each passing moment sapped more of my inner strength. I felt my spirit drain as if sacrificed to mend the fabric of time and undo my mistake. I had lost control and would soon disappear into the bewitchment unfolding. My amulet seared my skin, but I couldn't stop the rush of magic shooting out of my fingertips.

Unable to contain his enthusiasm, Jesse tackled me. His tight bear hug wrenched me into the present, shattering the enchantment and freeing me from the trance.

"Dude, that was epic." He grabbed my arm and raised it like a champion.

I managed a lopsided grin as my knees turned to jelly. Jesse steadied me, concern etched on his face. Thoughts slogged through my brain fog, but I couldn't form words. My body felt like rubber, and having exhausted my reserves, I struggled against the oncoming fatigue.

"That gained us some time," Jesse said, bubbling with excitement. "They won't know we're gone until breakfast."

Sara held the leathers while Orion pawed at the ground as if sensing the urgency. Bandit, in humanoid form, untied the rope and mounted his mono-wheel. Dizzy from the magical exertion, I stumbled, and Jesse helped me into the buckboard before swinging into the saddle.

"That's what I call a jailbreak," Headless Howard said, placing the reins into my numb hands.

"Go!" Sara said and gave her white pony a nudge.

The wagon wheels groaned as the goats lurched forward, following the ponies through the open gates. The guards were busy with an influx of new arrivals and paid us no mind. When I looked over my shoulder, Bandit covered our six o'clock, ensuring our jailbreak went undetected. As we exited The Tower of Song, birds twittered excitedly, chirping as if spreading gossip about our daring escape.

# CHAPTER 14

## *ON THE RUN*

Lester and Nester steadily put distance between us and The Tower of Song. The fog of magical exhaustion lifted, leaving me with a splitting headache. While rubbing the throbbing pain, I looked behind me, grateful to see Bandit and no posse in pursuit.

Worry gnawed at my gut, compelling me to ask Howie if he thought the provost would send troops to hunt us down.

Headless shook his hoody. "The provost's authority ends at the city walls. Everything will be fine now that the harp has *miraculously* returned." Howard gestured as if swatting a fly. "Algernon Flowers will forget about your jailbreak soon enough."

I slid my hand into my pocket, feeling the crumpled wanted notice tucked inside. The weight of it served as a reminder of an unseen enemy.

We plodded along the cobblestones, winding through a desolate land. The ancient lava flow had left parts of the landscape barren. Long ago, the molten rock flowed, blanketing what it touched with blackened rock. While leaving patches of flourishing grass and trees unscathed.

The sun beat down mercilessly on the Malpais Plateau, and heat shimmers rose in waves off the baked earth. Rivulets of sweat trickled down my neck as I sat on the buckboard, rolling onward, traversing the unpredictable terrain. We stopped only when Scout discovered occasional shaded pools tucked among the rocks. After a brief rest and drink, we continued our journey through this confusing landscape, heading deeper into the wilds of Goblin Valley.

Eventually, Bandit deemed us safe from pursuers. Eager to chase after the tiny fairy, he zoomed past on his mono-wheel, offering a jaunty salute.

The wagon rocked as Headless Howard alternated between bouts of silence and bursts of questions. "Restoring the jail was an impressive display of skill. I haven't seen magical finesse like that in ages. Where did you learn to wield such control?"

I cast a sideways glance at my travel companion. "Are you a wizard?"

Howard let out his gurgled laugh. "Oh, no, not a wizard. Although, now and then, I dabble in illusions."

"Cool, like what?"

"Mostly with cards," he replied in his hollow voice.

"You mean cheating?" I blurted, unable to hide my disapproval.

"Cheaters gonna cheat," Headless said with a shrug.

Nudging my pack closer with my boot, I tried to recall where I had heard that before.

The wagon squeaked while the goats scuffed their feet against the cobbles. My eyelids grew heavy to the rhythmic sway as we rolled along. The absence of hooves clacking startled me awake.

Surprised that the road had narrowed into a dirt path, I pulled back on the reins. "Did we miss a turn?"

"We haven't left the main road," Howard said, his tone laced with a hint of defensiveness.

I gave Headless a curious look. Obviously, we had left the cobblestones. I strained to listen for the sounds of my friends, the ponies, or Bandit's motorized unicycle, but all I could hear were cicadas.

"The trail is not much wider than the wagon," I said.

"These are Grimm Goats from Castle Dragon—known for their surefootedness and reliability." Howard waved his sleeve, and his Xs danced. "Let's see what they can do, shall we?"

"Um—I trust the goats, but the rickety buckboard is a different story."

After tugging the brake lever, I hopped down, lavishing Lester and Nester with affection. They nuzzled my palm eagerly as I offered them treats. "Hey, guys, the road ahead looks too steep. Can I count on you to get us through and to find Sara and Jesse?"

The goats seemed to understand and nodded in agreement, pawing the ground with anticipation.

"Howard says you can do it. I won't ask you to do anything reckless, so take your time." I leaned closer and whispered, "Besides, I trust you way more than I do, our *headless hitchhiker*."

The goats *baa'd* in a tone that made me think they agreed with my assessment. Lester nibbled at my fingers, and Nester winked his green eye while still eyeing me confidently with his brown one. I chuckled, scratching their furry heads one last time.

As I vaulted into the buckboard with renewed optimism, the Xs in Howard's missing face blazed, tracking me like laser beams. "What was that about?" Howard wanted to know.

In a display of faith, I wrapped the reins through the guide rail and brushed off Howie's prying questions with a noncommittal shrug. A faint sparkle of magic glittered, clinging to the sides of the buckboard. The wheels trundled forward, and the goats took the lead, bleating their eagerness.

While I busily secured my pack, Howard said in a monochrome voice, "Lean to the left and hang on."

Baffled by Howard's comment, I knitted my brow.

The road transformed as we rounded a bend. Steep granite towered above us, and the path narrowed even more. Lester nimble-footed over the wagon's tongue, twisting the yoke. The goats adjusted their positions, walking single-file. The buckboard groaned under the strain as the Grimm Goats nimble-footed the switchback trail.

My eyes bulged as the right side of the wagon teetered over the ledge, while the left wheels somehow clung to solid ground. We rolled forward on a shelf as wide as a horse. My duster brushed against the cliff, its protective wards sparking from the friction. The goats pulled the wagon up at a near-vertical angle. I blinked in disbelief at the impossible feat.

*This had to be the dumbest idea ever. Why had I let some headless guy talk me into this?*

I held my tongue—refusing to voice my doubts and empower my runaway thoughts. I had entrusted Lester and Nester to find my friends. So, I remained calm on the outside, but on the inside—I was freaking out and thought I might puke.

Upon reaching the summit, the vista unfolded into a breathtaking panorama. I scarcely dared guess how many wheels clung to the craggy peak. Perched perilously, I gulped thin air. Far below, the ribbon of cobblestones snaked along the winding river.

The goats bleated before surging forward with a burst of speed. My neck snapped back as gravity sent us racing down the sheer mountainside. The scenery blurred as we careened along the rugged pass, hooves hammering on the granite lip. At a sharp turn, the wagon swung out over the ridge. I gripped the railing, my knuckles turning white.

Howard had yet to move a muscle, and even his cloak refused to ripple. My stomach plummeted when I peered over the side, confronted by the gaping void. The adrenaline-fueled ride reminded me of the scene where the Grinch's dog, Max, pulled a sleigh loaded with packages down the mountain.

None too soon, my spine slammed onto the bench seat when the wagon bounced, landing on solid ground. I yelled in triumph, thankful to be upright on four wheels and alive to brag about it. My joy was short-lived when I realized it was not over yet. We were descending a shale rock slope. One false move and the mountain would come crashing down on us.

Nonetheless, Lester and Nester deftly piloted us through the slippery scree field. The springs screamed in protest as we bounced and bumped onward. When I was sure I'd shaken a kidney loose, we rolled onto the cobblestone road. The goats returned to their sedate pace and, once again, became evenly yoked.

As the sun dipped low in the sky, we arrived at a meadow

bordering a lazy river. Sara and Jesse stood beneath a sprawling oak tree while the unsaddled ponies grazed. Sara waved, and Jesse ran to meet us as we rolled to a stop.

"Where have you been?" Jesse asked. "Bandit thought you took a shortcut, and Sara was ready to send Scout to search for you."

"We were following you," I said, gesturing toward the trees. "How'd the horses manage on the narrow switchback trail?"

"Dude, what are you talking about?" Jesse scratched his chin. "We followed the cobblestone path and have been waiting for you in this meadow."

Confusion tightened my expression as I glanced at Headless, slinking away toward the river's edge.

"Hey, Howie," Jesse called. "Wait for me."

While Jesse dashed to catch Howard, I unhitched the goats. Their shaggy coats reeked of musk as I rubbed them down. Soaked with sweat and caked in dust, the Grimm Goats showed no signs of physical strain.

"That was a wild trip," I said, offering Nester and Lester a treat.

Bandit scampered over, his ringed tail bobbing. "Crikey, we thought we lost you."

"Were you worried?"

"Of course, mate, the wagon has all the food." Bandit delivered a toothy grin.

ΔΔΔ

After a quick meal, we gathered around a crackling campfire, ready to share the day's events.

"Thanks for the jailbreak rescue," I said to the group. "You planned and executed a flawless escape."

Scout puffed up at the compliment, and Bandit gave all the credit to Sara.

"What's the plan?" Sara asked, prodding the fire with a stick. The embers stirred, sending sparks dancing skyward.

"Same as before, we search for dragonroot," I said.

"And retrieve the Dragon Moonstone," Jesse said, staring into the flames. I clenched my jaw at Jesse's inability to keep a secret.

"Dragon Moonstone," Howard said. "Now, that's an old story."

"Tell us," Sara said, leaning forward with her elbows resting on her knees.

Howard had our undivided attention as he told his campfire tale.

"Once upon a time, nestled in the heart of Goblin Valley, there was a mystical cave where dragons made their home. Legends whispered of a bygone era when a wandering sorcerer forged an unlikely friendship with a lonesome dragon. The dragon, yearning for a friend and dreading solitude, found companionship in the wizard's company. Alas, the sorcerer became weary of staying in one place, and the allure of distant lands fed his wanderlust. Aware of the dragon's apprehension of being alone, the noble sage devised a magical solution. The wizard carved a dragon from an emerald crystal, placing it upon an enchanted pedestal deep within her lair. During the full moon, shafts of light shine through a dragon wing-shaped crack, showering the gemstone in moonbeams. The essence within the Dragon Moonstone soothes the beast, lulling her into a peaceful slumber. Should the dragon awake without the moonstone, her mood would sour, and her thirst would become insatiable. A foul and tempestuous loneliness would consume her, endangering not only Goblin Valley but those who dwell in the Otherlands."

Howard leaned forward, the flames of the fire casting a ghoulish shadow within the void of his absent head. "Some believe the lava in the Malpais Plateau resulted from a long ago fiery tantrum. And if the dragon breaches the veil into the mortal realm, untold peril will befall all who dare to stand in her path."

"Bwahaha!" Howie roared, waving his sleeves.

Jesse bucked, tumbling backward, treating us to a laugh.

"Well done," Sara said, clapping her hands in approval. "That was a fantastic campfire story."

"Only a myth. For whatever it's worth, where there are dragons, there will be dragonroot." Howard stretched. "Time for shut-eye," he said, wandering into the darkness.

ΔΔΔ

Before dawn, I shouldered my pack and hiked up a cluster of boulders to a higher point where I could watch the sunrise. I parked on a flat rock, allowing my eyes to sweep across the vista. I spotted a faraway campfire from my perch but failed to gauge the distance. A tingling intuition of danger added to my suspicion that we were being followed.

The snap of branches snagged my attention as Sara emerged from the jumble of rocks and brush. Sara offered an electric smile as she plopped down beside me. We'd been friends since the fifth grade, but after she left for college, we hadn't spent much time together. I worried we were drifting into different places of the heart. My heart longed to venture down a terrifying path. But I wasn't ready to risk our friendship for the remote possibility that Sara had deeper feelings.

I raked my fingers through my hair to untangle my muddled thoughts. "It's a beautiful morning, but I wish I had coffee."

Sara removed a thermos and a couple of mugs from her pack. A smile of gratitude spread across my face.

"What are you doing here, all by yourself?" Sara asked, handing me a cup of java.

"I thought I'd try meditation—because I didn't want to sit around doing nothing."

Sara swatted my arm at my corny joke, her silvery laugh blending with the chorus of morning songbirds.

I leaned into my cup, inhaling the steam while warming my hands. "I couldn't sleep with thoughts of a fiery dragon and a posse running through my mind, so I climbed here to check our back trail."

Sara lifted her brow. "Backtrail and posse—you sound like a spaghetti western."

A weary sigh escaped my lips. "It's been a whirlwind since Erik's unexpected arrival in my living room." I met her eyes. "I'm glad you're here. It's reassuring to have someone I can trust."

Sara's eyes warmed. "No matter what, I'm here for you."

We clinked cups. "Ditto," I said. We held our gaze for a bit too long.

Sara stood, moving closer to the rim. "What's that?" She pointed with her mug.

"Someone has a campfire," I said. "Either on the way to the festival or following us. Regardless, we'll keep a lookout."

"Following us? Why?"

"Well, we did just break out of jail," I said, pushing my hair from my face. "And from what I can tell, I'm still a vulnerable young wizard, and there are predators that would pay for my essence."

Sara frowned. "You don't believe old man Goodall's deathbed confession?" she said, referring to our trouble with magic awhile back in Sweetwater. When I first learned I had wizard blood, I attracted the attention of an evil witch. Coincidentally, she was Jesse's stepmother and related to Agnes, the witch in the well. The wanted poster crinkled as I unfolded it and handed it to her.

"So this was in Provost Algernon's pocket," Sara said as she read.

"Is that a question or a statement?" I asked.

"The provost rifled through a stack of papers at the jail. He became twitchy before stuffing it in his pocket."

"That was reckless, grabbing it from his pocket. What if the provost saw you?"

"First, I'm not reckless. Second, I was invisible." She huffed. "I pinched the slip of paper as he walked away and simply helped it fall." Sara studied the notice. "Hmm, this explains things. I tried to bail you out, but he wouldn't consider it. When I mentioned you were magically bound within the walls, he laughed so hard I thought he'd wet himself. But I didn't see the humor, so Bandit,

Scout, and I huddled and made a plan."

"But not Headless?"

"No, Howard showed up while we were hitching the wagons, and good thing because we could use the help."

"Sounds like Headless," I said. "He has perfected disappearing and reappearing at the right moment."

"What's wrong? Why the attitude?"

I shrugged. "I can't get a read on Howard—something's off."

"Yeah, he has no head." Sara chuckled. "Do you trust him?"

"I trust you and Bandit, that's all."

"And Jesse," Sara added.

"I dunno. Jesse's Jesse. He befriends everything with a pulse and can't keep his trap shut."

The bridge of Sara's nose creased when she frowned. "Jesse is your loyal friend." Her scowl deepened. "Pull the plank out of your eye before criticizing the speck in your friend's."

"And now you're quoting biblical verses," I said, "and incorrectly, I might add."

Sara's eyes darkened. "You know what I mean. You shouldn't judge. Don't go all doom and gloom. Try having a little faith in others for once," Sara said with heat in her voice.

"Look, this isn't summer camp!" I sipped from my mug to reset. The last thing I wanted was an argument. "I must find dragonroot and complete the Dragon Moonstone quest before it's too late."

Sara placed her hand on my arm. "Not I, we—We are in this together." She theatrically air-quoted. "There's no I in team."

I grinned at our inside joke.

"What else is bothering you? I can always tell when you are upset," Sara said, her face showing concern.

"The poster is from Sweetwater. Someone used our photo in the newspaper to create a wanted notice and sent it into the Otherlands, which means our enemies are supernatural."

I worked the knots in my neck and changed the subject. "Do you know how to get back home?"

"Not really. Shirley called, and before I knew it, Grandma was baking cookies and told me to pack. After that, we hurried to Shirley's house. Your Aunt Shirley said you were in a world of trouble and herded us up to the attic. Then she opened a door and gave me a shove, and that's when I stumbled through the portal at the archway."

"I'm puzzled why you passed through a portal when we risked life and limb on jumping over Dead Dragons Divide."

"That's five miles across," Sara said. "That's impossible."

I lifted a brow. "After all you've seen, you think that's impossible?"

We chuckled as the sunrise splashed the sky pink.

"How much further to Dragon Tooth Cave?" Sara asked.

After sliding the fairy globe from my pack, I shook it. When the snow cleared, a mountainous landscape with a river tumbling under a bridge emerged. A massive twisted tree stood sentinel with vibrant purple leaves, its roots clutching a jagged rock base.

"This tree was in my vision. If you look past it, there should be a cave."

Sara leaned closer, squinting at the terrain within the glass globe. "Try asking specific questions like a crystal ball."

With a theatrical flourish, I waved my hand. "All-knowing mighty globe, show me where to find dragonroot." With a dazzling spark, a red dotted line appeared, snaking down the valley, beyond the purple-leafed tree to the mouth of the cave.

"It actually worked," Sara said, her voice rising in surprise.

"It shouldn't be that easy. Something's off," I said, my doom and gloom returning.

# CHAPTER 15

## *FOLLOW THE COBBLESTONE ROAD*

The sunrise bathed the valley in soft light, painting the bronze cliffs with pastel hues. Blinded by the sun peering over the horizon, I turned and glimpsed movement. I gently tapped Sara, and we watched in silence as a woodland resident emerged from beneath a rock.

I felt confident he knew of our presence as he brushed off his green woolen britches. Standing eighteen inches tall, he wore a blue tunic cinched with a wide black belt and a silver buckle. An abundant beard concealed his chin, and a pointy red cap resting on his diamond-shaped ears hung low over his brows. He paid us no mind as another gnome emerged from the shadows. The second gnome was younger, sported a stubby beard and a twinkle in his eye, as if he held a treasure chest of secrets. He grinned, revealing a full set of teeth.

"Good Morning," Sara said, smiling to welcome the new arrivals.

The older gnome dipped his head. "Greetings, fair maiden," he said with a rich quality to his voice. He angled his chin toward me and gave me a scrutinizing stare.

I smiled politely but avoided prolonged eye contact. Considering our significant size difference, I didn't want to appear aggressive.

Seemingly unimpressed, he swung his attention to Sara. "Where do you call home?"

"We're from Sweetwater," Sara said in a cheerful tone.

"I once knew an accomplished wizard who hailed from that faraway land." The gnome rubbed his beard. "Yes, indeed, you are far from home. Are you lost, lass?"

"No sir, we are humble travelers. My name is Sara, and this is my friend, Noah."

I leaned forward, offering my hand.

The younger gnome laughed so hard that he tipped onto his back and kicked his legs. Not knowing what to do with the awkward gesture, I pretended to stretch.

*Okay, that just happened. Note to self—gnomes don't shake hands.*

Sara's eyes sparkled, amused by my social awkwardness. "And you are?" she asked, offering her brightest smile.

"Oh, I'd forgotten how casual your world is with names," the older gnome said, motioning toward his companion, who had finally composed himself. "This is my nephew, Thingamabob, and I'm Slumgullion, but you can call me Stu."

Thingamabob bowed to Sara with one hand on his middle and the other behind his back. He bent over so deep that one might think he had a stomachache. "My friends call me Bob." His cheeks flushed, and he looked down, scuffing the toe of his fine leather boot.

"We're enjoying the morning over a cup of coffee. Would you like to join us?" Sara asked.

"Yes, indeed. I'd never turn down coffee with a bonny lass." He wagged a finger at Thingamabob. "Could ya do me a favor and fetch our mugs?"

Bob dashed through the opening under the rocks.

"Do you live around here?" I motion to the tumble of boulders. Hoping I wouldn't make another cultural faux pas.

"Yes, this is our cap rock," Stu said, pointing to the boulder I sat upon and then to where Bob had gone. "And that is our burrow."

"Sara and I climbed the slope to watch the sunrise. I hope we didn't disturb you."

"You're fine." Stu waved his arm. "But creatures of the

Otherlands are often territorial, so it's best if travelers stick to the cobbles." He shifted his feet, moving toward a flat stone. "Although some parts are dangerous."

"Really? How so?" Sara asked, her voice laced with both curiosity and concern.

"Outlaws and hooligans." Stu motioned with open palms. "Goblin Valley is home to bands of renegades who don't respect the old code of wanderers. It used to be travelers needn't worry unless they left the sanctity of the cobblestones. But times have changed." He gestured to make his point. "Thieves are ransacking our sacred ruins and selling them to the highest bidder."

Stu paused as if struck with a random thought, hung his fists on his belt, and asked. "Are ye a fortune hunter, lad?"

"No, sir, I'm not. We have pressing business in Goblin Valley in search of dragonroot."

Stu's cheerful demeanor evaporated, his eyes narrowed to flinty slits as they raked over me with a glower that chilled me to the core. But when his gaze landed on Sara, his granite expression transformed, and his frigid glare thawed, melting into a warm smile.

Soon, Bob returned with two thimble-size cups, and Sara poured each a splash. Bob gripped his mug with both hands and took a deep breath, inhaling the aroma. A smile crept across my face at the familiar morning ritual while I also breathed in my mug's rich java scent.

The branches rustled and snapped as Jesse scrambled through the brush, stumbling to the overhang. His body quivered as he soaked in the glorious sunrise. "Wow, that view looks like a Monet painting." Jesse swept his hand toward the vista as his face erupted in a smile.

"So you're a friend of Claude Monet," Stu said in a friendly voice. "Most mundane believe Monet painted his landscapes in France." He leaned forward as if to reveal a secret. "Claude always said the Otherlands were the best place to capture the ephemeral qualities of light at sunrise."

Jesse pursed his lips but surprisingly remained mute.

"There haven't been many travelers of late." Stu gestured with his hands. "I was explaining to your fellow vagabonds how unsafe roads are these days."

"We're safe enough." Jesse puffed out his chest and pulled his shoulders back. "We travel under the protection of Castle Dragon."

Stu gave a half-hearted shrug. "That used to mean something, but now there's a growing lack of respect for the old ways."

"Have you heard? The Dragon Moonstone is missing," Bob said, wiggling his ears.

"The Dragon Moonstone? I heard it was a rumor and that there's no such thing." Jesse turned to me with an exaggerated wink. Subtle, he was not.

"That's how it starts, diluting words of wisdom into rumors and laws into suggestions," Stu said, shaking his head sideways. "Disrespect creates chaos." Stu drained his thimble-sized mug and handed it to Bob. "We should go. The truffles won't find themselves."

When Bob thanked Sara for the coffee, he gazed at her with adoration.

Stu wore a weighty expression. "Safe travels. And be aware, not everyone is as welcoming to trespassers."

I swallowed thickly at the backhanded warning. "Thank you for the advice, sir. We'll tread softly."

"And carry a big stick," Stu added, causing Bob to roll over in laughter, clutching his belly. When the laughter subsided, Stu's face grew stern. "You should be fine if you follow the cobblestone road, and whatever you do, stay out of the haunted forest."

We bid them goodbye and descended the hilltop. As we crossed the meadow, seeing the ponies saddled and the goats hitched was a pleasant surprise. When I thanked Jesse for saving us time, he explained Scout wanted an early start and had sent him to hurry us along.

A scowl creased my forehead, but I held back a negative retort. Exercising patience, I calmly asked, "Why didn't you say something as soon as you found us?"

"I didn't want to interrupt such a momentous event."

I tilted my head in confusion.

"It's not every day you make friends," Jesse said. As he sprinted toward the ponies, his laughter trailed in his wake.

ΔΔΔ

Headless Howard sat stiffly in the wagon while I took a moment to give the goats a hearty scratch. The goats responded with a cheerful bleat. After ensuring their comfort by making minor adjustments to the harness, I climbed into the wagon.

Howard tossed me the leather reins, his voice tinged with indignation. "I've been waiting by myself while you've been off doing who knows what."

"You're riding with me, not the other way around," I responded gruffly, taken aback by his sudden attitude.

After yesterday's demonstration, I didn't need to drive the goats, so I looped the reins through the railing. At my command, the goats lurched forward, pulling the wagon along the uneven cobblestone path. Bandit nodded, zooming past on his mono-wheel. With my pack between my feet, I leaned back and hoped Howard got over his morning grumps or it would make for a very long day.

As the miles rolled on by, something buzzed my ear. At first, I thought Scout was up to her old tricks, but a tiny bird with shimmering emerald wings and a yellow-tipped head zipped around my face. I'd never seen a bird so small.

"Ignore them, and they'll leave," Howard said. "Hummingbird Warriors—pesky little pests who play at provoking travelers."

The miniature birds became more daring, closing in closer. Another whizzed by my nose, and I shooed it away, but the mini-hummingbird persisted. I waved it off but ended up knocking it down. For a moment, I felt guilty as it lay there, wings glinting, its tiny chest throbbing. But as it rose to fly away, I couldn't resist taunting. "That'll teach you to mess with a wizard."

Big mistake. The warrior's green coloring blazed red, and a long, pointy stinger emerged from the tip of its beak. With a tweet, it shot up, circled back, and pricked my hand, leaving a stinging welt.

Howard snorted. "Told you not to provoke them." His hollow voice echoed with amusement.

"They started it," I said, rubbing my hand and waving them off.

Even more swarmed in, ignoring a stoic Howard, making me their primary target. No amount of shooing deterred the attacks. It only encouraged them to show their true colors and draw their stingers.

"Run!" I yelled, and the goats bolted, the Hummingbird Warriors hot on our trail.

Not long ago, I took an oath as an apprentice wizard and promised not to harm all creatures, great and small. *This must have been what Mrs. S meant, but I didn't want to be a pincushion, either!*

I waved them away as they stung my neck and hands. "Ouch, Howie, do something."

Howard laughed. "You're the wizard," Howard said, amused by my predicament. "Besides, I told you so."

*When is 'I told you so' ever helpful?*

Visualizing a bubble, I conjured a shield to enclose me in a layer of protection. The air sizzled, and an enchantment ward encircled me, blocking all sound. When I pressed against the sides, there was a slight give, but they held firm.

The tiny hummingbirds swooped in and bounced off. Their frustration grew, redoubling their efforts, but they couldn't get past my bubble. I laughed in victory.

The buckboard squeaked, jostling us in our seats as we hit every bump in the road. Safe in my protective shield, we lead the Warrior Hummingbirds on a wild chase. My defense worked perfectly. That is until the wheels hit a pothole and sent me and my bubble kangarooing over the wagon.

Howard waved as I bounded past.

Like a rubber ball, I bounced the cobblestones and sailed over a steep cliff. My pack whacked me in the skull while I spun head over heels inside the rolling sphere. Like a tumbling tumbleweed, I lost all sense of direction while tucked into a ball and waiting for it to end. As the land leveled off, the bubble rolled to a stop against a mossy log at the edge of a forest.

The good news was the shield had absorbed most of the impact. My heart jackhammered against my ribs, and I had a throbbing headache, but nothing was broken. And I had successfully outrun the Hummingbird Warriors. But the bad news was I had magically sealed myself in a transparent ball and had no idea how to get out.

Dizzy, I stumbled and pressed my hands against the unyielding shield that encased me. I hesitated to push too hard, fearing it might start rolling again. As usual, after magical exertion, a wave of exhaustion hit me like a ton of bricks, but I fought the overwhelming fatigue. I had to escape before succumbing to unconsciousness.

*How much air do I have left in this thing?*

*Oh, no, don't think about that!*

"You created the ward. So calm down and work through how to undo it," I said to myself.

But calming down seemed impossible while I waged an argument with my internal self.

*Not smart, trapping yourself in a bubble.*

*But I was trying to summon a shield to stop the wacko hummingbirds. How was I supposed to know?*

*You should've listened to Howard and ignored them.*

*How could I ignore an angry bird with a stinger?*

"This isn't working. Fix the problem, not the blame," I said out loud, asserting control.

My inner critic couldn't resist having the last word. *Good one, coming from the boy in a magic bubble.*

"Right—it's a bubble, and bubbles pop." I bobbed my head in excitement, and my headache protested sharply. So I rested my eyes while considering ways to pop it.

The sphere rocked, and my eyes shot open. Two bear cubs had discovered the shimmering ball.

"No! Go away!" I yelled. But I didn't think they heard me, so I flapped my arms to appear intimidating.

A paw the size of a dinner plate gave the bubble a playful swat, sending me rolling. The other bear with cinnamon fur nudged me with her nose. The cubs batted me about like a toy, pouncing, and romping. I did my best to stay on my feet, running wherever the bubble rolled with my arms in front of me for balance.

The cinnamon cub opened her mouth, but her sharp white teeth couldn't grasp the smooth surface. A surge of magic sparked when her slobbery tongue licked the outer shell. The cub yelped and swung her paw like a sledgehammer, popping the sphere like a balloon. Slimy ectoplasm sprayed in all directions. A wad of sticky goo clung to the cub's nose.

Bawling in frustration, she rose on her hind legs. We locked eyes for a tense moment until I unleashed my own panicked scream.

The cub scrambled back, and both bears fled into the woods. My legs kicked into gear, and I took off in the opposite direction. Fear of encountering a mama bear drove me. I dodged trees and hurdled logs, ignoring the burn in my thighs. But my foot snagged on a tangled root, and I face-planted the ground, my breath slammed from my lungs.

I couldn't catch my breath and wanted to rest, but I recalled the warning from the gnomes about the dangers lurking in the forest. Groaning, I rolled over and attempted to stand, only to have my ankle give way. With my last dregs of energy, I crawled under the sloping branches of a massive blue spruce, its boughs forming a natural canopy shielding me from sight. Satisfied with my hiding place, I leaned against the sturdy trunk and rummaged through my pack, my chest heaving.

My words came out between gasps. I could barely keep my eyes open, battling against fatigue. "*Mischief*, I need a security ward and quick. I can't afford to fall asleep without one."

The pages fluttered. "This page has an intriguing option," *Mischief* said, eyeing me curiously, "Unless you'd like me to do it."

"Please, wow, I didn't know you could *do* magic," I muttered as exhaustion closed in.

Twinkling stars floated from the page. The underside of the branches shimmered as the magic took shape. Soon, I curled into a ball and used my pack for a pillow.

"Get some rest, lad. Now and then, we can use a little help from our friends."

ΔΔΔ

An otherworldly silence descended upon the forest, as if nature held its breath while prodding me awake with a profound sense of danger. I shifted on my uncomfortable bed of pinecones, and every bone in my body complained. The sparkling magic within the boughs reassured me of *Mischief's* protective ward. Without hesitation, I crept toward a gap in the branches when muffled voices reached my ears.

The sun filtered between the trees, bathing the grass in a vibrant green. A scraggly bull moose heaved to a stop, tugging a ramshackle wagon to the far end of the clearing. The forlorn beast had a long snout with a pronounced upper lip, its head drooping under the weight of its impressive antlers. The boxy wagon, constructed from sturdy planks, featured a window with bars. While the driver was unfamiliar, the man standing alongside was Leo Parker.

"He came this way," Leo said, striding across the clearing. "But the tracks have disappeared."

The driver clumsily descended, dragging his foot when he scrambled to catch Leo. "Did you find something?"

"Frankie, you're messing up the tracks."

The pair stood close enough for me to untie their shoes. The sound of my thundering heart would've given me away if not for Frankie's ceaseless chatter. Leo stilled and tipped his head as if to use all of his senses.

Frankie limped toward the woods. "Did you look over here?"

Leo huffed. "Get back to the wagon before you trample every meaningful clue."

"Just trying to help," Frankie grumbled. "I thought you were a famous tracker."

"Hey, I can only work with what I'm given." Leo crouched, sniffing the ground, and after a moment, he began pacing as if measuring strides.

"Someone passed through, but I can't determine where he went." Leo gestured toward my hiding place.

I avoided looking directly at the men, worried they'd sense my gaze.

"Maybe it was a dragon," Frankie said, shielding his eyes as he scanned the trees.

"I don't know any six and a half feet dragons who wear boots," Leo said. "The young wizard was here and clever enough to cover his tracks."

"Why take the shortcut through the haunted forest?" Frankie shivered. "The place gives me the creeps."

"If you want to help, make breakfast. But this time, keep the fire small. The entire valley could've seen our last one."

"You'll find him," Frankie said, rubbing his hands together. "Big money."

Leo grunted in agreement, giving Frankie a friendly slap on the back, causing the shorter man to stumble. Frankie regained his balance, picked up a stick, and banged it against the wagon.

*Thump-thump-thump*!

"Rise and shine, Shorty! Time for breakfast. Oh, right, we don't feed the cargo," Frankie jeered.

"Don't pester the merchandise. Leave the gnome alone," Leo hollered from across the clearing.

My temper flared at the cruelty of capturing a gnome, and curiosity propelled me to investigate. The thick branches and the knotty trunk made for an effortless climb, with *Mischief's* glimmering wards advancing alongside me. When I reached a branch that offered a clear view, I tucked my feet and scooted along the limb.

The top of the wagon resembled a cage with bars evenly spaced. A gnome in a pointy hat stood on a hay bale, his face partially concealed by his cap as he looked out the window. "Where are you taking me?"

"To the Collector," Frankie said. "But if you tell me where you hid the treasure, I'll let you go."

"Treasure, what treasure?" The gnome adjusted his hat, revealing his face.

My eyes bulged, recognizing the captive as Thingamabob.

Frankie slammed the box with his fist. "Everyone knows gnomes guard treasure. Where is it?"

"I'm a simple farmer," Thingamabob said, running a hand across his face.

"You're as much a farmer as that young wizard," Frankie said. "Where's Noah?"

"I don't know anyone by that name." Thingamabob didn't miss a beat. He never considered ratting me out.

From that moment, no question about it—I had to rescue Bob. Another prison break was in order. But first, I needed a plan. While Frankie prepared breakfast and Leo sat on a log, I remained hidden in the spruce tree. Worried that *Mischief's* boisterous voice would betray my location, I whispered to him to show me how to make a sleeping potion rather than tell me. *Mischief* flipped open a page with the recipe, listing pinecone seeds, lavender, and valerian.

My time with Mrs. S had taught me to recognize plants, and I grinned at the picturesque glade below. It would serve as a veritable drugstore. I had what I needed as long as I didn't get caught. I brushed protection stars off the branches and sprinkled myself with the magical particles. Then, I focused my will, reciting the invisibility spell. With the added boost of my wristband, I faded into the shadows.

Keeping to the edges and with the utmost stealth, I scavenged for the sleeping potion ingredients. When I had stuffed my pockets, I retreated to the sanctuary of the spruce. Hidden beneath the sheltering boughs, I used my mortar and pestle to grind the ingredients into a fine, fluffy powder. The air was stuffy under the branches, and I wiped the sweat from my face. When I finished, I poured the powdery mixture into a pouch for safekeeping.

Meanwhile, as Frankie and Leo ate breakfast, the enticing aroma of bacon tempted my senses. My hollow stomach rumbled, and I dug into my pack, looking for one of Salty's box lunches I had stashed just in case.

A faraway rumble, followed by a shrill whistle, woke me from my deep sleep. Birds were singing, squirrels were chirping, and the sun was low in the sky. I buried my head in my hands and groaned at my foolishness.

# CHAPTER 16

## *THE MELANCHOLY MIST*

The sun's angle told me I had slept the day away. My sleeping potion worked, but not as planned. I must've gotten some on my hands—*another lesson learned the hard way.*

I snuck out of my hiding place, surprised by the oppressive humidity. The only evidence of Frankie and Leo was a wagon track heading deeper into Goblin Valley and an abandoned campfire. A gust of wind revived the smoldering embers into a flame. I shook my head at their carelessness. The forest floor, carpeted with dry needles, branches, and pinecones, lay dangerously close. One stray spark, and the evergreens would ignite like Roman candles.

While cicadas sang, I wracked my brain for a way to douse the flames. The camp shovel remained in the wagon, and I didn't have any water to spare. But then it hit me—I knew magic.

*Well, sort of.*

I used my staff to create a perimeter around the campfire before settling into a seated position within the circle. Next, I relaxed and focused on recalling a rainmaker spell.

*You can do this.*

"*Hagen Skerry Pluvia Nimbus,*" I pronounced each word carefully, understanding that a single mistake could trigger Noah's flood all over again.

Silence fell, and static crackled. Above the embers, a white cumulus rose skyward. A smile of satisfaction crept across my face at the first raindrop. The cloud swelled as its underbelly darkened. Then, a sudden downpour drenched the campfire and everything in the vicinity. Me included.

A bolt of lightning flashed, and the accompanying thunder echoed in my ears. As the storm's intensity increased, I hastily scraped away the magic circle with my boot. When the tenacious little rain cloud disappeared, I let out a sigh of relief. Although thoroughly soaked, it didn't dampen my spirits. I had successfully used magic to put out the fire or any chance of it re-igniting. Elated by my accomplishment, I yelled triumphantly and kicked my heels, shaking the water from my hair like a wet dog.

Darkness fell, and an icy chill ran through me, making my teeth chatter. I rubbed my hands together to warm them. It would be a cold night beneath the blue spruce. Buoyed by my success, I dismissed my concerns. I'd get through the night, and first thing in the morning, I'd rescue Bob.

*How hard could it be to find a moose pulling a wagon?*

Once I changed into dry clothes, I enlisted *Mischief's* help to create a luminous orb. We kept it dim and no bigger than my fist to avoid attracting attention. The light provided much-needed warmth and came in handy while I smoothed my bed of pine needles and organized the contents of my pack. Curious about what the fairy globe would show me, I shook it, but nothing happened. I inspected the glass, found no cracks, and wondered if it had run out of magic or didn't work in the haunted forest. The idea of spending the night in a haunted forest gave me goosebumps. But the sounds of crickets reassured me. I had nothing to fear.

*A noisy forest is a safe forest.* I repeated the mantra in my head.

The wind picked up, causing the trees to moan like restless spirits. An owl hooted. Then, the comforting symphony of crickets came to an abrupt halt. All that remained was a profound silence. A branch snapped. The wards clinging to the boughs sparked a warning. A vicious snarl shattered the stillness, turning my spine to jello. I tossed my duster over the orb, dimming the light. Then, straining my ears, my mind raced to identify what lurked outside my den.

"Crikey, let me in."

Relief washed over me, and I moved the branches aside, allowing my friend to cross the threshold. Uncovering the orb, his raccoon eyes glowed in the soft light's reflection.

"You gave me quite a fright, I—"

He lifted a paw to stop my words. "Sara and Jesse are in trouble," Bandit said.

I jumped to my feet, slipping into my duster. Without hesitation, I shouldered my pack and grabbed my wizard's staff. If only I hadn't stomped on the orb, crushing it in my haste.

ΔΔΔ

I raced after Bandit through the haunted forest, straining to keep the raccoon in view. Stumbling, I fell against the trunk of a colossal tree. My heart pounded against my chest as I fought to catch my breath. The towering giants of the forest resembled redwoods, but where the redwood forest inspired wonder, these giants exuded a foreboding presence. Unnatural shadows slithered like serpents while fog rose like hungry, reaching hands. Disoriented, I pressed against a tree, trying to gain my bearings. When I ran my hand across my head, the darkness was so intense I couldn't see my fingers.

"Bandit, where are you?"

"I'm here," he said, nudging my leg.

The fog thickened, and a heavy melancholy settled upon my spirit, smothering me with a deep sadness. I nervously wrung my hands, finding a brief respite when my fingers brushed against my wristband. "It's the mist. I can feel the evil spirits surrounding us." I tightened my grip, uncertain how long the wristband would protect me.

"Climb, mate!"

Guided by Bandit, I clambered up the colossal trunk, clawing for handholds to rise above the mind-altering shroud of mist.

Bandit halted when we had advanced safely beyond the ground fog. Only then did I straddle a sturdy limb and take deep, cleansing breaths.

I swiped a hand across my face. "That was a close one. You saved my skin. I almost curled into a ball of surrender." I rubbed at my eyes, trying to erase the fog's haunting memory. "The mist twisted my thoughts—I've never felt so hopeless," I said, pressing my palm against my wristband, comforted by its soothing influence. "But we are safe enough here."

"I felt the ghostly bogies, too." Bandit scratched his chin. "Crikey, I was a few sangers short of a picnic."

"Since I ate the last of my sandwiches, and we'll need to wait until this soup burns off, why don't you tell me what happened to Sara and Jesse," I said, changing the subject and trying to make light of this awful situation.

Bandit paced on the limb, updating me with the details and emphasizing key points with animated gestures. He explained how he and Scout had scoured the area looking for me while the others set up camp. The tiny fairy's lightning-fast speed allowed her to dart back and forth. During one of her visits, she discovered the Parker Brothers lurking nearby and hurried to alert him.

They hurried back to camp, and Sara, Jesse, and the animals were missing. The wagon had been ransacked, and even Bandit's beloved mono-wheel had been stolen. Scout darted off to track Sara and Jesse while Bandit resumed his search for me. However, tracking me inside the bubble was challenging because I left no scent. Bandit followed the trail of smoke. After discovering the soggy campfire, he caught a whiff of my box lunch right around the same time the other night crawlers did.

"The magic ward kept them away, but forest animals are persistent, so I ran them off," Bandit said.

Then, recalling the distant rumble I had heard in the clearing, I asked him about it.

"It's probably the train, mate—we're camped where the tracks meet the cobblestones."

ΔΔΔ

Worried I'd fall asleep and tumble on my head, I pulled a length of rope from my pack and tied myself to the tree. Bandit seemed unconcerned when he curled up and promptly nodded off. While Bandit slept, I leaned against the rough bark, contemplating my predicament.

The Parker's presence remained a looming threat. I wondered if they knew about the wanted poster. *And what about Bob? I had to rescue him!*

I dropped my head. "Why did I ever think being a wizard would be cool?"

When I heard *Mischief's* garbled voice, I pulled him from my pack, and a deep scowl greeted me. "What's with all the jibber-jabber?"

"Did I disturb you?" I snapped. "Besides, I wasn't talking to you, just thinking out loud. I do that when I'm stressed."

"Lad, what's troubling you?" *Mischief's* countenance softened, concern shown in his eyes.

"I'm no closer to my quest, and now my friends are missing." I sighed in frustration. "My so-called magical gift has given me nothing but grief. Whatever I do, I mess up. I am a lousy wizard."

"Enough of this nonsense. Wizards don't whine!"

"What kind of pep talk is that?" I crossed my arms, staring out at the milky stars. "Just forget it."

"Listen, lad—don't expect me to pander to your doubts. Doubt destroys hope and breeds fear. You must master your fear, or fear will control you. The same is true for magic. Master your gifts, or surrender them to fear. You're a wizard, so own it."

"But how do I master my magic?" I said, rubbing my neck. I hadn't considered magic as something I needed to own.

"Practice," *Mischief* said matter-of-factly. "We learn from our failures. Now tell me what you have learned."

I chuckled wryly. "Well, I've had my fair share of failures. It could take all night to list them."

"What else do you have to do?"

"Good point."

And so, while Bandit snored, we delved into a discussion, dissecting my magical mishaps one by one. *Mischief* listened, offering guidance. He pointed out where I could've made different choices and suggested alternative approaches. Before I knew it, the sky had transformed into hues of orange, and with the dawn of a new day, my burdens felt lighter.

I jostled the sleepy raccoon. Bandit stretched. "G'day, mate. So, what's the plan?"

"Since when do you need a plan?"

"Since I've been hanging out with you blokes and gone walkabout?" A sloppy raccoon grin spread across his snout.

"Return to the camp and search for clues," I said, with a renewed sense of courage to face whatever lay ahead.

"Right-o mate." Bandit, the raccoon, scuttled down the tree in a flash.

Even while my stiff joints protested, I climbed down, landed with a soft thud, and rebounded to a standing position, where I yawned and stretched. The sun streamed through the forest, and something white caught my eye. I cocked my head and blinked. My skin rippled with a sudden chill, and I ran my hands through my hair, struggling to make sense of the macabre scene.

Hanging from the branches were dolls, their faces streaked with mud. Some had tangled, matted hair, and others had molded plastic heads. Dozens of dolls were nailed to the trees, some with missing limbs and others without bodies.

"Ahhh—"

Bandit stood by my side. "What are you waffling on about?"

I pointed.

"Crikey," Bandit said, taking an involuntary step back, his hackles raised.

"Chucky would be my guess," I said, rubbing the creepiness off my arms.

The wind came up, the branches creaked, and the trees

moaned. A single doll's eyes snapped open, locking me with a malevolent stare.

"No worries, mate." Bandit scratched his head. "They're only toy dolls."

A heavy branch crashed, and breaking sticks rumbled from the undergrowth. The ground trembled.

"Run!" Bandit took off like a shot, and I followed in his wake.

We raced through the woods, desperate to outrun the unseen foe. But as I ran, something seized me by the scruff of my neck, picking me off the ground. My legs bicycled, and I thrashed about as it lifted me higher.

A round baby face with a tuft of purple hair and an emerald complexion eyed me curiously. My jaw dropped. Everything except the little giant's hair was green, including the snot dripping from her nose.

A snarl escaped her green lips. "You're not supposed to be here." Her breath carried a sour milk stench.

"Put me down." My voice came out in a squeak.

She shook me so hard my teeth rattled.

"Please, so we can talk?" I masked my fear in a neutral tone.

The little girl giant dumped me on a rock before flopping on the ground. She propped her chin with her palm and leaned in close. She sniffed, and a booger retreated into her flat nose.

"Dolly," she said in a childlike voice.

"No, my name is Noah. What's your name?" I asked, offering my best smile.

"Cassandra," she said warily.

"That's a pretty name."

"I want my dolly!"

She reminded me of a preschooler gearing up for an epic meltdown. "You have lots of dollies." I pointed at the freak show in the trees. "Did you hang those dolls?"

"Yes." She scooted up on her knees and crossed her arms, as if bracing for an argument. "But only the naughty ones."

*Yikes!*

"I don't like them. I want a new dolly." Her lip protruded in a pout.

"If you let me go, I'll bring you a doll."

"Fibber," she said, licking the snot from her upper lip. "You're saying that, so I'll let you go."

"I promise," I said, using my hand to draw a cross on my chest. "If I'm lying, I'm crying."

The little giant eyed me with interest. "I'm a collector, and I'm going to keep you," she said, her mouth tightening into a determined line.

"Cassie, I'm not a toy, but I'd like to be your friend." I faked a casual smile, doing my best to remain the adult in the conversation. "It's nice to have friends."

"Friend?" she said, as emotions danced across her face, like tasting a piece of sweet and sour candy for the first time. She furrowed her forehead. "You want to be my friend?" The little giant looked me in the eye as if to judge my honesty. "My dolly went away." Her chin quivered. "I guess she wasn't a friend."

"Cassie, sweetie, friendship isn't a thing. It's a million little things," I said, using a tone reminiscent of my father when dealing with my stubbornness as a child. "But I'll share a little secret with you—friends help friends." I ran my hand through my hair. "And I need your help. My people-friends are in trouble, and I must find them. Do you know where the train crosses the cobblestone road?"

She nodded. "I'm not allowed to leave the forest, but I can bring you to the edge."

"That would be a great help," I said.

"Friends help friends."

"That's right, Cassie." I offered an encouraging smile.

With her decision made, Cassandra plucked me off the rock, tucked me under her arm, and tromped through the trees. It wasn't long before the forest gave way to a meadow of yellow buttercups.

"This is as far as I can go," Cassie said, setting me firmly on the ground. "Daddy said I mustn't leave the forest." She squatted beside me, her green eyes searching my face.

"Where's your daddy?" I asked as I adjusted my pack.

"Daddy's at work. He has giant responsibilities," Cassie said, struggling to pronounce the six-syllable word.

I quirked my eyebrow when I imagined the height of the little girl's dad.

She pointed a stubby finger. "Over there is where the cobblestones cross the tracks. Daddy told me not to play on the tracks."

"Your father's right. It's not safe." With an exaggerated bow, I bid her farewell. "Until we meet again, fair lady."

"You go now," she said, wiping her nose with her sleeve. "Find your friends." Her eyes searched mine. "You'll remember my doll?"

"Uh yeah, sure, no problem." I held out my fist. "Forever friends."

Cassie grinned, revealing a single tooth. She bumped her fist against mine with such enthusiasm that it sent me stumbling. When I caught my balance, I offered a casual wave. Then, with a sense of urgency, I set off toward the cobblestone road where Sara and Jesse were last seen. When I looked over my shoulder, Cassie continued to wave. I returned the farewell gesture, increasing my pace into a sprint, thinking it best to get out of sight before the little green giant had a change of heart.

# CHAPTER 17

## *RESCUE MISSION*

A swath of clouds shared the sky as I ran, offering next to no protection against the unrelenting sun. I followed the bent grass and the unique evidence left by the moose until the tall prairie retreated to a jumble of misshapen rocks. I crested a hill and slowed, marveling at the whimsical nature of the stone menagerie below. Stacks of boulders, with arches, pits, and ridges, were sculpted into animals by time and wind.

While I worried about my friends, I couldn't help but wish the circumstances were different. It would've been fun to slow down and linger in this fantastical *rock-scape*. Sara would love to explore this boulder field. I pictured her delight at discovering the granite turtle poised in a cartwheel and grinned.

Sweat stung my eyes, snapping me out of my woolgathering. With a quickened pace, I continued along the wagon tracks that cut through the boulder field. A shadow darkened my path when I came across a rock shaped like a circus elephant. I shielded the sun's glare and watched an enormous raven soar through the currents. Iridescent wings glistened in the sunlight while it drifted closer, circling.

My jaw came unhinged, realizing it was no bird. Amazed, I marveled, admiring its grace and speed. But then a fright ran down my spine when the dragon's eyes locked onto mine and, with the maneuverability of a fighter jet, it dove. My veins flooded with fear-fueled adrenaline. I slid under the granite elephant, squeezing into a crevice while holding my breath.

I let the air out of my lungs at the unexpected reprieve. The dragon had changed direction and snatched up a wild boar, flying away with its squealing dinner held tightly in its grip. My heart slowed as the sound faded away, and I crawled out of my hiding place.

"Crikey, that was close."

I bucked at Bandit's voice.

"For a wizard, you're awfully jumpy," the raccoon said as he leaned against a bunny-shaped rock.

"Where have you been?" I asked, rubbing my lower back.

"Dodging feral pigs—and staying clear of the giant green kid because I didn't want her thinking I was a plush, cuddly toy."

"I can't blame you," I said, stepping from beneath the elephant rock. "How far to where Sara and Jesse had camped?"

"Three hundred yards. There's a guy with a moose camping there now."

We climbed a cluster of boulders, shimmying up what looked like a giraffe's neck to perch on its head. From our vantage point overlooking the cobblestone road, we spotted the jail wagon stopped by the river. Someone sat by a blazing fire, and from how he rubbed his leg, I guessed it was Frankie.

I scanned the sky. "Do you think the dragon will come back?"

"Hopefully, he filled his belly with pork," Bandit said.

"Barbecue pork sounds delicious, but we'll have to settle for an energy bar." As we ate, we planned our next steps. It was time to go on the offensive.

ΔΔΔ

Ten minutes later, I recognized Frankie as I strolled into camp without much of a disguise—A ball cap and sunglasses and my duster packed away. Frankie sat by the fire, rubbing his outstretched leg. I called out like they did in the old movies.

Frankie squinted, appearing surprised. "Howdy, stranger. I didn't expect to see anyone out here, especially on foot."

"It's a long story." I sighed, wiping my brow. "Is that coffee? I wouldn't say no to a cup if you're offering."

Frankie smiled, revealing teeth like crumbling tombstones. "I wouldn't mind the company, so have a seat." He pointed at the coffeepot. "Help yourself."

With the steaming mug in my hands, I feigned a bitter taste.

Frankie chuckled. "I like mine so strong it wakes the neighbors."

"Do you want sugar?" I said, digging into my pack.

Frankie's face split into a smile, displaying a missing molar. "I lost my sweet tooth, but not my craving." He snickered at his lame joke.

I dropped a pinch into his cup and pretended to do the same for mine. When I glanced at the moose, still hitched to the wagon, my eyes narrowed, hiding my disapproval behind my sunglasses. The pitiful animal stood panting in the blistering sun, with nothing to eat or drink, while the river babbled a few yards out of reach.

After taking a large gulp, Frankie nodded in pleasure. "So, what's your story? Why on foot?"

Using the time to make up a story that Frankie would believe, I swallowed my coffee. "An enormous beast spooked my horse." I gestured to the sky. "It dove from the clouds and grabbed a wild pig. It might've been a dragon," I said, letting fear creep into my voice.

"This is dragon country," Frankie said. "I've never seen one but heard tell that such monsters roam these parts, and more so the deeper you travel into Goblin Valley." Frankie's eyes took on a glassy shimmer.

Since I didn't know how long Peddler's truth powder would last, I started firing questions at Frankie. The man was forthcoming, bragging about how he and his cousin Leo had trapped a gnome and were on the trail of fugitives.

"There's big money in bounty hunting." A questioning expression shot across his face. "Say you haven't seen any wizards, have ya?"

"Nope," I said, shielding my chin behind my cup.

Frankie snorted. "Seems a young wizard and his friends annoyed a coven of witches from Estonia." He shuddered. "Dangerous bunch—wouldn't want to be on their bad side."

I raised my mug while considering Carla was from Estonia. Her sister, Agnes, the red witch from the well, must have been the one who created the wanted poster. "Where's your partner?" I asked, wanting to keep Frankie talking.

"Leo's on the way to the train station." He winced when he twisted, pointing toward the tracks.

"He left you here—injured?" I pretended to care. "Who does that?"

"Oh, my cousin's alright—my leg's always troubling me." Frankie massaged his knee. "We caught the Goodall kid, and Leo figured half a bounty was better than none, and besides, he expects the coven to pay extra for the girl."

"Girl?"

"Yep, she sure is feisty. She kicked me in my bum leg and put up a fight with fancy moves until Leo knocked her out." Frankie leaned in. "I don't abide hitting girls, but Leo's so mean, he'd fight a rattler and give him the first bite."

I ground my molars. *Leo would pay for that.*

"After the Collector's agent arrived, they rode the train."

"Collector's agent?" I asked, curious.

"He works for the witches and said the sooner we deliver our captives to Estonia, the better. He wasn't interested in the gnome, and Leo wasn't about to turn the goods over to a stranger, so he's traveling with the agent to see about the reward." Frankie motioned with his hand. "I'll meet up with Leo later after I finish with the gnome."

I kept from scowling when I pointed to my broken buckboard, wondering where Lester and Nester were. "Does that piece of junk belong to the gnome?"

"Nah, Leo busted it up to keep the girl and her red-headed friend from leaving." Frankie gulped his coffee.

"So why the gnome?"

"The gnome's treasure." Frankie's eyes sparked at the thought of money. "Leo's gonna split sixty-forty as soon as I convince the gnome to tell me where he hid it."

I prompted with silence.

"Never met anyone more stubborn. I tried to persuade him, but the filthy creature wouldn't give up his secrets." Frankie shook his head. "Even when I confronted him about colluding with wizards, he refused to answer."

"How did you connect him to the wizard?"

"Leo found their tracks." Frankie scratched his ear. "The way I figure it, he and the gnome are in cahoots. And the witches want the young wizard because he knows where the gnomes keep their treasure."

The more the man talked, the more I felt my temper rise. I told myself to remain calm while I refilled our mugs and spiked Frankie's cup, careful not to get any on my hands this time.

Frankie chugged his coffee. It wasn't long before he set his cup on a flat rock and yawned. Seconds later, his head dipped. I counted to ten before giving Frankie a hard shove. He responded with a snore. So I set my mug next to his and whistled for Bandit, who scampered down a nearby tree munching acorns.

"Our plan was iffy—truth serum and sleeping powder." Bandit pointed at Frankie. "But then that mongrel got to ear-bashing." Bandit crunched another acorn. "You learned plenty from that *Sleeping-Not-So-Beauty*. Good on ya."

I grinned at the raccoon. "We're not done yet. Keep an eye on things while I check on Thingamabob."

I hurried toward the jail wagon. Rusty hinges screeched when I threw open the door. The inside reeked of mildew while Thingamabob lay curled in the corner on a pile of straw, his beard matted with grime. "Bob, I'm getting you out of here."

The gnome groaned as he rolled to sit and tried to adjust his pointy hat. "You're the young wizard." Bob rubbed his eyes.

"I'm going to carry you." As gently as possible, I lifted the gnome and returned to the campfire, setting Bob on his feet. Thingamabob nearly toppled backward when he spotted Frankie slumped sideways.

"You needn't worry about him," I said, squatting, "you're safe now."

Bob sported a black eye and a misshaped shoulder. "Something's wrong with my arm." He sucked air between his teeth when he tried to move it.

As a kid, I had a dislocated shoulder, and I never forgot the biting pain. So, I asked Thingamabob if he wanted me to reset it. But first, I dragged a circle in the dirt, hoping magic would help with his discomfort. Then, concentrating on replacing Bob's pain with positive healing vibes, I repeated my mother's cantle—*out with the bad, in with the good.* My amulet hummed, and when I sensed a subtle shift of magic within the circle, I guided the gnome's dislocated bone into place.

*Snap!*

His shoulder joint rolled back into the socket, and I used my bandana as a sling. Thingamabob wiped the sweat from his brow and gave me a long, quizzical stare.

I motioned to the acorn-munching raccoon. "This is Bandit. He'll keep watch while you rest."

With calm, careful steps, I approached the weary moose. The whites of his eyes increased as the moose snorted and weakly tossed his head. His ribs protruded, and flies bothered pink sores where the harness had rubbed against his hide.

At the sight of the mistreated animal, dots clouded my vision. It might be an old saying, but I saw red. Making no sudden moves that might spook the anxious moose, I unhitched and coaxed him into the shade. The temperature dropped to comfortable beside the birch grove, and I searched my pack for a tube of ointment. The cream soothed the wound, and he lowered his head, appearing to relax. When I stroked his bony hide, blue sparks rippled across his back. "You look like you could sleep for a hundred years, so I'll call you Bull Van Winkle."

The moose munched on birch leaves, nodding at his new moniker, while I led him to the riverbank and unbuckled his halter. With plenty of water, food, and shade, it was the perfect place for him to recover.

A minute later, a train sounded in the distance. "I wish I could do more, but my friends are in trouble, and I've gotta hurry." I motioned toward the campfire. "Stay clear of Frankie. When he wakes up, he might come looking for you." I gave the moose a gentle slap on the rump. "You're free. Go in peace."

Bull Van Winkle slurped water while wading into the river until the level reached his neck.

As I approached the fire, I clenched my jaw at the sound of Frankie snoring like a chainsaw. But it wasn't Frankie—it was Bandit. I jostled the furball, but he didn't wake up.

"What happened?" I asked.

"I'm not sure. Your friend sat eating acorns, dunking them in coffee. The next thing I knew, the critter yawned and fell asleep," Bob said, stroking his beard. "The poor little guy is exhausted."

"I laced the coffee with a sleeping potion. Bandit must've used the wrong mug."

Still chuckling about Bandit, I found a shovel and extinguished the fire the old-school way. As I worked, my amusement faded, and soon, I was steaming at how Frankie had mistreated Bob and Bull Van Winkle.

*Frankie's a bully. He needs to be taught a lesson.*

With that thought in mind, a vengeful smile twisted my lips. I snatched Frankie's tattered boots and hurled them into the river with a satisfying splash. Frankie's stinky socks had a set of matching holes where his toes poked through.

The train whistled again, and I turned to Bob. "I'll see you get home, but first, I must save my friends. The Parker Gang is holding them prisoners on the train to Estonia." Then, realizing Bob couldn't match my stride with his short legs and arm in a sling, I asked. If he could ride on top of my pack.

The little gnome nodded and adjusted his pointy red cap. "We won't make this stop, but I can show you the shortcut to another station."

When I donned my duster, I felt its protective wards ripple with soothing magic. Thingamabob climbed aboard, and I scooped Bandit under my arm. With a last glance at Frankie, sleeping peacefully, Bob guided me to a natural bridge spanning the river shallows. With swift steps, I moved from stone to stone until we reached the other side, and from there, followed a narrow trail into the wilderness.

"We can meet the train at Dragon Dam. The lake is mesmerizing, so whatever you do, don't look at the water," Bob cautioned.

"I'm glad you know where you're going," I said, keeping my eyes on the uneven path through the thick brush. "Does the train have many stops?"

"The train is a gateway to the mortal realm and takes the scenic route through the Otherlands, stopping at various towns and forts along the way." After a quick beat, Bob asked. "Didn't you take the train when you crossed the veil?"

"We came through a portal at Dead Dragon Divide."

Bob let out a soft whistle. "You must have powerful connections because portals are restricted to VIPs. Most of us regular folk use the train."

I changed the subject, not wanting to discuss Castle Dragon business. "Can I ask why you didn't tell Frankie about me? Don't get me wrong, I'm grateful—You're one tough hombre."

"Guys like Frankie enjoy inflicting pain too much to listen," Bob said. "Besides, I'm not a snitch."

"Thanks," I said, impressed by Bob's attitude. "So, how did you know I was a wizard?"

Bob chuckled. "It wasn't hard. Gnomes recognize magic, and your power runs deep."

"This whole wizard thing is new to me. I'm what you might call a novice."

"Don't sell yourself short. You seemed to know what you were about when you healed my arm."

I shook my head no. "All I did was put your shoulder back in the socket. It hurt something awful when it happened to me as a kid. So I used a hint of magic to ease the pain."

"Wizard, you fixed more than my arm. I feel at least a hundred years younger." Bob did a tap dance on my pack.

I gnawed my lip, fretting, hoping I didn't borrow trouble.

# CHAPTER 18

## *THE VANISHING ACT*

Dragon Lake Station was a simple boardwalk with a water tower and a coal bin. Why anyone would build a train station in the middle of nowhere was beyond me. Bob climbed off my shoulder when I squatted to place Bandit on the grass. "Keep a lookout—I'll be right back," I said, giving the gnome a curt nod.

Ominous plumes of black smoke spewed from the locomotive as the workers diligently loaded the coal bins. I forced myself to amble at a casual pace because running might attract unwanted attention. The stock car's door stood ajar, granting a glimpse of Altair and Orion. Without a second thought, I slipped into the stock car and soothed the anxious ponies with hushed words. Although there was no sign of the goats, I stashed the ramp, closed the stock car, and secured the ponies' escape.

When we reached the trees, Bandit was awake. "How was your nap?" I asked.

"Ah yeah, 'bout that—" he rubbed his forehead with his paw and offered a sheepish grin.

The engine huffed, and the whistle blew, ramping up my sense of urgency.

"Can you guys ride?"

Bandit grinned. Bob's eyes widened, and then he turned even paler. His eyes darted to the train and back to me. He mumbled, but with no time to argue, I plucked Bob off the ground and set him in the saddle. I promptly introduced the ponies to the gnome. "Bob, they'll take you home, and please see to the horses until I return."

I gave the Fell Ponies a reassuring pat. "Take care of Bandit and Bob. I'm going after Sara and Jesse." Orion nodded, his white mane falling into his eyes, while Altair stamped his foot, seeming to understand the directive. Bandit stood on the saddle, one paw holding the reins.

"Noah, wait," Bob called as the ponies headed into the trees.

Waving off whatever Bob had to say, I hurried across the grass. I sauntered onto the weathered platform as if I intended to meet a passenger. When I heard my name, I turned around with surprise written all over my face.

"Your friends are in the caboose," Headless said, sweeping toward the last car and leading the way. "Hurry, the train is about to leave."

Relief washed over me—*Headless is here to help*!

The conductor hollered, "All aboard!"

The locomotive chugged, the train clunked, and its wheels clacked, grinding against the tracks as it gained traction. With no time to plan or think, I swung onto the balcony outside the caboose. The carriage rolled along, picking up speed. Stepping into the car, I faltered, sucking air between my teeth, taking it all in.

Leo Parker reclined on a couch, his floppy hat covering his brows. Across from Leo sat Sara and Jesse, both with dull, blank expressions. When I dared to open my third eye, I saw writhing tendrils wrapped around my friends, binding them in place. Sara's pupils dilated, but beyond that, she didn't move. Jesse's chin lolled against his chest with no recognition in his eyes.

Mahogany paneling and rich upholstery decorated the interior. Plush sofas, end tables, and Tiffany lamps adorned the opulent carriage. The air reeked of menace and deceit.

"Been wondering when you'd show up," Leo said, pointing to a velvet wing-backed chair. "Take a load off."

"What's going on?"

Leo shrugged indifferently, angling his chin toward Howard.

"Sit down, Noah," Headless Howard said, standing before the far door.

"Howie?" I questioned, raising my hands.

Prickling magic swelled inside the cabin, and I instinctively summoned a protective shield. Howard motioned toward the chair. I stiffened my spine, responding with an obstinate glare. Orange sparks exploded from Howard's sleeves and fizzled like wet sparklers against my invisible shield.

Howard let out a maniacal laugh at the failed attempt to subdue me. "Okay, we can do it the hard way." A long blade appeared in his hand.

I countered by unsheathing the Raven Moonstone sword from within my duster and pointing the tip at Howard.

Leo jumped to his feet, and I clobbered him with the sword's pommel, sending the lanky man sprawling back onto the couch. "That's for Sara."

Howard screamed, and brandishing his saber, he charged. Our blades sparked as metal clashed against metal. Howard had no talent for swordsmanship, but I kept my superior skill hidden, blocking while he struck again and again.

"What did you do to my friends?"

"A persuasive binding spell," Howard said.

"Let them go." I spat the words.

"If you cooperate, we can make a deal," he pushed the thought at me, and it rolled off my invisible ward. "We can talk this over as gentlemen. My client is eager to meet you."

"You're a double-crosser." I thrust my sword and forced Howard to step back. "We trusted you, and you betrayed us."

"That was your first mistake, Greenhorn—trusting a stranger."

"We tried to help you," I said through clenched teeth.

"You don't get it, young wizard. I played you like a fiddle from the start."

I channeled my frustrated anger into the sword, and the Raven Moonstone flared with vengeful light as I swiftly sliced through the magical bindings. When Sara's hands were free, she nudged Jesse into wakefulness with a slap. I stepped in front of

Sara as she pulled Jesse toward the door. While I kept Howard on guard, I directed them to the roof. "Outside—Use the ladder—climb."

The locomotive rumbled as it gained speed. Leo stumbled to his feet, his eyes blazed as he lunged. I sidestepped, and Leo's momentum blocked Howard.

"Get out of my way," Headless yelled, his hollow voice reverberating through the narrow carriage.

I lobbed a lamp and knocked over any furniture within reach before swinging onto the ladder attached to the outside of the car. By the time I clambered onto the roof and sheathed my sword, Jesse and Sara were already on the second, heading for the third.

Headless glided to the rooftop like a phantom, blocking the way to my friends. His flaming red Xs penetrated the dark space within his hood. I reached for my sheathed sword and came up empty-handed. Frantically, I patted my duster before I glimpsed it, hovering precariously close to the edge. The rail car rattled, and the blade wobbled. My wristband pulsed, and of its own accord, summoned my sword. The Raven Moonstone's hilt flew into my grasp.

With a steady hand, I raised my sword, its blade glinting with enchantment. "No more games," I said and lunged.

Howard parried, but he was no match for my skills. I sliced through him like a knife through butter.

*Snap! Crackle! Pop!*

In a blinding flash, Headless Howard vanished, his robe wilting into a pile of fabric. Confusion spread across my face. With the tip of my blade, I lifted the robe. Sewn into the hood was a black mask with two lifeless red Xs.

*What? It's a costume!*

Before Howard's disguise and disappearance distracted me further, Sara yelled and urged me forward. "Hurry!"

All thoughts of Howard disappeared as I jumped the gap between the rail cars. The fresh air had revived Jesse just in time to help steady my landing, as I crashed onto the roof with the grace of a gorilla.

The train jolted faster, the clamor amplifying as we crossed the wooden bridge spanning Dragon Dam. My duster flapped, and the wind pushed against my face. Vertical white cliffs lined the tranquil aquamarine reservoir. I felt the pull, even though I had only glanced at the lake for a split second. Bob's warning came to mind. "Don't look at the water!" I yelled.

But it was too late. Trance-like, Sara and Jesse stepped off the speeding train, succumbing to the call of the *Siren*.

"Noooo!" I cried, collapsing to my knees and pounding the running boards with my fists. "No! No! No!"

# CHAPTER 19
## *SHADOW VELVET*

I snuck a peek over the ledge, common sense unraveling my courage. Given more time, I knew I would've chickened out, but Sara and Jesse were in trouble, and I was determined to save them. So, without thinking further, I took a deep breath and jumped off the train. My heart pounded. Each passing second seemed like an eternity as my spiraling thoughts outpaced my rapid descent.

The rush of air stung my face. A constant reminder I was still alive. I spread my arms to slow my fall and struggled to devise a plan, but the pounding in my ears made it impossible to concentrate. As I plummeted, two majestic chargers rose beside me. Sara sat behind the plucky gnome, smiling so brightly it hurt my eyes. Jesse sprawled across Altair like a sack of potatoes while Bandit balanced on his back. With wings like Pegasus, the white ponies flew toward the horizon.

I couldn't understand why no one seemed to see me falling past them. But knowing they were safe, and with my heroics overshadowed by flying horses, my subconscious screamed at my recklessness.

*What were you thinking?*

*Give me a break. I was saving Sara.*

*When are you going to learn—Sara doesn't need saving? You're the one who needs his head examined.*

Diamonds danced on the water.

*What are you doing? Don't look at the mesmerizing dam*

*reservoir!*

I squeezed my eyes shut, bracing for the impact. My mother's amulet hummed, warming my chest and spreading fierce heat across my skin. Suddenly, a sharp tug changed my direction, propelling me upward. It took a moment for my brain to realize what was happening. A creature with oily wings carried me in its deadly talons. When I found my voice, I yelled for it to let me go.

And so it did.

The monster launched me into the air. I soared freely, peddling the empty blue sky until gravity butted in, and I went into a free fall. The winged beast swooped, rising to meet me. When my feet landed on its back, I fell to my knees and scrambled to secure a grip, much like straddling a horse. It had soft, black-bluish scales and a dragon's tail. My heart jackhammered, and my eyes watered. With golden eyes that radiated wisdom, I lost all fear when I met its gaze, knowing deep down that the dragon wouldn't harm me.

With a renewed sense of peace, we soared over Goblin Valley. It obliged all my directions as we glided over the Malpais. Soon, we came to high cliffs in a box canyon, and in the center stood an ancient tree with violet leaves. Exhilarated and in awe, I stroked the dragon's silken neck. "You're amazing."

*My personal dragon. How cool is that? Beyond epic, for sure!*

"You need a name. What should I call you?" I put my thumb on my chin while I contemplated. "I dub thee Shadow Velvet."

The dragon purred as if he approved. Shadow Velvet quickened his speed, and we raced across the bluest sky.

"Whoopee!"

*Oh, come on, you ride a dragon, and your manly response is whoopee?*

A snort escaped my lips as I chuckled at my childishness. I shoved my hair out of my face and gathered my thoughts, deciding it was time I stopped fooling around. When I asked Shadow Velvet to find my friends, the dragon responded, flying low over the hillside. Fifteen minutes later, I spotted Jesse's trademark fire. Jesse could start fires by snapping his fingers, but the embers were never orange—they always glowed purple.

Shadow Velvet flew to a nearby knoll and back-flapped his wings, clawing the dirt with its feet. At the sudden stop, I lost my grip and somersaulted onto the grass with a *thud*. The young dragon eyed me with an equal mix of curiosity and amusement.

"Thank you. Will you stay here a moment? I want you to meet my friends."

Jesse and Sara had camped close to the trestle bridge. As I ran, an iridescent, feathery scale drifted to the ground. When I picked it up, the dragon flew away into the bright sunlight.

Arriving at camp, a flurry of voices assaulted me, asking where I'd been. Sara grabbed me in a hug. "Noah! We thought we lost you again."

Relieved, I stepped back, brushing a tear from her cheek. But the savory scent of food cooking over an open fire made my stomach growl loudly. Sara laughed, shook her head, and dragged me to the food.

My friends gathered around the fire for a hearty meal of beans, bacon, and bread. The comforting lavender flames of the campfire brought us together, and we laughed and relaxed. After a while, I mentioned Shadow Velvet, and everyone stared at me, dumbfounded. "You didn't see the dragon when we flew over the camp?" I asked, sounding disappointed.

"Nope, we thought you were still on the top of the train," Jesse said.

"How could you miss me falling between the flying ponies before soaring away on a dragon?" When I looked at Bob and Bandit, they offered bemused shrugs. As my gaze swept over Sara, she smiled sweetly, as if she didn't believe a single word.

"Dude, did you hit your head?"

In disbelief, I gawked at my friends. *They didn't believe me.*

A while later, I asked about Scout. "We figured she was with you," Sara said in a questioning voice.

"No dramas, mate. Scout's probably chucked a *U-ey*." Bandit gave a thumbs-up with his paw.

"As in a U-turn, and went home. After all, she wasn't supposed to go beyond The Tower of Song," Jesse said, as if we didn't understand the Aussie lingo.

"Scout wouldn't leave without saying goodbye," Sara said, worry spreading across her face. "When's the last time anyone saw her?"

Bandit explained they separated at the knoll overlooking the prison wagon. Scout went after Sara and Jesse while he searched for me.

"You shouldn't have split up," I said roughly. "There's safety in numbers."

"Crikey, mate, we couldn't be in two places at once. Besides, someone had to save your tush."

Heat flooded my cheeks. I hated I turned scarlet when frustrated, which only infuriated me even more.

"Hey, Dude, I'm worried about Scout," Jesse said, and with a hopeful expression, added, "Maybe she flew to Castle Dragon for reinforcements."

"It's more likely the Parkers captured her. They've been suspected of poaching Fae folk for profit, but it could never be proven."

All eyes were on Bob. Then, in two beats, Jesse jumped up. "Let's go save Scout," Jesse said, shouldering his pack, and we all scrambled.

"Hold on, we can't—not yet, anyway. Not until we find the dragonroot," I said, making a sweeping motion with my hands to emphasize my point.

"Come on, Noah, you can't just abandon Scout," Jesse protested, sounding genuinely shocked.

I pushed my hair away from my eyes. "That's not what I'm saying, but Mrs. S is depending on us for the dragonroot."

"And don't forget Erik," Sara said.

"Yeah, right—Your precious popsicle," I said, tossing my hands and stepping back.

"No one's forgetting about Erik or Mrs. S," Jesse said, "But Scout's in trouble."

I turned to Jesse and sighed. "Dunno, man, I just dunno." Guilt roiled in my stomach. I couldn't meet his eyes. Scout was our friend, but Mrs. S's life depended on dragonroot. My guts twisted like I was being ripped in half.

Jesse continued to argue, but I couldn't think, so I took a few steps toward the river to clear my head.

"That's what you always do," Sara snapped.

I stopped. "What's that supposed to mean?" I matched her angry tone.

"When you don't like the direction a conversation is going, you leave." She folded her arms, her glare unwavering.

"I wanted some fresh air—to think," I said, tossing my hand up.

"What—the air here is not good enough for you?" Sara said, her lips forming a thin line.

"Stop it!" Bob's voice bellowed. He stood on a rock with his hands on his hips. "Everyone sit down." The atmosphere sizzled with frustration and angst. "I never met such a dysfunctional set of misfits." Bob shook his stubby finger at me. "You want to do everything yourself, but that isn't working."

Sara made a noise—but Bob wasn't done. "And you—" he pointed at Sara. "Now is not the time to pick a fight." Sara knitted her brow and looked at her feet.

"Jesse's right. Scout needs help. But what good is it to rush off pell-mell? You can't lead if you don't know where you're going." Bob gestured. "The only one with half a brain is Bandit.

"Ah, thanks, mate."

"I said—*half* a brain. You need to use both halves." Bob softened his tone as he continued. "I sense magic among all of you. Combining your talents will make you a formidable team, but only if you cooperate."

Properly chastised, my temper evaporated. I nudged Jesse with my elbow and smiled an apology at Sara. Bandit gestured with his paws. "Let's make a plan."

We all started talking. "Whoa, one at a time." the gnome lifted his hand to stop the commotion.

"Noah, use your globe," Sara said.

"It's broken. When I tried it in the forest, it only spun."

"Magic doesn't work near Wail Mist Forest," Bob said. His eyes grew wide. "Wait, you entered the Wail Mist Forest and lived to talk about it? Stu told you to stay out of the haunted forest? What didn't you understand about don't take shortcuts through the woods?"

While Bob continued his rant about *not listening to my elders*, I dug into my pack in search of the globe. When my hand brushed against the smooth glass, I said, "Bob's right. It's time to pull ourselves together and work as a team."

The globe displayed our current position, and I handed it to Sara, grateful it wasn't broken. Jesse grabbed a branch and etched a perimeter in the soft dirt. Bob grumbled something like that's more like it and joined our circle of friends.

"We need better light." Jesse rubbed his palms, and a radiant lavender ball appeared.

Sara placed the globe in the center of the circle and waved her hand. The scenery projected against the backstop of an invisible shield, much like a movie theater.

"Cool," Jesse said, impressed with Sara's ingenuity. "Now that we're all together, we should each share our thoughts," he added.

"Not yet." All eyes turned to me while I set *Mischief* beside the globe. His soft leather cover tingled at my touch. "Everyone, this is *Mischief*." His pages fluttered.

"Dude, what's the big deal? We've seen Ezra's journal. It's just a book."

"Show respect, young man," *Mischief* said as his weathered face emerged and a grin spread across the volume. A collective gasp erupted, except for Bob. He was the only one who didn't seem surprised.

"*Mischief*, is it?" Bob said. "I know you by a different name."

"It's the moniker the lad stuck me with—catchy, don't ya think?" *Mischief* said. "Been a while, Thingamabob. I'm glad to see you're keeping better company these days."

It was my turn to be shocked. "Wait—you two have met?"

"Seems that way," *Mischief* said in a neutral tone.

"How is that possible?"

Bob chuckled. "Anyone who has lived as long as I have is bound to have met some questionable characters, Ezra and *Mischief*, to name a few."

"You know Ezra?" I sat up, eager to learn about my ancestor.

"Sure, you remind me of him." Bob traded glances with *Mischief*, and I could've sworn a message passed between them. "That's a story for another day." Bob gestured dismissively. "We were about to brainstorm."

I frowned at the lack of information about Ezra, but Sara jumped in, changing the subject. "We should plan our next steps."

"Show us the Tree of Apotheosis," I said, touching the globe's base. The globe's landscape shifted, revealing a sprawling tree with a purple canopy.

I recalled Mrs. S's words. *Travel deep into Goblin Valley until you reach the Tree of Apotheosis. Rumor has it that is where you will find dragonroot.*

"Where's the dragonroot?" Jesse asked, and the screen changed. "All I see is black rock."

Bob explained the globe displayed the Malpais Plateau, a desolate landscape of molten rock and ancient lava flows crisscrossed with trails. In the outer reaches, there was volcanic activity, including Mount Drakon, an active volcano with magma close to the surface. But the land wasn't entirely volcanic rock. The Tree of Apotheosis thrived in a volcanic oasis, where patches of greenery emerged among rugged formations. Our quest for dragonroot would lead us to an ancient lava field covered in Obsidian, a glassy volcanic rock with sharp edges but no flowing lava. Beneath the surface lay a labyrinth of caves and sinkholes. Even with an expert guide, the journey promised grave danger.

As my mouth went dry, making it hard to swallow, Jesse examined his designer Louis Vuitton hiking boots. "We can't risk walking across a lava field—those rocks would shred our boots."

"I'll guide you to a secret entrance known only to gnomes," Bob said. "But from there, you're on your own. You'll have to search the labyrinth until you find what you seek. It's a shortcut, but not without risks." Bob's shudder sent a shiver down my back.

"How far are we from Dragon Tooth Cave?" Sara asked.

"About 15 minutes as the crow flies," I said.

"You mean as the dragon flies?" Jesse laughed and gave me a playful shove. "Did the baby dragon give you an aerial tour of the entire valley?" His tone suggested he wasn't buying my dragon story.

"His name is Shadow Velvet, and yes, I recognized a few landmarks," I said. "He's an excellent tour guide, by the way." I pointed toward the screen. "Here's the railroad track and there's the train."

"What's that?" Bandit pointed to a pulsing red light. The screen zoomed in on the train. The light flashed at regular intervals from a window.

"That's Morse code." Jesse leaned closer, squinting. "SOS—It's Scout! She's a prisoner and is on the way to Estonia."

"Estonia," Sara said, as expressions of surprise, worry, and dread traded across her face.

"Come on, let's go! Jesse's right—we can't leave Scout," I said, relieved to have made a decision.

"Hold on a moment," Bob said. "In the Otherlands, trains don't travel in the dark. You have plenty of time before it arrives in Estonia."

"Why doesn't the train travel at night?" Sara asked.

"Because of The-Things-That-Go-Bump-In-The-Night," Bob said, as if talking to children. He yawned and stretched. "Get some sleep. We won't travel at night, either. You should all take turns keeping watch, and we'll leave at first light." Bob curled into a ball, making a pillow with his hat. "Stay close to the fire, and you will be safe," he said, closing his eyes.

When it was my shift, Jesse woke me and then, just like

Bob, fell fast asleep. It was a moonless night, with a swirl of stars reflecting off the river. The only sound was the occasional snore and the water babbling against the rocks. The current was strong, unlike downriver. I sat alone with my thoughts and stared into the darkness until Bandit came to relieve me. But it soon became apparent I wouldn't be able to go back to sleep, so I decided I'd move closer to the river.

Mrs. S had suggested I meditate to cleanse negative energy by pulling positivity from the environment. The river was an excellent source of pure power. I hoped to refresh my reserves before we headed into the *big unknown*. So I removed my boots, waded out onto a flat rock, and focused on breathing. With my palm on my mother's amulet, I relaxed.

*Out with the bad—in with the good.*

I repeated the mantra, concentrating on drawing pure essence from the water. Each deep, calming breath eased the weight from my body, my eyelids softening as tension unraveled. A hiss sliced through the tranquility. And then a snarl. My eyes popped open, only to discover that I had been floating four feet off the ground. My reaction was to flail, and gravity did the rest. I hit the rock hard and struggled not to slide into the water.

Sara screamed.

I bolted, jumping the rocks to shore, only to come skidding to a stop. Sara stood by the river's edge, her eyes round and shiny in the moonlight. A giant octopus held her with a florescent green arm. Its single yellow eye darted as the *kraken* used its other arms to scoot backward into the river. It loosened its grip as it wobbled, giving Sara enough room to reach into her boot and pull out a knife. With a swift flick of the blade, she severed the slimy limb and spun from its grasp.

The wounded creature shrieked, retreating into the river while green slime oozed from its stump. It disappeared into the water with a splash. Then, with our jaws agape, the detached limb wormed back to the river and swam like an eel, hurrying to catch up with its body.

A large cat snarled. Bandit's hackles were raised, and he

positioned himself in front of Sara. A pack of feral cats with glowing red eyes crept from the shadows. Bandit rose on his hind legs and growled, baring a sharp set of teeth.

I sprang into action, leaping the rocks to get to Sara. But the beasts tucked their tails and ran at the sound of Bandit's war cry. When I reached Sara, she shook with sobs.

But then I realized she was laughing. "What's so funny?"

"Did you see those cats run from Bandit?"

I eyed her as if she were crazy. She hiccupped. "I put a magnification spell on Bandit. They fled from a giant snarling raccoon." Sara wiped her eyes. "But don't tell Bandit—he's so proud."

We returned to find Bob sitting by the campfire, unimpressed with our adventure. He promptly reminded us he had said to stay by the fire. And that we shouldn't have wandered off. About that time, Jesse woke up, wanting to know what he had missed. I winked at Sara, and she smiled when Bandit dove into a monologue of how he scared off some red-eyed scaredy-cats.

Once the danger had passed, I hotfooted it back to where I left my boots. Jesse called out to check for spiders, taking his advice, I tipped my boot, and a scorpion slid out. I yelped, jumping on top of a rock. Bandit, Sara, and Jesse came running.

"What's wrong?" Jesse asked, swiveling his head as if searching for monsters.

I pointed with a shaky hand at the scorpion, scurrying for cover. "That—that arachnid was in my boot."

"Well, they do that," Jesse said. "That's why I said to check."

Sara laughed. "A *kraken* and a pack of angry feral cats threaten us, and we hardly get a peep out of you. But a tiny scorpion taking a nap scares the heebie-jeebies out of you?"

"It wasn't so tiny," I grumbled, returning to the fire while my friends snickered behind me.

ΔΔΔ

The early morning sky had turned gray. Bob assured us the power of the night creatures waned at dawn. And that *The-Things-That-Go-Bump-In-The-Night* had retreated into nothingness well before sunrise. I cocked my head at the sudden realization. "Is that their real name?"

Bob looked at me quizzically and nodded. "Isn't that what I said?"

"So we're safe now? Is it okay to travel?"

"Not entirely, young wizard," Bob said, gesturing with his hands. "The Fae folk and the inhabitants of the Otherlands are a bartering society, trading on promises. The wanted poster will attract many unsavory characters."

"You heard about that?" I bit my lip.

Bob gave me a sideways look as if to say *who hasn't*. "You're not safe here with a bounty on your heads. It would be best to leave the Otherlands and return to your realm."

"Well, that's the thing. I have my obligations. I can't return to Castle Dragon without dragonroot or the Dragon Moonstone."

Bob nodded his understanding. "You can't escape the responsibilities of tomorrow by evading them today," he said, appearing unsurprised by the admission of the true nature of our quest.

"Maybe I can talk with the witch and explain our innocence," I said.

"Good luck with that," Bob said. "There's no negotiating with evil."

# CHAPTER 20

## *THE GROTTO WEEPS*

Bob guided us along the trails that crisscrossed the Malpais Plateau. The paths often came to what appeared to be dead-ends, but we ducked under overhangs or squeezed through gaps between sharp rocks and kept to a steady pace. Without his expertise, we would've had to check the globe and risked getting lost. Bob led confidently, keeping us on soft sand.

As we walked, my thoughts drifted to Lester and Nester. Bandit assured me the goats were clever, and with those corkscrew horns, they had the accessories to take care of themselves. But uncertainty gnawed at me, and I wished I could be sure.

A few hours later, Bob halted beside a sharp rock outcropping. "This is as far as I go," our gnome guide said.

The narrow cave loomed ahead, shrouded in a sinister foreboding. Its gaping mouth exposed jagged teeth as waves of frigid air rolled from the abyss. From the depths of the darkness, a moan, much like a death rattle, marked the cave's next breath.

"Crikey, what was that?" Bandit rocked on his heels.

"We call it the Grotto Weeps for a reason," Bob said, backing away from the palpable malice lurking at the entrance.

Sara bit her lip and rubbed the gooseflesh, dimpling her arms.

The thought of venturing into the dark churned my insides, and I shoved my clammy hands in my pockets.

"Bob, are you sure you won't come with us?" I asked.

The gnome shook his head. "No, nope, nada, no can do," he

said, adjusting his cap. "The last time I harvested dragonroot, I nearly lost my legs," Bob said as he paced, running his hand over his beard, glancing every so often to the mouth of the cave. "I swore I'd never return to this place."

I swallowed hard. "But that's why we need your help. You know the dangers better than anyone."

Jesse's leg bounced, betraying his nervous energy. "What are we looking for exactly?" he asked, as his eyes swung like a pendulum from the cave to the gnome and back again.

Bob stroked his beard, appearing relieved to change the subject. "Dragonroot is a mushroom with a blue cap and white stalk." He clasped his hands. "I'll keep watch, but I won't be going any further." His tone sounded final.

Then, having decided, he relaxed. He crossed his ankles and leaned back while Sara fumbled with a flashlight. Bob chuckled. "Those gadgets don't work in the Malpais. You'll have to rely on your own powers."

The cave seemed aware, almost taunting, daring anyone to trespass. I shuddered, attempting to dispel the unsettling notion. Gathering my thoughts, I contemplated how to persuade Thingamabob to change his mind.

"We need a guide," I said, giving Bob an intense stare.

In return, he gave me the cold shoulder, showing a sudden interest in his fingernails.

"You owe me."

As soon as the words slipped out, I wanted to shove them back in, but it was too late. The burden of the implication slammed down between us. Bob's eyes widened, and his mouth hung open, but then his expression changed, his eyes tightened, and his mouth drew into a thin line. Before us stood an angry gnome. I took an involuntary step back, embarrassed by my ingratitude.

Sara's whole body tensed, and a deep frown creased her forehead. "Noah, don't be a jerk." She pushed past me to sit beside Bob. "We aren't pressuring anyone to do more than they're comfortable with," Sara said, her voice compassionate and kind. "Bob, you've already been a tremendous help, and we appreciate what you've done for us."

"Bob, I'm sorry. I shouldn't have said that." Squatting on my haunches, I met the gnome's distressed eyes. "But I'm scared, in over my head, and desperate for your help." I swiped at my eyes. "Please."

He gnawed his lip and shifted his weight. "I'm not a coward."

I rocked back as if slapped. "Bob, I didn't say you were, and I don't believe it for a minute." I pushed the hair from my eyes. "Sara's right. I'm a jerk." I felt awful and didn't know where to put my hands. They felt heavy and clumsy when I stuffed them in my pockets.

"Little dude-man, we've got this covered." Jesse flashed a reassuring smile. "We'll be in and out, like the burger joint."

The tension broke when the gnome chuckled at Jesse's words.

With several deep breaths, I turned toward the cave, preparing to face my fear of creepy, confined, dark spaces. "Okay, let's go."

"Wait. I'm coming." Bob stepped forward. "You rescued me from the Parkers—and gnomes pay our debts."

Sara put her arm on his shoulder. "Friends don't keep score. You don't owe us. Noah helped you because it was the right thing to do."

Bob's cheeks tinged pink. "It was—my short legs—I wouldn't keep up."

"Dude, you can ride on Noah's back. He already walks like he carries the weight of the world," Jesse said, gesturing to me.

As I nodded, the cave interrupted with a low, mournful sound, akin to a woman sobbing.

"Crikey, if Bob's going, then I'm staying," Bandit said, leaping onto the saddle. Orion nickered, tossing his head agreeably.

"Sounds like an excellent plan. Someone should stay with the horses. We'll see you on the later." Jesse let out a nervous laugh.

Standing before the cave, Jesse rubbed his palms, conjuring a radiant lavender orb. Then, leading the way with the soft purple glow, we sidestepped the jagged teeth at the mouth of the cave and ventured into the belly of the beast. The sphere couldn't push back the inky blackness more than a step ahead. I tapped my staff, summoning light. The eye of the raven moonstone glowed. Still, the combined light couldn't fully penetrate the suffocating void.

The darkness pressed against my spirit. And to make matters worse, I couldn't shake the feeling of being watched by hundreds of eyes as we inched forward into the dank, crypt-like cave. The sticky air clung to the walls, making the passage slick. I stumbled and reached out, sliming my hands as they slid off the greasy walls. "It's still too dark—I just tripped on a stalactite," I said, wiping my hand on my pants.

"They're stalagmites," Jesse said. "Remember it this way—stalactites hang down from the *top,* and stalagmites rise up."

The glow against Jesse's profile cast an eerie shadow when he eyed me curiously. "Noah, you're sweating and awfully pale. What's the matter? Haven't you ever been spelunking? Exploring caves is an amazing adventure."

"I don't like dark, confined spaces," I said, hiding my trembling hands. "I'm fine—keep moving."

Jesse scrunched his face in concentration, and the light flickered. "I cannot make it any brighter."

Sara leaned closer and blew on the orb, and like a glowing dandelion in the wind, tiny fireflies of light scattered, shining into the cave's nooks and crannies like a thousand stars.

"Nice teamwork." Jesse bounced on his heels. "It makes this place sparkle like an underground utopia!"

"I wouldn't go that far," I protested.

With the darkness overpowered, we increased our pace, venturing deeper into the passageway.

"How much further?" Jesse asked.

I responded by rolling my eyes.

"The texture of the walls has changed," Sara said. "It's as if something drilled through the rock and created a smooth tunnel."

Jesse leaned in closer, inspecting the sides. "Are those tiny teeth marks?"

Sara released a nervous laugh.

"Not funny," I said through a clenched jaw.

"Just kidding, you make it too easy. Besides, dude, like, what would eat rocks?"

"We're not in Sweetwater anymore," I said. "The impossible is probable in the Otherlands."

Sara grabbed my arm, pulling me forward. "We should keep moving."

Silence fell. The cave wind had stopped. And irrational as it seemed, the quiet added to my anxiety. The sporadic moans had mentally anchored me to the exit. I strained to hear beyond our echoing footfalls, the stillness amplifying my fear. I wrestled with thoughts of retreat, but forced my wobbly legs to continue, resisting the urge to run.

The tunnel, shaped like a polished tube, glistened as it snaked through the ancient volcanic rock. At last, we arrived at a fork. Not knowing the direction, we pondered our choices until Bob gestured for us to keep to the left. He hadn't spoken since entering the cave. Jesse took a piece of chalk from his pack and marked our trail. With a few more tight twists and turns, the cramped space expanded into a massive chamber. Relief washed over me until a putrid stench punched me in my gut, making me gag.

"Get your gloves ready," Jesse said, covering his nose with his hand.

"Do you see any dragonroot?"

"No, but those piles look like the poop emojis, and from their smell, I'm guessing that's where you dig."

"Me?"

"Hey, this is your quest. We're here for moral support and the adventure." Jesse handed me a camp shovel, grinning like a fool.

I kicked at the mound with disgust.

"Get going. We don't have all day." Jesse chuckled, enjoying my discomfort.

"You guys could help."

"Nope," Sara said. "I distinctly remember Mrs. S saying you

had to dig deep. Besides, we need to keep watch."

"What for?" I asked as I broke the crust with my shovel.

"Dude, where do you suppose the dung piles came from?" Jesse's grin faltered. "Start digging," he said, his voice having lost its bravado.

We put aside all joking. I dug for mushrooms, and the others stood guard along the outer chamber. I tried to breathe through my mouth to keep the foul smell from burning my nose. All the while, I felt as if I were being watched. When I glanced over my shoulder, I half-expected to see something lurking in the shadows. The odd feeling fueled my motivation. I gripped the shovel and dug, faster and faster, pile after pile, until my hands blistered.

"This is useless, a waste of time." I stretched the kinks out. "Nothing's here."

"What's that?" Jesse asked, pointing at a white object.

I scraped the ground and uncovered the mushrooms. Jesse pulled the dragonroot from the manure pile. I had found the motherlode. We quickly stuffed the canvas bag, and Jesse slung it over his shoulder.

As I filled a second pouch, the hairs on my neck tap-danced. "Wh—what was that?"

Sara *sshhed* us, tilting her head to listen.

It sounded like gravel under tires and grew louder as it moved closer. The floor trembled before a thunderous crack reverberated in the chamber. Bits of rock spewed as something bored through the wall.

A red beetle emerged. Not a Volkswagen, mind you, but a dung beetle the size of a football.

"Time to leave!" Bob yelled, running one way and then the other, unsure of the best retreat as more red bugs appeared.

The beetles made a dull clicking sound with their antennae. When one noticed us, it opened its mouth and hissed through four rows of teeth. The mound we hid behind exploded, and we scattered as dozens of red beetles swarmed out of the floor.

"We can't go back! The beetles blocked the tunnel," I

stammered, my heart pounding like a war drum.

A beetle charged, and like a hockey stick, I delivered a powerful blow with my staff. The bug sailed across the floor and splattered against the wall.

"Over here," Sara's voice bounced off the chamber walls. It was as if she was everywhere but nowhere.

"Where are you?" Cold sweat beaded my temples.

Jesse released a purple flash. I scrambled, using my staff to knock beetles out of my way as I followed the light.

The insects spilled out of the rocks. It was a numbers game, and they vastly outnumbered us. They were backing us into a corner, boxing us in. Fear gripped me, my mind paralyzed by the futility. But then, a cry for help reached my ears, and I turned to my friends. "Find a way out—I'm going for Bob."

As I sprinted toward Bob, I could hear the panic in his voice. I channeled my concern for my friend into my staff. The carvings glowed with magic as I swept away the beetles. Sparks flew with every splat. Two beetles struggled to roll Bob into a side tunnel. But the gnome had wedged his boots into a crevice and had a tight grip above his head. "Oh no, you don't!" I swung my staff with all my might and sent the bugs sailing.

A huge scarab rose on its hind legs and snapped its jaws. I jabbed it with the end of my staff, piercing its underbelly. The beetle dangled, and with a mighty thrust, I flung the bug at a swarm, sending them scurrying for cover.

Bob lay limp, lifeless, as more clicking bugs poured out of the walls. I gasped for breath, my mind searching for answers. Jesse sent another beacon of light, yelling to get my attention. I scooped Bob up, tucked him under my arm, and ran. When I reached Jesse and Sara, we scrambled over rocks and climbed to higher ground. We stopped on a ledge where sunlight filtered through a gap in the ceiling, granting a full view of the chamber below.

"That's a lot of beetles," Jesse said between breaths. "I hope they can't fly."

I groaned, handing Bob over to Jesse. "Be ready to run if this goes bad."

Leaning over the edge, I pointed my staff at the thousands of dull black eyes and shouted, "*Pruina receptum!*"

The air crackled with a subzero blast. A moment later, a drizzle of frost trickled from the end of my wizard's staff. "Come on," I groaned at the feeble results and gripped my staff tighter, applying more pressure.

Sara placed her hand on my shoulder. "Wait for it."

And sure enough, the frost unfurled. The temperature plummeted. Ice formed, spreading on contact, freezing the first beetle, the next, and the next. The hoar frost gained momentum, rolling over the bugs and deep-freezing everything in its path.

Magic poured out of the staff, burning through my reserves. An electrifying rush ran up my arms and down my neck as I struggled to sever the connection. With a final effort, I wrenched my hand free, and my staff clattered to the floor. Drenched in sweat, my chest heaving, I slumped against the cold rock wall, utterly drained.

"Dude, that's so cool."

I pushed the damp curls from my eyes and fought the burning sensation of fatigue in my muscles. With effort, I pushed myself up, forcing the weariness aside. "We need to go! No telling how long the ice will last."

"This way," Sara said, clamoring over the jumble of rock.

Jesse carried Bob and kept pace. When we reached the gap where light beckoned, we squeezed through the crack.

The cramped space unfolded into an expansive dome-like room with a dizzyingly high ceiling. Positioned in the heart of the stone floor stood a black obelisk. A shaft of light landed on the beveled stone, refracting it into thousands of sparkling diamonds. Magic prickled as if the air held a charge. The cathedral-like atmosphere stole my breath, a sanctity difficult to define. I sensed an eerie familiarity and a spiritual connection to the cave.

Curiosity lured me forward, but caution slowed my steps as I approached the carved pillar. Etched into the obelisk was a message in a style similar to that of the hunger stone, but this time in English.

In the lair where the moonstone gleams,

My dearest sleeps in peaceful dreams.

Disturb her not, lest wrath shall rise,

With fury fierce, 'neath starlit skies.

Angry dragon, rivers dry,

Spreading havoc 'neath heavens high.

Wizard's kin soothes the beast,

With enchanted stone, discord cease.

Thieves, be warned, heed these words,

The dragon wakes if the stone disturbed.

Respect the treasure, let it be.

Or brave her wrath and misery.

"Check it out," came Jesse's voice. Still cradling an unconscious Bob, he pointed to a pile of grass and leaves. Remnants of sticks, twigs, and shiny trinkets were woven into what looked like a giant bird's nest.

Sara motioned to a dual set of boot prints in the fine dust. It was easy to imagine robbers sneaking past a sleeping dragon, snatching the Dragon Moonstone, and running away.

"Let's backtrack the footsteps," Sara said, her eyes curious and excited about the clue.

"Okay, *Nancy Drew*, lead the way," I said.

The footprints wound through one chamber after another, each room smaller than the other. The cavern shrank until my hair brushed against the ceiling. I hunched forward, headed toward the light that drew us closer to what I hoped was the exit. We hurried out of the confining space, slipped into an alcove, and waited for our eyes to adjust.

Outside the cave, sunshine shimmered off the black volcanic sand. In the distance, the majestic Tree of Apotheosis towered, its purple canopy basking in its grandeur. A shadow crossed the opening, and a screech shattered the silence. We ducked for cover. Finally, curiosity won, and we chanced a look-see.

Wrapped around its leg was a thick chain. A man snapped a whip. Sara gasped, and I tensed. But before we could make a plan, Jesse shoved Bob into my arms and stormed out of the cave.

"Stop that!" Jesse yelled, putting himself between Leo Parker and the dragon. With a defiant stance, he held his ground, fists clenched, his face flushed to match his fiery red hair.

"Hey, look who's here," Leo sneered as he rolled his bullwhip. "Where are your friends?"

"Leave him alone."

The young dragon spread its wings and pulled against his restraints, dwarfing Jesse.

Leo flipped the whip, emitting a mini sonic boom.

Jesse didn't flinch. "Don't, you're hurting him."

"The dragon needs to learn who's in charge," Leo said, rolling his whip.

Jesse moved forward. "Stay where you are, kid. Don't get any ideas." Leo snapped the whip at Jesse, kicking up a cloud of dust.

Jesse remained steadfast, trapped between the dragon and Leo.

"Where's your friend?"

"But it's only a youngster."

"The best age for training is before they've bonded and have learned to breathe fire."

"Let it go."

"Nope, mind your own business," Leo snarled, snapping the whip. "That was a warning. The next one will hurt worse. Answer my question."

Jesse sucked the back of his hand, ignoring Leo's demands.

Out of the blue, Max Parker jumped from behind a rock and grabbed Jesse, catching him unaware. Jesse struggled, but Max only twisted Jesse's arm further.

I began to lunge, but Sara stopped me. "The reinforcements have arrived," she whispered.

Dozens of angry gnomes with clubs charged out of the Malpais. In the mayhem, Jesse wrangled free, punching Max in the nose. Max dropped to his knees, screaming in pain. That gave the gnomes their advantage.

In the meantime, Leo used his bullwhip to fend off the gnomes.

Like Gulliver, Max lay helpless. With his feet and hands tied to wooden pegs, his desperate pleas for help fell on deaf ears.

Without a backward glance at his brother, Leo sidestepped onto a magic carpet and flew away, ending the skirmish.

Slumgullion smacked his club in his palm. "We meet again, young wizard."

"Bob's in trouble," I said cautiously, unsure if Stu was friend or foe.

"I expect so. When Thingamabob didn't return, we followed the tracks. We met up with Frankie, and he confessed. Well, not before we promised him a pair of boots." Stu grinned wickedly. "Later, we came upon Bandit, and he filled us in on the rest of the story."

Slumgullion didn't appear concerned when he spied Bob in my arms. He simply motioned for me to set Bob on the ground.

Thingamabob moaned. "Where am I?" he asked, raising a weary hand to his forehead. Then he bounded to his feet, and sporting a satisfied grin, he winked at Sara.

"Been playing possum, have you?" Stu said, grinning. "But I'm surprised you'd go anywhere near Grotto Weeps after the last time. I didn't think you were a beetles fan."

Bob took off his hat and bowed to his elder. Bob's head was as pointy as his cap, and there wasn't a lick of hair on his dome. "I couldn't leave the youngsters to have all the fun."

Stu and Bob both laughed while clutching their bellies. And

that's when the Fell Ponies rounded the bend.

Bandit jumped from the saddle, arching his tail. "Crikey, you stink like a pigpen."

The dragon pulled at its chain and whimpered. I walked toward the beast. "Easy now."

"Stop!" Stu said, his tone commanding. "What are you doing?"

"I know this dragon. I'm going to let it go."

"Not while we're here. Dragons consider gnomes a delicacy."

I looked at Stu to see if he was kidding. Stu's eyes were enormous, and his mouth drew a tight line.

"Right, no gnomes on the menu today." Jesse joked. Fortunately, the gnomes found Jesse amusing.

I turned my attention to the dragon. With a hungry gleam in its eye, it licked its lips while watching the gnomes. "Easy, Shadow Velvet."

The young dragon hopped closer, and with bright green eyes, it gave me a questioning stare. And that's when I realized it wasn't my dragon.

I stepped back and turned to Stu. "But I can't leave it chained." I motioned to the shackle.

"Of course not, but a few minutes longer won't matter," Stu said, scratching his beard. He looked at Bob, who nodded to some unspoken question. "You saved my nephew. It appears we gnomes owe you a debt of gratitude."

"Thank you, we—"

Jesse stepped forward, words tumbling out of his mouth, "The Parkers kidnapped Scout. She's on the train to Estonia."

Then Sara added, "We must bring dragonroot to Mrs. Shea at Castle Dragon."

"Any suggestions?" I said, smiling at the gnomes.

Stu pointed toward a split in the rock. "Follow the path through there, and it will lead you to a natural arch bridge. If you time it properly, you can hobo the train."

It took us only a few minutes to come up with a plan, which was a good thing because that's when we heard the distant whistle. Bandit would take the dragonroot and the ponies to

Castle Dragon, and we'd go after Scout. The plan had risks, but we had little choice. We wouldn't leave Goblin Valley without our fairy guide.

Soon, the gnomes bid us farewell. They had rigged a cart, with Max trussed up as their prisoner. Bob walked alongside Stu, no worse for wear, filling in the details of his brave adventure.

Sara and Jesse went on up the trail, and I stayed behind. One swift blow with my sword and the shackle broke apart.

"You're safe now," I told the green-eyed dragon. "My name is Noah. I hope I see you again under better circumstances."

The dragon nuzzled my sleeve with its velvety snout, purring softly as if to thank me for his rescue.

"Hurry, we can see the train," Sara yelled, her voice sounding far.

"Sorry, I have to go." I left the dragon at the mouth of the cave when I turned and ran to meet up with Sara and Jesse.

They stood before a natural rock bridge overlooking a deep ravine where part of the arch had broken, leaving a gap. "We'll have to jump," Jesse said as he looked at Sara. "Can you make it?"

"Just watch me." With a brilliant smile, she took off at a run and sailed over the opening. When Sara landed on the other side, pieces of rock broke, widening the breach. When it was Jesse's turn, he slipped and scrambled for footing, the ledge crumbling under his feet. Sara pulled him up by his arm. As they backed away, the entire bridge gave way with a thunderous crash.

When the dust cleared, we heard the sharp whistle, much louder this time. "I'll catch up." I waved them on.

"Are you sure?" Sara asked, her voice tinged with uncertainty.

"Yes, we must save Scout!

And with that, Jesse and Sara ran to catch a train while I circled back to hitch a ride on a dragon.

# CHAPTER 21

## *THE TREE OF APOTHEOSIS*

After retracing my steps to the cave, I gazed at the Tree of Apotheosis, towering in the distance. Its essence inexplicably called to me, and knowing I might not get another chance to see the tree up close, I made the short, brisk walk. Its twisted limbs sprawled, hosting a canopy of rippling purple leaves. The tree urged me closer, drawing me in.

I climbed its low-hanging branches until I reached a fork high enough to survey the valley. When I brushed against a cluster of figs, the ripe fruit dropped into my lap. I bit into the fig, and my senses went into overdrive. The sweet, intense flavor spread a pleasant warmth throughout my body, revitalizing my tired muscles and clearing my cluttered mind. An overwhelming sense of peace and joy filled me with renewed confidence and enthusiasm. My face erupted with an uninhibited smile, and I didn't hold back my spontaneous, ecstatic *whoop* that echoed across Goblin Valley.

"Let me out," *Mischief* called from deep within my pack.

I greeted the book like a long-lost friend. "Hey, long time no read. You're a bit dog-eared and long on the page count, but that adds character—if you ask me."

The book's face blinked to life, carrying a bemused expression. "Lad, what have you done?"

"Nothing much. I simply grasped its ancient, twisted limbs and hoisted myself up. Humbled before her wisdom. I breathed in her sweet perfume as leaves whispered tales of centuries past."

"Did you, by chance, eat any figs?"

"Yes, I detected notes of honey, brown sugar, and exotic florals in each bite."

"Why are you sitting in the Tree of Apotheosis indulging in forbidden fruit?"

"I came to contemplate and devise a strategy—Did you say forbidden fruit?"

"You're not dead, so never mind. Fill me in on what I missed, and Noah, stick to the facts."

It didn't take long to bring *Mischief* up to speed. I explained the urgency of catching the train. After asking the globe to locate Scout's SOS beacon, we determined the fastest route.

"There's a boulder blocking the tracks. It appears someone is buying us time," *Mischief* said, "but whom?"

"That would be who."

"Lad, I don't need a grammar lesson. Focus on clarity."

"My dear fellow, allow me to elucidate. I have gained abundant mental clarity from ingesting the fruit of the venerable Tree of Apotheosis. My intellect is prodigiously stimulated, and my faculties are remarkably sharpened. In brief, I have attained sagacious lucidity and an invaluable perspicacity. I am empowered, enlightened, and enthused by these gifts of mental endowment."

"You're fortunate it didn't kill you. The fruit is fickle, appearing at a whim. If it doesn't poison, then only a few receive its blessings."

"Interesting. Please elaborate."

"We don't have time for philosophical discussions. Keep it simple and use your old self to talk to me. I can't stand pretentious snobs," *Mischief* said.

Disappointed that I couldn't showcase more of my new and improved brain, I clutched *Mischief* and climbed down. As I reached a branch extending over the soft sand, I had a sudden burst of energy. With a wild cry, I executed a flawless backflip, landing with a flourish worthy of Bandit's praise.

"Why the acrobatics?" *Mischief* asked.

"Just having some fun," I said, motioning toward my backpack. "In or out?"

"Fresh air would be nice. Your pack stinks of dirty socks. Besides, I should keep an eye on you until the euphoria wears off."

"Okey-dokey," I said, securing *Mischief* in an outside pocket where he could see over the flap. "Let's go catch a train."

And so I took off running, pumping my arms to propel my body forward. My breathing settled into a steady rhythm, and my mind emptied of thoughts. I ran in a trance-like state, my feet eating up the ground.

A voice cut through my rhythmic cadence. "Noah, where are you going?"

In an instant, *Mischief's* inquiry snapped me back to reality. I turned in a circle, surveying the volcanic landscape. The terrain had become severe and inhospitable. The lava rippled with serrated edges, and steam hissed from fissures. A mountain loomed on the horizon, where smoke plumed skyward.

"There's Mount Drakon. We're definitely off course."

After checking the globe, I learned I had unknowingly taken a shortcut. Fortunately, cutting across the lava field would reach the train much quicker, even though it would be hard on my boots. The ground radiated heat from the ancient molten flow, venting sulfurous fumes. The expanse of onyx-hued rock crunched underfoot.

When a shrill whistle sounded, I pressed onward with renewed vigor. But as soon as I shifted my weight, the brittle lava splintered like glass. Before I could react, the bottom fell out. I plunged, spiraling helplessly into an abyss. The rocky walls blurred past with no hope of stopping my descent into the fathomless darkness. I screamed, but I couldn't hear my voice above the rush of wind. My mother's amulet vibrated against my chest. And to my surprise, wings swooped, and a magnificent dragon stared at me with curious golden eyes. It wasn't fear that gripped me, but relief. Shadow Velvet's timing was nothing short of a miracle. The dragon swooped beneath me, and I landed softly, scrambling for footing on his velveteen scales.

My heart surged with awe and gratitude for this amazing creature who saved my life, not once, but twice. I tightened my grip as Shadow Velvet soared, banking at breakneck speed and hugging the cliffs. As we flew along the jagged edges of lava, some patches were wafer thin.

"That was a close call, lad. Has the side effects of the fruit worn off yet?" *Mischief* asked, appearing unsurprised by riding on the back of a dragon.

"Leave it to a near-death experience to sober me up."

*Mischief* barked a laugh. "One adventure after another, you remind me of Ezra, a bold dragon whisperer himself."

I grinned and stroked my dragon's velvety neck. "Thank you, Shadow Velvet. You arrived in the nick of time. But quit showing off with these crazy maneuvers. It's time we caught a train."

ΔΔΔ

We flew over the Malpais badlands until the blackened earth gave way to lush rolling hills. The dragon's wings cast imposing shadows along the meadow, and the scent of apple blossoms filled the air. Pollen flooded my eyes and tickled my nose. A sneeze ripped out of me—a thunderous *achoo*! I reeled backward, windmilling, and Shadow Velvet instinctively adjusted, steadying me. I ran a shaky hand over my face.

When we spotted the locomotive, my dragon landed on a knoll, hidden from the men who were clearing boulders off the tracks. I motioned to Shadow Velvet to wait and belly-crawled along the grass, disturbing a nest of grasshoppers, and hoping my allergies wouldn't blow my cover. Determined, I crept forward for a better view of the scene below. When I was close enough to hear voices, I rested my chin on my arms and hid behind round tufts of prairie grass. I blew at a pesky fly and peered between the mounds.

A man in fancy Western attire yelled to get the train moving and that he had a schedule to keep. Oddly, his warbly voice sounded familiar, but I couldn't place him. I knew I hadn't seen him before. In that outfit, he'd be hard to miss.

Zeb Parker, a chicken bone in his mouth, complained as the dandy insisted on taking charge. Their argument heated up when Zeb bellowed, accusing the man he called Doc of cheating him out of his bounty.

While the two argued, I slipped through trees toward the passenger car. After scaling the ladder to the roof, I leaned over and peeked through the window. Sara's bright eyes grew round, and then she subtly signaled a single guard with her hand.

The train rumbled to life. I scrambled to the landing, pulling the release lever to uncouple the railcar, leaving it stranded on the tracks. I hoped surprise would be my advantage. With sword drawn, I swept in and swiftly sliced through Jesse and Sara's restraints. The guard had his nose in a book. When he finally noticed me, he sighed, set his paperback down, and didn't resist when Sara tied him up with enchanted knots.

Jesse's words spilled out in a chaotic retelling of their capture and our fairy guide's whereabouts. I grabbed his arm when he mentioned Scout's whereabouts and rushed to the door. At Sara's cry, I whipped around to see Zeb pressing her windpipe in a chokehold.

"Drop your weapon, or else!" Zeb hissed. He tightened his grip. "You heard me."

In a flash, Sara struck—an elbow to Zeb's nose, a knee to his groin. As he crumpled, she trussed him up with magic.

I waited until Sara was out of earshot and inspected the enchanted bindings. "That'll teach you to underestimate my girl," I said, strolling out of the coach car and throwing the lock.

ΔΔΔ

Jesse and Sara struggled with the boxcar door. It had a spring-loaded latch, and when I pulled up on it, the door slid open, revealing a jumbled mess of toppled crates and overflowing barrels. The interior reeked of stale magic and mildew as I stood bewildered at the cache of old toys.

Sara elbowed past me, toppling containers and calling for Scout. "I'm here!" came the muffled reply.

Sara climbed the rickety stacks and yanked a basket, discovering Scout locked in a birdcage. Jesse jumped with a yelp when he grabbed the door.

"The lock's enchanted," Scout said.

"You could've warned me," Jesse said, blowing on his singed fingers.

*Mischief* chimed in, "As if you'd listen."

Jesse laughed, noticing the harness I rigged for *Mischief* outside my pack.

"Open, says me," I commanded, and the lock fizzled.

Now free, the fairy buzzed the boxcar, jarring Sara on her makeshift staircase. I caught Sara by the waist as the pile collapsed, spinning her in circles. Sara's laughter filled the boxcar.

"Hey, settle down. I heard something," Jesse said, following the sound to reveal a toppled basket overflowing with dolls wrapped in burlap. One doll crawled forward, with chubby cheeks daubed cherry red, large expressive eyes, and yarn hair fashioned into braids. As Jesse snatched up the doll, her cloth limbs squirmed and kicked. "Let me go, you beast!" she screamed in a high little kid's voice.

"You're okay. I won't hurt you," Jesse said, holding the wiggling doll out in front of him.

I couldn't help but smile because my mom had a Cabbage Patch Kid from way back, packed away somewhere. They were goofy-looking dolls with *adoption papers* you could fill out when you bought them from the store. If my memory serves, Mom named her doll Melinda.

Suddenly, a snarling tangle of matted fur leaped out, latching onto Jesse's leg. Jesse kicked out, trying to shake the angry stuffed monkey loose. I pried it off, holding my breath as it stunk like a wet dog.

"Put the Cabbage Patch Kid down," Sara said, motioning to Jesse, "the monkey, too."

I shrugged and sat the cloth monkey on top of a box. The Cabbage Patch Doll hugged the monkey. "Chico, are you okay?"

The monkey jumped down, chittering as he aggressively threw a few air punches at Jesse. His chest and arms were marred with uneven stitches where he had once been mended. Although ragged, he had spunk, evidenced by his attempt to protect his Cabbage Patch friend.

The doll patted Chico's arm. "My brave monkey." Then she turned to Jesse with her hands on her hips. "And what's your problem?"

I smiled at Jesse's lack of words. His expression swung between annoyance and confusion. His mouth opened and closed, but nothing came out.

Scout fluttered her wings between them. "They're my friends—here to rescue us."

"Some rescue," the doll huffed, smoothing out her dress.

"What's your name?" Sara asked.

"Lily," the doll said guardedly. Sara smiled and introduced us.

Lily scratched her head. "How did you undo the sleeping spell?"

"Love," *Mischief* said from behind me.

Embarrassment burned my cheeks while I busily removed my pack.

"Love and laughter are potent forces that can disrupt magical enchantments. And in this case, gave the cast-offs the strength to break free from their spell-induced slumber," *Mischief* said.

"I'm not a cast-off—I was kidnapped." Lily stomped her foot and folded her arms, scrunching her face into a pout.

"But why take old warn-out toys?" Jesse asked.

Lily gasped, her mouth shaped in an O, with a look of outrage.

*Mischief* explained toys absorb a child's unconditional love. And that magic thieves covet such beloved possessions. But they can't wait long before they harvest the magic because love fades when forgotten. *Mischief* went on to say, "I don't want to get into the gory details, but it is an aggressive boiling down process to extract the raw essence."

"Yeah, no gory details," Jesse said, making a face.

Sensing an unusual presence. I asked *Mischief* if other cast-offs could be alive.

"Trust your instincts," he said.

And with that, a disorganized, free-for-all ensued. We rifled through the baskets of discarded toys, crates of trinkets, and boxes of arcane relics. As I dug into a corner, potent magic emanated from an old-fashioned tin canister. It fit squarely in my hand, and when I yanked the lid, it made a *Pfft* sound like opening a can of Pepsi. A sugary, sweet-scented fog wafted over the edges. A green crystal dragon peered back at me when the smoke cleared.

"The Dragon Moonstone," I said, shaking with excitement. My sense of urgency kicked in. "I got it! Grab your stuff. Let's go!" I leaned out of the train, pressed my fingers to my lips, and released a piercing whistle.

"What are you doing?" Sara asked.

"Calling for Shadow Velvet before it's too late."

Jesse pointed. "Too late."

Four horsemen rode up fast. The Doc Holliday doppelgänger tipped his hat in greeting. Reacting quickly, Jesse slammed the freight door.

Laughter erupted outside. "Thanks for making this easy," Doc said. With a *sizzle* and a *snap*, cold blue waves of magic sealed the boxcar.

I glowered at Jesse. "You really messed up this time."

"Sorry, dude."

"You react without thinking."

"Sounds familiar," he shot back.

Sara stepped between us. "Noah, that's unfair."

Frustrated, I waved my hands but got too close to the shimmering force field, and a *zap* of static crackled against my fingertips.

"Some rescue," Lily scoffed.

"Who asked you?" I snapped.

"Stop it, all of you. We're a team—remember." Sara said firmly. "Let's fix the blame, not the problem."

"It's the other way around," I said irritably.

"Whatever," Sara huffed. "You know what I mean."

When Jesse couldn't hold back his laugh, I offered my hand. "Sorry. I lost my temper."

"Dude, it was never lost—you've always had one!"

The train lurched as it picked up speed. Light streamed in through a broken board in the boxcar door. I tried wedging my staff to pry it loose, but I couldn't get close enough. The ward repelled my efforts like opposing magnets.

"If only we could fit through that hole," Sara said. "I'd like to gather intel on the Parker Gang and see if we can trip the lock."

Scout darted around the boxcar, sizing up the opening. I attempted to talk her out of it, knowing full well how ruthless the Parker Gang was, but she shot through the gap before I could make a convincing argument. She returned in a flash, collapsing to the floor, gasping for breath.

"What happened?" Jesse asked, dropping to his knees and leaning over Scout.

"Jeez, give her a moment," Lily said. "Can't you see she's exhausted?"

"Yeah, that's why I was asking," Jesse said impatiently.

Scout's words came out in bursts. She explained Doc and the Parker Gang had loaded their horses in the livestock car and had gathered in one of the passenger cars.

"Hey, this might work," Jesse said, pulling threads from the burlap packing material.

Together, we unraveled burlap and braided the strips to create a lengthy rope. Jesse asked Scout if she could thread the looped end through the gap and hook it to the latch. Scout admitted she wasn't strong enough to breach the ward again so soon. But she believed Chico might be immune to this type of magic because he wasn't Fae.

Eager to put Jesse's plan into action, Chico leaped through the gap in the door. After the third attempt, the boxcar door slid open. Cool air rushed in. Sara smiled, sweeping her hair out of her face. Blue static pulsated along the threshold as the security ward held. Chico swung by his tail from a side handle on the outside of the train, making happy monkey noises. Suddenly, Jesse hurled a barrel at the opening. As it crashed against the ward, it detonated in a shower of shrapnel. Lily screamed and dove for cover.

"Warn us next time," I said, brushing splinters off my duster.

"Sorry, dude, I thought I could short-circuit the force field."

I grumbled, but kept my temper in check.

"Water might work," Sara said. "If they were sloppy and didn't make the ward waterproof, water often nullifies magic."

"Does anyone know how to make it rain?" Jesse asked.

"Without drenching all of us, I'd have to think about it," I said.

A definite *splash* resounded when Chico lifted his leg and made water. The magical barrier *crackled* and then vanished. "Ew, Chico! That was disgusting!" Lily scolded.

Chico leaped through the door, chittering proudly. Seeing how Chico took care of business, Jesse laughed and gave him a high-five.

With the coast clear, we climbed onto the roof. Soon, we were all seated, watching the scenery roll by. Sara tucked Lily under her arm while Chico cuddled in close. Out of immediate danger, I reflected on the Dragon Moonstone and all we had been through to find it. I considered the ruthless Parker Gang and what they had done to my friends and, yes, even that brat, Lily.

"Noah, I've seen that gleam in your eye before—what are you scheming?" Sara asked.

"We can't let them win," I said as my mind spun with past events. "The Parker Gang needs to be taught a lesson."

"Revenge," Jesse said.

I shook my head. "Not revenge—justice."

# CHAPTER 22

## *DISGUISES AND DARING DEEDS*

The train rumbled down the tracks, billowing smoke. We huddled atop the swaying car, finalizing our plan to capture the Parker Gang and haul them to Castle Dragon to face justice.

"Are you sure about this?" Sara asked, tucking her hair behind her ear.

"It's our best option," I said, trying to sound convincing. Then, steeling myself for what came next, I gave the signal, and we dispersed, each taking our agreed-upon positions.

My heart hammered as I slipped into the caboose, bracing for a confrontation. The brown robe settled around me, its illusion masking my identity.

"Thought you could double-cross me?" I said in Howard's menacing, warbly voice.

Zeb bolted to attention. "Headless? But you were—"

"Gone for good? Not a chance." I loomed closer, the costume swirling. Improvising a script was risky, but I had to sell the act.

The eldest Parker shrank into the cushions. "Now hold on, this is all a misunderstanding—"

From my periphery, I glimpsed a shimmer as my friends closed in. I needed to keep Zeb distracted.

"Save it," I said, the costume's red Xs flaring.

Zeb raised his palms in a calm-down gesture. I glared and waited. Zeb's gangly frame crumpled, and his head lolled to the side. His eyes rolled back, and the chicken bone clattered to the floor.

"He's sound asleep," Jesse said, materializing beside me. "That sleeping potion sure works fast."

Silver threads wove around Zeb. When Sara finished the binding spell, she appeared. My eyebrows lifted as Lily and Chico emerged from Sara's invisibility shield.

"We didn't want to stay behind," Lily said, flipping a braid over her shoulder and lifting her chin.

"Fair enough," I said. "But we're on a tight timeline. We need to stop this train."

"What about the rest of the gang?" Jesse shifted his feet, his face tense with concern. "We only caught Zeb."

"We'll have to split up—You go with Scout and search the compartments while I handle the conductor."

Sara held my wrist. "Be careful, Noah."

I gave her hand a reassuring squeeze before turning to go. "When aren't I?"

Sara scoffed and punched my arm. "All the time, you doofus!"

ΔΔΔ

Howard's magical robe buoyed me over the gaps as I raced across the spine of the train. Up ahead loomed the engine compartment.

*No time for doubts.*

I charged through the door. "Stop the train!"

The conductor spun, his jowls quivering. "How dare you barge into my locomotive cab!" He glared at me, his eyes blazing.

I faltered, bewilderment dampening my bravado as I recognized him. *What's the mayor doing here?*

Before I could recover my wits, a warbly voice interjected. "I'll take the train hopper into my custody."

My blood turned to ice. I whipped around to find Doc Holliday smirking at me.

"You have no authority here," the conductor said. "I insist you return to your assigned seat.

Doc Holliday smiled coldly. "Not without him," Doc said,

reaching for my arm.

I ducked out of his way and pulled back my hood, revealing my face and dispelling the illusion.

Mayor Spychalla of Sweetwater, aka the conductor, froze, recognition dawning. "Noah Farmer? What in blazes are you doing on my train?"

I took a deep breath. "Mayor, this man is working with the Parker Gang to smuggle illegal cargo. You have to stop the train before we reach Estonia."

Doc Holliday bristled, his charming facade cracking. "Preposterous. Don't listen to this delusional young man."

I stood up straight and met the mayor's gaze. "He kidnapped my friends."

The mayor's eyes narrowed, scrutinizing us with razor-sharp focus. After a tense moment, he turned to Doc Holliday. "We can sort this out at the next stop. In the meantime, return to your seat."

Just then, Jesse and Sara materialized. "Noah's telling the truth, and we have the rest of the Parker Gang tied up in the dining car, along with a boxcar full of stolen relics to prove it!" Jesse said.

The mayor twisted his handlebar mustache, indecision etched on his forehead.

"But Mayor, we have the drag—"

*Ooof*!

I jabbed my elbow into Jesse, mouthing, "Need to know."

"Mister," came a child's voice. The Cabbage Patch Kid tugged on the mayor's striped jacket.

The mayor smiled. "And who are you, little one?" he softened his tone.

"My name is Lily, and bad guys took me from my person." The Cabbage Kid's eyes glistened as she continued. "And now they plan to take me to the magic rendering plant in Estonia." Her chin trembled. "But Sara and her friends saved me and Chico."

Chico squeaked and jumped onto the instrument panel. His monkey limbs danced over the controls.

"Get down from there!" Mayor Spychalla shouted.

Undeterred, the stuffed primate scampered across the maze of gauges and levers.

"Mayor, please stop the train," I begged.

But where Lily had softened the conductor's heart, Chico's antics had strengthened his resolve. "Impossible! I have a schedule." The mayor's voice grew sharper, and his patience was wearing thin. "Everyone out!"

Chico chattered, swinging on a lever with his tail.

"Don't touch that!"

The train jolted. A sudden darkness engulfed the cab. Chico screeched. Chaos erupted. Fingers clenched my collar, yanking me sideways. I jabbed with my elbow, striking a solid form. A pained grunt echoed through the blackness, followed by a muffled cry.

Moments later, sunlight flooded the locomotive as we emerged from the tunnel. A dazed Mayor Spychalla sprawled on the floor. Blinking, I whirled around, braced for another attack. But my assailant had vanished, and so had Sara. To my astonishment, Chico swung on the emergency brake, bringing the train to a jarring stop.

"Doc Holliday has Sara," I yelled. "Lily, look after the mayor. Jesse, let's go!" I jumped from the train and landed on a floating platform.

A sign with faded letters spelling out *Sweetwater* swayed in the cool breeze. There were no outbuildings, only a suspended boardwalk with an elaborate pergola guarded by a pair of gargoyles. A queasy feeling and fear clouded my thoughts as I tried to find my bearings.

Jesse bounded next to me. "Over there, reinforcements." He pointed.

Laying prone next to Zeb Parker was Doc Holliday. Ranger had his boot on Doc's back. Erik stood beside Ranger, dressed in his trademark white. I stepped off the boardwalk, sighing in relief to see Sara unharmed and talking animatedly. They were too far away to catch any words.

Then, to my shock, Sara threw her arms around Erik and planted a kiss on his cheek. My steps faltered. Heat flooded my neck, and my hands curled into fists. I burned with emotions I didn't recognize. At that moment, I wanted nothing more than to wipe the smug look off Erik's face.

Someone tackled me from behind. "Don't do it, dude," Jesse said. "Calm down. You have no reason to be jealous."

"Get off me," I said, spitting gravel.

"Not until you promise you won't do anything stupid."

"What are you talking about?" I said, struggling to squirm free, but Jesse had me pinned.

"Dude, I stopped you from making a mess of things. You're letting jealousy make decisions."

"I wasn't—"

"Noah, are you okay?" Sara called as she ran toward us.

"It was an accident. I tripped and knocked Noah down," Jesse said, bouncing to his feet and shooting me a stern, cautionary glare.

I feigned a smile, gripped Jesse's extended hand, and let him pull me up.

Sara grabbed me in a hug.

"I'm glad you're safe," I whispered, hugging her tightly.

Sara stepped back. "I was so scared when Doc Holliday dragged me from the train. But then suddenly, Erik and Ranger appeared, and when Doc made a run for it, Erik lassoed him with magic." She pointed at the wardens as they strolled forward. "Erik saved me."

My smile dropped like a rock.

"I saved you, too," Ranger said, offering Sara a confident smile.

"Thank you," Sara said, giving Ranger a quick peck on the cheek.

I scoffed.

*He makes it seem so easy.*

Ranger's sunglasses hid his eyes, but his smirk taunted me.

"Hey, where's mine?" I said, faking a cocky grin.

Sara responded with a sharp jab to my arm.

"Ow! What was that for?"

Sara rolled her eyes.

"How did you find us?" Jesse asked.

"The Grimm Goats returned to the castle and alerted us," Ranger said, placing his hands on his hips. "I had a rough time tracking you. I lost your trail when you left the cobblestones. Eventually, I met up with Bandit and the Fell Ponies, who filled me in on the details. I escorted them the rest of the way to Castle Dragon."

My shoulders relaxed, learning that the supply of dragonroot had made it into Mrs. S's hands. Ranger clarified that Mrs. Shea promptly revived Erik once she concocted the cure. And even though Mrs. Shea advised against it, Erik insisted on coming along.

I tipped my chin. "I see you've thawed out."

Erik sneezed, folded his arms, and shot daggers with his eyes.

"Bandit returned to Castle Dragon just in time," Ranger said.

Erik trumpeted into a handkerchief.

"That's some cold," Jesse said.

"He's much better now that he's defrosted. Lost his voice, but some say it's an upgrade." Ranger nudged Erik, barking a laugh. Sara's giggle tinkled like wind chimes. "You should have seen him when he was a human-popsicle. Oh, that's right, you did!"

Jesse snorted.

Erik's eyes held me in the crosshairs of his anger.

I took a sharp inhale and avoided Erik's glare. *Obviously, you don't have to be big to carry a grudge.*

"Excuse me, mister." Lily tugged on Ranger's duster. "The conductor gentleman could use some help." She gestured toward the platform, where Mayor Spychalla sat with a bandage wrapped around his forehead.

We hurried to check on the mayor.

"All's well that ends well," the mayor said, working his way into a bowlegged stance. He patted Chico on the head. "Your little friend here administered excellent first aid." Chico hooted and danced at the praise.

"I helped, too," Lily added.

"You sure did, little darling. An excellent job at that."

I smiled, remembering *excellent* was the mayor's go-to word.

"What are you doing here?" Sara asked.

"I could ask you the same thing," Mayor Spychalla responded. "Why don't we take a seat and sort things out?"

Doc Holliday and Zeb Parker sat on a side bench secured by handcuffs. I absentmindedly rubbed my wrists, recalling the feel of Erik's cuffs. Zeb pouted while Doc Holliday seemed amused.

Jesse shuddered, staring at the menacing gargoyles on each end of the platform. I smirked as he rubbed the gooseflesh from his arms. The mayor asked me to bring him up to date, so I recounted our run-in with the Parkers and how the witches of Estonia had it in for us.

When I mentioned Doc Holliday, Ranger shot me a quizzical glance. "Doc Holliday?"

"Oh, that's what we call him," Jesse said. "He's decked out like a gunslinger in the Old West.

Ranger tipped his chin toward Doc. "That man is the notorious criminal mastermind, Duncan Sinclair, aka *The Pretender*, *Headless Howard*, and now *Doc Holliday*.

"Doc Holliday is Headless Howard," Jesse repeated, his mouth hung open in surprise.

"The infamous Duncan Sinclair is a master of illusions." Ranger adjusted his aviators. "He's a cunning mercenary who will work magic for the highest bidder. The Parkers are two-bit peddlers who sometimes traffic in questionable transactions." Ranger acknowledged the oldest brother. "It's been a while, Zeb."

Zeb's mouth quirked into a half smile. "Howdy. How's that mare I sold you?"

"You know horse flesh, that's for sure—she's a fine animal. The Mayor's been after me to sell her for some time now."

"Wait—you guys are friends?" I folded my arms in disbelief.

"Friends—no. Zeb's a shyster and not an okay guy," Ranger said. "I might've bought a horse or two from him, but I always make sure I get proper papers."

I cast a glance at Zeb, who held a crooked smile.

Ranger crossed his arms. "Zeb, I'm surprised to see you mixed up with the likes of Duncan Sinclair. This man's a different cut of meat—a dangerous predator." Ranger shifted his attention to us. "If I had known Duncan was involved, I wouldn't have stayed so long at The Tower of Song. But the festival was in full swing, and the provost told a convincing story."

"Provost Flowers was in on it," Sara said, stamping her foot in annoyance.

Ranger grunted and then explained that he'd take Doc Holliday to answer to the Warden's Council and see that he receives a speedy trial.

"As for Zeb and the stolen artifacts, I trust Erik can handle that aspect of the caper," Ranger said, looking at Erik. "Deliver the Parker Gang to Castle Dragon and let Wizard Dragon deal with them."

Erik gave a firm nod. He had a chalky complexion with no color to his cheeks.

I realized I had no idea how law and order worked in the Otherlands. But before I could ask about the Warden's Council, Ranger gripped my shoulder, and magical muscle radiated, catching me off guard. "You showed real mettle. Well done."

Then Ranger grabbed Duncan Sinclair-Doc Holliday—or whoever he was—by the collar, lifting him off his feet, and stepped off the rear of the platform. There was a crackle of energy and a loud *pop* as they vanished into thin air.

Erik put a handkerchief to his nose, and a comical car horn-like sound escaped. *AROOOGAA!*

My friends stood beside me, their faces radiating the joy of our achievement. We had been through so much already, proving we could tackle any challenge as a team. Mrs. Shea had received the dragonroot in time to save her garden and Erik. We had also captured the Parker Gang. I grinned at a gargoyle, unable to resist, sending it a triumphant wink. My eyes widened when it returned the gesture.

"So, Mayor, what brings you here?" Jesse asked.

"Oh, just helping a friend. I drive this route now and then. Fortunately, I agreed to fill in today. Casey Jones doesn't cotton to such shenanigans. He would've tossed all of you off, without a doubt."

"Does this train stop at Castle Dragon?" Sara asked sweetly.

"It does if I say so." The mayor adjusted his conductor's jacket and gave her a sly smile.

"Would you take us?"

"Of course, dear, what an excellent idea."

The Mayor shifted his gaze toward the gargoyles and cleared his throat. "Come on—If we hurry, we can make it in time for dinner."

The number of gargoyles had grown. One menacing statue—a prehistoric cat with curved fangs had fixed its empty eyes on me. The tiny hairs on the back of my neck quivered. My excitement faded as my sense of foreboding grew.

I knew in a flash that this adventure was far from over. I hurried to catch up with Mayor Spychalla and the others as they strode purposefully toward the train.

# CHAPTER 23

## *TROUBLE ON THE TRACKS*

When we arrived at the train, we met up with Scout. She informed us that Duncan Sinclair had only freed Zeb, leaving the rest of the Parker Gang tied up in the dining car and that she had been standing guard. Scout then confided a worried pang of guilt about venturing beyond The Tower of Song without permission. She said it was time she went home and faced the consequences, having had enough of trains for a while. We bid the tiny fairy a swift farewell, and the little fairy disappeared in the blink of an eye.

Sara sweet-talked Mayor Spychalla into letting us ride up front. The mayor agreed but, given Chico's past behavior, refused to allow the little monkey into his locomotive cab. Since Erik would guard the prisoners, Lily and a sulking Chico followed him to the dining car. Jesse crowded into the forward cab with Sara and me.

"Noah, I want you to keep a hold of this lever. When I give you the signal, move it down a notch. You're the engineer today," Mayor Spychalla said.

A goofy grin spread across my face. I gazed in awe at the intricate machinery—rows of polished brass gauges, steam hissing from ancient pistons, and the maze of pipes. I almost laughed aloud, scarcely believing I was about to bring this powerful locomotive to life.

"Jesse and Sara, there's a jump seat on either side. Strap in," the mayor said.

Jesse clicked the strap across his chest, his eyes flashing with excitement.

The mayor leaned out the window, waving his arm. "All aboard!"

I stifled an eye-roll—after all, we were the only passengers. Still, experience told me the mayor insisted on protocol.

"I didn't know you were a wizard," Jesse said. "I thought you were just the mayor."

The mayor twisted his mustache. "Just the mayor? Son, we are all more than *just* one thing. Magic abounds in Sweetwater, and our talents come in many shades."

"Sorry, that didn't come out right. It's just that people keep surprising us."

"Better to be surprised than disappointed." The mayor reached past my shoulder and pressed *start*. The train's engine chugged, setting us in motion. "Engineer, give us some power."

With a bemused expression, the mayor waited until I grasped he meant me. When I touched the lever, my hand tingled. I jerked in surprise, but the mayor cautioned me not to let go and break the connection once the train started rolling. He explained I should move the handle down a half-tic whenever he asked for speed.

I bit my lip, feeling the weight of the sudden responsibility. I didn't want to let the mayor down.

"And when you're on my train, address me as conductor."

"Yes, sir, conductor, sir." Ignoring the unusual pinch of magic, I slid the lever to the next notch, and the engine rumbled. We rolled along the rails, crossing a flat prairie at a steady clip.

Conductor Spychalla whipped out a thin stick from his sleeve that I assumed was a magic wand, waving it to the rhythm of a symphony only he could hear. Soon, he called for another notch of speed.

The cab rattled as the train sped up. A metallic screech echoed, resembling pulling nails as the railway ripped from the ground. My white-knuckled grip didn't falter as confusion took over. "The tracks are pulling out of the ground," I said, blinking in disbelief. The tracks repositioned themselves, forming a sweeping arc in time for the train's advance.

"I'm altering the route, laying the tracks as we progress," the conductor said.

"But they aren't connected to anything, only empty air."

The conductor looked at me as if I were five years old, questioning why the sky was blue. "The fastest route back to Castle Dragon is as the dragon flies, hence the rerouting." His wand swayed as if directing an orchestra while the train rattled along the dynamic railroad.

"This is like a roller coaster," Jesse said, laughing.

"Do you enjoy rollercoasters?" the conductor asked over the rumbling train.

"Yes," Jesse and Sara said in harmony.

The conductor smiled. "Do you want to have some fun?"

Jesse's eyes widened, along with his smile, as he bobbed his head. "I've got a need for speed."

"Engineer, more power."

I pulled the lever, and the train surged forward. Amidst the rush of air pushing against my face, the tracks corkscrewed. Sara's death grip on the jump seat handle and her bright eyes, widened my grin.

*Bang!*

The locomotive rocked when something hard smacked against it. A crack splintered across the front window. I reeled, straining to comprehend the impossibility. Dozens of stone gargoyles pelted the train, smashing into the sides, clawing and biting to grab hold.

"The gargoyles are coming. The gargoyles are coming," Jesse yelled over the racket, raking his hand through his hair.

With the agility of a much younger man, the conductor dropped-kicked a gargoyle out of the broken window. The beast shrieked as it fell.

"This animation spell is over my pay grade. The witches of Estonia must really want you," the conductor said. His eyebrows shot up when an exceptionally resourceful beast wrestled with the tracks.

"More power!" Conductor Spychalla yelled.

I seized the handle with both hands. The train rocketed forward, and the force lifted me off my feet. The conductor had looped his boots through a bar and remained steadfast and upright. We flipped, twisted, and turned, flying along the tracks more like a spaceship than a train.

"This is better than Six Flags!" Jesse whooped over the noise.

*Typical—only Jesse would call riding a roller-coastering bullet train while being chased by monsters, fun. Meanwhile, it's all I can do to keep from tossing my cookies.*

The train spiraled through the atmosphere. It seemed like forever, but soon we outran the onslaught of reanimated gargoyles.

"Whew, that was a close call," the conductor said.

The tracks leveled out, and the train sped along, blurring the landscape.

"Uh, Engineer, give me more power."

"I can't. It's jammed."

"I need warp speed now, or we're in trouble." The conductor's voice had lost its whimsical tone.

*What could be worse than a horde of maniac gargoyles?*

The answer loomed in front of us in the form of a mountain. We were headed for a granite wall with a thunderous waterfall cascading over the edge.

The conductor's eyes glazed over as he waved his wand in a vigorous figure-eight motion. The tracks reassembled themselves and shot straight up.

I fought to move the lever. My arms strained, but the handle wouldn't budge. I used my legs and pushed against the wall for leverage. Sweat rolled off my temples.

"Noah, if you have any magical reserves, we need everything you've got, or this will be our last train ride," the conductor said. His use of my name spoke volumes.

I concentrated on drawing on the energy of the waterfall. My mother's amulet vibrated against my chest, and I connected with the water's essence. The charm grew warm, and a surge of strength rippled through my body. With a fierce yank, the lever moved the last four notches to full speed ahead. The train pitched, hugging the rails at a vertical angle. Air rushed through the cabin with so much force I couldn't turn my head. I managed a sideways glimpse at the conductor. He focused solely on moving his wand and humming a strange tune.

The train kept to its tracks, pulling the string of boxcars up and over the waterfall. Without warning, we lunged and flew down the rails at a steep angle.

"Pull back, too fast, pull back."

What I had thought was fast before we now raced beyond what I could describe. I pulled on the lever, clicking at each backward notch. We left the red and entered yellow on the speed gauge.

"Slow down," he yelled.

Drenched with sweat, I strained to pull the lever back. My muscles screamed in protest. The train showed no sign of reducing speed. We rocketed down the rails and plunged into a gray cloud, engulfing the cab with smoke.

"Hit the brakes," the mayor yelled. "I can't see in this soup."

The fog reeked of a putrid swamp. The stench clawed at my nostrils, burning my lungs and stinging my eyes. I frantically looked for the brake, but it was too dark to see.

*Note to self: Know where the brakes are BEFORE driving a magical train!*

"Where's the brake?" I shouted. The dense smoke filled the cabin, and I couldn't distinguish one lever from the next.

"Over there," the conductor motioned in a vague direction while blindly setting the tracks one section at a time.

Jesse leaped from his seat, grabbed hold of a handle, and yanked. The brakes smoked and squealed. The biting stench of burned steel mixed with the already foul odor of the fog.

A massive explosion jolted the train, throwing us around like rag dolls. We somersaulted, boxcars colliding in an agonizing cacophony. The roof peeled back like a tin can. I lost my grip, and the impact ejected me through the opening. The last thing I heard was a scream that I recognized as my own.

When I opened my eyes, acrid smoke filled my nose and burned my throat. My ears rang. I pushed myself to my knees. "Sara?" I coughed. "Jesse?"

I crawled over the sand toward the black smoke. Below me, hot, twisted metal. Nausea made my knees weak. My palms stung from where I hit the sand, but the wards woven through my duster cushioned my landing. I gathered my strength and stood, relying on my staff for support.

The boxcars were scattered helter-skelter across a rocky canyon. I skidded down the embankment, calling for my friends. The wreckage was complete. No car remained unscathed. The derailment was a jumble of boxcars stacked and twisted atop one another. Green liquid spilled from overturned containers. A pungent chemical smell assaulted my nose as I yelled for my friends.

"Here," a faint voice called behind an overturned boxcar. I clambered over the smoldering wreckage to find Jesse pinned, face ashen and beaded with sweat. He gritted his teeth against the pain.

"I've got you. Hang on." I heaved with everything I had. The beam shifted slightly, but enough for Jesse to haul himself out. Battered but unbroken, Jesse slung an arm over my shoulder.

We limped onward, searching for our friends. Sara's voice rang out as she waved both arms from the far side of the ravine. Lily stood beside her, with Chico clinging to the little doll's hand. Mayor Spychalla, spry on his feet for a bowlegged cowboy, scrambled up the draw toward them.

A sudden flash and a series of boxcars exploded, sending shrapnel flying in all directions. The blast knocked Jesse and me to the ground. I hit the sandy embankment and rolled, instinctively covering my head. After a few minutes, the fire burned itself out.

A loud snarl echoed across the wreckage. I propped on my forearms as an enormous cat jumped onto a toppled freight car. This was no ordinary fat house cat. The beast resembled a prehistoric saber-toothed tiger. It had perked ears and curved fangs and sat with its tail wrapped around its hindquarters. Pitch black with lavender eyes, the animal remained motionless, staring across the divide.

I nudged Jesse and motioned toward the giant cat. Jesse flinched, but I cautioned him to stay down. We didn't move, both of us too scared to breathe. Mayor Spychalla's deep voice sounded across the canyon, calling for me and Jesse. The cat arched its back and hissed.

I jumped to my feet. "I'm over here," I yelled, waving my arms to attract attention.

Mayor Spychalla yelled, pointing up the mountain. "Head for Castle Dragon."

I looked at Jesse. "Can you run?"

"Always," he said with a grin, springing to his feet.

"Get to Sara and see her safely to the castle." I pointed to the black saber-tooth monster. "I'll distract the cat."

Jesse met my gaze, hesitation clouding his face.

"Wait for my signal," I said, running toward the opposite hillside and away from Jesse.

The cat snarled and paced, agitated by the smoke and commotion. It jumped from one overturned boxcar to another.

I reached a cluster of boulders and clambered to the top. Before grabbing my slingshot, I scooped up a handful of rocks. "Here, kitty, kitty."

The cat turned his lavender eyes on me. I whistled, and Jesse jackrabbited, scrambling across the wreckage toward Sara. My first shot hit the cat on the behind. It yelped and spun as I ducked behind a boulder. I waited. When I braved a peek, *Saber-Tooth* was gone.

I crept from my hideout and ventured to the edge with cautious steps. Green, steaming liquid spilled from the wreckage, creating a small river. As I squinted to make out what was swimming in the pool, a hot breath reached my neck.

A fierce *meow*.

I turned my head slowly and peered at the enormous cat with its maw opened wide. Its gums were black, and its teeth yellow.

Cornered between the smirking cat and the rocky ledge, I couldn't help but think I was Jerry in the old cartoon *Tom and Jerry*. I raised my hands, my voice shaking, "Easy there, good kitty. Nice *Saber-Tooth*," I offered it my cheesy grin.

Its eyes twinkled as it swatted me with its paw. I fought to keep my feet under me, but ultimately lost the battle. I tucked and rolled, coming to a stop before the scattered wreckage. Boxes had split open, their contents soaking in a bubbling green liquid. The air was thick with the sulfurous odor of rotten eggs. I sidestepped the goo and placed my foot next to a three-toe footprint. The prints in the sand looked like arrows and pointed in the direction that Jesse had run.

*Cluck-cluck.*

I whipped my head around. A giant prehistoric rooster with laced wings and a long tail feather faced off against *Saber-Tooth*. Sure, you might think, no contest. But this chicken towered over the cat. It had a red comb resembling horns and a massive beak. The rooster crowed, and the cat backed up, hissing.

I stilled my urge to run, fearing it might provoke both creatures to join forces and chase me. My heart raced. I desperately searched with my eyes for a place to hide. With precise steps, I slipped away toward the trees.

*Saber-Tooth* snarled, and the rooster responded with an impressive *cock-a-doodle-doo*. It was a standoff until suddenly, the cat leaped at the rooster, who jumped into the air and slashed with its razor claws. I grabbed a branch and climbed until I was far above the fight.

*Wonder-Chicke*n fought like it was demon-possessed. *Saber-Tooth* tried biting the chicken's neck, but its fangs were more of a hindrance than a help. The rooster kicked with both feet and struck the cat, launching it backward. It landed on its feet as felines are apt to do. But then *Saber-Tooth* spun and ran into the forest.

*Wonder-Chicke*n strutted, clucked, and pecked at the tiny

creatures crawling from the ectoplasmic puddle. From my hidden perch, I sucked in a breath at the realization. A crate had been filled with plastic dinosaurs, and the green liquid pooling around the boxcars was re-animating toys into monsters. The rooster ate the tadpole-like creatures as fast as they emerged.

The sun hung low in the skyline as I left the chicken to its dinner. With as much stealth as possible, I slipped out of the tree. A brisk wind stirred the trees. It would be a chilly night, and I didn't want to spend it in the forest. So, as quietly as I could, I slipped through the trees. Once out of sight of *Wonder-Chicken*, I took off running toward what I hoped was Castle Dragon.

The hill was steep. I trudged into the late afternoon sun and soon arrived at a field of sunflowers. Castle Dragon's outer wall stood proudly in the distance. As I weaved through the stalks, a shadow crossed my path from overhead. Then, something coiled around my waist, lifting me off the ground. Panic churned in my stomach. I thrashed, trying to break free. But I was headed skyward rapidly, and my fear of falling outweighed my fear of flying. I dangled at an odd angle and couldn't glimpse what new beast had ahold of me. At that moment, screaming seemed my only viable option.

"Don't be such a baby. Grab the rope."

I craned my neck and spied Sara, wearing a mischievous smile, standing at the reins of a golden chariot. As the tingle of magic brushed against my senses, I grappled for the rope. The magic lifeline worked like a pulley system, helping me climb. Hand over hand, I pulled myself up. Finally, I reached the carriage, threw my leg over the rail, and flopped aboard. Chico hooted, scratching under his arm.

Lily greeted me with a gap-toothed grin and apple cheeks. "There you are. We've been looking all over."

I would've preferred to remain on my hands and knees until my pounding heart calmed. But Sara's smile anchored me, and I stood up and donned a brave face.

"Hi," I said and offered a sheepish grin.

"That's all you have to say after we saved your life?" Lily said.

"You didn't save my life. You almost killed me." I ran my hand through my hair and looked at my saviors. They were staring at me with an expectant look.

"Is everyone okay?" I asked.

Sara smiled and pushed back her hair. "Yes, Jesse stayed with Erik to give a full report to Mrs. S, and Mayor Spychalla has already returned to Sweetwater. But I don't know what happened to the Parker Gang."

Standing beside Sara in the golden chariot, Castle Dragon appeared further away. "Where are we headed?" I asked, confused by the change in direction.

"Thought we could survey the wreckage," Sara said, her eyes sparkling with curiosity.

Our flight path formed a wide arc as we circled the crash site. Lily held onto Chico, whose tail wound around the railing. The Cabbage Patch Kid leaned into the wind—her yarn braids sailing away from her head. Lily whistled. "What a mess." She pointed to a freight car that had been ripped in half. "Look, that's the car we were in." Burned remnants were strewn and smashed.

"What's that green stuff?" Sara asked.

"Condensed magic residue," Lily said. "It's what *Mischief* talked about. But instead of boiling the magic, extreme heat burns off the organics. What's left is the poisonous ectoplasmic material."

"When did you get so smart?" I teased.

Lily huffed in response.

"The spill will contaminate the environment," Sara said. "Who knows what could happen?"

"I know," I said, pointing to the gigantic rooster.

"Is that a chicken?" Sara asked.

"Chicken—rooster, tomato—tom-ay-toe." I gestured with my hands. "But I named it *Wonder-Chicken*."

"Of course you did," Sara said with a chuckle.

"Hey, it tussled with *Saber-Tooth* and emerged the victor."

That's when we heard the snarl. The giant cat had returned, seeking revenge.

Sara snapped the reigns, and Orion climbed higher, continuing our tour of the surrounding crash site.

"How do we contain the spill?" Sara asked, wiping the hair from her eyes.

I shrugged ignorance and retrieved *Mischief*, but the book didn't respond, and his pages remained blank.

"Oh, come on, not again," I grumbled.

"It's like he expects you to know the answer," Lily said.

I glanced at Sara and tilted my head. "Let's think this through."

Sara chewed on her lower lip, her brain working overtime. "How do we counteract magic?" she asked, a sense of urgency tightening her voice.

"Water." Sara and I said at the same time, the solution sparking between us. Mrs. S taught us that water was the great neutralizer. With enough water, it could dissolve the ectoplasmic magical residue.

Orion soared above the wreckage while I closed my eyes and focused on absorbing the surrounding energy. My amulet pulsated as I commanded rain with the same spell I used to extinguish Frankie's campfire. A single cumulus materialized, gradually darkening its underbelly.

Sara joined in the effort. A subtle motion of her hand wove a delicate thread. One end fastened to the cloud, and the other she deftly tied to the chariot. The cloud floated skyward, tugging on its shimmering tether. With careful aim, I launch a stone from my slingshot. The cloud sprung a leak and drifted in Orion's wake. We flew over the wreckage, sprinkling the derailment as we passed.

*Wonder-Chicken* strutted out from behind a boxcar, with Zeb Parker dangling from his beak. Zeb struggled to squirm free. Careful not to fly too close, we directed the rain toward the rooster, hoping to neutralize the mutant magic. Water and magic usually don't mix, and when the rain showered the chicken, it squawked in protest, dropping Zeb. He hit the ground running. The lanky man sprinted for the trees where the rest of his gang huddled, appearing no worse for wear.

"We need more pressure. At this rate, it'll take all night," Sara said.

The rain cloud tugged against the wind like a kite. I lifted my staff and commanded more rain. The cloud doubled in size and let loose a deluge. *Wonder-Chicken* flapped its wings, which only quickened the results. With a final *cock-a-doodle-doo,* the mighty rooster dissolved into a pile of wet ash.

We kept the water flowing, diluting the green ectoplasm, until only ashes remained. There was a sizzle like water on grease, and before we knew it, the train and its tracks melted away.

"We've gone too far," Sara said. "The rain destroyed all the arcane artifacts. The Dragon Moonstone—it's gone." Tears threatened, and she wiped them away. "What about the imbalance the hunger stone warned about?"

"Sara, stop. It's not a problem."

"Not a problem? Of course, it's a problem! The Dragon Moonstone anchors the Otherlands. Without it, we won't restore balance." Sara wrung her hands. "We saw the river. The drought has already begun."

"Don't worry—I got this."

"Oh, really?" She arched an eyebrow, her tone laced with sarcasm. "You got this?"

I grabbed the canister from my pack and opened it, showing Sara the crystal.

"You had the Dragon Moonstone in your pack—all this time?"

"Yes, I couldn't risk losing it to chance."

"That's awesome." She hugged me, then pushed me. Scowling. "Why'd you let me go on about not having the Dragon Moonstone? Why didn't you tell me?"

"It's hard to interrupt when you're on one of your tirades. Besides, you're cute when you're mad."

"Cute?" She stamped her foot. "There's nothing attractive about being mad." Sara's cheeks flushed. Wisps of hair framed her high cheekbones, and her lips formed into a pout.

"If you say so," I said, offering her my brightest smile.

"Humph!"

The sun slipped below the horizon, and a silvery blue moon took its place. The air held an icy nip, and Sara shivered.

"We better head back," I said. "One thing for sure, we shouldn't be out after dark."

# CHAPTER 24

## *THE WITCH'S ULTIMATUM*

Chico's incessant monkey chatter woke me. Still half asleep, I shuffled into the dining room, a blanket wrapped around my shoulders.

"Erik lit a fire. It should warm up soon," Sara said, glimpsing my discomfort. When I nodded to Erik in thanks, he turned away.

Jesse's eyes were fixed on the window, his breath fogging the glass. Bandit lifted Lily, the Cabbage Patch Kid, so she could see. Chico chittered, tugging his tail, unsettled by Lily's lack of attention.

Shivering, I pulled my wrap tighter. The rich aroma of coffee lured me into the kitchen, where I poured myself a steaming mug before joining the group. Outside, the trees bowed, weighed down by a foot of blue snow, sparkling like diamonds in the morning sun.

"Grandma would love this," Sara said wistfully as she gazed at the wintry scene.

A smile broke through my groggy haze. "She sure would."

Mrs. S burst into the room with an icy blast, directing her bony finger at the cerulean ocean of snow. "Noah Farmer, what have you done?"

Realization hit me. I shoved my feet into my boots and hurried outside. From high above, blue snowflakes drifted over the castle grounds. The snowdrifts piled waist-deep, blanketing the golden carriage, but the path to the barn had been wind-swept clean. I brushed the powder aside, searching for the gossamer thread to reel in the cloud. I clumsily worked my stiff fingers to wring it out and stuff the icy squishiness into a jar.

Mrs. S fixed me with a stern gaze, her eyes boring into mine. "Come inside where it's warm," she instructed, her tone brooking no argument.

I swallowed hard. *This wasn't over.*

In the short time we secured the cloud, unseen chefs prepared a breakfast feast. Despite the anxious knot in my stomach, the savory scent of sizzling sausage made my mouth water.

"Eat up," Mrs. S said. "We have important matters to discuss."

I wolfed down my eggs, paying no mind, as Bandit chugged syrup straight from the bottle.

"Ew, disgusting," Sara said. "That's for your pancakes."

Bandit speared a stack with his fork and submerged it in orange juice. "It all ends up in the same place," he said through sloppy bites.

Mrs. S dabbed her mouth with a napkin. "Noah, I'd like an explanation about this unprecedented weather anomaly."

I sputtered, swallowing my mouthful as every eye turned to me. "It was an accident—"

"An accident?" she echoed, her brow arched. "You unintentionally conjured a supernatural snowstorm?"

"Not exactly." I caught Sara's gaze, encouraging me to come clean. "The train crash caused an ectoplasmic spill. We worried it would contaminate the environment, so we cleaned it with rainwater. We returned after dark, and I saw to Orion. But I was bone tired and left the chariot outside, forgetting about the mighty super-soaker rain cloud. Besides, I didn't expect the temperature to drop below freezing overnight."

"Fretting is fruitless." Mrs. S sighed. "But you must be more careful. You know better than to leave enchantments unattended."

Relieved Mrs. S wasn't angry—I savored my last bite. "So, are you okay? Did the dragonroot cure you?"

She smiled. "Bandit arrived in time, and yes, I restored my

garden and defrosted Erik with no lasting side effects."

At his name, Erik glanced up. He grabbed a napkin and blew his nose like a baying hound dog.

"You poor guy," Sara said. "You should get some rest. I'll order chicken soup for lunch."

"I'll be fine," he rasped, giving her an oily yet pitiful smile.

When Jesse asked our mentor if there was anything she could do to help Erik, Mrs. S responded that the cold would have to run its course.

"Is Erik contagious?" I hid my smug grin behind the rim of my mug as an awkward hush fell. "Oh, is it too soon to joke about it?"

Erik's expression told me he had more to say. But then, a silent message transpired between him and Mrs. S, and he turned away.

"Quick thinking, neutralizing the spill with rainwater," Mrs. S said. "You two prevented a disaster. Unfortunately, rumors suggest the Dragon Moonstone was on the train. If true, it's lost forever." She sipped her tea, pondering. "No telling what that means for the supernatural world."

"But it's not lost," Sara said. "We have it."

Surprised, Mrs. S sloshed her Earl Grey. "My goodness, this changes everything."

"I'll be right back." My chair scraped the floor.

I returned to find breakfast over and the group gathering in the sitting room. The roaring fire in the hearth battled against the chill. I dropped my pack on the coffee table and kneeled, rifling through its contents.

When I pulled out the globe, its glass had turned milky. Sara took it from my puzzled grasp and gave it a shake, but nothing happened. She shrugged and set the useless globe aside.

Next, I grabbed the once-weathered journal—now oddly smooth and when I urged *Mischief* to speak, he remained mute. "He's moody," I said, flipping through the blank pages.

Mrs. S furrowed her brow. "The moonstone, do you have it?"

I scrounged in my pack, pulling out a tin canister. Its lid sat askew, coated with a dried, crusty substance. As I attempted to twist it open, Mrs. S stopped me.

"What? I've opened it before. It's packed in a stinky gel and gives off fumes, but nothing too serious," I said in response to the concerned look in her eyes.

"Well, it's potent enough to nullify your arcane enchantments." She gestured toward *Mischief*.

*What had I done?* My eyes darted to the lifeless journal, and a sharp pang of fear knotted my stomach. "Is he dead?"

"Let's say he's in a coma," Mrs. S said gently. "Everyone, come with me."

In a daze, I followed as Mrs. S led us to the kitchen. She wrapped the Dragon Moonstone canister in a towel, her tone brisk. "Wash up to your elbows, hot water—soap. Scrub."

Mrs. S sighed in frustration. She explained the thieves had sealed the Dragon Moonstone in a shoddy anti-magic substance. It served as a temporary safeguard to protect elementary enchantments during transport. However, when the mixture leaked into my pack, it proved disastrous for extraordinary artifacts like the globe and *Mischief*. Adding an explosive train wreck to the mix of charms, ruins, and relics created a catastrophic combination. A perfect storm resulted in a toxic aftermath of ectoplasmic residue.

Erik noisily interrupted by wiping his nose with a white handkerchief.

Mrs. S patted him on the shoulder. "Erik, rest. Everyone else, meet me in my lab when you're done washing."

ΔΔΔ

Mrs. S had us don what resembled hazmat suits, each with a pointy witch's hat. Once we were ready, she conjured a magical vacuum to collect the anti-magic. Only then did she examine the emerald crystal cradled within her gloved palm. "Amazing artistry," she said, her voice laced with awe.

The dragon's eye sparkled, and I was hit by a wave of dizziness. I reached for the counter to steady myself. Mrs. S deposited the moonstone in a small satchel, and my vertigo eased. I swiped my hand across my face. "Okay, that was weird. A freaky fog of confusion clouded my brain."

"Not unexpected," Mrs. S said. "Your wizard lineage has a unique connection to the crystal. The moonstone will attempt to find another dragon to soothe, and if it can't find a dragon, it will look for the next best thing." She eyed me with a knowing look. "You must return the Dragon Moonstone before it causes an irreversible disruption."

"Return it where?" I asked, even though I knew what she'd say.

"Where it belongs, in Dragon Tooth Cave, where your ancestor left it."

"No way—been there, done that!" I folded my arms across my chest. "That cave's infested with man-eating beetles."

Mrs. S clasped her hands, fixing her eyes on me, but remained mute.

"Can't someone else do it?" I whined, rolling my shoulders. "I brought you the dragonroot. Wasn't that good enough?"

"Well, technically, that was me, mate," Bandit said, leaning against the wall with a satisfied smirk.

I shot him a dirty look.

"So, if we don't, what happens?" Sara asked, ignoring my discomfort.

"I'm sure you've seen the effects of the drought already. The snow helped. But the valley remains in jeopardy until the river covers the hunger stone and the dragon returns to her lair. Without the Dragon Moonstone to soothe her, chaos will rule. The rivers run dry, and the dragons run a muck."

"Do we have to coax the dragon back into the cave?" I asked, tugging at my lip with my teeth as the squealing bore came to mind.

Mrs. S lifted an eyebrow in response.

"Maybe they'll think the Dragon Moonstone was destroyed in the crash," Sara said.

"That'll buy us some time," Jesse said. "But as long as the witches are after us, we won't have any peace."

Tension pulled across shoulders. "Dragon Tooth Cave is deep in Goblin Valley. That's a long way. And nothing's changed. The witches of Estonia are still after us. The Parkers Gang escaped, and soon they'll figure out we have the Dragon Moonstone and set their sights on us."

Mrs. S placed her hand on my arm, locking her eyes on mine. "We are often called to do things we don't want to. But doing what needs to be done is a sign of strong character."

I exhaled deeply and ran my hand through my hair, grappling with the reality of what I had to do.

"What about Noah's new friend, the young dragon—maybe it could help?" Jesse said with a gleam in his eye.

"What's its name?" Sara asked.

"There are two. I only named Shadow Velvet." The conversation made me uneasy. I thought they were mocking me about my so-called *yet-to-be-seen-by-anyone* dragon.

Jesse jumped in and recounted how Leo Parker had caught the young dragon and tried to tame it with a bullwhip. Afterward, I mentioned I knew it wasn't my dragon because it had green eyes and Shadow Velvet's were gold.

Mrs. S's eyebrows shot up in surprise. "Golden eyes? Are you sure? How extraordinary." She stiffed her spine. "The imbalance is growing stronger. This is Noah's quest, and he must see it through." Mrs. S said, leaving no room for argument. "First things first—Return the Dragon Moonstone, and I'll talk to the Council about the troublesome Estonian coven." She patted my shoulder, her violet eyes sparkling. "I knew you wouldn't let us down. Your destiny awaits."

Sara pushed her hair behind her ear, laughing. "Sounds like a plan."

ΔΔΔ

As the others headed to the guesthouse, Mrs. S asked me to stay. She insisted on a medical-magical checkup. She slipped into a white lab coat and stuck an otoscope in my ear. Next, she instructed me to open my mouth and say *ah*. After that, she withdrew a small hammer from her pocket and whacked my kneecap.

I yelped, grabbing my knee. "What was that for?"

"Nothing. I simply find it amusing." A smile played across her face.

Mrs. S folded her arms, the overhead lights dimming. "Lie down, close your eyes, and clear your mind." Her tone sharpened. "Don't move a muscle until I return."

I mumbled, sank back onto the cot, took a few deep breaths, and soon slipped into a vivid dream.

*I sat under a tree with purple leaves, its canopy shading me from the harsh sun. Half-moon shadows danced across the warm sand. A stiff wind blew from the mouth of a cave where a stone obelisk stood, etched with an ancient warning. Scattered bones lay strewn on the rocky floor inside. A specter drifted into view, pacing back and forth. I recognized the ghost—Ezra, my grandfather's grandfather. He met my eyes with a piercing gaze and shouted, "Ogre awakens!"*

I opened my eyes to bright lights, and Mrs. S was staring at me. I pulled the pillow over my head, groaning.

"Well, well. If it isn't Sleeping Beauty," she said.

Swinging my legs off the cot, I stood and stretched. "Nothing better than a catnap."

Mrs. S smiled as if we shared a secret. "You dreamed of the Tree of Apotheosis."

"Sorta," I said, pushing my sweaty curls out of my eyes.

"I know you ate the forbidden fruit." Mrs. S rested her hand on her chin. "It's time to fulfill your destiny."

"Wait—what about my checkup?"

"Your magic has centered with the help of the fruit. Risky, but it served you well. Your physical self has melded with your spiritual self and now accurately processes magical residue. You're healed. It's up to you to accept who you are."

I scratched my head. "What do I do?"

"Wizardry is not something you do. It's something you are.

You are a wizard, so be a wizard. Your gifts dwell within your core. Respect them by caring for your body, mind, and spirit. Develop your talents. Don't hide or fear them. Guide and challenge them, and embrace possibilities. Let the magic flow."

"Okay..." I dragged the word out.

"I have high expectations for you, young wizard. Use your abilities for justice, not evil."

"I'm not ready."

"We're seldom ready to face our most significant challenges. Life doesn't work that way." Mrs. S gave me a gentle shove. "Clean your pack thoroughly and remove all traces of the anti-magic that leaked into your pack. You leave at dawn."

"Why is it always dawn? What's wrong with after lunch?" I grumbled, dragging my feet to my room.

ΔΔΔ

Dawn arrived all too soon. I trudged outside, hoisting my squeaky-clean backpack, and headed toward my friends. Orion and Altair stood harnessed to chariots. Sara and Eric occupied one, and Jesse and Bandit, in human form, crewed the other.

As I strode toward Sara, Mrs. S snatched my sleeve. "This is your ride." She pulled the cork from the jar and poured the cloud out onto the ground.

I stepped onto the plush pillow as Mrs. S secured it to the chariot. Jesse, his eyes gleaming with excitement, explained that we would travel in style to Goblin Valley. While I rode the rain cloud, they'd fly the chariots. And by following the river, *the little rain cloud that could,* would replenish the water levels.

"Whose brainchild was it for me to ride this?" I asked, frowning, wondering how I'd balance.

"Mine," Erik croaked. His lips twisted into an arrogant smile.

"It sure beats riding a buckboard, mate," Bandit added.

"Say, that reminds me, what stall do you keep Lester and Nester in?" I asked Mrs. S. "I'd like to thank them for sending the cavalry."

Mrs. S smiled and explained that the Grimm Goats weren't domestic animals. They were members of the Gruff Clan who went home to attend to family business. The goats only agreed to pull the wagon as a favor for Castle Dragon. Before I could ask any of the questions that came to mind, Lily skipped over, plopping down on the cloud with Chico. "We volunteered to keep you company."

"Sure, okay, but what about breakfast?" My stomach rumbled.

Sara tossed me a paper bag containing a couple of sandwiches. "You snooze, you lose."

The cloud wobbled beneath me. "This doesn't feel stable." I windmilled my arms, recalling my near-drowning disk-boarding experience last summer.

"Sit or stand, your choice. The cloud won't let you fall," Mrs. S said. "Godspeed!"

The chariot's sudden jerk threatened to topple me, but the cloud rose to meet me, forming into a cozy chair. I sank into the cushiony puff.

Orion pulled us along at a steady clip, tracing the river's winding path while the underbelly of the cloud showered the land below. A couple of hours later, I called to Sara, using both hands to mimic breaking a stick. She nodded, grasping the idea of time for a break, and guided Orion to a soft landing, leaving the cloud floating at the river's edge.

Lily perched atop the dripping cloud, eyeing the growing puddle. "I don't like getting my feet wet," she said, shifting from side to side. With a grin, I plucked the Cabbage Patch Kid off the cloud and set her on her MaryJanes. Chico grunted, and I extended a hand and helped him swing to dry land.

Erik marched over. "I didn't say we could stop." He rasped in a hoarse voice. "This isn't a vacation," his last words came out breathy, barely in a whisper.

"Save your voice for when it matters," I said, rolling my eyes at Erik's leadership skills.

Jesse raced over. "Erik, you gotta see the hunger stone. It's just down the gully. Come on, let's check it out."

A flicker of curiosity crossed Erik's face as he followed in Jesse's wake. When we arrived at the obelisk, I sensed the familiar magic. Erik examined the ancient writing on the stone, his forehead wrinkled in concentration. He cleared his throat with a gruff cough. "I can only make out some of this archaic language. But it's something about thirst and grief—" His voice gave out.

I splayed my palm against the cool surface of the stone and recited the verse.

Erik's eyes widened with surprise as the last words left my lips. He stumbled back a step, cocking his head as if seeing me for the first time. His pale eyes bore into me like I had grown a second head.

A mournful howl of wind echoed among the rocks. Jesse beckoned us to follow as he led the way around a large boulder, revealing a secluded marble basin. "This is where we saw the witch in the well," Jesse said, his trembling hands telegraphing his anxiety when he pointed at the cistern.

But it was empty—not a drop of water remained.

Erik frowned and motioned questioningly with his hands. When I didn't respond, he crossed his arms, tapped his foot, and glared at me, his neck flushing crimson with frustration.

"No big deal," I shrugged, eager to change the subject.

"It kinda was," Sara said, flipping her hair back.

"Well then, enlighten him," I said.

As Sara recounted our witchy encounter, Erik listened, his eyes round as saucers. Then Jesse urged us to show Erik the well and how it worked as a window into the witch's realm. Even when I reminded him that the last time had been intense, Jesse insisted.

Stepping forward, I shrugged off an icy chill. The cistern appeared empty except for an impenetrable darkness. I strained to connect to its essence but felt only a void.

"Nothingness," I said, with a shake of my head.

Jesse's eager smile waned.

I sighed, meeting Jesse's earnest gaze. "It's impossible to feel nothing—there's always something, but this here is a complete void, total darkness—it's unnatural."

"Try again," he pressed.

I took a deep breath and leaned into the murky well, opening my mind to any flicker of essence. A slithering warmth rose from the void—coiling, smothering. Mystic threads wrapped around my psyche, tugging as if to pull me into the abyss. I tore free, stumbling back. A ghostly moan sent shivers up my neck as a plume of smoke billowed from the cistern. Erik raised his palms, restraining the fog as Jesse yanked me to my feet.

A spectral, disembodied hand formed. It curled into a clenched fist, one finger pointing at me. From the shadowy depths, a voice reverberated as if from a thousand buzzing bees. "Bring me the Dragon Moonstone, young wizard, and I'll spare the others. With it and yourself, I shall be satisfied."

I stepped forward, balling my fists. "Never!" The entire valley depended on us to return the moonstone, and there was no way I'd let Mrs. S down.

"We shall see," came the voice.

The fist melted into a swirling blur of smoke and shadows. The vortex slowed, colors and shapes materializing to reveal Aunt Shirley's house and the giant elm in her yard. Tendrils slithered out from the whirlpool, weaving together to form the image of a pulsating cocoon bulging and clinging to the Elm's sturdy branch. As the apparition gained clarity, it revealed Aunt Shirley's horrified face pushed against the silk.

Sara gasped, hands flying to her mouth, and my jaw clenched as the mist transformed again. The witch, Agnes, appeared in smoke, overlapping the ghastly image of my aunt imprisoned in a cocoon.

"Kin for kin," she hissed. "Hand over the Dragon Moonstone, submit yourself for reprisal, and your dear auntie goes free."

"You can't get away with this," Jesse yelled.

"I already have," the witch said.

"Meet me at Dragon Tooth Cave in two days," I said, my chest heaving. “And let Aunt Shirley go!”

“Auntie’s napping, but we shall see.” She cackled. “Noon, the day after tomorrow, young wizard.” The spectral witch disappeared.

“That was foolish,” Erik croaked in his voice raspy.

I shrugged. “But now we know where to find her.” I met his gaze. “Are you with us on this?”

The corner of Erik’s mouth twitched into a hint of a smile. “Sure, count me in.” Then, with a nod, Erik turned and marched toward the chariots.

# CHAPTER 25

## *GIANT TROUBLES*

Grinding my teeth, I surfed the silver cloud, riding behind Sara and Erik's golden chariot. Sara's occasional laughter floated back on the breeze, a constant reminder of their cozy seating arrangement. I couldn't hear their words, but Erik's body language conveyed everything. He'd brush back his hair and lean in, chatting with Sara. He'd smirk and glance my way when she wasn't looking, working his laryngitis to full advantage.

*What did she see in him?*

With an exasperated huff, I turned around, shoulders sagging. I couldn't let my imagination run wild—We were best friends, nothing more. Sure, we had hung out but never officially dated.

"*Why not take a chance?*" my inner voice nudged. *"You miss every shot you don't take."*

"Stop obsessing—Now's not the time to indulge in mental debates. Not while a witch is looming. And then there's Aunt Shirley to consider. Let alone the whole Dragon Moonstone fiasco to sort out," I muttered.

"She doesn't like him that way," Lily said with a know-it-all expression. "And don't pretend you don't know what I mean."

I sprawled out on the pillowy cloud, crossing my arms behind my head. "Can we drop it? I need a nap to recharge, and maybe, just maybe, I'll come up with a plan to untangle this mess."

With the night settling in, we coasted to a stop in a mountain clearing—the same meadow where I had freed Bob and Bull Van Winkle from Frankie. After setting up camp and repurposing the carriages as the base for our tent, Bandit and I ventured out to explore. We searched for clues left behind by the Parkers, traces of the moose, and remnants of recent events. But it was as if the forest swallowed all evidence of the tussle and dramatic escape. We found no trace of our splintered buckboard, and Bandit attributed its disappearance to woodland scavengers.

Lily and Chico's childish antics echoed across the meadow, reminding me of Cassandra, the spirited little green giant. A faint smile tugged at my lips.

The others had gathered around the crackling campfire. Its flickering purple flames and dancing shadows captured their attention. I grabbed a stick and idly scratched shapes in the dirt.

"Do you think that awful vision of Shirley was real?" Sara asked, her eyebrows knitted with concern.

I shrugged. "It's hard to decipher reality in the spirit world. But I guarantee she meant it as a threat." I continued scribbling, thoughts churning. "No one threatens my family and gets away with it."

Sara leaned over, curious. "Hey, that could work." She pointed at my unconscious doodles, and I blinked in surprise and then grinned. I had sketched an outline of a plan.

ΔΔΔ

We took turns keeping watch. My shift ended when the night yielded to dawn. Morning birds serenaded overhead as I ambled to the river's edge. The river slapped against the rocks. Our rain cloud had done its job—the water level had risen overnight. It had a long way to go to return to its once mighty flow, but our efforts were helping, and I smiled at the thought.

The earth rumbled beneath me, not from earthquake tremors but because of a rhythmic thumping. I wheeled toward the thunderous footfalls, eyes ballooning as I recognized the figure stomping through the trees.

Cassie, the little green giant, hesitated at the edge of the clearing before lumbering over. I greeted her with a wave, but her watery eyes hinted at something amiss.

"What's the matter, kiddo?"

Cassie's chin quivered as she plopped down on the dewy grass. "Daddy doesn't care about me. He won't help find my dolly." She crossed her arms with a huff.

I settled beside her. "Your daddy loves you, Cassie. But grown-ups get busy with work sometimes."

She jutted her chin. "I miss my dolly and ran away to find her."

"When I was about your age, I ran away."

Cassie's eyes widened with interest. "You did?"

"I was really mad about something, and with a pout, I grabbed my backpack and stormed out of the house. I stomped around the block a few times but wasn't allowed to cross the street, so eventually, I grew tired and sat on the curb. Then, when it started getting dark, the streetlights came on, and guess what? Mom showed up. We didn't say much—we just sat together. After a while, I forgot why I was even sad." I smiled gently. "Sometimes it helps to have someone who cares sit with you until you're ready to go home. Even when you're feeling upset, it's nice not to be alone."

"My mommy died," Cassie said, her voice tinged with sorrow.

"Mine too, and I miss her every day." A cloud passed over the morning sun while my heart ached at the memory.

"But you have a daddy who loves you." I glanced at the towering giant casting a massive shadow. "I bet he's worried sick about you. Should we look for him—tell him you're running away? You know—so he doesn't worry?"

"Okay—"

"Cassandra," came a deep, rumbling voice.

"Daddy!" Cassie cried, leaping into his arms. "I'm sorry." She sniffed, wiping her eyes. "I missed you."

The giant smiled. "We can discuss it at home. But first, introduce me to your friend."

Cassie's father resembled a giant-sized version of the already huge Incredible Hulk. He said his name was Skogvarder, but to call him Skog.

Soon, Chico's excited grunts filled the air. Lily came running, laughing, and chasing after the silly monkey. While Jesse ambled along behind them.

"Dolly!" Cassie ran for the Cabbage Patch Kid.

I pivoted Lily out of her reach. Cassie lunged again, and I stepped away. The little giant's mouth tightened, not liking the game.

I scooted back and held up my hand. "Sweetie, there's a misunderstanding. I know I promised to bring you a doll, but she's not the one—"

"But I am!" Lily cried.

I scratched my chin, setting Lily on the grass. Lily bobbed her head with a gapped-tooth grin. "The Parker Brothers stole me from Cassandra."

Cassie jumped up and down, clapping her hands. "I knew you'd find my dolly!"

Lily put her hands on her hips and glared at the little giant. "You left me outside—in the rain!"

"I'm sorry," Cassie's voice cracked. "I went to find you, but you were gone. Will you forgive me?"

Lily beamed, jumping into Cassie's arms. "Yes, of course! You're my person, always and forever."

At her words, Chico whimpered, his tail drooping, and slunk away. I scooped the pitiful monkey into my arms.

"Chico, what's wrong?" Lily asked.

Chico's face fell into a frown, eyes downcast.

I turned to Cassie. "It seems Chico feels left out."

"Chico is my friend, Cassandra," Lily said, her round eyes threatening tears. "He has no one else."

"Daddy, can we keep Chico, too?" Cassie pleaded with giant puppy dog eyes.

Skog beamed at his daughter. "Of course, the more friends, the better."

Cassie, Lily, and Chico cheered.

Skog shielded his eyes from the climbing sun. "But it's time we headed home." Skog grew serious. "Thank you for returning my daughter's doll. Lily has been part of our family for ages, and Chico is welcome for as long as he likes." His voice rumbled. "If you ever need my help, summon me, young wizard."

Skog scooped up his beaming daughter and her two friends and lumbered off into the woods. His laughter sounded long after he disappeared among the trees.

Jesse blinked after him. "How *exactly* do you summon a giant?"

"Good question. I wish I knew," I said, hanging my arm over Jesse's shoulder as we returned to camp.

ΔΔΔ

It was a relaxing flight over Goblin Valley. I slept most of the day with the cloud to myself as we cruised along at a steady clip. We landed in a clearing, a short walk to the Grotto Weeps. The sun hung low over the jagged rocks as we set up camp in a grassy cul-de-sac enclosed by blackened stone.

Erik's voice had recovered, and to my dismay, he grew increasingly talkative. He boasted about quitting his lucrative chimney sweep job to become a seasoned warrior and officer in the warden's ranks. Our conversation shifted to what Erik called *strategic planning*. I suggested arriving a day early to catch the witch off guard. While Erik agreed with the element of surprise, he proposed splitting our efforts. He'd take the trail to the Tree of Apotheosis while we retraced our steps through the caves.

My stomach soured and churned, recalling the rock-crushing beetles' double row of gnashing teeth.

Erik brushed me off. "The beetles are more afraid of you than you are of them. Besides, I must witness Agnes, the Witch of Estonia, break the MSC."

"What's MSC?" I asked, but then quickly wished I kept my mouth shut.

Erik scowled, his frustration simmering. "The Magical

Standards of Compliance—Foundations that you should know inside and out. You were provided a list of the rules. And, yet, you remain as ignorant as ever." The fire crackled as Erik regarded me with disdain, the dancing flames distorting his face into ghastly shadows.

"Why not arrest her on sight?" With an eager grin, Jesse karate-chopped the air. "We'll back you up."

Erik shook his head no. "Hearsay and circumstantial evidence won't suffice."

I couldn't believe my ears. "But the witch threatened my family, trapping Aunt Shirley in a cocoon-thing." My fists clenched as I remembered the horrifying scene.

Erik's eyes squinted into a glare. "You don't know that. It could've been an elaborate illusion of smoke and mirror magic designed to intimidate you. And judging by your reaction, it worked."

I bristled at the implication. "I'm not scared of no stinkin' witch."

"Well, you should be," Erik retorted.

I clamped my jaw shut, holding back a flood of objections.

Sara intervened and calmly asked, "What are the grounds for arrest?"

"Using magic to harm—Wizard, Witch, Fae, or any supernatural being, including inept magical mundanes like those two." Erik tipped his chin my way.

Erik's omission of Sara from his disparaging comments spoke volumes. But before I could form a snarky comeback, Jesse said, "We're not mundane." His brow scrunched in disagreement.

"You might as well be." Erik's comment stung, and then he held up his hand to hold off the expected rebuttal. "It's all irrelevant—unless I witness Agnes commit a criminal act, my hands are tied."

Then Jesse made a screw face, spotting Bandit in human form by a rotten log. "Ugh, what are you eating?"

"Ants." Bandit extended a finger with a wriggling ant before popping it into his mouth. "Yum, spicy-hot, and amazingly delicious." He revealed a fistful of ants. "Fancy a taste?"

Jesse recoiled, laughing and thrusting his hands out to keep Bandit away.

Bandit shrugged and asked Erik, "Any bright ideas, champ?"

Erik lifted his chin, his gaze brimming with conceit. "Agnes wouldn't dare try anything with a first-class warden like myself present," he said. "While I keep to the shadows, you'll have to goad her."

I bit my tongue at his arrogance. "What if the witch steals the Dragon Moonstone from the cave?"

Erik gave me a patronizing glare. "The Dragon Moonstone technically lacks an owner. Its purpose is to soothe the dragon. Thus, taking it isn't illegal, just unwise. Stupidity isn't a crime."

"Stupidity landed most people in jail," Jessie said, earning a few chuckles.

Erik rolled his eyes and took a step as if to walk away. "Do you want my help or not?"

Bandit clamped his hand on Erik's shoulder, tossing me a mischievous smile. "No worries, mate, we're all ears."

Erik paced, yammering endless strings of words. An ant crawled along his cheekbone, making his eye twitch. He brushed it away and droned on. Another explored beneath his collar as he rubbed his neck and scratched. When he finally came to the point, his plan was simple—I was the bait.

Jesse and Sara erupted in protests, their voices piling on top of one another. Though it was a terrible idea, I agreed. We had little choice but to go along with Erik's plan if we wanted to stop Agnes. Besides, I wouldn't have been able to keep a straight face much longer, watching Erik squirm like he had ants in his pants.

With a basic plan in place, restlessness tugged me toward the ponies. Offering them a treat, I ran my hand along Altair's side, marveling at the hidden wings that allowed flight but disappeared when on the ground.

"Hey, boy," I murmured, stroking Orion's neck. "Did you catch all that?"

Orion huffed, shaking his mane and stamping a hoof in

response.

"If things go south, don't hesitate. I have a feeling we'll need a fast getaway." I grabbed a brush and curried the ponies as darkness blanketed the campsite with only the stars and fading embers for light.

"You look troubled, mate."

I jumped at Bandit's sudden voice, spotting him lounging on an overhanging branch. "What are you doing up there?"

"Just hanging out—Why so tense?"

"It's hard to explain, but I have a nagging sense we're walking into a trap while Erik waits for something to happen." I stroked Orion's silky coat, taking comfort in his warmth.

"This is your party—You invited the witch." Bandit's comment hit home.

"That's right." My brows furrowed in determination. "And I'm tired of this cat-and-mouse game. I want to end it on my terms."

"Then do it. Unleash your inner dragon," Bandit said, chomping on the tree's red leaves. "Don't worry, mate. I've got your back."

My gloomy mood broke. "Thanks, Bandit, you're a true friend. Get some rest. We ride at first light."

ΔΔΔ

Morning arrived, brushing the sky in vibrant colors. Erik snored, mumbling in his sleep. His hike to the Dragon Tooth Cave was straightforward, so we didn't wake him to tell him goodbye. As for the fearless ponies, we left them with confidence, trusting in their ability to fend for themselves.

Bandit, the raccoon, insisted his place was with us. He jumped onto the cushiony cloud while I fastened the line to my backpack. With the cloud in tow, we walked side by side, making our way to the Grotto Weeps.

After a while, Sara broke the silence. "We need a plan."

"We have one. Enter the cave, return the Dragon Moonstone,

wait for the witch to attack me, and let Erik save the day. What more do we need?"

"More details," Jesse said.

"We each should have a specific task to help us navigate the caves and achieve our goal," Sara said.

"You sound like a candidate for upper management," I said with a chuckle.

Jesse scratched his chin. "I've been practicing creating light. We can use the cloud as a lantern." Jesse pinched his eyes, and a shimmering light appeared in his palm. Then, plunging his arm deep into the puffy folds, the rain cloud pitched.

Bandit grabbed hold. "Hey, warn me next time."

Jesse withdrew his hand, and the rain cloud lit up like a light bulb.

"That was a great idea. Now, what about those rock-eating beetles?" I said, cringing at the thought.

"I remember they didn't like ice," Sara said. "Noah, can you drop the temperature?"

"Yes, but not while I pushing the cloud forward."

"I'll make wind," Sara said, and we howled with laughter. "What's so funny?" Sara said defensively. "Wind is one of my specialties."

Jesse laughed so hard he struggled to speak. "Breaking wind. You know—passing gas," he said, slapping his thighs. "As in the musical fruit."

"Make wind, not break wind. You're so juvenile." Sara rolled her eyes, though a wisp of a smile graced her lips.

The comic relief faded when we arrived at the mouth of Grotto Weeps.

"Ready?" I huffed out a breath, steeling my nerves to face the claustrophobic cave once again.

*The second time had to be easier, right?*

Jesse rocked on the balls of his feet, eyes shining.

"We can do this," Sara said, offering a subdued smile while staring into the dreadful darkness.

The lack of sound was oppressive. Where before, the cavern

echoed with sporadic gusts of air—now—there was only dead silence.

"Crickey, you all looked like you came across a spotted croc in the dunny." Bandit motioned with his paw. "How nasty can a few bugs be?"

We responded with a nervous laugh.

Sara conjured a steady gust, sending the cloud forward.

"Tally Ho," Bandit said, piloting the silver rain cloud like the captain of his ship through the mouth of the cave.

In single file, we followed Bandit through the narrow tunnels, our determination driving us onward. I trailed behind, sloshing through the stream of water and summoning cold while dragging my staff along the wet stone. The air in the cave was naturally cool, and soon, the temperature dropped below freezing.

Glancing over my shoulder, a web of ice formed in our wake. "Brrr, this should keep the bugs away," Sara said, rubbing her hands to stave off the chill. No beetles skittered into view as we hustled through the cloud-lit passageway.

We followed Jesse's prior chalk marks, trekking through the labyrinth. In the dragonroot chamber, we stopped to catch our breath. Our eyes darted nervously around the unfamiliar surroundings.

"Where's the backdoor into Dragon Tooth cave?" Jesse asked, scanning the uneven walls.

"I don't know. It looks different. There are holes everywhere, and parts have collapsed. We need to spread out and search," Sara said.

"Be careful. This honeycomb of beetle tunnels has likely undermined the entire labyrinth," I added, still on edge thinking about the beetles.

We scattered, leaving the cloud tied to a rock in pursuit of the opening. It wasn't long before Jesse came sailing toward me. The cavern floor had turned into a massive skating rink.

He slid sideways. "Dudes, you gotta try this," Jesse said with contagious excitement.

Bandit and I mimicked Jesse's actions. We glided across the ice with our arms outstretched, one-upping each other until Sara, arms crossed and tapping her foot, reminded us of our mission. Her scowl told us she was clearly unimpressed with our skating abilities.

Sara found the passageway, scrambling up a boulder, and motioned us to follow. While I secured the cloud, Jesse pushed past me, following Sara deeper into the cave, oblivious to the atmospheric charge of magic.

As I paused and held my breath, I once again felt a profound mystical connection to the sanctity of the cathedral-like cavern, which rocked me on my heels. The marble obelisk, etched with a message and decorated with intricate designs, drew me closer, looming like a sentinel. It warned of the dangers of disturbing the Dragon Moonstone. I reread the poem that cautioned thieves of the consequences of disturbing the crystal. With reverence, I freed the crystal from its satchel and placed it into the tapered, pyramid-like top.

"There you go, back where you belong," I said, caressing the dragon's head. "Magnificent as a museum display."

High above, a split in the ceiling, shaped like a dragon's wing, allowed a cascade of sunlight. The sunbeams danced and sparkled in the dragon's eyes, creating a mesmerizing play of light. As I fixed my eyes on the dragons, a profound mixture of awe and solidarity engulfed me as a tidal wave of magic hit me head-on.

*"Open your mind to all you can be,"* a voice echoed in my head. *"You are one with the dragon—Be the dragon wizard."*

Startled, I rubbed my eyes, blinking hard. *Had the Dragon Moonstone just spoken to me?*

The electrifying magical energy crackled, filling the space surrounding the moonstone with a mystical effervescence. I opened myself to acceptance, taking deep breaths and filling my lungs with fresh, enchanted air. Waves of power surged through my veins as my senses heightened. The cavern no longer smelled dank and musty. It now carried scents of lavender and mint. And despite the dim light, I could see into the shadows. With newfound clarity, I understood the magic within me. The teachings of Mrs. S and *Mischief* were within reach not as facts but as an innate understanding.

The revelation ignited an idea, and I rifled through my pack for the book that housed so much ancient wisdom. *Mischief's* cover had corroded, and his pages appeared dry and cracked. With shaking hands, I held the withered tome toward the Dragon Moonstone like an offering at an altar. *Mischief's* binding crunched under my grip. "Please heal my friend."

Beams of golden light shot from the dragon's eyes, bouncing off *Mischief's* fragile cover. I wrestled to hold *Mischief* steady as the book convulsed under the force. His quakes transitioned into spasms, and *Mischief's* voice emerged amidst erratic hiccups. "Enough, lad—Stop."

I moved away from the intense rays of light and severed the spell.

"*Mischief*, you're back!" My eyes brimmed, and I used my sleeve to wipe away the tears as I looked at my friend's prominent nose and bushy eyebrows appearing on the revitalized cover.

"Well done. You saved me. The Dragon Moonstone burned away the magical mildew that nullified my powers. Much longer, and it would've been too late."

Elated by *Mischief*'s recovery, I couldn't stop smiling. I brought him up to speed and described my sudden magical bond to the Dragon Moonstone. Then I filled in the details of our journey and ended my summary with the bombshell we planned to confront the witch.

"You must be ready for treachery," *Mischief* said. "But first, let's ensure the Dragon Moonstone is secure, once and for all."

My eyebrows popped as an idea formed.

"I can see you know what to do, so if you don't mind, I'd like a nap." *Mischief* yawned. "That cure took its toll, but I'll be alright soon enough."

After stowing *Mischief*, I created a series of wards and

booby traps. I made a small trench encompassing the obelisk while mumbling magic words and sprinkling dragonroot in the grooves.

As I finished surveying my handiwork, Jesse yelled, "Turn off the AC." He stood with his arms wrapped tight across his chest, his teeth chattering loudly. I chuckled, having forgotten about the icy cold emanating from my staff. Jesse pointed to the crack we used to enter the grand chamber. "The wall is solid ice. There's only one way out now. And that's the way the witch will come."

I reassured my friends we had a whole day before the witch made her appearance. Sara directed us to a bottomless pit in a side alcove that would be a perfect spot to catch the rainwater. As I prepared to position the cloud, Jesse inched toward the abyss and leaned over to peer inside.

"Don't slip," Sara said, grabbing Jesse's coattails and faking a push.

Jesse jumped back, clawing at the wall. "Not funny."

Sara giggled.

"Crikey, mate, you're too easy," Bandit said with a sloppy grin.

The group huddled for lunch. But I shook off the offer, too keyed up to eat. This provoked Sara's surprised look, as it wasn't often I turned down food. Instead, I dropped my pack into the corner and wandered off to explore the cave's recesses. But mostly, I needed to think because I didn't want to be caught off guard if the witch took a page from our playbook and showed up early.

As it happened, the day's surprises were only beginning.

# CHAPTER 26

## *THE SHOWDOWN IN GOBLIN VALLEY*

My footsteps echoed as I mentally mapped the cavern, envisioning it as a clover with four sizable chambers among uneven pockets. Light spilled through a gap in the towering ceiling, creating shifting patterns on the walls. Two opposing energies clashed, charging the atmosphere with a perplexing vibe. I needed to ready myself for the witch's showdown, yet this place put me on edge. I pushed my hair out of my eyes, damp with sweat. Meeting Agnes, the witch outside in the fresh air and sunlight, might be a better option, but I wanted to take a stand between her and the Dragon Moonstone.

The Dragon Moonstone hummed with enchantment as the cave thrummed an ominous warning. If I ventured beyond the sight of the obelisk, my connection to the crystal faded, replaced by an oppressive heat and inhospitable presence. It was as if the crystal held the cave's anger at bay. We weren't welcome, and the cave wanted me to know it resented my intrusion. A sudden prickle crept along my neck, sending a wave of unease washing over me. I slowed my pace as my senses heightened. With a palpable sense of wickedness, heat poured out of the tunnels like a blast furnace.

*Caves are supposed to be cool, but this place burns with a vengeance—ready to explode.*

Before charging in unprepared, I wanted to understand what was happening, so I searched for a better vantage point. About twenty feet above, a ridge protruded. I secured a foothold, climbed the wall, rolled onto the flat surface, and wedged into the gap. Tucked under a narrow tapered crevice, I inched forward on my elbows until I gained a bird's-eye view.

Jesse and Sara's amicable chatter rose to meet my ears.

"Man, I'm boiling," Jesse said. "Who cranked the thermostat?"

Sara and Jesse huddled in a tight alcove, relaxing against an interior wall. Scattered rocks blocked their view of the Dragon Moonstone. They didn't notice when an elongated slab emanated scarlet light, which coalesced into a dense mist. The fog swirled into a portal, revealing a woman draped in a billowing crimson cloak. She moved like a bird, her steps tiny and quick, while spiked heels clicked against the stone floor.

With an unmistakable air of authority, she demanded, "Tell me where the wizard is, and you both can continue to draw breath."

Sara and Jesse shot to their feet, backing up until their backs plastered against the rough wall. Sara stood silent, her dark eyes wide, white rims glinting with fear. Jesse's leg bounced with nervous energy.

"Where's that troublesome wizard?" The woman in red locked eyes with Sara and Jesse. A tense silence stretched between them. "I don't enjoy repeating myself," she spat, her voice dripping with venom.

"Hey, wait a minute—I remember you—you're Agnes, the witch," Jesse said, stepping away from Sara with a confident smile. "Well, you've found me."

My jaw tightened as Jesse strutted forward. *What's he playing at?*

"You? The wizard?" Agnes sounded skeptical. "You don't look like much."

"I'm often underestimated," Jesse said, his expression mirroring one of my trademark scowls.

"You're coming with me," Agnes said, her gaze flickering to the lingering portal.

"Nope," Jesse said, folding his arms as I often did.

Agnes lunged.

"Get away from me, you nut." Jesse vaulted, performing a flip that sent him into a controlled tumble and landing squarely on his feet.

"Adorable—But I don't have time for games." The red witch hissed, her fingertips crackling with lightning. A bolt shot forth, striking Jesse and propelling him backward until he collided with the wall.

"Jesse," Sara yelled, running over to where he landed. Jesse pushed himself up, swiping a shaky hand through his tousled hair.

"A-ha! You're not the young wizard." The witch's voice rang with amusement. She tapped a finger to her chin, lips curling into a scornful smile. "You're that troublesome red-headed stepchild my sister Carla used to complain about. Not the sharpest tool in the shed, are you?"

"Wait, a second—"

Sara touched Jesse's shoulder. "It's rhetorical. Don't answer," she whispered, yet the cave acoustics carried her words to my ears. She must've sensed me watching when she turned her head toward me. I pressed a finger to my lips. Sara gave the slightest nod before averting her eyes.

"You there," the witch pointed a painted fingernail at Sara, "Where's the young wizard?"

"He's not here. He went outside to wait for you," Sara said, her voice unwavering. "You're early."

"Leave us alone," Jesse said. "Go back on the broom you came in on."

"Broom?" she scoffed. "Brooms are old school. I assure you that my entrance through the portal was much more dramatic." She glanced behind her at the mist. "Temperamental, I must admit."

"Come back tomorrow," Sara said, putting her hands on her hips.

The red witch turned her gaze to Sara. "We haven't met—and you are?"

"A concerned citizen," Sara responded coolly.

"I have no patience for impertinence." With a pointed finger, the witch uttered, "*Aevus*!" The word reverberated through the cave, its echo growing stronger as stars encircled Sara.

Time seemed to slow as an hourglass materialized, encasing Sara and silencing her piercing scream. White grains of sand trickled from the upper chamber. As I jerked forward, my boot wedged into a crevice. I labored to pull free but sensed a stubborn resistance, as if the cave had grabbed my foot and refused to let go.

Bandit's paw pressed against my hand. "Stay down, mate."

"Wizard, I shan't wait long. Reveal yourself before the dear girl's fate is sealed. Remember, time waits for no one."

Jesse's voice sliced through the air as he flung a ball of fire. "Let Sara go!" His fiery missile shot forward, a comet ablaze in hues of purple and gold. Yet with uncanny grace, the witch sidestepped, her movement as fluid as a dancer's twirl. Agnes countered with a searing lightning bolt. Jesse's instincts kicked in, and he zipped behind a boulder just as showers of sparks erupted like the 4$^{th}$ of July.

"Remain in your corner. I'm not interested in you," Agnes said, her voice loaded with disdain.

The witch spiraled in widening circles. Then, with a sudden stop, she jerked her head. "Wizard, where art thou?" Her nostrils flared like a bloodhound trying to catch my scent. "Interesting." She licked her lips. "I smell young wizard blood." Her sharp laugh sent shivers down my spine.

Jesse persisted, launching another barrage of purple flames at the witch. Undeterred, the witch swatted the fireballs like mosquitos.

"Don't annoy me. The wizard's all I want." With a dismissive wave, the red witch continued her search, scrutinizing every shadowy crevice.

Sara's fist rained desperate blows upon the glass, but no sound escaped. All the while, I twisted and squirmed, trying to free my trapped boot. Jesse pounded the hourglass, and his determined strikes met with a crackling burst of magic. His sharp cry of pain echoed as the swirling magic burned his skin.

"Run along and find your wizard friend. I don't have time for hide-and-seek." Agnes cackled the way witches do. "And neither does the lovely Sara."

The red witch persisted in her search, venturing deeper into the shadows. She stumbled, wobbling on her heels. She then muttered an incantation and the offending rock exploded in a thunderous flurry.

"Agnes, did you get him?" yelled a familiar voice.

"That double-crosser, I knew it—"

"Shh!" Bandit warned. "They'll hear you."

"My foot's stuck," I whispered. "I can't see behind me to free it."

The witch turned to Erik. "I told you to wait."

"Where's the kid?" he asked, marching forward with his usual arrogance.

"I haven't found him. The girl claims he's outside."

"He's not. I would've seen him." Erik skidded to a halt when he noticed Sara trapped in the hourglass, sand collecting around her feet. "What did you do? You promised not to harm the others." Erik's voice carried a mix of concern and accusation.

"Oh, the girl's fine," Agnes crooned, her tone laced with a sinister edge. "If we find the wizard in time—that is." Her malicious laughter bounced through the chamber.

"We had a deal, and you broke it." Erik's eyes darted between Sara and the witch.

"Oh, please," Agnes scoffed. "I don't have the luxury of indulging your complaints. The portal won't stay open indefinitely." The red witch's heels echoed as she paced. "Tick-Tock, wizard."

"Just take the Dragon Moonstone and leave. Forget about the kid wizard," Erik said.

Agnes whirled around, her gaze burning into Erik. "The wizard murdered my sister."

"You know that's a lie," Erik said. "Besides, you didn't even like her."

"That's irrelevant. I have a duty to avenge the coven."

Erik scanned the surroundings. "Where's Jesse?"

"The red-headed pest?" She waved dismissively. "Over there somewhere."

Jesse poked his head out from behind a boulder. "Erik, help us."

The scar on Erik's face stretched as he stiffened his back and faced Agnes. "Release Sara at once."

"And if I refuse?" The witch's hand found her hip, and a sly smile graced her lips. "You're adorable when angry," she purred.

"The Dragon Moonstone is more valuable than that troublemaker and his companions," Erik said.

The witch continued to sniff the air and scan the shadows. "Good point. I shall take both," she said without looking at Erik. "But make it quick."

"Have you searched his belongings?" Erik asked, gesturing toward the alcove.

The witch rushed forward, but Erik outpaced her. Agnes lunged for it, but Erik evaded her grasp. "Release Sara and the crystal is yours," he said, waving the backpack to catch the witch's attention.

"Give me that." The red witch made a second grab for my bag.

Erik was nimble, if not quick, staying just out of reach, jumping on a rock. With one swift motion, Erik tossed her the old-fashioned tin canister. He then flung my backpack at Jesse, who caught it with a grunt.

"There you have your precious stone. Now reverse the spell on Sara," Erik said, stamping his foot.

"I'm beginning to think you harbor tender feelings for the girl. How unoriginal." The witch barely glanced at Erik as she struggled with the stubborn lid.

My hands clenched and unclenched as I wracked my brain for ideas. I was trapped, powerless to help Sara. She had stuffed her duster into the funnel to slow the flow, but even so, sand had piled over her Doc Martens.

And then it struck me—I had Ezra's sling. I wormed it out

of my pocket and scooped a handful of walnut-sized stones. Frustrated, I tried to kick free.

"Be still," Bandit said. "I'm working on loosening your boot."

"Agnes, Witch of Estonia, I demand you undo the hourglass spell," Erik said, squaring his shoulders. He wasn't as tall as the red witch, even standing on the rock.

The witch wrestled with the lid. "Why is it so hot?" she muttered, dabbing her brow.

"Give me that," Erik said, grabbing the bottom of the canister. A tug of war ensued until the lid popped off, triggering an explosion of powder covering the witch. Agnes screamed in pain as blisters formed on her face and hands. She blindly used the edge of her cape to wipe her eyes.

"Hey, witchy face," Jesse yelled, his voice brimming with bravado. He had hold of the cloud and sprayed it like a firehose. I stifled a laugh as Agnes screeched even louder, while Jesse gave her a good soaking.

Unfortunately, Jesse's timing couldn't have been worse because the water neutralized my poisonous trap. Jesse's antics triggered a swift and fiery reprisal. He yelped and darted for cover as rocks shattered all around him.

"Crikey, Jesse's fearless," Bandit said, sounding impressed. "And stop moving your foot—I'm almost finished here."

"The wizard will pay for his tricks," the witch hissed with each word. "As for pretty Sara, well—how unfortunate—her untimely demise."

She wiped the water off her face, and where mascara dripped, she left black smudges. The witch lowered her cape's hood, revealing a towering cone of curls in what I could only describe as a red version of Marge Simpson's hairdo.

Agnes extracted a hairpin that extended into a sword. "Find the wizard," the red witch commanded. And as her locks unraveled, I gasped at the revolting spectacle.

An outpouring of rats tumbled from the tangle of her curls. The rodents scattered in every direction. One bounced off her breast before she caught it. The witch's gaze lingered on her pet for a moment longer, a twisted smile forming on her lips. "Off you go, my sweet. Find that deplorable wizard." She kissed its head and lowered the toothy rat to the ground.

"Enough. You're under arrest," Erik's voice boomed. "I'm a warden of the council."

"Only when it suits you."

Erik unsheathed his sword with a steely resolve etched in his expression. "Agnes, I mean it."

"Oh, Erik, you're hilarious. You're not seriously thinking you are strong enough to beat me."

The witch launched into a frenzy, slashing her sword with one hand and shooting lightning with the other. The thunder of enchanted steel filled the chamber as lightning cracked and blades crossed.

"Now," said Bandit.

I pulled my foot free, wiggled out from under the crevice, and crawled onto the overhang. Bandit handed me my boot, and I rushed to put it on.

Sara tried to stem the sand as it spilled through the folds of her duster like water. I launched a rock toward the hourglass, but the glass held firm. Again, I sent a rock flying, to no avail. Sweat ran from my brows, stinging my eyes. Heatwaves radiated from the cave walls, and I harnessed the heat's essence, channeling it into my sling. The stone struck the glass with a resounding *crack*.

At the thunderous sound, the witch screeched, targeting a fire blast toward me. The fireball fizzled when it hit my protective shield. She sprung to a ledge out of Eriks' reach.

"The young wizard has arrived in the nick of time," Agnes said, her words dripping with sarcasm.

The red witch's eyes blazed with vengeance and longing as her gaze swept to the fading portal and back to Erik.

"Erik, it's not just about revenge. The young wizard possesses a core that could shift the balance of power in realms beyond your comprehension. And with the Dragon Moonstone, we would be unstoppable."

Erik hesitated, appearing conflicted. He looked at Sara's futile efforts to break free, tears streaming down her cheeks. Relentlessly, Sara pummeled the glass. The sand poured unabated, rising above her knees and threatening to reach her waist.

"You're under arrest for violating the MSC," Erik said unconvincingly.

Agnes laughed, a disturbing blend of mirth and madness. Her cackles echoed through the cave, an eerie backdrop to the unfolding chaos. She hurled a fireball at Erik's boots, missing him on purpose. It was then I realized she wasn't interested in hurting Erik. It was me she wanted.

A horde of rats swarmed over the ledge. I kicked two away as more surged forward. Bandit furiously fought them off, using his raccoon teeth and sharp claws to defend our position. I drew in a breath and aimed for the center of the crack. The rock hit its mark, puncturing the glass but only creating the tiniest hole. It did nothing to stop the sand from cascading above Sara's head.

"Draw on your powers, mate. Be the dragon," Bandit urged between snarls.

Erik slashed and parried and the battle raged on, each clash of sword punctuating the air with bursts of light and sound. Amidst the chaos, the Dragon Moonstone's glow intensified. I collected its energy swirling around the crystal, drawing it into my staff, wristband, and core.

Sara's fists hammered her glass prison with waning strength. All the while, the suffocating sand poured in at an alarming rate. Jesse ignored the sparks, hurling himself against the outer glass. With each strike, the wards flung him down. But Jesse rebounded, roaring as he rammed the hourglass again and again.

I couldn't launch a spell without hitting Jesse. So I jumped from the ledge onto another and then another, following a makeshift staircase to Sara. The ongoing sand avalanche had buried her up to her chin, seconds from burying her alive. Sara's eyes bulged. Our gazes locked—Hers pleading, mine determined.

With all the strength I could muster, I rammed my staff against the hourglass. "*Frangere*!" I roared.

The glass exploded outwards. Sara tumbled forth, carried by the wave of sand. I wrenched Sara free, relief flooding my senses. She retched, gasping for air, her terror-filled eyes brimmed. But then she swiped her eyes, and they narrowed with determination. With a ferocious intensity, Sara summoned a whirlwind of glass and sand, directing it toward the witch.

Agnes shielded her eyes from Sara's onslaught, and Erik seized the opportunity, grazing the witch with his blade. The impact of Erik's strike elicited a piercing scream from the red witch, and she retaliated by unleashing a swirling vortex in her fury.

We ran for cover as rocks exploded one after another. But then I stopped, doubled my shield, and held my ground against the witch's wrath. Although I couldn't see the Dragon Moonstone, given the rate at which Agnes was demolishing boulders, it wouldn't be long before the obelisk came into view. I wasn't sure if she could tap into its power, but I didn't want to find out. With my staff, I hurled a shockwave blast. It was my best shot, but it didn't faze her.

Unabated, the red witch drove fire and lightning in all directions. Her eyes flashed with a crazed frenzy as rats swarmed, taking bites from Erik's legs as he battled the witch. I jumped onto the rock Erik had once commanded, willing the cave's exhaustive heat to feed an invisible shield. I widened my perimeter, stretching my limits to provide Bandit with similar protection as he fought against the scourge of rats.

"Stop," I yelled. "By the powers vested in me as an Apprentice Wizard of Castle Dragon, I hereby place you under arrest." I had no idea if that was possible, but it sounded impressive.

Agnes turned to me with a sinister smile. "Well, aren't you special—standing on that stone like a fledgling warrior? Time flies when we're having fun." With a few choice words and a swift gesture, the witch sent a fire dervish that flung Erik into the abandoned dragon's nest, setting it ablaze. Landing hard, he crab-crawled away from the flames.

Above me, Bandit snarled at the rats swarming over the ledge. He fought with the ferocity of a Tasmanian devil.

The red witch summoned a lightning blast, and my shield reflected the energy. Her eyebrows lifted, and her lips pursed in appraisal. "Hmm, perhaps the wizard has some skills. Only time will tell," she said, sending another blast.

My shield held, but barely.

"Come with me," Agnes said. "I can teach you to harness your power. We can be friends."

"I don't believe that for one minute." The Raven Moonstone pulsated from my staff's hilt as power surged. "This ends here and now." I let loose a bolt of lightning.

The witch blocked my blasts as the ground rumbled and walls cracked. She rocked, cocking her head in surprise at the tremor.

But it wasn't me—I sensed the cave's angry impatience. The earthquake was a warning shot. It wanted us to leave.

I chanced a glance at Erik. He hastily tossed debris aside, struggling to wrench a wooden chest from underneath the dragon's bedding. I quirked an eyebrow at his discovery. In that distracted moment, the witch hit me with a full-on assault of lightning and razor-sharp star-shaped blades. They pinged as they bounced off my invisible shield, but the force pushed me backward several steps.

"The portal is closing," Agnes yelled. "One way or another, you're coming with me."

Sweat pooled at the small of my back. I gritted my teeth, drawing power from the cave's hostile vibes to bend my shield. Like a fisherman casting a net, I uttered the command and turned my shield inside out. While the witch spun, hurling her blades in every direction, my force field landed, wrapping her in a shimmering transparent bubble. Her circular momentum hit against the shimmering walls and sent the witch bouncing like a super ball. The inside was a spiral of red lightning.

But then the witch calmed her physical fury, and the ball rolled to a stop before the Dragon Moonstone. Agnes's eyes popped with surprise and outrage.

"Sara, Jesse, are you okay?" I yelled, scanning the cave until Sara and Jesse appeared at the entrance.

Jesse bounded on his feet, pointing. "The witch is escaping!"

Agnes had made a tear and had jammed her fingers through the opening. A blue vein in her temple bulged as she concentrated her powers to rip the ward apart.

My vision blurred, and I stumbled. Exhausted, I clenched my teeth and pushed beyond my reserves, straining every fiber of my being. My knees wavered, and my muscles threatened to seize. I stayed on my feet by sheer determination, raised my shaking arm, and lifted my staff, the weight of it almost overwhelming. "*Glacio*!" I roared.

An icy blast erupted, and the witch's bubble turned into solid ice. I reached out to steady myself on the wall. My chest heaving as I tried to catch my breath.

The sound of Bandit's battle with the rats died as Jesse and Sara sprinted toward me.

"Is she dead?" Sara asked.

"Cryo-magically frozen," I said, staring into the witch's dull eyes.

"That was amazing," Sara said, running over and giving me a hug. "You're my hero." When she stepped back, she left her arm around me. I smiled at the comforting gesture.

"Dude, you were like some warrior wizard. How'd you do that?"

"It's the cave," I said. "I tapped into the blistering anger. I don't think it likes trespassers."

"Huh? I can't hear over the ringing." Jesse put a finger in his ear and jiggled it. "The first blast was a doozy." He looked around, and confusion crossed his face. "Where's Erik?"

"The last time I saw Erik, the witch tossed him into the dragon's nest," I said, shrugging indifference. Then, realizing Jesse couldn't hear me, I pointed.

Jesse grabbed the cloud, using it to put out the small fires while yelling for Erik.

Sara hadn't let go of me, and I wasn't about to be the first to break the connection. But then Jesse yelled, "Hey guys, check this out!"

He had found a small chest, with the sides collapsed, spilling over with gold coins and precious gems.

"I wonder if this is the gnomes' treasure—the one that Frankie was so set on finding," I said, cautioning with my hands. "Don't touch anything. I'm exhausted and not in the mood to fight off gnomes protecting their treasure." I grinned half-heartedly at Jesse, and that's when he told us his ears had finally stopped ringing.

Sara crouched for a closer look and pointed at what resulted in a trail of gemstones heading for the portal. As we stepped closer, the remaining mist disappeared, and there was a *sizzle* and a *snap* as the portal blinked out.

"Looks like Erik ran off with as much loot as he could carry," Jesse said.

A grin tugged my lips. *Better Jesse voices what I dare not say.*

"Erik—Really?" Sara actually looked surprised.

I snorted. "What did you hear when Erik approached the red witch?" I asked, careful to keep my tone neutral.

"Nothing," Sara said, her voice still hoarse from swallowing sand. "I couldn't hear a thing in that hourglass." She shuddered. "That was so awful. I can't speak of it."

We stood at the cave's opening, and heat poured out, mixing with the cool evening air. The sun had already set, turning the sky a deep purple. A faint hum emanated from the mouth of the cave. I knew it to be the crystal calling the dragon home.

"Look," Jesse said, pointing to the sky.

"Hurry, get back behind these rocks," I said, tugging Sara's sleeve while Jesse ran up behind us.

"There are two of them," Sara said, peeking through the gap in the boulders. We huddled while the dragons circled before landing at the cave's entrance.

"Which one is your dragon?" Jesse asked in a low tone.

*Neither*. I remained mute as we watched the dragons approach the cave.

Though graceful in flight, the dragons wobbled with an endearing awkwardness like ungainly ducks on land. The young dragon dawdled, stopping at the entrance, a moment of uncertainty in its stance. Meanwhile, the beast we assumed to be his mother entered the cave.

The moon had risen. Moonbeams fell upon the Dragon Moonstone crystal, bathing the cavern in a mystical golden light. Positioned in front of the obelisk, the red witch remained suspended in her frozen state. The dragon crept closer, pushing the ice ball with her snout. The frozen witch rolled along the floor, propelled by the curious dragon. She toyed with the witch but soon grew bored. Then, as if struck by an impulsive thought, the dragon swung her head, jaws parting wide, and swallowed the red witch in a single gulp.

"Well, that takes care of that," Bandit said, walking with a limp, chewing on a rat's tail.

"Ew, what are you eating?" Sara said, scrunching her face.

But the mother dragon grumbled before we could discuss the perils of eating rats. She circled once, then twice more, before tucking her tail and settling beside the pedestal. She released a toothy yawn and closed her eyes.

The young dragon waddled forward and tilted his head when he saw us.

*The little dragon with green eyes remembers us.*

I walked up and offered him my hand, and he sniffed it. "Hello again." I sensed no fear when he eyed me with curiosity. "We have to go now. You'll be safe here. Time for a long nap."

The green-eyed dragon nodded, continued into the cave, and plopped down beside his mother.

"Bandit, are you okay?" Sara asked, her voice laced with concern, and she furrowed her brow

"I'm knackered," he said, leaning against a rock and clenching his stomach. "I don't feel so good."

"Maybe you shouldn't eat rats," Jesse quipped.

Confusion crossed Bandit's face when he withdrew his bloody paw.

"Bandit, you're hurt," I said, rushing forward and dropping to my knees. "Let me see."

Sara gasped. One of Agnes's star blades had penetrated deep into his neck.

"Stop!" I said, reaching for his paw.

But it was too late. Blood gushed from the piercing wound when Bandit wrenched the blade free. His legs buckled, and he collapsed with a whimper.

Tears brimmed as Sara kneeled over Bandit. "Stay with me—Look at me," she pleaded.

I pressed on the gushing gash, feeling his lifeblood spill over my fingers. "Jesse—My pack. Get something to stop the bleeding!" My voice shook. I poured my energy into staunching the blood, but my abilities failed me. Bandit's breath came in ragged gasps, his body shuddering. Our eyes locked. His gaze reflected all the words left unsaid and all the adventures left undone.

*What was taking Jesse so long?*

"See you on the other side, mate," he said, just above a whisper.

The spark in his eyes retreated to vacant glass as Bandit's last rattling breath echoed in my ears. Tears scalded my cheeks while I threw back my head and howled, cursing the unfairness.

# CHAPTER 27

## *FAREWELL*

I dug the grave beneath the sprawling oak, refusing help. Mrs. S stood beside me, her usual glint absent from her eyes. Numb, I remained motionless, unable to comprehend.

*Why?*

My heart—a ravaged and raw wound.

The fairies played a mournful tune as the small wooden coffin hovered over the grave, yawning like a gaping mouth. Fae from all over Goblin Valley gathered. Mourners shook with muffled sobs. A swell of grief surged as, one by one, they placed tokens on the casket. Bandit's tattered duster. A honey cake dolloped with ranch dressing. A clutch of his beloved acorns. Each object landed heavily, carrying memories that dragged my heart down. Slowly, they lowered him into the earth. I wanted to scream to demand that they stop and bring him back. Instead, I stared dry-eyed.

Long after the others departed, I lingered alone. *If only—Why couldn't I save him?* Another death would haunt me forever.

"It's time to go," Sara said softly. "Mayor Spychalla will escort us through the veil."

"You two go ahead. I've decided to stay."

"You're serious?" Sara's eyes widened with dismay, her smile fading.

I affirmed with a nod. "You both have classes starting a new semester and need to head back. I'm in no hurry to return to Sweetwater. Ranger assured us the well incident was a scare tactic, and Aunt Shirley and Mercy were off on a Caribbean cruise."

Mayor Spychalla stood by the portal. He tapped his foot, checked his pocket watch, and cleared his throat in a not-so-subtle manner.

Jesse pulled me into a bear hug that nearly swept me off my feet. "If you ever need me, call," he said, his voice muffled against my shoulder. Then he released me and dashed off to catch up with the mayor, his footsteps muffled against the grass.

Sara smiled knowingly, and I let her think what she said next was true. "You want to continue your training with Mrs. S." She gave me a quick embrace. "Be sure to come home for the holiday break. We'll catch up then."

My mother's amulet warmed my chest as a sense of urgency washed over me.

*Don't let her get away without knowing how you feel. Speak from your heart.*

My breath escaped with a sigh. "Sara, wait."

She turned with an eager, questioning look. I stepped forward, clutching her hand tightly, my heart thudding in my chest. Sara stiffened, hesitation shadowing her face.

"When I return, there's something important I want to share," I said, my voice trembling with emotion. I looked at my hand and loosened my grip before meeting Sara's warm eyes. "But first, I have unfinished business with Erik." My tone sharpened, and my eyes hardened at the thought of Erik's betrayal.

Sara wrenched her hand away, eyes flashing with anger. "What's with this weird obsession with Erik?" she snapped. "You have no reason to be jealous! Get over yourself. There's nothing between us!" Sara pivoted, and with a huff, she stormed toward the gateway.

Stunned, I struggled to breathe and ran my hand through my hair, swiping at my eyes when they suddenly blurred. The weight of her rejection pressed against my heart as I watched Sara vanish beyond the shimmering veil.

A firm grip on my shoulder broke my numb stare, and I turned to face Ranger—The only one I had confided in about Erik's betrayal.

Ranger regarded me through his aviators, his words carrying a hint of warning. "I hope you're not planning something foolish." His grip tightened. "Vengeance leads to anguish."

I balled my fists, anger and betrayal searing through my veins. "Erik must answer for what he did to Bandit. Are you with me or not?"

The End.

# ACKNOWLEDGEMENT

I want to thank my awesome family and friends—you guys rock! You've always had my back, cheering me on and encouraging me to keep Noah and the gang's adventures going.

A special nod to my super chill husband, who's put up with endless "what-if" scenarios and even made sure I didn't forget to eat or move around when I was deep in my writing zone.

A massive shout-out to my beta readers—Rachel, Brenda, John, Ben, and Tom—you all kept me on the right track and with insightful feedback.

And for you, dear reader, you're the real MVP. In a world bursting with books, it's seriously mind-blowing that you picked mine. I hope you had a blast reading it.

If you enjoyed the story, please tell your friends. Word of mouth is like magic for authors. And hey, if you're feeling extra awesome, leaving a review on Amazon is always appreciated.

# BOOKS BY THIS AUTHOR

## The Raven Moonstone

Noah never expected to find a wizard's journal in his hometown library, but when he does, he unleashes a wave of unintended magic with outrageous consequences.

He also discovered that his town is full of secrets. Secrets about magic and family. Secrets that could change everything. With each new revelation, he realizes the stakes are higher than ever imagined.

Now he must embark on a perilous quest to find the Raven Moonstone, a legendary artifact that can reverse his magical mistakes. But that's not all. He's determined to unravel the mystery of his great-great-great-grandfather's disappearance.

Time is slipping away, and dark forces are closing in. Can Noah save his town from a magical apocalypse?

Don't miss this rural coming-of-age magical adventure.

Printed in Great Britain
by Amazon

36145920R00165